I0603967

PARALLEL LINES

DAVID MYRCOTT

CRAIG TUCK

ADEN SIMPSON

*Writing to impress is the surest path
towards undeniable mediocrity.
Nevertheless, we hope you enjoy our stories.*

David Myrcott

is a Melbourne-based writer, editor and artist. His written work has appeared in *Voiceworks, Wet Ink, Tincture, Eureka Street, Page Seventeen, The Brag, Lucky, jmag, Beat, Ripples, Van Helsing's Journal* and elsewhere.

tiktok.com/@david.myrkr

instagram.com/phqllic_bqldwin

Craig Tuck

The man behind the YouTube phenomenon, Ghost Crayfish Productions. Producer, director, actor, plus self-published author of 'Of hat-tricks and heroism', Craig adores words. Adores them.

youtube.com/@crajmahal

Aden Simpson

is filled with rage. Burning Rage. His novels include *The Illusionists* (2016), *The Reincarnation of Tom* (2020) and *Invisible York* (2023).

adensimpson.com

CONTENTS

The Egg

David Myrcott

The problem was he couldn't remember having ever been trapped in the damn thing. It seemed as though he'd been confined in it for as long as he could remember. There was no recollection of sleeping or waking, no memories of dreaming, eating, breathing – he just *was*. Like an insect simply exists, so he existed.

He had vision, that much was certain, for he could clearly see the membranous walls which hemmed him in on every side; he had hearing too, for could occasionally discern the muffled crashings and roarings that went on outside, as though taking place in an entirely separate reality. Most of the time however he lived in a state of suspended animation, with little in the way of thoughts to distract him.

There were endless days, endless nights, each signified by a gradual change in the amount of light which permeated the bounds of his tiny enclosure. He had no words for night and day however; there was simply the ceaseless rotation of twelve hours of veiled radiance coupled with twelve hours, give or take, of pitch black. In the blackness especially even his primitive thought processes abandoned him. It seemed that in the absence of such phenomena as masked sunlight glowing red through the cutaneous layers of his confines his mind had nothing to attach itself to, was lost to the depths of its own weak orbit. Each darkness was a little death, a dark mouth come to devour him. Yet he continued to function, and with each dull morning grew slightly more alive.

* * *

Gradually his perceptions began to awaken. He regarded his surroundings with increasing discernment, noting with some interest that the walls which encircled him were latticed with thick veins, some bloody red and others a deep, pungent blue. Though words did not yet exist he couldn't help noticing the tangle of tubes which swarmed wormlike wherever he looked, causing the light to splinter into grotesque tongues of stained glass.

He had other realisations, began to notice that he had hands, and feet, and arms. If he cast his eyes down he could see the hazy outline of a nose protruding useless and proboscis-like from the centre of his face. He began to appreciate a simple relativity: those organs responsible for sight occupied a space somewhat higher than this nose, which seemed to serve no purpose at all. Higher still was the crown of his head, as he perceived in the many hours spent running his hands over his body, feeling out the parts with naïve wonderment. He had a torso, knobbly joints, legs covered in downy hair, toes which he individually felt out by hand. He noted his body had remained the same size for quite some time, and that he did not appear to be getting larger. In other words he was a fully grown man.

As countless days and nights passed he began to develop a rudimentary vocabulary, saying words like 'aah' and 'aum,' drawing them out, experimenting with various combinations of sound, applying them to different sections of his body.

In time he had a crude sort of language. He came up with a name for his cell. It was 'Gulah.' He named some of the larger veins, most of his limbs, and even started singing to himself in a peculiar caveman grunt. He spent hours in this fashion, droning on with nonsense syllables until the darkness came, bringing with it an end to thoughts, a total unconscious. Then the day came once more, he gradually accustomed himself to his surroundings, and began again the ritual of greeting himself and his confines, with their curious crimson glow and expanse of swollen, mottled veins.

Two things dawned on him surprisingly late. The first was the sudden realisation that he had been crouched in essentially the same position for as long as he could recall, in fact could remember occupying the confines of his little space in no other manner. The more he considered it the more he longed to stretch out as far as he could, to flex his shoulders, to arch his spine and work some life into his unused muscles. He was hunched over, knees drawn up almost to his chin, as though whoever designed his womblike enclosure had intended it to be inhabited by a much smaller creature. If it wasn't for the regular periods of darkness and the sleep or lack of consciousness they brought he might well have gone insane.

His little shell hovered over him, pressing against him, holding him completely captive. Practically immobilised in the way he could only explore his body with his hands, curl his fingers and toes in protest and sing his odd little songs. He explored the walls around him too, running his fingertips along the plump veins, observing the firm suppleness of the substructure which ensnared him. Its tactility fascinated him, kept him occupied for entire days. 'Gulah' he mumbled to himself as his fingers roamed in curiosity. 'Gulah.'

The second thought that came astonishingly late was that his conical prison was filled to the brim with a viscous, transparent brine. So completely suffused in fact that he had simply failed to notice it was there. He gained the first sense of its presence when composing one of his earliest sentences, many nights or days ago, but his mind had not really registered anything out of the ordinary. It was unavoidable however, for whilst his throat remained as clogged as though it had been stuffed with gauze he was capable of opening his mouth a fraction.

This tiny motion was in large part how he came

to invent new sounds and words, and he sometimes observed that a little of the liquid would seep into his mouth as he muttered away to himself. The taste was not altogether unpleasant, though the sensation itself was an unusual one and an impediment to the murmured utterances that constituted his speech.

Soon he began to resent the intrusion of the thick fluid he swam in, and its presence occupied his thoughts to an ever greater degree. He named this irritating bile 'Holra' and spent hours willing it into non-existence, longing for some respite from the liquid which filled his unblinking eyes, wrapped itself cloyingly around his body, even clogged up his mouth when he spoke. 'Holra' he burbled accusatorily. 'Holra.'

But the watery cocoon refused to abate or even to acknowledge him. It remained as impassive of the walls of the spongy structure in which he was imprisoned.

He was in an egg. He had realised that some time ago, however now another, markedly more insistent thought began to dominate; he didn't *want* to be in an egg any longer, was tired of squatting, hunched over, crippled, eyes and mouth and pores engorged with revolting translucent slime, nothing to do but contemplate his confinement, his body, his useless existence. Whereas formerly the darkness had been his mind's cue to shut off, an escape mechanism of sorts, he now found himself waking in a gloomy hell, spending hours immersed in blackness with no stimulus except the occasional deadened moan from the world outside his shell.

That was it! There was another world, a world out there! His legs, immobile all this time, proved surprisingly and wonderfully equal to the task ahead of them. He kicked strongly, lashing out again and again at the blotchy red interior of the egg which had kept him captive for so long. Its walls were apparently not as immutable as he had supposed, and with each frenzied heave of his legs he noticed them weakening more and more.

He cursed himself for not having thought of this earlier, for waiting until he had almost been driven mad with immobility and boredom before choosing to make his escape. He was through with this womb and its cloying, claustrophobic hold on him. He struck again and felt the walls of the egg beginning to crack. The amniotic fluid slushed around in protest but was powerless to stop the imminent birth.

With one final kick his right foot completely pierced the surface of the shell and protruded into the outside world all the way to mid-calf. He held it there for a moment in amazement, savouring the sweet extension of his half-atrophied limb. Then came a different sensation, no less unique or enjoyable. It was the feeling of a cool breeze gently lapping against the wet skin of his leg. It felt exquisite.

He quickly pushed his other leg through the cavity, which obligingly yielded just enough to allow for the intrusion. The lukewarm fluid which had previously occupied every inch of the egg, clung to his skin for God knows how long, suffocating him, now began to seep slowly out from the perforation he had created. Both lower limbs now experienced the indescribable joy of liberation from their former bounds. He easily spent an hour this way, gradually forcing more and more of his legs through until both now penetrated well past the knee. By arching his back he was able to stretch out almost fully, a pleasure he had scarce dreamt of knowing. Liquid continued to gently weep from the hole.

He remained supine, immersed in the remnants of his damp amnion, knowing his escape would soon come. He luxuriated in this certainty, until finally he decided he must know liberty in its entirety. He drew his legs slowly back into the confines of his shell and reached up through the muck to tear at the opening he had made earlier, ripping off chunks of white shell with his hands until the chasm was large enough to crawl through. Sunlight streamed in, diffusing its warmth over him.

Without pausing to take one last look around the interior of the only home he had ever known, he thrust upwards with all his might, arms extended, and wriggled serpent-like to freedom. The cavity he had torn open split complaisantly, and after a little effort he was freed completely from the egg, flopping like a fish onto the hard ground.

He looked around with cloudy eyes at the world, unable to distinguish anything except the monstrous beauty of the light. The light was everywhere, it filled him to bursting, dried off his shining skin, sang to him. He choked up the last remnants of the womb which had so long ensnared him, threw back his head, and screamed.

Waking

Craig Tuck

The mourners gathered in their thousands for the occasion, disparate in background, united in grief. Today was no ordinary day. Nothing made sense.

'It's hard to cop when they die this young,' an inconsolable, vaguely familiar man said to no one in particular.

'Particularly when they were so talented,' the artist formerly known as Prince replied, resplendent in glitter, greatly troubled by the world's sad loss. 'I don't know if I'll ever recover.'

The ink, only just dry on the front pages of all the world's major newspapers, was now being moistened once more by the free-flowing tears of the multitudes. George Radley had died and there was nothing now for the beautiful girls to do but weep.

The eulogy said it all:

A sad, lonely child with a penchant for dreaming, George struggled initially for solace in a world unprepared for a musician of his like. Eventually, as his ability and willingness to adapt and prosper in this world developed, George came to accept that he was both the man and the

Rock God the world had unknowingly yearned.

As George's adulthood bloomed and his gifts flowered, the world was delivered not the hero it deserved, but the hero it needed. Admired as much in adulthood for his numerous philanthropic endeavours as he was adored for his sparkling charisma and rugged good looks, George was looked upon by many as more God than Man. Certainly he had been a fine singer/songwriter.

Blessed with a uniquely humble perfection, George came to represent everything good about music and, indeed, life in general. His earthly presence seemed testament to God's benevolence. By fans and collaborators alike, George was loved greatly and as was his way, made love greatly in return. George was a Saint, and the world is poorer for his passing.

The words did their best, but some forms of perfection cannot be captured by modern prose. So it was with the humble perfection applicable to George; a perfection that perplexed all thinking, literate beings. It was this indefinable, incorruptible excellence, lost, that had caused the world's collective heart to sink.

And yet in defiance of the gloom, music came. Inexplicably, unperturbed by the sadness and ignorant of the tears, joyous, optimistic, vulgar pop music now enveloped the occasion. It grew louder with each moment.

The vocals soared with optimism.

Inappropriate and invasive, the jubilant rhythm lurched forward like Dr Frankenstein's monster, clumsily unaware of the destruction it wreaked. The pulsing jangle turned heads and inspired revulsion.

'Not today!' the multitudes cried. 'Not now!'

The grief was raw, but still the beat marched on.

'They say we're young and we don't know

We won't find out until we grow

Well I don't know if all that's true

'Cause you got me, and baby I got you...'

The mourners searched the area in confused despondency. Unsatisfied, they lifted their gaze from their pooling tears below and beckoned instead of the harsh storm clouds above. The world's populace held its collective gaze, beseeching God for address. Today was a day, it seemed, when anything was possible.

Suddenly the storm clouds began to part, the ambience began to lighten, and the voice soared into a message of majestic intent, erupting into an emotional crescendo that confirmed the wonder of the occasion.

'Babe, I Got You Babe!'

And then, amidst the swirling bliss of this heavenly address, George opened his eyes, resurrected. A new beginning!

Immediately the mourners disappeared. Flowers, banners and placards vanishing with them. The TV news crews vanished too. All that had been was now gone. Only George remained. Alone, awake, alive, and left rueing the fact, wishing he were anywhere but at the early dawning of yet another work day.

He yawned grimly.

What day was it? Tuesday? Wednesday? There was no difference, the alarm clock marched on regardless, belting out the Sonny and Cher classic *I Got You Babe* until George had no choice but to concede that he was indeed awake. Prince had not been mourning his passing; there was no denying that now.

George stirred restlessly from within the depths of his lonely, spacious double bed, hesitantly pushing his arm from his blanketed cocoon to fondle his alarm clock. After a few brief, painful fumbles, George was able to turn the music off. He celebrated a mild victory with its departure.

The effort, though successful in its basic ambition, was entirely fruitless in another, deeper sense; the music had been vanquished, but the gates of hell had been irrevocably opened. There was no escaping the fresh torment the day had in store for him.

As grim as the reality was for him to accept, or me to recount, the truth is that George's alarm clock had deliberately plunged him into another workday as a Junior Grants Administration Officer with the Department of Community Restoration and Proliferation.

George took a deep breath, stretched a little, and eyed his alarm clock closely. In red, bold numbering, the message it sent was brutal in its finality:

7:16 am

Time to get up.

George looked around his room, pleading for some unknown mercy; a murderer, perhaps? But there was nothing. He glanced back at the alarm clock. This was no joke; it really was time to get up.

'Fuck,' George whispered quietly to himself.

He climbed out from under his warm blankets and stood, with as much certainty as he would all day, on his own two feet.

It was freezing, so there was no time to waste.

He began scanning the room for his glasses and was surprised by their absence. It was strange; he usually left them *somewhere*. Usually, he left them on his desk, so this was the first place he decided to examine in closer detail; at first with his eyes and then, luckless, with his hands.

The perverse tragic comedy of the situation, of which George was well aware, belied the importance of the search. How could he hope to find his glasses when they were the very thing he required in order to see?

He pushed on though, despite the absurdity. Without them, the day would be lost.

The monumental clutter in which George lived his life also made things difficult. His hands careened blindly and unsuccessfully over and through a motley collection of cups, plates, cutlery, coins, newspapers, magazines, CDs, empty juice poppers, almost-full juice poppers, condom wrappers (displayed with meticulous abandon throughout his room, as Proof for any friends that may ever visit) and other bin-worthy memorabilia of his life.

Thankfully, the whirlwind search knocked over nothing which could spill or stain, though he still had no luck in finding his glasses.

'Fuck,' he whispered to himself once more.

George was by this stage wide awake and beginning to panic. If he were a sweater he would have been sweating now, despite the cold. Instead, he stood motionless, shaken.

He took a step back and assessed.

Without his glasses, George would struggle to do much with his day at all. His eyes darted around the round with nervous energy until his blurred gaze eventually stumbled back upon his desk.

'Shit!'

He began to rummage some more before bending down, bringing his face as close as he could to his computer desk to speak quietly to the mess below.

'Please, I know I left you here,' he began. 'I just need you to show yourself.'

He glanced at his alarm clock.

7:22 am

'Fucking hell,' he muttered.

George began to pick up the pace of his search, throwing everything he could pick up someplace else, presumably to see under each item. The glasses were in none of these places. He couldn't believe it. He'd *lost* his glasses.

Without his glasses he would not be able to work, he would not even be able to drive himself to work. With eyesight as poor as his, even leaving his room could be a risky proposition.

Panic quickly became resignation. He would not be able to go to work today.

Resignation quickly became relief. He would not be able to go to work today.

Relief approached jubilation. He would *not* be able to go to work today.

George even allowed himself to smile a little at the thought, though not too much. This was his livelihood we're talking about, after all.

George resigned himself easily to his fate and turned his thoughts to tactics for the all-important office phone call. The hardest part of any sickie is the office phone call: you must sound apologetic, but sincere. You must seem too weak and affected to work, but be firm and clear in how you express it.

It is real tight rope stuff, not for the faint of heart (unless that is your chosen ailment for the day): go too far with your apologetic rhetoric and you run the risk of exposing yourself an insincere liar, but sound too unconcerned and your commitment will be called into serious question.

George paused thoughtfully to consider his approach. The cold was no longer a factor. His focus lay only on getting this one thing right.

'Get it done,' George thought, '...and the day is mine.'

While George did have a *legitimate* reason to miss work for the day, it was still a ridiculous and somewhat embarrassing tale to recount. There was no doubt Margaret, his manager, would be judgemental about the matter, particularly since his most recent Performance Review had lambasted George for his 'deficiencies in the field of attention to detail' and 'prolific absent-mindedness'.

Understandably, George was reticent to concede that he was taking the day off work because he had misplaced his glasses. But what could he say?

After brief deliberation, George settled on the story that he had accidentally broken them. No! Even better, his housemate had accidentally broken them. Yes, he thought, that was better. He steeled himself.

'This does not make me sound like an idiot.'

He took a deep breath and eyed up his desk one more time, this time in search of his phone. It wasn't there. He brightened further. If he couldn't find his phone, he would be able to email in to work instead! Anyone can email in an excuse for absenteeism! That stuff is child's play!

'Brilliant!' George exclaimed, grinning wildly now. He hadn't glowed with that much misguided optimism since the day Margaret had first offered him his job.

Much like his previous optimistic outburst, the wild grin faded quickly. George's memory kicked into gear and gave him all the information necessary.

In a stroke of instant, horrific misfortune, George could see it all: his mobile phone carefully placed between his wallet *and* his glasses, on a shelf in his bedroom cupboard. He turned to face the offending cupboard, suddenly feeling the bite of the morning chill.

As he shivered his way towards the culprit, George put his hands together in a silent plea, begging the Gods (though subscribing to no *particular* God) to be wrong. If not about all items, as an error in memory of that size could spell early onset Alzheimer's (no laughing matter), George hoped to at least be wrong about the glasses.

He trudged to the door and opened it quickly.

No point wasting time now.

Everything was as his memory had belatedly told him it would be: the glasses, the phone, the wallet.

'Fuck.'

Despite his disappointment, somewhere deep down, George knew that it really was better that he went to work.

George sighed quietly, put his glasses on, and made his way for the bathroom.

He was now running late and would not have time for breakfast.

The Last Day to Die
Aden Simpson

I watch the needle drool ever so slightly before it slides into my vein. I wince at the cold invasion but remind myself of its necessity. The yellow liquid, thick in texture like flavoured kid's medicine, finds its way in and my head rolls upward. I close my eyes, my heart racing. Five minutes. Five minutes till the mind turns on itself and I become convinced that this is my last day left on earth.

The kids did it for many reasons but I always felt it boiled down to just one: Life was boring; everything was safe with all corners sanded down these days. There were no real experiences anymore. People were putting them off till they never came true. Sure, you could do a whole heap of drugs, they still had the classics available for hijinks, but there was none more elusive, nor life-affirming than the spiritual kick of that yellow liquid.

The concept was simple. Take a shot and become gripped with the impenetrable 'truth' that this day was your last. A personal apocalypse; all brought to you by a few tricks of the brain. There would be no more tomorrows, just one mad day to take it all in. The legend goes that this liquid was conceived by a suicidal freak that had bumped uglies with an extraterrestrial. This alien had then started to pulsate a yellowy goo from which our interstellar gift was born. Not the most realistic of stories, but what did you care if you thought it was all going to end by sundown that day?

As you can imagine, anything can happen when all signs point to impending doom. Some would take it to feel crazy. Some were already crazy and just wanted that extra push before they went postal. Some sought inspiration. Some were seeking clarity in their life (and the after-kick was just as good, apparently). Some even did it for major sporting events; those wanting to play the game as if they had nothing left to lose.

Some would cry a lot. Throw a premium pity party for themselves. Go through the textbook stages of accepting one's own demise. If they were new to it all they'd request a friend to hold their hand and let them get all emotional about an end with no real consequences. People say the truest things when they think their seconds are short.

Simply put, everybody had their reasons.

* * *

I took my shot in the bathroom, before they got to the, "If anyone has a reason why these two should not be wed, speak now or forever hold your peace." I certainly wasn't the first and I certainly won't be the last for this kind of reason. And, as a first timer, to be perfectly honest, my timing was off. I didn't account for the clenching of everything as the brain came to its false conclusion. There were many ways the rationalisations found their way in: often, it went that you had just received news of a dreaded poison or illness that was going to wreak havoc throughout your body within only a matter of hours. For others, it came a manic certainty that there was a car out on the road speeding along— your destiny at 60km/h while you looked the other way crossing the street.

Either way, I'm not ready for it.

The tears roll out as I look in the mirror, dressed all prim and proper. The door to the bathroom swings open and I hastily change tune to washing my hands, washing my hands, feeling the softness within the warmth of the running stream; softness just like how it used to be with Mel.

I enjoy the feeling as I come to realise that these last moments are to be treasured, my assured mortality throbbing through my brain. It was cancer; the doctors had found it too late and though I felt fine now, tomorrow the cancer would cause a stroke while I cruised through an intersection. A semi would then collect me. It was all so beautiful and very unavoidable.

"Shouldn't you be out there by now?"

I turn to see the old man who'd come in, sparking my nonchalant hand washing. "Yes, just washing my hands."

"You've been doing that for a while... Everything okay, chief?"

Well, I've got inoperable cancer and the girl I love is making a huge mistake.

"Yeah," I eventually reply. "Guess I was just taking stock. I'll see you out there."

The old man nods and follows me out casually, but I make sure to skip ahead.

Gabe the Groom urges me to take my place. I nod sharply and make my way down the centre aisle. I feel every step, the sweat flowing heavy all over my body. At one stage I glance at the sunlight streaking in through the window. It is a beautiful day outside, a lovely last day. If only I'd known about it earlier. If only I'd confessed to Mel earlier. Time is a cruel bitch and the withdrawals of hindsight are a kick in the teeth.

The organ begins playing. I realise I've stopped mid-stride and am now just gazing out the window, eyes stupefied like some invalid. Everyone is now watching me, so Jonathan, one of the groomsmen, urges me over like I'm a cat stuck up a tree. I pick up my pace as Gabe gives me an "are you on drugs?" kind of stare. I want to tell him that I'm going to die, that all the light and the beauty in the world is being sucked up and taken in for the last time, but I don't want to ruin his big day, even if mine is more significant.

The people in the pews turn and the little shit with

the flowers strolls through. And then I see her, the one that got away all those years ago. She is an angel and floats that way too, breaking me with every step forward, her face one of pure happiness.

And then I remember what it was to feel her; a picnic at Linley's Point, one of our first dates. The show reel begins to press into my brain, the big "flash before my eyes" coming a little sooner than expected. And then I remember what I was supposed to say, what I needed to do, what must be lifted from my soul before I leave this world: the truth.

Parkinson's law relates to the notion that the longer one has to complete a task, then the longer its completion will be stretched out. I didn't have that much time left, so for these last moments, I was going to put it all to good use.

Mel takes her place at the Altar. I can feel all the cheeks in the room rising and booming as a sea of smiles direct their flow to Mel and Gabe, as if there was nobody in the world but just them two.

I stare as intently at Mel as she stares at Gabe. And when the priest man makes his spiel about objections...

It all rises out of my throat as the memories spill out of me, leaving me overwhelmed. This is it.

"I obj—"

I'm cut off.

My interruption has been interrupted.

The man next to me, Gabe's best buddy Jonathan

has broken the peace. Everyone in the pews is trying to outdo each other with their gasps. Jonathan steps forward in front of the two lovebirds. I grit my teeth—*the raw nerve of him!* Jonathan hasn't said anything else yet and this leaves everyone frozen, waiting for it all to come blurting out: Jonathan's in love with Mel! My instincts kick in, and I grab Jonathan by the shoulders and hurl him off the stage before the words leave his mouth. There are more gasps, more family members fainting at this sordid spectacle. Now they're all looking at me.

Trembling, I stare into Mel's eyes. She isn't mad, in fact her face, like all those nights we used to spend curled up into one another, is very understanding. Gabe, on the other hand, is clenched up in white-hot rage.

"What the fuck are you two doing?" He screams at Jonathan and myself.

I take one more look at Mel for courage and then clear my throat.

"I don't have long for this world, and I just wanted Mel to know that I'm still in love with her—even after all these years—and I guess Jonathan had similar thoughts, though to be honest I really didn't see that coming."

"That's because I don't love Mel," says Jonathan, rising to his feet. "I love you, Gabe."

There are more gasps at this point. I'd burst out laughing like a nutter if I didn't think it was all so tragic.

Gabe's eyeballs have burst out of their sockets.

"What?"

"It's true," Jonathan gushes. "Ever since grade school... and now I think I've played my hand too late: I just found out I'd ingested the poisonous part of a puffer fish last night. There's nothing the doctors can do. Today was my last day to tell you."

Now I'm confused. "Wait. You're dying too?"

"Yeah."

"But we had burgers yesterday?"

Jonathan's brain locks up. "No—I was at this Japanese restaurant and I had this special puffer fish, but the main chef was sick and so this trainee chef—"

"That's an episode from *The Simpsons*," Gabe interrupts. "You're not dying. What the hell is... wait— have you taken Death Wish?"

"No, I—"

"That's fucked up, man." I declare. "Especially for those of us who are *really* about to die!"

"And you're probably not dying either!" screams Gabe.

I'm taken aback, absolutely indignant. "How dare you! I don't have to put up with this shit on my last day." My attention then turns to Mel. "Mel, please. I just want you to know that I love you more than anything in the world, and I couldn't go knowing I'd never said that."

Mel's eyes well up, "I love you too."

Gabe stomps his foot on the ground like a little brat.

"WHAT?"

Her tears are now flowing freely. But she is not sad at all. She looks free of all guilt in my eyes and I am the happiest I will ever be. I reach forward to embrace her, but she stops me.

"I love both of you, and all of you." She gestures to the crowd.

Gabe and I trade looks of furthered confusion (I'm expecting more gasps from the crowd at this point).

"I wanted you all to know this before...before the accident."

"What accident?"

Mel clutches Gabe's wrist. "We are driving away. We've just been married. You lean in to kiss me. And then a drunk driver collects us. I don't make it, babe. I don't make it..."

"Wait—are you fucking kidding me? You've taken it too?" On our wedding day?"

Gabe takes a giant step back from us all, shaking his head in disbelief. "I can't deal with this," he throws his hands up as he then plods heavy down the steps and rushes back up the aisle. Jonathan cries out to him but Gabe is having none of it.

Then there's just the three of us and a silent crowd of once well-wishers, their faces twisted, ready to erupt into whatever emotion best accompanies a two-way Death Wish admission (I don't know, Jonathan's the writer).

Unsure of where to go to from here, I turn to Jonathan. "So, you're a fag then?"

"Not for much longer."

"Why not? Oh, the whole dying thing..."

It is then that Gabe's mom finally explodes. She screams before she charges, vindicating her thoughts that Mel was indeed a bitch and that Gabe was too good for her. Gabe's father doesn't try to stop his dear Charlotte. The mother lunges at Mel, but not before Mel has stepped up to the plate and knocked Gabe's mum out with a well-timed haymaker. Now the father is up, and most of the crowd too. Jonathan and I are staring dumbfounded at Mrs. Bennett.

Mel lets out a sigh of relief. "I always wanted to do that!" she exclaims like a manic child. The others in the crowd are now getting a sense of the ground once shaken—and they are all pissed. The father leads the second charge and I suggest we get the hell out of there.

The cans bounce along behind our getaway car. Gabe's father gains close for the first few yards and I imagine him lunging for the cans in mad desperation, but he eventually stops and is left kicking at gravel.

No one in the car talks for a long time, our direction aimless.

Mel is driving. I gaze into her, those dark eyes bereft of that life that would often burst forth into the world, ready for anything. Instead, everything in her is now droopy and slack as she comes to terms with the life she once had. The Death Wish is a wild ride, so I've heard.

"Well, since we all don't have long, do you guys want to go out to Linley's point?" I finally suggest.

"Watch our last sunset?" asks Jonathan.

"Sure," says Mel, speeding the car up and cutting into a lane before boosting through a red. Our hearts race once more and the caucus of honking from other drivers lifts a smile in Mel.

"Have you told your parents yet?" she asks us both as the car speeds up.

"I'll do it when we get there, I'll tell them before the sun sets. And then, when it's setting, we'll kiss like we used to," I say, anxious for her response.

"I don't think my parents would care, to be honest," Jonathan utters.

I turn around and look at his ruffled state, his weathered eyes. "Did they know?"

"I don't know... Maybe Dad knew. That's why things were never right... That's why I never..."

"May as well tell them now," Mel says, matter-of-factly.

Jonathan goes quiet for a moment, before time gets the better of him and he decides why the hell not. "Mel, what if Gabe came?"

I lock up at the idea, but Mel seems to pay it no mind. "Sure, if he doesn't try to throw us off the cliff. Shit, we can even get naked and have ourselves an orgy, if you guys are up for it."

I can't say it didn't make me feel insecure at first, but then again, I was going to die tomorrow. Any sense of reservation was criminally repugnant at this point.

* * *

Linley's Point is beautiful. Beautiful and somewhat occupied by other love-struck couples. I snarkily suggest we get rid of everyone and Jonathan, to my surprise, follows this suggestion as if God himself has decreed it. There is a lot of swearing and shouting and some of the men in these peaceful duets try their hardest to stand up for themselves, but Mel waddles up in her wedding gown and sets them straight, blurting out a sad tale of her husband leaving her at the alter. Within ten minutes of them getting aggressive and myself losing all clothes we finally reserve this exquisite bit of real estate for a sunset viewing of a premium last will and testament order.

"Think they'll call the cops?" Mel finally asks.

"What's it matter, this is a great place for a last stand anyhow," says Jonathan, "...nice dick by the way, Pete."

"Thanks, Jonathan."

"Is it worth getting naked too?"

"It's not as liberating as I thought it'd be."

I take Mel's hand. "Hey... if you didn't drive away with Gabe, then maybe you won't get in an accident like

28

you said would happen?"

Mel gives me a soft smile of reassurance. She grabs my hand. "The accident's inevitable, Pete. When we're finished here, Gabe's going to take me away and I will say goodbye to all this."

"But if you don't! I don't want you to. Even if I can't have you, that doesn't mean I want you to die."

Mel doesn't respond. She simply smiles softly, and then I see it. The resignation. That was the Death Wish's real purpose: letting go and enjoying the moment.

"And you? You say you've got incurable cancer. But you look just fine to me. Just like you used to look, when it was just the two of us."

I want to correct her and explicitly repeat the doctor's news, but there it was: the resignation and a moment that needed to be enjoyed.

"You look just as beautiful too."

The sound of a car pulling up some ways behind us gets all our heads turning. No, it's not the local SWAT team, but a groom and my drug dealer, Randy.

"You actually messaged him?" I turn to Jonathan, but Jonathon's already making his way over to Gabe. Gabe hesitates as Jonathan's arms open up, offering a hug.

Gabe puts a hand up, "One thing at a time, Johnny. First, Mel." He brushes past Jonathan and comes straight towards us. I watch as his feet begin to slow down, his composure dribbling out with each step closer. He stares at me, trying to hide his disgust, before focusing on Mel.

He wants to start simple.

"What're you guys doing here?" It's then I feel Mel's hand leave mine. She's edging backwards. I do the same.

"It's our last sunset."

"It doesn't have to be. Look, baby, you're not dying—Randy told me how he sold *all three of you* Death Wish." Gabe glances beyond us to the cliff's edge. "You're not in your right minds—any of you. Now, please, I know you're scared. We don't have to go through with this wedding. We don't even have to be together..." I watch his face as those words tear away at his insides, cutting all the roots away. I see his love for her like I see my own.

"We don't have to get in a car; we don't even have to do anything. We can all just watch this sunset," he turns back to Jonathan, "All of us, together."

And suddenly, I find my hand at Mel's back, urging her back from the cliff, back to sanity, as it seemed. It was wrong of me to say anything today, even if it were my last. Mel turns to me and smiles, that reassuring soft smile I knew so well, all those years ago. She then lifts her wedding gown, ready to walk back into the safety of Gabe's arms.

Gabe doesn't drop his gaze until they embrace.

I am happy for them. And that is the truth.

Gabe and Mel then turn to face me, both of them corralling me over, if not for an actual orgy, then something emotionally similar.

"C'mon, Pete, come back to us. It's going to be okay."

I smile and I laugh, shaking my head. "Don't worry about me, it was inoperable anyway. I Love you guys, all of you."

And then I step back into nothingness, enjoying the moment as I finally let go.

A Beginner's Guide to Revenge
David Myrcott

Like most people I have a number of interesting and rewarding hobbies. Restoring antique parasols to their former glory, putting tiny bow ties on tadpoles then releasing them back into the wild, seeing how many dead otters it takes to fill a vivarium — these are just some of the ways I choose to enjoy my leisure time. None of these experiences, however, comes close to giving me the satisfaction I derive from obtaining revenge on all the people who have ever wronged me in any way, no matter how trivial the transgression.

Allow me to explain. As a bitter and resentful individual I am often on the lookout for ways in which to feel indignant. What I then like to do is seek redress in a manner entirely out of proportion to the alleged slight, thus ensuring I not only feel empowered, but that the person who's wronged me will know never to cross me again. It's like Gandhi said: an eye for an eye teaches people not to fuck with people's eyes. I got the idea whilst watching *Oprah* one day. She was talking about making a list of all the bad things people have done to you throughout your life, then tracking those people down one by one and making them suffer. Or something. I wasn't really listening. At any rate that's exactly what I did, and I couldn't be more satisfied with the results.

In the event you want to make a list of your own but don't know where to start or how best to repay a lifetime's worth of transgressors, the following examples of my own retaliatory accomplishments may provide a useful starting point.

Marbles

The first person I took revenge on after deciding to finally chuck in several decades worth of religious upbringing and associated prattle about forgiveness was an old primary school acquaintance named Jess Wakefield. This irksome little shit used to continually cheat me at marbles when we were in grade one, pocketing the best of my collection, and I was too meek and mild-mannered at the time to do anything about it. Well, not anymore.

Having tracked him down through a mutual acquaintance I arrived on his doorstep one grey September morn, thoughts of revenge coursing through me like some delicious aperitif. When he answered my knock and opened the front door I pulled out a Polaroid camera, snapped a photo of him then turned and walked away without a word. I then boarded a flight to Haiti, found the most wizened and unscrupulous voodoo high priest money could buy and had a potent curse put on the incorrigible marble-pilferer. Now his ghost is destined to wander the afterlife, blind, with excrement clogging his nostrils and the screams of tortured souls ceaselessly besieging his ears. That'll teach him to take my marbles, the thieving cunt.

Queue Jumpers

If there's one thing I despise in this life (and there's not, there are hundreds) it's someone cutting in front of me in a queue. The last time this happened I was standing in line waiting to be served at a busy inner-city pizzeria. 'Who was next?' called the assistant, and I moved forward to place my order as it was indeed my turn to be served. Imagine my horror when before I could utter a word some bloated suit barged in front of me with his Bluetooth earpiece and aftershave reek and said 'I'll have a large...'

That was as far as he managed to get, because the next moment my fist was making decisive contact with his Adam's apple. Shrieking like Bruce Lee in *Enter the Dragon* I lashed the miscreant repeatedly about the head and neck with one of his own shoelaces, then slapped him hard with a slice of Margarita as I rained insults and abuse (or what I like to term life advice) upon him.

As a throng of horrified onlookers watched on helplessly, I then proceeded to remove the adder I keep inside my sock at all times for just such an event and allowed the fanged beast to have its fill of the recumbent queue-jumper's horrid little face. When he had been savaged to my satisfaction I then returned the serpent to his home inside my Chuck Taylors and made my way through the crowd. If he did happen to survive the ordeal I almost guarantee that's one fellow who won't ever be cutting in line again. This incident is also important as it highlights the fact that new enemies can be made at almost every turn, and need to be dealt with summarily with the weapons at hand or, as in my own case, a sock-adder.

Deities

There are times in life when misfortunes befall one and no earthly agent appears upon which to seek redress. Accidents, illness, natural disasters — these can all throw a spanner in the works of the serious revenge devotee. Who to take your ire out on I such instances? The answer is obvious — God. No matter what your spiritual affinities, your denomination is bound to have a place where members of that faith habitually gather to praise their chosen deity. Churches, mosques and synagogues are all highly flammable and arson is one thing you certainly don't need to be a genius in order to grasp: match + petrol = kaboom.

That's all well and good for churchgoers and the devout, but what about us atheists? Let's say there's a torrential downpour and several houses on your street, including yours, are badly damaged. Why should your house get flooded during a heavy storm but your neighbour's house be spared? That isn't fair. If something like this has happened to you, simply hide in your neighbour's front yard and wait until they go to work. Smash a small hole in a side window using the butt of a screwdriver, then insert their garden hose and turn it on full blast. By the time they get home at least 70% of their downstairs carpeting is bound to be ruined beyond repair, and if you're lucky they will have been in the midst of rehanging some artwork and left several expensive originals leaning against the wall waiting to be destroyed by your watery torrent of hate. Parfait.

Remember, the above is intended as a rough guide only. Get creative with it. If you happen to be beating a philandering ex-boyfriend with a crowbar and you eventually tire of the dull thwack of metal on bone, try running him over with your car for a while. Similarly, after your third or fourth stair-pushing you may notice a certain nonchalance creeping in. At this point it might be best to utilise an abandoned elevator shaft or even to try an old-fashioned method such as the garrotte or rack (this may require the aid of one or several accomplices). A fully functional Iron Maiden can be easily constructed from just a few thousand nails, some broken glass and a man-sized, hinged sarcophagus.

But I'm just an average person I hear you cry, *What do I know about constructing medieval torture devices?*

Don't worry! As you progress through your own list and your hatred and thirst for retribution becomes all-encompassing, you'll find the motivation you need to see things through to their logical, illegal and probably highly bloody conclusion. Happy revenging...

How T-Bone Learned to Stop Worrying and Love Happy Gilmore

Craig Tuck

He was a man who'd always loved a fight, a drink, a smoke, and a woman, but one thing T-Bone Pickens had never expected to love was the Adam Sandler film *Happy Gilmore* — that came as a surprise.

Prison life was hard, but the little things made all the difference. Adam Sandler made all the difference.

In Windy Hill Penitentiary, breaks in the routine of violent intimidation and casual degradation weren't common. But on the fourth Friday of every third month, the prisoners who weren't in the hole, infirmary, or morgue would call a truce, and gather in the rec hall for movie night.

Movie night was the only time when the neo-Nazis and the Latino gangs associated in relative non-violent harmony, kindly moving their legs so enemies could pass unobstructed along the aisle. Movie night was the only time when the fresh meat wasn't ritualistically paraded around the room in women's clothing, the only night when the ageing 'lifers' didn't cower in the corner with fear and confusion, as new generations of increasingly violent criminals swept through their home in waves.

Even though Windy Hill Penitentiary only had one video left that hadn't been weaponised and destroyed, movie night remained sacrosanct. It was the most important unofficial rule of life in gen pop: on the fourth Friday of every third month, retributional shankings were unquestionably postponed.

If ever an inmate broke the laws of movie night (no cutting, no kicking, no kissing) they would pay a hefty price. In fact, the last man who'd started trouble on movie night actually begged to be put into solitary confinement, such was his need for protection.

Frustrated by an obstructed view, he'd jabbed the tall jewellery thief seated in front of him with an AIDS-infected needle. The ensuing brawl ensured the cancellation of movie night before Happy had even learned how to putt. The violence in the air was palpable as the bloodlust surged to awful extremes, even for gen pop.

Mindful of the danger the man was now in, prison authorities granted him his wish for isolation. However, once he had been safely locked away inside, the guards settled the score themselves — repeatedly, for six consecutive weeks.

In Windy Hill Penitentiary, everyone loved movie night. The entire prison population, inmates and guards alike, had been won over by *Happy Gilmore*'s sweet life-affirming blend of violence and golfing.

Everyone looked forward to that magical night on the fourth Friday of every third month, when they could enjoy the character's beautiful story arc once more. Even inmates who had never watched films on the outside loved movie night; even men like T-Bone Pickens.

The first time he saw Happy mock 'Shooter' McGavin for speaking in rhymes, he laughed so hard he cried. That simple joy of pure, innocent laughter was a pleasure the recently incarcerated T-Bone had thought he'd left behind. To experience it there, in that place, was incredibly emotional.

As his fellow inmates reached out to him that night, patting him on the back to let him know they were right there with him, T-Bone felt the ache of a familial bond he'd been searching for his entire life. At that beautiful moment, right there in the filthy rec hall of Windy Hill Penitentiary, T-Bone felt community. T-Bone felt love.

And it was that bond — a love which only became more intense over time — that put T-Bone in such a bind on his final movie night, just six days from his scheduled release.

By 2016, the prison was undergoing a significant facility upgrade, after the ambitious new Mayor of Windy Hill, the Hon Stephen Mathison, had successfully campaigned on a platform of prison reform. Prisoners shouldn't be left to rot in overcrowded, poorly maintained facilities, he had said in the lead-up to the election. He held firm to that line after he won, too.

'Prisons should be modern, secure and safe for inmates and staff alike!' he thundered in front of the gathered media throng, as he approached City Hall for the first time as Mayor.

'How can prisoners be expected to truly rehabilitate themselves when they live an existence that is so far removed from the outside world?

'When prisoners are left without access to even the most rudimentary of training equipment, in a facility where it is considered a privilege to be granted access to broken down old typewriters, how are they meant to grow?

'How are they meant to build up relevant skills for the future?'

It was a speech he had given many times before, except with each performance he added another new example to further illustrate the facility's inadequacy. By the time his agenda had reached the hallowed halls of the Senate Expenditure Review Committee, it had become a convincing list indeed.

As he stood before the foremost bean counters in the land, the Hon Stephen Mathison detailed his request for maintenance funding. It was the performance of his life, and he rammed his argument home with a powerful final point to the committee.

'...and if all of that is not enough,' he said, 'I am told

that on the fourth Friday of every third month, these poor men — and despite their crimes, we must remember that they remain men — are herded into the rec hall like cattle, where they are forced to watch a crackly television recording of that terrible Adam Sandler film, *Happy Gilmore!*'

To this day, government insiders on both sides maintain that this was the point that got the bill over the line. In fact, there was hardly a dry eye in the house.

When Mayor Mathison added that the inmates were also being forced to sit through the same TV broadcast commercials that interrupted each screening, the committee couldn't approve the funding boost quickly enough.

'Get those poor fools a DVD player!' became the common cry. 'At least then they'll have a remote!'

And so it was.

As the inmates gathered for the gala premiere screening in the newly upgraded facilities, they couldn't help but be impressed by their first glimpses of the new equipment being deployed. They adored the big new flat screen TV and gasped when they saw a shiny disc being slipped into the attached DVD drive.

Had the outside world really progressed this much? The casual conversation among some of the younger prisoners suggested that indeed it had, and terminology like *digital restoration*, *high definition* and *surround sound* had the gen pop veterans like T-Bone Pickens buzzing with excitement.

That is, at least, until the film started.

"What the hell is *Twilight*?" one of the neo-Nazis yelled as the title screen appeared.

"No estoy impresionado por esta tontería!" added one of the Mexican gang leaders.

One of the quieter inmates — often reduced to whimpering in the corner — threw his box of popcorn at the screen. Many other inmates followed his lead, such was the outrage. But not T-Bone. T-Bone was too stunned for that.

In his time behind bars, T-Bone had learnt a lot about life. He learned a lot about the importance of love, respect, commitment and conviction. It wasn't his time in the yard or the kitchen that taught him those lessons; it was his time in front of the old crackly TV screen. Those tri-monthly screenings taught T-Bone more about the enduring value of friendship and the undeniable bond between a man and his dreams than anything else life had thrown at him.

In 18 years' hard time at Windy Hill Penitentiary, T-Bone had suffered every indignity known to man, but that powerful story of a failed hockey player who was forced to take up golf had always been there for comfort.

Sitting in the refurbished rec hall as a rehabilitated and almost free man, T-Bone reflected on the role that beautiful film had played in his life. Thanks to the lessons he had learned studying Happy's inspirational character arc, T-Bone had managed to rebuild his marriage and establish a relationship with the kids he had never held in his own hands or seen with his own eyes.

In prison, T-Bone found a confidence — an inner peace — which had eluded him throughout his years on the outside. And in just six days, T-Bone was going to return to that world a new man: a husband, a father, a provider. He was finally going to live a life of substance, and it was all because of *Happy Gilmore*.

Now, on the verge of returning to the family he had failed, with a new chance for redemption, he couldn't help but worry about what the future held for the new blood around him. What had this political refurbishment really given them? *Twilight*?

T-Bone felt sick. He looked at the agitated men who filled the halls; just kids, a lot of them. There was so much that Chubbs could teach them.

And as the riot gathered steam around him — chairs and fists alike flying about the room — he decided he couldn't just sit by and do nothing. Considering the terrible fate that had befallen Windy Hill Penitentiary, T-Bone made a choice. It was the same choice Happy had made when his Grandma's house was in peril — he chose to fight.

In a swift movement which showed that time — and Chubbs' calming influence — hadn't dulled his fire completely, T-Bone leapt from his chair, advanced over the concussed neo-Nazis, past the guard with the shotgun, to the locked video cabinet. As the guard turned towards him, T-Bone grabbed the shotgun from his hands, dug the barrel into his chest, and told him to step back.

'In fact, all you mother fuckers stand back!' he added loudly to the room.

The crowd did as instructed, and with a sudden, violent jab, T-Bone used the butt of the shotgun to smash open the video cabinet lock. Without taking his eyes (or his gun) off the many dangerous men around him, T-Bone opened the cabinet, reached inside, and grabbed a VHS. When he held the video aloft, the inmates cheered. The guards did too.

'This!' he yelled, to thunderous applause, 'This is the movie we will watch tonight!'

Again, the people cheered.

'Happy! Happy! Happy!' they chanted.

Triumphant, T-Bone turned to face the new TV and his eyes darted around the shiny new technology, looking for the spot to insert the video. The new equipment was complicated. He couldn't find a hole big enough. Puzzled, he scratched his head.

'Man, you trippin!' one of the younger inmates yelled. 'Trippin' like Scottie Pippen! There ain't no VHS spot in a modern DVD player!'

The blood drained from T-Bone's face. No place to

put the VHS? No room for *Happy Gilmore*?

Stunned, the shotgun slipped from his grip. Before he noticed that he had dropped the weapon, the guard had picked it up and pointed it directly at T-Bone's face.

'Listen boy, you just took a weapon from a prison officer,' the guard said. 'And worse than that, you got my hopes up about watching *Happy Gilmore*!'

'I'm sorry!' T-Bone wailed. 'I didn't mean no harm, I just wanted to watch this movie!'

T-Bone held the video demonstratively aloft once more, and the guard snatched it away.

'This video...this video is useless!' he snapped. 'It is obsolete, and I am going to destroy it!'

The guard threw the old VHS copy of the Adam Sandler classic to the ground and pointed his shotgun at it.

'It's time we all just move on!'

It was instinct that made T-Bone dive over the video, as the guard prepared to pull the trigger. It was love that drove him to protect the sacred VHS, as the bullet burst from the barrel.

The shot was fired the moment T-Bone left the ground, and that man who had always loved a fight, a drink, a smoke, and a woman, took the bullet that was meant for *Happy Gilmore*.

T-Bone was killed almost instantly.

Before he died however, there was time for a big smile to form on his face, as his final moment of life was a proud one; he had finally become a man of conviction. T-Bone loved the thought: after a lifetime filled with hate, he would die protecting what he loved.

As his last breath gently slipped away, T-Bone knew that right there on the cold concrete floor of Windy Hill Penitentiary, he had finally found his happy place.

T-Bone's bags were packed, and he was finally going home.

Dreamers

Aden Simpson

Dream Men

Noun.

A small subset of humans that, while dreaming, have the ability to inhabit and alter the waking reality around them, within a certain radius.

See also: Bigfoot, Area 51, the Loch Ness Monster

An Assassination

All his men were dead.

And he was running, faster than he'd ever run before, like his life depended on it (which it did). Lights flicked on wherever he went, whether this being the work of the curious residents of the barrio or the entity that chased him, he couldn't tell.

Previously, he'd only made it about five hundred metres with the Bentley before the bonnet sparked up and the wheels lost traction, as the car began to levitate off the ground. He leapt out of the vehicle when it rose from the ground and was lucky not to shatter both his ankles. Sensing this may happen to all the cars he hopped in, he decided to run the last 1.5 km to theoretical freedom, not that he could see any reason why the entity could not do the same thing to him as it had the car.

He'd progressed another five hundred metres or so before he noticed that the road further up had disappeared and dipped into a large pond, a family of ducks gliding peacefully along the surface. He froze, sweat pouring out, fully aware whose calling card the duck-pond setup represented. He turned down onto another road, this one thankfully sans duck pond, and continued his marathon for life. His heart pounding, he kept telling himself just a little bit further, just one more kilometre before he was out of reach, that's what the myths alluded. It felt like he'd run the required kilometre down this street before he sensed the shadow from above. He spun his head around to find the car he had previously ditched, still airborne, veering down on him at a leisurely pace, like a wolf toying with its prey. In the driver's seat, one arm casually out the window, sat the supernatural figure that conjoured this nightmare.

He ducked into a side alley adjoining the main street, only to realise too late it was a dead end. He turned and there his assailant stood. The assailant was tall and lean; his naked skin a sickly black of pulsating fluid, shimmering at the edges, but in direct contrast his face was a bulbous, cartoonish yellow smiley face, the kind you'd see on a cheap novelty t-shirt.

"Please," the minister begged, "I'll do whatever you

want. I'll leave. I'll sign the agreement!"

"It's just a job for me, minister," said the smiley-face creature, his smile somewhat dissipating, "I just do what they tell me. Sorry."

Doomed, the minister stumbled backwards until he was up against the brick wall that had cut his escape and ended his life.

The smiley-face creature was now frowning, as he produced a banana from thin air. The minister shrieked, for he'd seen the same innocuous banana used on one of his bodyguards earlier that night, culminating in a horrible, inexplicable end.

"Sorry," the smiley-face man muttered as he carefully lined up the terrified minister and shouted, "Banana Republic!" as he threw the banana at the minister's heart, only for the banana to stop just short of the man, disappearing into thin air.

The minister opened his eyes when he realised he wasn't dead.

Smiley Face had turned to a frown once more, his eyebrows raised as he scratched his chin, deep in thought. He then began inspecting a watch on his wrist while doing some calculations in his head. Smiley Face then talked into the watch, "Doug, all I need is about another couple of metres north-west, please."

The minister looked on in confusion as Smiley Face raised his hand in acknowledgement. "Sorry about this, it should only take a second."

Somewhere in a sleepy motel, an exact 2.005 kilometres away, a disgruntled Doug pushed with all his might against a futuristic black coffin with red lights whirring along its sides. Doug pushed it to the corner of the room and pressed the recalibration button on the coffin's lid. He waited, until the sound of Smiley Face cracked through the air again. "Going to need just a little more line here, Doug. Our friend is starting to get wise."

Throwing his hands up in frustration, Doug looked out the window and did the requisite calculations, including the estimated fall. These things were pretty sturdy, he figured.

Out the coffin slid.

The minister was growing bolder now; though he kept his back against the wall, he started looking at the sidewalls of the alley, searching for an escape route. When that failed, he reached for his phone and started going through his contacts, the screen having stopped melting in front of his eyes since he left the 'zone' of his assailant's influence. He dialed the emergency number, but dropped the phone when he heard a polite cough. He looked up to see the smiley-face man once more pointing a banana at his chest.

Smiley Face grinned. "Sorry, this will only hurt a lot."

* * *

Charlie opened his eyes to Doug Shraeder and the night sky.

"I could have sworn we were in a hotel room."

"Accommodations had to be changed, *because of you.*"

"The bad guy is dead, by the way. I ended up saying 'Banana Republic'."

"Congratulations," mocked Doug, "but that's not really the issue right now. We need to eviscerate the coffin—second one this month—and evac to rendezvous in what I can only assume is now a very awakened city."

Charlie stood up and smiled at Doug. "Then why are you wasting our time berating me?"

Doug slapped Charlie in the face.

There wasn't going to be any sympathy from Doug for the punk during debrief, if they were ever going to make it to debrief at all.

Debrief

Two tense border smugglings and one leech-infested trek through Central American jungle later, Charlie found himself in an interrogation room for his usual game of debrief. Sitting across from him were the Top Brass, Colonel MacCready and his brown-nosing, bean-counting subordinate, Cedric Hayes.

Next to Charlie was his handler, Doug Schraeder, who for the last fifteen days had been constantly reminding Charlie that he was looking forward to saying absolutely nothing in his defence this time. Charlie merely laughed at this; for all his talk, Doug had a soft heart and Charlie was certain Doug wasn't going to let him hang out to dry.

"What are we going to do with you, Charlie my boy?" MacCready shook his head.

"What indeed," parroted Cedric Hayes, unnecessarily, as usual.

"Well, here's an idea," Charlie began, "How about you decommission me and, I dunno, shut down the program? Because as you can see, from the last two times, the publicity and conspiracy theory venting could be getting a bit too much. Maybe you should go back to just using those guns of yours—you know, the ones you bought for our military industrial complex?"

Charlie never used to joke like this, at least not to such an extent. He seldom went out of his way to rattle the cage. But he was growing tired of this cage, and something had to give.

"This attitude change has been very disappointing," said Colonel MacCready.

"Yeah, well, so have my twenties, so far."

"You know we can't shut down the program, Charlie. There's too much potential in it."

If anyone wanted to know the real reason as to why they kept on with the program of dream men doing paranormal assassinations for the US government, then quite frankly they did it because they could, because it was a toy that simply had to be played with, even if the toy could be a little difficult at times.

"I just don't feel I should still be punished for something I didn't mean to do, something I did when I was basically just a kid."

"You're not being punished. You're serving your country," said MacCready.

"With pride," added Cedric, once again wrong.

"Haven't I served my country enough? How much longer can you keep me in here? I've paid for my mistake and then some."

The Top Brass looked over to Doug, who still hadn't said anything. Eventually, that soft heart of Doug's relented. "Maybe we could scale back the assignment load, until we find a suitable replacement of Charlie's calibre?"

The Top Brass considered this for a moment, before MacCready nodded.

"We do have that bunker-busting field test in Pashawan coming up."

"We could throw someone else in the deep end for that, perhaps?"

"Hmmm..." the Top Brass thought allowed in unison.

Finally, MacCready relented. "We'll consider it on the condition that during his remaining missions, Charlie will refrain from applying his recent dream style and stick to the allowed dream tactics."

"And no more feeding the ducks," added Cedric, this being less a matter of efficacy and more as a form of punishment.

"I can't always help that!" Charlie shot back.

"Well you'll just have to; your calling card has become more of an unnecessary sideshow than striking fear into the hearts of America's enemies."

Charlie leapt to protest, but Doug drew a hand across him. "It's a good deal. Just take it."

With his head drooped, Charlie complied.

A Brief Brief

The Top Brass kept their word. There were no missions sought for Charlie, and with the bunker-buster trial in Pashawan a complete success (the rookie recruit managing to hone his flying skills) Charlie hoped he would soon be on his way out. He didn't do much at the barracks but daydream about his new life. He'd saved enough over the years, and even entertained the thought of asking for a severance (if that was a thing in the army—unless Doug was lying) and maybe finding somewhere peaceful for a while, let his dreams get quiet again so he didn't hurt any civs on the outside.

These thoughts of the future put him in a good mood and in turn he'd go off around the barracks, playing pranks in the day and spooking those on duty as Smiley Face at night. This didn't last long, of course, and he was reprimanded and reminded that these barracks were the very place he'd made that fatal mistake that kept him tied up in the military. Charlie apologised and then went back to just feeding the ducks in his night time incursions, only for someone to slip and fall when they failed to notice that the floor had become pond. One bruised ass later, Charlie found himself back on the meds until his next, and hopefully last, assignment.

He didn't see Doug the entire time either, this probably a good thing, as a break would do wonders for the family man's patience and blood pressure.

It was precisely thirty-two days of lounging about in leisure before the Top Brass finally came calling. Charlie met with Doug before the briefing and admired his handler's new tan.

"South Lake with the family," explained Doug.

"How are the wife 'n kids?"

"They're good, thanks for asking."

"And Heather, how's she doing?"

"She's fine, Charlie."

"18 yet?"

Doug rolled his eyes. "How was your downtime?"

"Better than expected, thanks. I'm thinking North Dakota once I get out.

"North Dakota, huh."

"Somewhere quiet. Maybe get a job on one of the rigs, if this severance thing doesn't transpire."

"How many times do I have to tell you, Charlie? There is no severance package."

"Change only starts when we take action, Doug."

"Where'd you hear that?"

"Saw it on some poster in Santiago on the last mission… It's either severance or I take a quick detour into the local bank on our next job."

"…So North Dakota, huh."

Truth was, Doug didn't think they were going to let Charlie go. He was just too dangerous to just be set free among the civilians, and he wouldn't know how to take care of himself anyway. Despite the fact that he was a soldier, the kid was treated like an army brat. And if it got to the point where Charlie refused all other assignments, Doug knew that deep down they wouldn't go for a dishonourable discharge. No, young Charlie would be taken care of, and Doug had a sneaking suspicion who they'd ask to make sure this happened.

The Top Brass were already smiling when Charlie and Doug entered.

"Good news, Charlie."

"It's Heather's birthday?"

"Yes—no! Goddamn it! Charlie, we've got one more assignment for you."

"Your *last one*," said Cedric.

Charlie's eyes lit up. His grin pancaked from ear to ear. He even smiled at bean-counter Cedric.

"Really?"

"Absolutely," Colonel MacCready confirmed.

Doug waited for it all to sink in for Charlie, before he made his questions. He was already sceptical.

"What's the last mission?"

Cedric scratched his head, "Err, well this one will be a little different, actually..."

Charlie had stopped his grinning.

"How so?" asked Doug.

"The target will not need to be eliminated, but instead made to understand our thoughts on recent relations in order to come to a more positive outlook."

Charlie raised his eyebrows and sat back in his chair, folding his arms. "So you want me to intimidate someone?"

"Exactly. And you won't need to discuss the finer points of our disagreement with them either. Just make your presence known and they should come to their senses soon enough."

Doug was not sold, but Charlie was blinded by the light at the end of the tunnel. "So, I don't have to kill anyone *and* this will be my last assignment?"

"You can even feed the ducks, if that's how you want to make your presence known."

"Oh, boy!" cheered Charlie.

The dossiers were all dispensed with in less than a minute and a gleeful Charlie smiled as he stood to salute the Top Brass on his way out, before Colonel MacCready asked Doug to stay back. Doug didn't like the sound of that and even Charlie couldn't help but hesitate in his joy.

"Go on, Charlie. We won't be long."

A French Autumn

It was strange that Charlie didn't bring up Doug's private conversation with the Top Brass until they reached their quaint homely hotel in the canal-lined city of Sainte-Rêver after two draining flights.

"You waited all this time to ask me about that?" asked Doug, surprised the relentless Charlie had not pestered him earlier.

"I didn't want anyone else to hear."

Doug couldn't argue with that, nor with Charlie's obvious yet unspoken feeling throughout the plane ride that something was up.

"So?" Charlie prompted once more.

"So what? They were discussing my reassignment. It had nothing to do with you."

They stared each other down for a hot minute. Eventually, Charlie buckled. "Well, all right then. You should've just said that instead of making it weird the whole plane trip."

"You're the one who made it weird," countered Doug. "Besides, there was nothing to tell..."

Doug tried to resume setting up the coffin in their hotel room, before Charlie resumed his grilling. "Who did you get for reassignment? Was it Morris—that atrocious fuck?"

"That was the offer, but I turned it down and applied for a desk job."

Charlie was stunned. "That wife of yours put you up

to it?"

"I want to see my kids become adults, Charlie, so I can protect Heather from deviants like you."

"Hey I'd treat her with respect, dammit!" Charlie declared, distracted by Doug's joke, to Doug's quiet relief.

The coffin now set up, reconnaissance became their next order of business. It was a warm autumn day when they stepped out, cameras in tow. Charlie loved the early part of reconnaissance the most, the first day was really just a day of sight-seeing, taking in all the landmarks, choke points, escape routes, all important features captured under the guise of a curious tourist. Charlie had a lot of photos developed on the barracks and his Nikon D3300 HDSLR camera was his most treasured possession. He had quite a photo collection built up, and, unlike the travel snaps of people his age, all of Charlie's photos had to be printed and approved by the US military for personal keepsake. He couldn't just go posting them on Facebook saying "These are the sixty-eight cities and towns I've visited across the globe with my military salary—don't read too much into it!" Such as it was, Charlie wasn't actually allowed a Facebook account, though he heard and seen a whole lot about it from the others on the barracks. And not wanting to be left behind in the race to make memories, Charlie was steadfast in building his collection for his retirement so that he could one day meet someone and show them all the places he'd been, as if to say "I had a life too."

Together with Doug, Charlie walked around the beautiful town, lined with cobblestone streets and Victorian street lamps, and took photos of the church, the river and the stone bridge they crossed to get to the north side where their target would be holed up for a few days with his mistress in a luxury suite. Doug also engaged in the exact same kind of recon, albeit, in Charlie's opinion, in a less artful way.

As they crossed a bridge over one of the river canals, Charlie found himself drawn to the water below, where the river widened and became a riverbank, and along this bank Charlie saw a bench and a family of ducks floating in the water. Charlie's eyes lit up and he was off. Doug was about to raise his voice until he saw what Charlie was racing toward at the end of the bridge and down the stairs. He thought about following, before deciding to ease up on the boy. The river glistened exquisitely in the afternoon sun, and, with everything in town layered with this fairytale enchantment, Doug couldn't help but relax. They had time. Doug could wait.

There was a young child feeding the family of ducks with his grandma. Charlie exchanged smiles with the grandma, who offered him some bread to throw to the ducklings. Charlie knelt down next to the young child and cheered when the kid threw in his bread piece. Charlie then dropped his own bread piece in the water and chuckled as ducklings scrambled to catch a nibble.

Watching the kid and the grandma smile together while the sun shone off the water, he couldn't help but wonder if he would ever have a family of his own. After the grandma ran out of bread, she took the boy to leave, but not before the boy said goodbye to Charlie, which made him go all warm and fuzzy inside. Taken with this feeling, Charlie continued to watch the ducks for a little while longer, content in the moment. When he finally decided to move on and continue his reconnaissance, he crossed paths with a beautiful girl, only slightly younger than him, on his way up the stairs to the bridge. Strawberry blonde hair dangled to her shoulders underneath a purple beanie, framing her perfect freckled cheeks. They locked eyes for the slightest moment, Charlie's heart skipping a beat, before Charlie was met with Doug's harried look that said, *let's get the rest of this show over with.* Looking back, Charlie swore he caught the girl glancing back at him, before she produced some food, knelt down and threw it to the ducklings.

The rest of their scan went without incident. They proceeded to stake out the target as he did some shopping with the mistress, Doug believing his surveillance had successfully netted him the location of their dinner plans. "They're going to La Bella Rousseau, which means if they decide a leisurely stroll back to the apartment is in order, we could intercept our man here," said Doug, pointing at the map on his phone. "Or, meet them in their room and discreetly scare the pants off of them."

Charlie shrugged. "I'm easy. Both sound good."

"Then how about the first one, intercepting them by the riverbank?"

"Sure."

"No questions?"

"You seem to have it all worked out...listen, after this is done, do you think it would be so terrible if we stuck around, just for a little while?"

"We've got a flight scheduled tomorrow morning."

"I know; it'd only be an extra day... I guess I just want to take it all in, I suppose."

Doug hesitated. "Okay, sure. I'll see what I can do, but we can only do this if you don't attract any unnecessary attention in your dream tonight. How does that sound?" Doug felt like a mother bargaining with her offspring, but it had to be this way sometimes with Charlie, who was really more like a boy stuck in a man's body.

"Yes, mother." Charlie relented.

"Ok then, so what are you going to do?"

"City-wide aerial assault—just kidding! I was thinking of feeding the ducks at the riverbank and then staring at our guy, perhaps while masturbating, making him *very* uncomfortable."

"Maybe lose the masturbation part."

"How else will I stroke fear into the heart of America's

greatest enemy?"

"They did say you could do the duck feeding this one last time...but I'd rather you be more certain than that. According to our man's dossier, his natural fears include spiders, snakes and, strangely, fortune tellers."

"Fortune tellers?"

"Did you read the file?"

"I did...but refresh my memory."

"A fortune teller predicted his father's death...you're going to read the file before we have dinner."

"Absolutely, without a doubt... Maybe I could force a detour to a fortune teller stand, where I reveal a note that tells him to 'step off' whatever he's doing?"

Doug was surprised by this relatively simple suggestion. "You're showing a lot of restraint, where was that before?"

"Well you said if I did, we could stay a little longer. Besides, this way is kind of funny, no? God knows how many tax dollars just to send a guy a letter."

Doug chuckled. "It's your call."

They had a light meal in the lobby downstairs before they went back to their room where the coffin had to be prepped. Developed by one of the first dream men, the coffin had become integral to keeping a dream man dreaming and allowing the handler to monitor a dreamer's status and vital signs, with some communication allowed from the handler through a series of colour-coded prompts that would appear to the dreamer. Doug reiterated the radius Charlie's dreamwaves could extend and, in this case, with the town itself not that big and the task of little strain, all the ducks were lined up, so to speak. Doug had Charlie sit in the chair and wait while the sedative was prepared.

"I think I've decided the title of my memoir: *Dream Men: The Shockingly True Story of Charlie Wax.*"

Doug, usually one to dismiss the joke, given the vast protocols and ramifications both were well aware of, asked who would play him in the movie.

"It's such a complex role, I may have to play it myself."

"I thought you wanted to look good?"

"Hardy fucking har."

Doug nodded over to the Coffin. Charlie sighed as he stepped in.

"Not going to miss this."

Doug stopped. "You never mentioned any discomfort before."

"The sedative is fine. It's afterwards—bad dreams." Charlie snorted. Doug rolled his eyes, humouring Charlie.

"And you promise, an extra day?"

"I already put the request into HQ," Doug said as the veins were lined up and the sedative was slowly injected.

"Good. Thank you. Doug... I'm sorry about the last mission. Sorry about all the times I went too far... But it wasn't all bad, was it? We made a good team, didn't we?"

Doug smiled as Charlie's eyes began to droop. "No, it's okay. It was good; we were a good team." And when Charlie's eyes were fully closed and the visuals on the coffin highlighting his vitals dropped to their sleeping states, pre-REM, Doug removed his glasses and wiped his eyes. "I'm sorry too, Charlie."

The Job

A dream can be a beautiful thing, a place where anything, including flying, is possible; where all the moments are as mysterious as they are tantalising. They can inspire, offer telling truths to those seeking advice or scare the living daylights out of a soul. Charlie had a strange gift, a beautiful gift and it depressed him to know that the only kind of dreams he needed to have; the only kind of truths he needed to tell came from dark corners to suck the light out. A boogeyman, that's what he was but often he wondered if he really needed to be. There was no respite for him, no chance to regather and recalibrate each night. It was either take the pills that blacked him out OR become the thing that goes bump in the night.

There are good people that do good and there are bad people that do good, Charlie. That's what the Top Brass had said, defining Charlie before he had a chance.

The sun was just setting as the target finished his exquisite roast duck and green sprouts with a glass of white, while his ever-slim and ever-vigilant mistress dutifully ate her salad and a naughty bite of Chocolate éclair.

Entering reality as the dream man was always weird, like how one never remembers how their dream starts. Over the years Charlie had honed this into a well-refined art of appearing inconspicuous at first close to the target, and then beginning the slow stalk of the hunter as Smiley Face. There was no risk of being recorded, Charlie never showed up on any videos or CCTV footage, much to the despair of several conspiracy theorists looking to prove the existence of paranormal government spooks.

Sometimes, Charlie used to come in from the ceiling, covering the whole ceiling with dark wraith-like cloth and chains. In this particular instance he appeared out of thin air on the street outside La Bella Rousseau. This came as somewhat of a shock to an oncoming UPS delivery van that tried to swerve in time—but couldn't—careering through Charlie as if he were a ghost (which was essentially true in this form). The swerve directed the delivery driver to a nearby seasoned oak tree on the canal side of the road, smashing most of the bonnet and sending nearby pedestrians howling in shock. A crowd gathered and Charlie casually joined them, avoiding detection. Dazed, the delivery driver stumbled out of the van with mild whiplash and Charlie blew a sigh of relief. Leaving the crowd, he radioed in to Doug: "Slight mishap on entry. He's going to live though!"

Doug could not see what Charlie was seeing (this being Charlie's choice) nor could he really respond, but it was not hard to imagine what had transpired and Doug could do nothing but shake his head.

Charlie searched the crowd to see if the target had come out to witness the spectacle, but found the man and his mistress were already making their way back to their room, presumably for a no-holds barred sex romp of the highest order.

Charlie then floated, as discreetly as he liked, over to the bridge with the side stairs that led down to the riverbank where the ducks had been feeding earlier. Charlie twisted the world ever so slightly so that a detour of bright orange and yellow road signs would guide his target through to Charlie's fortune telling booth. The sun was making its final descent and the streetlights blinked on.

Floating over for a double-check of the target's status, Charlie found the pair were still a good five minutes away, and thankfully, had slowed down to a pleasant stroll, absorbing the beauty of the twilight draping over this enchanting place. Sensing time on his side, Charlie relaxed and made some bread to feed the ducks (both real and his own) appearing along the bank while he waited.

"They're hungry today," a soft voice crept up on Charlie, whose creepy yellow smiley face was immediately plastered over his face, like a chameleon changing colour when threatened. He turned to see the girl he'd passed before on the stairs looking at him, now taken aback by his yellow smiley face. Seeing her in all her beauty, Charlie was right then and there able to confirm the existence of angels. She was the reason he'd asked to stay another day and she was the reason he believed that, just maybe, this was the end of all his nightmares. Standing there, stupefied by her and unable to respond with anything more than an um-ing and uh-ing, the girl was taken aback, clearly regretting her approach.

"Okay then..." she whispered, turning away and having just decided to never speak to another stranger again, before Charlie finally found his tongue.

"Wait!" he blurted. "Sorry, you just startled me." He extended his hand out, a piece of bread offered as a token. "Do ya wanna feed 'em?"

The girl smiled and took the piece of bread and Charlie's relief was unending. She walked over to the side of the river and knelt down. Charlie followed and got one of the ducks that he generated with his mind to come over and quack happily at the girl, eagerly snapping away at the piece the girl threw.

"I think he likes you," said Charlie.

"I think I like him too," said the girl, her French accent only increasing her cuteness. "Why do you wear that mask? I don't want to be rude, just curious."

Charlie didn't have any answer that was good so he just told the truth. "I was going to scare someone with it. And while I'm spilling secrets, I should probably just tell you that I'm also a secret agent for the US government."

"Oh, that sounds like fun," the girl laughed nervously. She looked at the fortune telling stall set up behind them. "Is that yours?"

Charlie nodded. "What's scarier than the future?"

The girl thought about this for a while and eventually muttered, "I guess existential terror works too."

His heart racing and desperate to keep her attention, Charlie gulped. "Want me to do a reading? I'm sure it will be good."

"Sounds fun."

Charlie led her over to the fortune telling stand and moved behind the booth. Twilight was over, and the lamps became their only illumination. Some wit came to him and Charlie said, "Just one second, I need to get my official fortune telling hat." He then proceeded, to the girl's amusement, to look as if he was walking downstairs in an Illusion of perception (though to make it look even more realistic he did in fact create stairs leading down to nowhere) and fetched a large over-the-top purple turban with a glass mirror appearing in the centre to go on top of his smiley face. "Are you ready?"

"How does this work?"

"Give me your hand, please."

She extended her elegant hand out to Charlie, ready to do a palm reading, and as Charlie brought his hands to reach her, the softness of her skin sunk warm fuzzies all over him. Deeply overwhelmed, he felt the heat burst through his body and inadvertently caused the street lamps that barely lit her beautiful features to surge with light, one even exploding in a rain of sparks. The girl turned around in shock and other pedestrians on the bridge also stopped to see what all the commotion was.

"Sorry," said Charlie, before raising his other hand and snapping his fingers, returning the lights to their original states. "Now, where were we?"

Untroubled, the girl said, "You were going to tell my future."

"Of course," Charlie nodded, taking his other hand, and this time just managing to keep it together as he ran a finger across the lines of her palm. "Oh, yes. This looks like a happy life indeed."

"Will I get the job I always wanted?"

Charlie pretended to re-study the lines, clearly enjoying the touch of her skin. And because she didn't seem to mind, Charlie was willing to re-study extensively. "Yes, you get the job you always wanted, and from this line which details your finances and retirement savings, it also looks like you will be very filthy rich too."

The girl laughed. "Maybe this is true, but money isn't

everything, no?"

"Of course," said Charlie backtracking, "but if I look further, it seems you will also live a long and healthy life too."

"Will I have children?"

"Three."

"And their father. Will we be in love forever?"

Charlie did nothing but stare. He did nothing, because that's all he could do as he fell into her eyes and was swallowed by her mere existence. Whatever she wanted was what he would give.

"Absolutely."

"And who will he be, this husband of mine?"

Charlie smiled cheekily, "I can't tell you."

The girl raised her eyebrows, as if to say, *oh really?*

"I don't want to ruin the surprise."

"Can you tell me something about him?"

"What do you want to know?"

"What is his favourite thing?"

"He likes to feed the ducks."

"And why does he do that?"

Charlie drew a breath. "Because he used to go to the pond with his mum before she died, and they'd feed the ducks together, and they were happy, and since then he's never been more at peace than when he feeds the ducks."

The girl took her other hand and placed it on Charlie. The street lamps began to overheat again.

"And what is in this man's future?"

"He takes this girl out on a date and they fall in love and feed the ducks with their children."

"How many children will this man have?"

"Three, of course."

The girl smiled and then an abrupt seriousness drew upon her face, "And what is this man's name?"

Charlie knew he could give no such thing away. What was the point of altering your face if you told them your name? But then again, what was the point of wearing a mask when all you wanted to do was open everything up inside and leave yourself at the mercy of this woman who you wanted to run away with and leave this pointless dream killing behind?

No. This was his future. This was the only dream he wanted to have ever again. And as he went to remove the mask and tell her his name and everything that he was, he felt the familiar prompt in his head, a collection of colours in wriggly lines streaking through his vision, sent from Doug via the coffin, asking for a status on the mission. Charlie glanced over at the empty bridge and realised his target was probably already in bed with his mistress, blissfully unaware how scared he should be of the US government.

Charlie cursed. "Fuck!"

He stood and turned to the girl. "There's just one thing I need to do. A real quick thing. Please, stay here and I'll be right back."

The girl was scared, broken from the spell of their romantic bubble. "What's going on? Where are you going?"

"Tell me your name and I'll be right back." Charlie pleaded, clinging onto her hand.

"Sophie—what's yours?"

"Charlie," said Charlie before reaching in for a kiss on the cheek. "Stay right here."

"Where can I find you?"

The coloured wriggly lines blurred his vision again. Charlie brought his watch up to his mouth and screeched back at Doug, "I'm doing it! Jesus Christ!"

Charlie then became a dark blur as he left Sophie and snaked through the streets, stunning those who thought they saw (and felt) some dark apparition speed right through them. Charlie hit the target's bedroom like a freight train on an unsuspecting peacock, blending through the walls so fast he ran into the back of the target, already busy with his mistress.

"Jesus Christ!" the target yelped, as the mistress also turned around to shriek in horror at Smiley Face.

Charlie slapped the man across the face, and in his limited French, explained to the man that he was to think twice about his banking policy manoeuvring lest he want to be haunted every time he made love.

After the man and woman did nothing but cower and shrivel, Charlie threw his hastily-written letter of caution like a paper airplane at the man's chest.

"Do not fuck with us!" Charlie threatened and then he said a final "Boo!" to the woman before he disappeared right in front of their eyes. The target fainted and the mistress screamed, not for the first time that night.

Like a bullet, Charlie shot back to the fortune stand by the bridge, ignoring the colourful wriggling line prompts going haywire through his head, Doug trying desperately for a status update.

When Charlie hit the bridge he stopped, startling some bystanders at his sudden appearance. He had only eyes for Sophie however, and standing there, enraptured by her beauty, Charlie planned how he'd sweep her off her feet and take her flying around what he presumed was her home town. But as his feet reached for the stairs, he felt a familiar tug on the back of his head, the simulation of falling, sent by Doug via the coffin. Yellow warning flashes and whirling sirens then engulfed Charlie's senses. Charlie knew what it meant and in pure desperation he called out her name, but when she turned to see him, he was gone.

Charlie sped back, the sirens blaring inside him. They were a call to return, to defend the coffin and its handler in a measure of last resort. Charlie made it back to the hotel and hovered over it, scanning for signs of approaching enemies. After finding the coast clear he bled in through the wall to find Doug sitting in the chair next to the coffin, his gun drawn. The room was dark.

Charlie's smiley face disappeared. "What the hell's

going on, where's the bad guys?"

"Why were you taking so long? I got worried."

"Are you fucking kidding me right now?" hissed Charlie.

Doug looked overly confused, morose. His gun was drawn. "The lights in the room all blew out. Your earpiece (a severed ear acting as a receiver, courtesy of Charlie's sick humour) heated up and exploded, and the coffin was giving off these strange readings and there was a thumping, like a heartbeat—your heartbeat— shaking the room. I wasn't under attack. You were."

Charlie laughed. "I wasn't under attack."

"Then did you complete the mission?"

"Yeah, the target fainted. Lovely end to his evening. Now if there's no danger here, you'll have to excuse me, I have to get back to a meeting."

"A meeting? But the mission is done?"

"It's with a woman—before you say anything— she's different. All those weird things that happened in this room—the heart beating, the lights burning out—that's love."

Doug winced as he saw all control being lost. "Love?"

"Yes. Love."

"I can't authorise that."

"You can't authorise love?"

Doug shook his head. "I can't authorise you using your powers unnecessarily once the mission has been completed. You know this."

Charlie was indignant. "But the mission's over. It's done. We're free! I just need to dream for a little longer, let me go back and impress her."

"If you go out that door, I'll have to push the button."

Charlie stood back. He looked at the coffin where his real body slept and then at the red button at the front of the coffin, which if coded and pressed by Doug, would incinerate the coffin and Charlie. All evidence gone.

A tear was rolling down Doug's cheek. "They're not going to let you go, Charlie."

Charlie was speechless. He lay down on the bed and sunk into the blanket. Finally he said, "That's what they wanted to talk to you about."

"Yes."

Charlie sat up. "It doesn't have to be this way. You could let me escape. You don't have to follow their orders."

"I've thought about that. Lord knows I've wrestled with it...but I don't just put myself at risk defying them. I put my family at risk too."

Charlie stood up, took one look at Doug and then materialised a net that pinned Doug against the wall. Charlie then pulled Doug's gun from him. "You said you'd give me one more day. We'll talk about it then."

And then Charlie was out and flying through the night, back to the fortune telling stand by the bridge. But Sophie wasn't there. Instead there was a man inspecting the fortune telling stand. Charlie swooped down beside the man and said, "Can I help you?" Startled, the man went to reach for something in his coat but Charlie said, "Nuh-uh," and lifted the man up with one hand.

"There was a girl here before. Where is she?"

The man was struggling to breathe a little too much and Charlie dropped him down but shuffled him backwards towards the ducks in the river, who begun to grow larger and hungrier...

"I saw you. You were trying to take something from the fortune telling stand."

"I was just looking," the man gasped.

"If you're interested in a reading, here's one on the house: tell me where the girl is and you don't get fed to the ducks."

The man said the girl ran off crying.

"What direction?"

The man pointed off towards the bridge and the wider city. Charlie dropped the man off in the river and flew out, shooting through the amber-lit city filled with crowds of people with rosy cheeks that drank beer in their bars and ate heartily in their restaurants to escape the cold, while a man with an unnerving smiley face zipped through the city like the flash, leaving those he passed in a cloud of bewilderment, unsure of what the hell just happened. Charlie searched in every public house, church, restaurant, street he could within his radius. He knocked on doors and asked the residents in a futile attempt if they knew a Sophie—about this tall, strawberry blonde hair, face of an angel—and for those who didn't scream or faint at his eerie smiley face and pulsating black body, the others were simply confused and wondering why a person would be singing carols so early before Christmas.

Charlie checked everywhere, he held up pictures of her like she was a lost dog, but no one could recall this angel from the sky.

Meanwhile, all over town, talk was buzzing of a mysterious figure—a ghost, a strange dark flash—blitzing through the cold streets, haunting folk and asking about his dead lover. The police were going door to door, taking notes about a man in a smiley-face mask knocking on the doors of people and scaring the bejesus out of them.

These were the usual complaints raised when things got hairy on assignment, and usually by this time Charlie and Doug would be well on their way out, but of course this time had to be different. He had to find her; he just had to.

Despondent, Charlie went to the town square and in his final act of desperation he erected a fifty-foot, life-like statue of Sophie, replicating her perfection the best he could. He then yelled at the top of his lungs, all across his radius, "Sophie, meet me where we first met!"

He flew back to the platform by the bridge, where

the fortune telling stand had been taken and Charlie waited in the dark for her.

He waited.

And waited.

And just when he heard footsteps coming down the stairs, he woke up.

Charlie hit his head on the coffin as he shuddered awake. When he opened his eyes, he saw Doug, gun in hand, aimed squarely at his temple.

"Get up. Slowly."

A Question of Loyalties

They were going to talk, at least that's what Doug intimated. What happened after the talk was over was the real question. When Charlie was a dream man he was, for all intents and purposes, invincible. He'd been stabbed, shot, and exploded—or at least each action had been attempted, only for the object of affliction to pass right through. One cannot help but grow a sense of invulnerability with that kind of experience. But he knew deep down that no matter how much of a team they were (despite their ups and downs), Doug's fierce loyalty would naturally fall with his family, and that would be that. Charlie asked Doug what the deal was, trying to pick up where he'd left off after the whole putting Doug in a net incident; a net that Charlie *should* have imagined to be of stronger fibre.

Doug was frank: if he followed through with

disposing Charlie, his loyalty with the program would forever be unquestioned and treated as tenure, meaning his knowledge would never have to be silenced with a silencer.

If he let Charlie go, a dishonourable discharge was the best-case scenario. Otherwise he'd be looking over his shoulder for the rest of his days.

"This isn't easy, Charlie."

"Why don't we swap positions then? See how we feel when our best friend has a gun pointed at us."

"If I let you go, and you get caught, spotted, any kind of trouble with a foreign force, they'll kill me too. I've got my family, Charlie."

Charlie sighed. Who could argue against family? (Though he was still going to try.) "Sophie."

"What?"

"Her name is Sophie. I saw her by the river, where the target was supposed to divert to. She was an angel, Doug." Silent tears made their way from Charlie's eyes. "Please. Let me find her and start again."

Doug looked Charlie over, studied the kid and thought about how he'd grown since their first day together. The bags under Charlie's eyes had grown to carry the guilt applied in sleep, and this was Doug's fault too, the same way it was his job. Doug was tired of that job. He was tired of putting Charlie to sleep and though he reasoned that this would be the last time he'd have to do such a thing, it was something he couldn't do. The gun trained on Charlie was finally lowered, both Charlie and Doug breathing a sigh of relief.

"How about we get a drink?" said Charlie.

"How about fifteen?"

Charlie smiled. "I'm buying."

Charlie peeled off the bed and went to wash his face in the bathroom.

"We'll need to come up with a believable story of your exodus tonight," said Doug.

Charlie began brushing his teeth. When he finished, he went in with puppy-dog eyes ready to request a favour. "We can *discuss* that tonight, but I can't leave yet. I have to look for Sophie, and I'm not leaving town without her."

"Charlie, it's going to draw suspicion if we stay another day on the books..."

"You said we could stay another day, before."

"Well that was before, when I was *still* intending to press the red button."

"I see..."

"You know the protocol, Charlie. We don't stay in town after a mission. You've just been given life, but it needs to happen away from here. We need to be smart— let's just make it one beer, actually. What's the status out there, anyway?"

Charlie recalled all the mayhem he'd caused in every inch of the city within his radius trying to find Sophie. Maybe it wasn't such a good idea to go for a beer, but he couldn't tell Doug that. "There was nothing. I saw Sophie, I told her to wait while I did the job. I did the job and no one saw me, except for the mistress of course. Then I went back and looked for Sophie but she wasn't there."

"No usual commotion?"

"No."

Doug seemed satisfied with the answer. They were about to disassemble the coffin and pack it away when there was a knocking on their door. They both shared a glance before both drew their sidearms. After some silence, Doug asked them to identify themselves. No one answered, so Doug motioned for Charlie to turn on the coffin's self-destruct button. As Charlie nudged his way over to the coffin and reached for the button, the door was blown out with a shotgun blast. Charlie immediately returned fire with his pistol. The shots echoed around the room with a deafening roar, the dividing wall being chewed up into Swiss cheddar. Charlie emptied his clip as he retreated to the bedside drawer before glancing at Doug, who remained still by the foot of the bed right next to the floor.

Charlie kept his gun on the buckshot door as he edged forward to Doug, who was still not moving. Charlie grabbed his shoulder and shook lightly, but Doug did not move. Charlie forgot about the door and whoever was still behind it, turning to face Doug's eyes, motionless, an entry wound to the right of his temple.

Charlie clenched up, his face boiling red with rage as he tried to hold it all in, keep the shock in him at bay as it revereberated all over his body. Doug was dead, and Charlie was left to wonder what could have been different. *He does his mission on time and Doug kills him and exits safely. Doug goes home to his family and Heather grows up with a Dad that protects her from people like Charlie. Life goes a different way, a better way.*

But this does not happen, and now nothing will ever be the same for the Schraeders.

Charlie was ready to collapse and hold his best friend, the one who had saved his life countless times and granted him this last gift of freedom when so much was at stake. In a daze, he zipped up Doug's jacket to hide the buckshot in his chest, tidy him up and make his soul more comfortable in whatever afterlife he found his way to. Charlie would've stayed there, rocking away forever in his guilt if he didn't hear the sound of shuffling in the hallway. Charlie swung the door wide open, ignoring the body slumped against the wall and set his fury on the lone survivor crawling away. The man turned, his hands and face smeared with blood, as Charlie raised the gun and sent the man still. He returned to the room and allowed himself a minute, a crucial minute, given that there would be more folks with guns coming soon. But he needed this minute—demanded it—to say goodbye to his friend. Closing Doug's eyes, he dragged the body outside the room, down the hall as quickly as possible. Charlie returned to the room and set the coffin to self-destruct. He then tried sliding it under the bed to discourage shrapnel. The faint sound of sirens in the distance raised his panic level and he abandoned his attempt, the coffin only halfway under the bed, but hopefully it was enough. The sirens wailed closer to the hotel and Charlie knew it was too late to escape down the hallway. He reached for a lighter and held it above the smoke alarm, which began its incessant, high-pitched whining. He then decided he'd have to get the coffin fully under the bed before leaving, wanting to make sure the explosion hurt no one else. He set the timer for the coffin, took the case of sedatives from Doug's bag and threw it in his backpack, before opening the window and sliding down a drainpipe, dropping to the ground from a safe distance. His window backed out onto the small rear garden (a tactical decision) and Charlie climbed over the garden wall onto a back street, bolting away as the coffin exploded, rocking the room.

Charlie didn't look back, running down the alleyway and turning any random direction down dark streets, his memory of an exit strategy gone with the panic. At first, Charlie had the darkness to his advantage, but this did not last as the lights from all the houses gradually began to flick on to investigate the explosion. Everywhere Charlie went, the silhouettes of faces crowded front windows, and Charlie could do nothing but keep on running.

He needed a quiet place, a dark place, to take his sedatives and plot his revenge.

Eventually, Charlie made his way to the outskirts of town, where the homeless and afflicted sought refuge. He entered an industrial yard and checked for security. He knew he'd be safe there, the sirens having dissipated, but another part of him realised he'd need to be closer to town to ensure his radius could cover its full potential. They knew he was here, they must've known, it was just a question of whether they were his own men or the local intelligence. He could flee, start a new life anywhere else but here, but he knew he'd be hunted to the ends of the earth if he went down that path. So he decided on revenge. Revenge and then eloping with Sophie, with maybe a confession in between. He slumped his shoulders and made his way back to the centre of the city, trying hard to think of the nooks and crannies he wouldn't be found. It was getting to midnight and though it was a Saturday night, the streets had gone into lockdown, patrolled by all local authorities available. Wearing a beanie as his only means of cover, Charlie felt truly exposed each harried step forward into town. He got a decent way in from the outskirts and found a side alley with several dumpsters lining its walls. It was merely a matter of picking the most comfortable and suitable to his needs. Slushing into its juicy surface, Charlie adjusted the bags until nothing was sticking into him that shouldn't have. He closed the door on himself and used his lighter to illuminate the box of sedatives.

Charlie opened the box and did a double take, there was only one vial left when there should have been three, four, perhaps even five. Furious and broken by this, Charlie then remembered that the true purpose of the mission had been to terminate him, and any extra sedatives would only play to his advantage were he to obtain them, like he had now. Charlie cursed and kicked at the garbage bags as softly as he could, screaming inside himself. He tipped the dumpster lid open to allow the right kind of light for his syringe. Finding the vein whilst holding the lighter was incredibly difficult and clumsy and after much excruciating fanfare, Charlie just said, "Fuck it," and stabbed away. He used the whole vial, otherwise it wouldn't have worked. Feeling it making his head light, Charlie barely reached for the dumpster lid, managing to close it just as his head hit garbage.

Revenge

Charlie transformed into his Smiley-Faced self atop the building overlooking the dumpster. He gazed over to the distant hotel where red-and-blue lights still flashed and then he took flight.

Outside the hotel all the resident were being comforted with blankets and assurances of refunds while men with guns stood guard and local detectives argued with a mysterious, moustached man about credentials and jurisdictions: "Well I've never heard of this Dark Matter Defence Department before, let me speak to your superior!"—"I am your superior!" Etc.

Charlie went invisible in his own discreet way and floated gently towards the hotel lobby, where he went behind the desk and melted the hard drives containing records of his name. He then went back to the police van and melted their systems too, causing deep confusion for the technician manning the computer. Charlie then left the van, and reappeared from behind some bushes. Charlie put on one of his non-descript government agent faces and acted like he was taking notes as he edged his way closer to the mysterious Moustached Man calling the shots.

The Moustached Man noticed Charlie straight away. "Who are you?" asked the Moustached Man. As Charlie wasn't well versed in French, he went straight for his good ol' American.

"Sir, I don't believe we've met. I'm Agent Johnson, a local emissary from one of our specialist branches and I would be more than happy to extend an offer of assistance to your boys."

The Moustached Man smiled curtly, "I'm sorry, Agent Johnson, but this is a local matter of quite technical terms that is..." (and he was definitely enjoying his power trip) "perhaps above your pay grade."

"Like I said, I'm happy to offer another set of eyes in what looks like one hell of a supernatural clusterfuck, wouldn't you say?"

Just then, the technician from the van came to complain about the hard drives completely melting. The Moustached Man regarded this information with quiet interest before turning back to Charlie's Agent Johnson. The Moustached Man then gave the tech an order in French, and then put his hand out to Charlie, who shook it likewise. "Perhaps I should give you a tour."

They began walking into the hotel.

"It is quite strange you use the word supernatural for a triple-homicide."

"I was more thinking about the strange reports going around town of a masked man appearing in many places at once."

The Moustached Man feigned surprise. "Oh, and you think they are connected?"

"I wouldn't be here otherwise."

They passed Doug's body in the hallway. Charlie tried to avoid looking at Doug's body, and the Moustache Man seemed to make note of this. He calmly reached for his walkie and made a quick order. The Moustached Man then pushed up ahead to the other men in the hallway. "This is what happens when your subordinates don't wait for backup."

Charlie laughed. "I don't think it would've helped."

The Moustached Man turned back to Charlie, "Oh,

no?" before his walkie went off again. The Moustached Man repeated the order, this time a greater sense of urgency in his voice.

"Something the matter?" Charlie asked, smiling.

"Let me show you the room," said the Moustached Man, his hands visibly shaking.

They walked into the room, everything still smoggy and smelling of ash as investigators took samples. The Moustached Man ordered everyone to leave the room. Once they had left, the man undid the button on his collar. "The coffin is an interesting contraption, tell me, does it improve the radius of your travels?"

"A lady never tells," said Charlie as he ripped his Agent Johnson face off to reveal his smiley face. The Moustached Man reached for his walkie and hissed into it once more.

"Backup won't help. If y'all speak of radiuses and coffins the way you do, you should already know that."

"I have a wife and kids," the Moustached Man stated, though this was expressed more as a fact than anything, the Moustached Man knowing full well how far that would get with Smiley Face.

"So did my friend," Charlie curtly replied.

"They disobeyed orders."

"So did my *best* friend. Someone's got to pay for his death. Unless you want it to be the rest of your men, that person must be you."

The Moustached Man swallowed his remaining fear.

"Then please make it quick."

"I'm going to tear your head off and let it gravitate around me so you get to watch me kill all of your friends."

"If you sever my head, I will be dead, and subsequently unable to watch the awful acts you wish to inflict on my men."

Charlie stopped to consider this. "You may be right; I'll get your heart too." And then, without further adieu, Charlie grabbed the Moustached Man by the face and punched into his chest, working his way around the rib cage until he felt a large pulse. He ripped the head, spine and heart out at the same time like the tablecloth trick a waiter pulls to impress (the rest of the body in this case being the cutlery and dinner plates). A truly sadistic and blood-gushing sight, the Moustached Man gasped over and over as the chords to his heart were wrapped around his spine like a tetherball so it wouldn't dangle needlessly.

"Beautiful," Charlie grinned, his Smiley Face at its absolute brightest. "Now let's go meet your friends."

Charlie was going to kill them all. This was the rage coursing through his black, pulsating body and revenge was surely justified beyond reproach. He skipped down the stairs into the hotel lobby. The men had guns, assault rifles of all kinds of badassery, but it would make no difference. They gasped when they saw their superior's head, still bobbing up and down as it made its gravitational circle round the smiley-faced dream man.

"Get out, you fools!" the Moustached Man slurred with his final breaths.

"Terrific advice, though difficult given the circumstances," said Charlie as he lined up his next victims.

Unsure of what to do, they began shooting, as this was what thousands of movies, training, books, history and instincts had taught them to do with the modern marvels they held in their hands. Thirty men, firing machine guns in a hotel lobby of no more than twenty square metres. It was obscenely loud, and poor Charlie had to imagine some earplugs.

When they ran out of ammo and realised nothing had worked; Charlie still standing his ground, perhaps even more relaxed than before, whatever was left in their bowels oozed its way out in muddy surrender. Charlie lined up his next victim and was about to strike—before through the lobby door came a gust of energy so powerful it threw Charlie against the wall, forcing his gravitational hold of the Moustached Man loose. As the Moustached Man's head was about to drop and splat, the gust of energy caught it and suspended it in mid-air.

Charlie's eyes opened wide. It was another dream man.

"That's mine!" shouted Charlie.

And all he heard was the echoed voice of *"No..."*

before the gust was out the door and Charlie gave chase, sparing all the terrified men in the hotel lobby of their floating head fate.

The gust of energy was lean and agile, zipping through tight laneways and tighter turns—up, down, left and right—firing off rounds of fireworks to blind Charlie in his pursuit, but to no avail. The gust then settled on gliding through the river canal, leaving small waves in its wake, the head of the Moustached Man at its head. Charlie gained with each turn, his speed honed after years of hunting. Snaking along the river, Charlie recognised the bridge up ahead and its memory gave him a plan. Just as the dream man went under the bridge, a gigantic duck with a bill the width of the river burst forth from the water, the Moustached Man's lollypop remains having to pull straight up to avoid the duckbill lined with serrated shark teeth, allowing Charlie to go over the top of the bridge and snatch the Moustached Man in mid-air.

The dream man kept climbing and Charlie gave chase, flying upward into the heavens, the Moustached Man now rightfully by his side, but the higher he flew the slower he got, as somewhere back on earth his brain was finding this all a little too much, and when Charlie had seemingly reached the end of his radius tether, the other dream man still continued, well beyond Charlie's radius. When the dream man realised Charlie was unable to follow, he stopped his ascent and returned to Charlie, staying just out of reach. All Charlie could see was the outline of his enemy, who seemed to regard him and his twisted Smiley Face with boiling hatred.

Despite the lack of face and eyes, Charlie sensed the dreamer was transfixed by the head of the Moustached Man and as Charlie realised this, a droplet of water, possibly a tear, softly dropped onto his face.

The dream man was despondent at losing his handler.

"Now you know how I feel," said Charlie, no sympathy escaping him. "You want the rest of your friend, come get him." And then Charlie let go of the Moustached Man's head and spine, as it plummeted to the earth and the tears began to flow from the dream man, falling like rain drops upon Charlie's face, who kept his smile burning.

Until he noticed the wings...

Or at least, the outline of them.

They were flapping gently behind the dreamer, keeping him afloat, and the longer they both floated, regarding each other until the Moustached Man went splat, the more this crying dreamer revealed itself to Charlie. The soft face, the hair, and all the transparent lines slowly crystallizing into the shape of an angel...

Sophie.

Charlie's eyes lit up, and, realising what he'd done, woke up screaming in his dumpster.

The Enemy

Sophie did not wake that night like she usually did when her dreaming became too overwhelming. When Charlie disappeared, she drifted slowly down, like a feather that weighed a thousand pounds, to collect what little remained of the man she had mistakenly called "father" on one too many occassions. Cradling his lifeless head atop an empty rooftop, her tears filled the sky and cast a downpour on the town.

Eventually heeding the call of her other heads of command, she returned to the hotel and was provided with the passport pictures of her mentor's killer. She showed no emotion when she recognised the American dreamer, codename: Smiley Face, as the man she passed by the bridge in the afternoon, unbeknownst to her that his dreamer alter-ego would be her target only hours later.

With identification of the target's human face now known, Sophie was sent like a hound to hunt. She spent the rest of the night roaming the streets, tasked with finding Charlie, and wherever she went, the rain of her tears followed.

Back at the hotel, the French agents were packing up the evidence and making themselves sparse lest Smiley Face return. Media news crews were treated with talk of a terror plot successfully foiled in a raid that claimed the life of brave French counter-terrorism security advisor Jacques Dusautoir.

Sophie woke in the early hours of the morning to a glass of water and her daily dose of tablets. Sitting at the foot of her bed was Madame Pascal. The Madame was dressed in her professional attire and her commiserations about the late Dusautoir were brief and to the point, betraying the fact that she had just lost a dear friend too; because this was part of the job, as young Sophie was to learn.

"Mademoiselle, we cannot bring him back, we can only honour his memory by continuing his work, his belief in you. You broke a record last night, your submersion was over four hours, quite a feat."

Sophie did not react to this.

Madame Pascal sighed. "The people that support us do so out of a love we can sometimes feel we can never fully reciprocate, though it is our duty to try. We will get this man, Mademoiselle, and to do this you need to keep yourself ready for your next submersion, no matter how difficult it must be to focus right now."

"I'm sorry I didn't enter in time."

"No, Sophie, You did your best. Those men shouldn't have jumped the gun, so to speak. Don't worry, we will track down the American and when we have his position, you will have your opportunity to take your revenge, and it will be yours Sophie, we promise you that."

"I will do you proud."

"You will do Monsieur Dusautoir proud. Now, while

we search for the American, you will do your exercises, so that you will be ready, understood?"

Sophie nodded and Madame Pascal left the room, leaving Sophie to her water, pills and tedius breathing exercises in an empty white room bereft of natural light while the rest of the department hunted her mentor's killer.

Thoughts of guilt and the feel of her mentor's head—the absence of life in his eyes—clouded Sophie as she tried to stay focused on her exercises, the dull monotony meant to lower her stress levels and increase lucidity, thus enhancing the control of her gift during submersion.

Breathe in...

Breath out...

Breath in (Smiley-Faced pig)

Breath out (ducks, their necks wrung)

She waited.

And waited...

And then she stopped the exercises. They were utterly useless, just like her. The American was probably long gone by now, and Sophie would have no chance of avenging her mentor as she promised. She yearned to sleep and become the angel of death, putting that wretched Smiley Face on those ducks he loved so much and napalming them with her fury.

And as these vicious fantasies reached fever pitch, there was a knock at her door.

The American was at the river, by the bridge.

The End

The sniper team watched over Charlie from a nearby rooftop with a view of the riverbank. Across from Charlie, on the other side of the river where trees and brush of falling autumn leaves completed a Grimm fairytale picture, strike teams edged carefully through the trees, setting up positions against the American sitting on a bench, throwing bread into the bank and feeding a family of ducks.

Sophie joined Madame Pascal and the sniper team observing from the rooftop. Madame Pascal flinched when she realised Sophie was there. "Goodness, Mademoiselle. You can't sneak up on your own team like that."

"Is it him?"

"Yes."

"Is he dreaming?"

"Scanners aren't working from this range."

"There are no glitches in his image, though," added the sniper.

Madame Pascal smiled at Sophie, whose eyes never left Charlie sitting in the distance, throwing bits of bread to hungry bills. "Make us proud, Sophie."

Sophie climbed up onto the ledge and stepped off, the sniper instinctively trying to reach out and stop her from falling, before his eyes bulged as Sophie floated like a ghost slowly to the American.

Charlie stood when he saw Sophie floating over, his peace at feeding the ducks dissipating in his harrowed features. When Sophie landed, they both regarded each other in silence while the ducks quacked away with glee and the strike teams flicked their safeties off.

"I wrote you something," said Charlie, as he reached inside his coat to produce several rumpled pieces of paper. He held them together and studied them like a child about to read his speech in front of class for the first time. "It's an apology, a confessional of sorts, and hopefully maybe a how-to guide for dreaming a better life—like, what pills work best and, um…" Charlie stopped because Sophie had not removed her piercing gaze from his sorry face. She then raised her head by the slightest and the pages wriggled free from Charlie's grasp and flew over to her, reassembling in her hands to which she scrunched up into a ball and tossed in the river, the ducks scrambling to investigate.

"You killed my mentor."

"I'm sorry. You killed mine too, though…" said Charlie, "…there were some good notes on there…"

"They're gone now. Say your last words before I finish this," declared Sophie.

Charlie closed his eyes, holding back tears. It wasn't because of all the bad he had done his whole life; he'd made his peace with that a long time ago. It was absorbing the sense of absolute loss behind the fury in

Sophie's eyes and knowing he was the cause.

Charlie thought long and hard, and then swallowed his fear. Here went nothing.

"I made a lot of mistakes in my life, wrote as many down as I could on those pieces of paper and yet that still didn't cover it—wasn't even close. I didn't sleep a single second last night and I don't think I'll sleep again. But that's okay, because I'm tired of sleeping, dreaming, except, maybe one last dream: That stuff I said to you, about the kids, a happy future. Maybe you can still have that—I hope you do. Because of all the dreams I ever made, I think that was my favourite one."

Sophie's jaw unclenched, her fury faltering as she became lost for words.

Unable to bear the silence, Charlie kept talking, "You know, in the beginning, I thought there were things we could've done, good dreams, not the nightmares we became. We could generate food, enough for anyone, least while we were still sleeping or something like that. Enchant the air and make happy zones for the people..." Charlie stopped and chuckled to himself. "You know what I thought I could be: a superhero, and of all the people I knew, I actually had the power to be something like that..."

Sophie perked up, her wrath unwinding further. "I thought that too."

"But that's not how it went," revealed Charlie, "they forced me to kill, over and over. You've seen what I'm capable of, and they'll make you do the same. Sooner or later. I wish I could say otherwise, but that's what people will want from you: to do the dirty work. Least that's all they came to expect from me. Don't let them do that to you, Sophie. Don't become like me."

Clouded in confusion and unable to respond to this truth, Sophie looked to stall; she conjured a piece of bread and threw it to the ducks.

Back on the rooftop, the sniper noted this to Madame Pascal.

"She's getting cold feet. I have a shot. Strike teams are advising the same thing."

"No," said Madame Pascal. "She must learn."

"It's okay you can finish me," said Charlie. "Make them believe you're on their side. But then you need to leave, go anywhere you want."

"I can't... I..."

"You don't owe them anything."

"I owe them more than you know," Sophie countered, and Charlie flinched.

"But you haven't killed for them yet," he said, hopeful it was a statement and not a question.

"No. You will be my first."

Relief flushed his face, relaxing everything within him. "I'm okay with that, as long as I'll be your last," he smiled, and attempted a cheeky wink, one that said it wasn't going to hurt, before a tear rolled from his eye that he wiped away.

"I'm sorry," he finished.

"I'm sorry it went this way," said Sophie.

And her hand was then raised, ready to apply whatever she wanted to him, all of it at her will, limitless imagination at hand.

She could have fired a gun, a single bullet right in the area (to the millimetre) where he would feel nothing, not an absolute thing.

She could have burned him alive, one limb at a time or all limbs at once. Destroyed him slowly for everything he deserved.

She could have spared him. Saved him. Forgiven him. Maybe even grown to love him.

Eventually.

It was all at her command. Whatever she dreamed.

And yet it wasn't going to be that simple. There wasn't going to be any of that dream that Charlie said— or hers, for that matter.

Because the world was going to keep spinning and wear her down and make its demands; from Madame Pascal to her deceased mentor and all the systems that willed it be.

And for that, it was to be—but not by her doing, vengeance or otherwise.

"I won't," she relented.

"And I hope you won't ever have too, Sophie. So please: dream of me, dream of us, feeding the ducks," said Charlie, as he pulled out his gun and slid it up into his chin.

The strike teams saw a weapon and they fired.
The sniper saw a weapon and he fired.
Charlie fired too.

Mark the Immaculate

David Myrcott

First the pains came, then his water broke. It felt a bit like wetting the bed. He winced and gave a groan.

'Better see a doctor,' said the site supervisor.

'You aren't kidding,' said the man. His rendering trowel fell to the ground with a splash. Doubled over in agony, he made his way outside to his ute and fumbled for his keys.

Kidney stones. It had to be kidney stones.

'Mop up whatever that is,' said the site supervisor to another of the workers.

* * *

On the way to the hospital things got really weird. An apparition slid into the passenger seat.

'Hello,' said the angel.

'Jesus Christ!' said the man.

'Not quite,' replied the angel. 'Tell me, how well do you know the Bible?'

'Not all that well, actually.' The man clutched at his belly and moaned.

'Labour pains,' said the angel. 'You are blessed and

highly favoured—'

'Hold on,' said the man, grimacing. 'What was that about labour pains?'

'Oh, I'm sorry! Wasn't that clear? It's been a while since I've done this. Let me start at the beginning.' *[talking slowly]* 'We've made you pregnant, and you're going to give birth to the new Messiah.'

The man stared at the angel.

'That's right! He's getting it now. Lucky you, huh?'

The man stared.

'Well, naturally it couldn't be a woman this time. It was a woman last time, and the time before that, and frankly all the times before that. It wasn't until the 21st century rolled around that we realised we were being a tiny bit sexist about the whole thing. That's where you came in. It had to be an everyman this time. Literally.'

The man continued staring. The angel looked uncertain.

'I mean, we took care of everything, pretty much. Your health's fine. The cavity for the baby was created supernaturally and just sort of inserted into you from the other side, as it were. You didn't even notice it before today, did you? That's where a bit of a paunch comes in handy. Not saying you're out of shape or anything. The light's gone green by the way.'

The man drove on in stunned silence, one hand on the steering wheel and the other on his stomach.

'Look at the positives though. You just became part

of history. A big part! You're going to get millions and millions of Facebook followers from this, you know. Maybe even a billion. That's a considerable revenue stream, no? Look at the Kardashians.'

The man exploded.

'I don't want millions of Facebook followers! I don't want this! Is this even real? Is this actually happening?'

'Oh, it's happening,' said the angel. 'It's really real. Take a moment to get your head around it. I'm just going to fiddle about with the radio if you don't mind. I've heard that you can twist this dial, and anywhere you twist it a different song is playing.'

Suddenly the man gave a yelp of pain.

'Ooh. I bet those are the contractions starting.'

'Shut up,' said the man. 'Shut up, shut up, shut up, shut up, shut up!'

'Alright,' replied the angel. 'I can take a hint.'

They drove on.

'I think you'll find you should take a left up here.'

The man glared at him.

* * *

More silence, occasionally punctuated by pain. Then the man thought of something.

'How... how exactly is this baby gonna get out of me?'

There was no answer. He turned to look at the angel.

The angel avoided his gaze, fidgeted a bit with the

ashtray in the passenger door, opening and closing the lid.

'No...'

The angel avoided his gaze.

'Dear God...'

'It might be best not to think about that just for now.'

'Oh God! Oh, my God, oh God...'

'He isn't happy about it either, if that's any consolation. The Big Guy I mean. We considered a C-section. Obviously we did. But it turned out the whole artificial womb thing had its limitations. It had to be attached somewhere, I mean... the baby has to come out of *somewhere*, do you see what I'm saying? It can't be removed surgically. It has to be a natural birth without human interference. That's a direct quote. Believe me, we went over the rulebook with a fine-tooth comb. It *has* to be a natural birth, and it *has* to be a man this time.'

'But why me?' wailed the man. 'Why out of all the men on earth did He pick *me*? You said I'm an everyman, but there's plenty of those knocking around. That's kind of the definition of it.'

'Um, well, your name's Mark for one thing. That's a good biblical name. It even sounds a bit like Mary.'

'No it doesn't. What do you mean? It doesn't sound at all like Mary.'

'Well... the start's the same. Same first three letters. It's only the *k* and the *y* that are different.' The angel paused. 'It's a bit of a pun, I guess. Mary-Mark. That and other factors. The why of it isn't really the most important thing. Frankly, I thought you'd be more excited than this.'

'Well I'm not, okay? And telling me God picked me more or less for a lark isn't helping. He sounds like a bit of a prick, if I'm being honest. So let's just get to the hospital in silence, get this fucking thing out of me, and I can try to forget about all this or... or... wake up from this *nightmare*, somehow.'

'Fine with me,' said the angel, flicking the lid of the ashtray up and down some more.

'Don't do that,' said the man.

* * *

Later, at the hospital.

A nurse poked her head in the door. 'Excuse me, but there are three men here to see you. They have gifts and they're claiming to be wise? They said you'd know what that meant.'

'Let them in,' replied the man, slurring, swathed in bandages from his abdomen to his thighs. *Ledd-dum-inn.*

The baby looked happy.

The man looked deflated.

The angel was reading the newspaper, and sporadically monitoring the drip.

'Is this him?' enquired the first wise man. 'The one they call Mark?'

'It sure is,' replied the angel. 'Best not to chat with him just yet though. He's on quite a heavy dose of morphine. He's on a lot of stuff, actually. God felt a bit bad about the whole "baby coming out the urethra" thing, so He mixed him up a special elixir. I've been adding a few drops here and there to his IV.'

'*Blurbleglah,*' said the man, Mark.

'That's right,' responded the angel soothingly. He attempted to offer a reassuring pat on the hand, but the man snatched his hand away. *[To the wise men]* 'He's off his rocker, frankly. This whole thing has been supremely unorthodox. I kept trying to deliver my speech about being blessed and highly favoured, then before you knew it he'd delivered a baby through his penis. I should have amended the wording slightly. It was my own fault. As soon as he wakes up properly, I'm going to apologise profusely about the whole exploding cock thing. He's right really, we shouldn't have used him as a guinea pig, we should've chosen someone with a womb and a vagina like all the other times. We were just trying to think outside the box, so to speak.'

'And the Messiah?' asked the second wise man.

'Perfectly fine,' said the angel, beaming. 'Couldn't be better. You can hold her if you want. And say, could I get a whiff of that myrrh? I adore the scent and it's been ever so long.'

The third wise man duly unstoppered the gilded container of myrrh, holding it up to the angel's nose. The angel inhaled deeply.

'Oh, that's nice isn't it? I miss that smell.'

They nodded in quiet contemplation. The baby grasped contentedly at the second wise man's beard when he bent to kiss her forehead. He indulged her for a while, making the appropriate cooing sounds, then smiled at her fondly as he stood back up.

'She's beautiful,' he said, wiping away a tear. 'All hail the new Messiah.'

'All hail,' offered the other wise men and the angel in perfect unison. More contemplation followed. The heart monitor beeped every few seconds. It was kind of annoying, but nobody said anything on account of the magnitude of the situation. This type of thing happened only once in a thousand years, if that. It was a great celebration day in heaven. There was a bit more silence.

'Got any of that elixir left?' asked the first wise man.

Shopping

Craig Tuck

'This is it boys,' Skip said to the team of social cricketers gathered eagerly around him. 'Breathe in the air. Taste's good doesn't it? You know what it is?'

The troops shrugged.

'I'll tell you what it is, boys: it is destiny. Drink it down; let it fill your lungs.'

The troops took a deep, collective breath.

'I can guarantee you that our competitors – all those bastards who edged us in the important moments last season – have not been out netting through winter.

'Last season we were 5 per cent behind, but we are now 5 per cent in front...' Skip paused, shrugging. 'Fuck...maybe even more.'

It had been a long pre-season.

'We've put in the hard yards, we've worked on our weaknesses and we've turned them into strengths!'

The troops cheered.

'We've also improved what we were already good at! Our old strengths are now stronger than ever!'

The troops cheered again, but Skip's brow furrowed.

'Which I guess means that our old weaknesses, I suppose, could still be considered our weaknesses...'

Skip paused, collecting his thoughts. His troops silently urged him on.

'...but, what strong weaknesses they are!'

The troops applauded. Then cheered. Then applauded louder.

Skips's address had been a success.

Pre-season had been a success.

There was no doubt the season to come would continue the trend. Now, the team agreed, it was time to get drunk.

Packing up the cricket equipment after Skip's address had finished, Tom turned to his friend George.

'Pumped for tonight mate?'

'Yeah,' George shrugged. 'Should be OK.'

'OK?' Tom replied. 'OK? Shit mate, this is gonna be classic. Did you bring your clothes or do you need to go back to yours?'

George smiled confidently and reached into his bag. He pulled out a scrunched up grey t-shirt and unfolded it for Tom to see. It was tattered and wrinkled, with a picture of 1990s basketballer Dennis Rodman's head on the front. Tom frowned; he had seen the T-shirt before. It was old, frayed, and had a few holes in it.

Tom turned away without comment to collect the stray gloves, thigh pads and cricket balls strewn across the ground at the end of the netted cricket practice facility.

'Cool, right?' George asked.

'You are not wearing that,' Tom said, as he packed the stray cricket equipment away. 'I won't let you.'

'I like this shirt!'

'Come on mate, it's an Obnoxious Boys Night Out – you've gotta look the part. If you get yourself a sweet new getup, the women are in for a treat! But if you wear that...'

George eyed his friend warily.

'I'll just stick with this – I can't be bothered going home. Let's just go to yours and have a few beers.'

Suddenly Tom lashed out, snatching the T-shirt from George.

'This is an old, shitty shirt that looks ridiculous. I will not have this in my house!'

Tom threw the shirt in the bin next to the cricket nets.

'I'm sorry I've had to do this, but it's for your own good. The shops are still open – we're going. You will thank me, believe me!'

George sighed, too exasperated to argue. The T-shirt had been a $3 purchase at the Salvos several years ago, so he couldn't be too upset. Shaking his head, he packed away his expensive new cricket bat, the Slazenger 580. It had thick edges and an expanded, 'meaty' hitting zone.

'Don't worry George – tonight you are going to look good. I will help you.'

It was the same conversation that had been raging

for weeks, ever since the duo first began planning for their last big night of drinking before the start of the new social cricket season.

As usual, Tom had been the instigator of the plans for both the drinking and the shopping.

With cricket season fast approaching, it had been Tom's strong contention that the end of pre-season training would need to be celebrated with a night that was rowdy, drunken and well-dressed. Tom ceaselessly maintained that no proper Obnoxious Boys Night could be conducted in rags.

'I've got a $50 limit,' George sighed.

Tom wasn't convinced.

'That might need to be raised...'

Meanwhile at the roadside, captain and elder statesman, Skip, had already left the cricket nets and was standing impatiently by the road, waiting for his wife to collect him. Unfortunately, Skip had lost his Driver's Licence following the club's Christmas party and, following further alcohol-related mishaps, had recently been banned from all alcohol by his wife, Christy.

The cricket club meant the world to Skip and to him, Obnoxious Boys Nights were occasions to be treasured. Skip was desperately unhappy to be missing out, but had maintained a brave face for the club, the boys and his marriage.

Christy pulled up and tooted the horn cheerfully. Skip

nodded his head sternly, though a wry grin escaped his lips. After leaning across to open the passenger door of her funky-styled, three-door hatch, Christy was greeted by the surging aroma of cigarette breath and paternal pride.

'God the boys done real fuckin' good today,' Skip gushed as he forced his large frame gracelessly into the vehicle.

Unable to conceive following a childhood boating accident, Skip regarded the younger members of the cricket team as his children.

'They've really earned a night out tonight.'

'Yeah?' Christy replied with vacant enthusiasm. 'That's good!'

'I mean Tom? That guy is such an athlete; he has such perfect poise.'

'Yeah?'

'He's fit, he's strong. Shit, I mean, real fuckin' strong. He really looks *good* out there, you know?'

'Just how *good* did Tom look?' Christy asked, giggling with mock concern.

'I mean...physically...athletically...technically ...not, like... geez, love...not, like...aww geez!'

Christy laughed cheerfully.

'You know I'm not like...I'm not like that! OK!'

Skip realised he was yelling. He took a breath and softened his tone.

'I mean, look at you...you know that you're the

only one for me, don't you?' Skip said sweetly, before leaning in to give his wife a quick, passionless peck on the cheek.

His feigned enthusiasm barely masked a sighing heart that was miles away.

Back at the cricket nets, George and Tom finished packing up the kit bag and, after further negotiation, agreed to head to Greensborough Plaza to pick up some new clothes.

All the while, George remained wary of putting any effort into his appearance, reasoning that it is easier to look terrible if it seems deliberate. Irony is hip they say. Still, despite his reservations, he went along with Tom's scheme.

It was not long before the two pulled into a parking space at the megaplex shopping plaza. George sat fidgeting in the passenger seat. Tom had noticed that anxiety loomed large for his friend, so he tried to make light of the situation.

'Well, here we are buddy!' Tom wailed with exaggerated delight as he grinned in George's sullen direction. *Let's go shopping!*'

As with all metropolitan shopping centres, the halls of the megaplex maintained an overwhelming daily flow of indifferent stroller-pushers, obese couples and bratty, sociopathic teenagers, surging from store to store.

Tom led George forward, weaving his way through

the loud, heaving mass of humanity, while George did his best to ignore the troubling hordes of teenagers who gleefully strode the halls, berating each other with all manner of horrific taunting.

While the crowds were the most loathsome aspect of shopping, another added menace was the possibility, however slight, of an awkward encounter with a work colleague. Memories of George's never-to-be-forgotten bump into Kenneth, the IT guy, as he passed through the Big W Lingerie Section a few months prior, served as a constant warning of the dangerous possibilities.

Walking through the halls of Greensborough Plaza, beaten into a bruised bloody mess by the stray elbows, knees and strollers common to this depraved circus, George eyed the faces of approaching strangers, desperate to spot and avoid anyone he knew.

George wondered how he had allowed himself to be conned so thoroughly. What was he doing here?

He turned to his right and saw his friend, Tom, drifting poetically through the crowd. Even the most sociopathic teenagers parted in deference to the passing of Tom's masculine grace. Eventually, after much jostling on George's part, the contrasting duo found a quieter area of floor space and stopped to assess their position.

'OK, Man to Man is just over there,' Tom said, pointing to a store that looked ominously classy. 'You can go in there and make a start if you want; I'm just gonna go grab a quick ice cream.'

'You're gonna send me in there alone?'

'You'll be right mate, just stick close to the Exit and say nothing until I get back.'

George edged forward into the throng of moody consumers, uncertainly shuffling towards the clothing retailer while Tom slipped effortlessly towards the Food Court. As much as he told himself that shopping at Man to Man was nothing to be afraid of, George was clearly intimidated by the prospect at hand.

Approaching the store, George felt the grip of unease squeezing him tightly. Examining the shimmering clothes racks, he wondered how any clothing collection could look so immaculate.

Good, proper clothes shops felt like a foreign world to George; part of a secret society that he had no right entering. Regardless, he shuffled forward, all the while wondering what a mumbled secret password, delivered with just the right knowing look, could achieve in such a place.

'Enter through the third changing room,' he imagined the shop assistant whispering.

'Remember, there's no use of mobile phones allowed back there; but everything else is, of course, totally fine!'

Before George's thoughts could explore the possibilities any further, he was jolted back to reality when a stroller ran over his foot.

'Move out of the way would you?' a mother said as

she passed him by. If she was apologising, it was very subtle.

Eager to avoid further trouble, George entered the store and registered with surprise that the shop assistant at Man to Man was a sexy, yawning young half-Asian woman with red streaks through her hair. George offered an awkward, unreturned smile to the appealingly bored shop assistant.

Much like girls who kept their natural hair colour, girls with dyed streaks in their hair rarely smiled at George. He shifted his focus back to the task at hand. A bright sign advertising a Crazy Clearance Sale, standing proudly atop a shirt rack, caught his attention.

'Now then, time to find me a shirt...'

He steeled himself. He moved forward decisively. Before long, he found something that seemed appropriate: it was a cotton blend long-sleeve, black-striped shirt with a double inner collar, Italian sizing and centre front button closure and button fastening cuffs.

George pulled the relevant coat hanger clumsily out from amongst the others and checked the size of the shirt. It was small. George held the shirt to his torso and made a hasty comparison: it seemed okay.

He looked out to the front of the store and noticed Tom sitting on a bench, eating an ice cream and watching on. George gave his friend an exaggerated shrug as he held the shirt aloft. Tom replied with an exuberant thumbs up.

With all the approval George needed, he carried the shirt towards the front of the store, where the improbably beautiful shop assistant stood engrossed with the screen of her mobile phone. George placed the shirt on the counter and reached for his wallet.

'Hey, just this, thanks,' he said, smiling.

'$80 please,' the shop assistant replied, barely glancing up from her phone.

'Oh, but the sign says this is reduced to $40,' George replied, pointing at the Crazy Clearance Sale sign.

'Yeah, but that sale is discretionary,' the shop assistant replied.

'Excuse me?'

'We use discretion in our application of the advertised sale price,' the shop assistant explained with disinterest.

'Um...' George began, 'what?'

'Do I need to talk slower, or use smaller words, or both?'

The shop assistant seemed displeased.

George looked around eagerly, seeking a witness to the bizarre conversation and could perhaps offer some moral support. Unfortunately, he was alone.

He turned back to the shop assistant in bewilderment and her raised eyebrow challenged him to pursue the matter further. George collected his thoughts.

'Can you explain the nature of this discretionary policy?' he asked after a moment.

'OK,' the shop assistant began. 'I study business at uni, so maybe this comes easier to me than to you, but here at Man to Man we don't just sell because of our prices, we sell because of our image.'

'OK...'

'If you don't uphold that image, we do not uphold our sales price,' she explained, as if reading from a script.

'Every person we sell to becomes a walking billboard for our store. We want prime advertising space that will accurately reflect the prestige of our brand. You get what I'm saying?'

'No.'

The shop assistant adopted a more aggressive tone now.

'You do *not* uphold our required image,' she said coldly.

'We charge you more for our shirt because your wearing of our clothes will *adversely impact* our sales.

'The extra charge is our *compensation* for your sullying of our name. We will improve your look, but you will hurt ours. You get it?'

'Yea...' George began uncertainly.

'*You* are poor advertising,' she continued, placing even more emphasis on her words now. 'So we must *adjust* the price accordingly...'

George was stunned as the shop assistant continued her explanation, her tone softening now.

'But if, for example, your friend out there were to

buy the shirt...well, we'd probably only charge $30 or so,' she said, gesturing at Tom, who was sitting with perfect posture on the seat outside the store.

'You'd actually *lower* the sale price for Tom?' George asked, turning to see his friend gracefully finish his ice cream.

'Yes, he is very pretty,' the shop assistant said, smiling.

'Pretty?!'

The shop assistant nodded absent-mindedly, eyes sparkling as she watched Tom stand and enter the store.

'Hey Tom, can you buy this shirt?' George asked.

'Sure,' Tom said, unfazed by the strange request.

'I'll pay you back,' George said.

Tom nodded as he stepped towards the register with his wallet already open.

'No,' the shop assistant said, shaking her head whilst also somehow maintaining her glare at George.

'It does not work that way. I know this shirt is for you! I want you both out of the store *now*!'

George turned furiously to leave and Tom followed along, though unsure what had actually just happened. Before Tom could leave though, he felt a tap on his shoulder and turned to face the shop assistant once more.

'Call me?' she asked hopefully, holding her business card outstretched.

'Sorry...I've got a girlfriend,' Tom shrugged.

Five minutes later, Tom and George were rummaging through the t-shirt rack at Just Jeans when suddenly the shirt appeared; it was a pre-stained, pre-torn, pre-faded grey t-shirt with Dennis Rodman's face on it. It cost $50.

'Hey!' Tom cried. 'We're gonna stick to your limit after all!'

The Circle

Aden Simpson

Crawford, Indiana. Population 14,362.

When he first saw the circle, or at least its plain, chalky circumference outside the dilapidated house, Sheriff Stuart Stuckey was compelled to consider the issue from two different perspectives, that of a husband and one of a policeman. As a husband, he thought of finding the love of his life, Deputy Jane Stuckey, and taking her as far away from this town as possible— far from the storm of panic and blood that would run through every street of Crawford as things were to unfold.

That was the first thought, and the Sheriff did well not to act on it, given the way those sparse news stories and conspiracy theory websites had reported the fates of those who found themselves encircled.

The second thought, that of a duty to the law, understood that with any crime there was a perpetrator. Stuckey believed he knew the culprit, a face that up until two days ago he hadn't seen in Crawford since high school, Thomas Holt. This town had not been nice to Thomas Holt and Stuckey suspected Thomas wasn't back in town for nostalgic tidings.

Stuckey realised he'd been frozen on the sidewalk

gazing at the circle for a good number of minutes, deliberating his duties, before a girl riding her bike along the sidewalk toward him, mere feet from the circle, sprung him into action. He pulled his gun, a very un-Stuckey thing to do, and rushed the girl, who instinctively veered off the path towards the very circle he was trying to ward her from. He caught her just in time, while the bicycle rolled itself into the circle. It was a long while before he could calm her hysterical screaming. The neighbours soon came out to see what all the fuss was about. Stuckey turned to see Stephanie McRae out on her porch, squinting her eyes in confusion.

"Everything OK, Sheriff?"

"Stay right where you are, Steph! I'm coming to you," said Stuckey, taking the little girl by the arm and telling her she had to come with. When he got to Steph's porch he told the girl to go back home.

"But my bicycle!"

"Leave it! Don't touch it!"

The girl was shocked, on the verge of tears, "But why?"

Steph was also confused. "Yeah, why?"

"It's contaminated," said Stuckey, "I want you to go home and stay home. In fact, tell your mother to keep the doors locked."

"What the heck is going on, Sheriff?" asked Steph, her anxiety building as she saw Stuckey's harried face begin to sweat all over.

"I'm not a hundred percent sure what's going on," he said, "but I think we may be under attack."

After rolling the police tape around the house, specifically the circle that surrounded it, Stuckey grabbed Ralph Riggins' phone number from Steph and called the man inside the circle.

"Who's this?" said the gruff voice.

"Ralph, it's Sheriff Stuckey here."

"The fuck you want?"

Charming, thought Stuckey, before the gravity of the situation roped him back in. "Listen, are the kids with you?"

"Yeah, it's the weekend."

Stuckey cringed and turned back to his vehicle, only to find a note stapled on a tree by the sidewalk, facing the house. Stuckey honed in on the note, an old parchment of paper nailed into the oak. Written in ink with cursive were the words:

A food circle:

Once you start

You cannot stop

A hunger never satisfied

Is a dangerous hunger indeed.

Ingredients:

A small baseball

A worn glove,

An object loved,

An object loathed,

An object...

The rest was cut out, torn off deliberately. Stuckey understood the ingredients portion. They were the keys to Ralph and his children's salvation, but their display was merely a means of false hope. Stuckey remembered from those news reports that the ingredients required to make the circle could also be found and gathered and then taken out to break the circle. But this was just the beginning, a taunt. Ralph's assailants didn't need to leave the note there. Ralph, none the wiser, would have walked out of that circle and undergone an unspeakable fate, or broken the rules of the circle and suffered a similarly awful end.

One time in middle school, Ralph Riggins stole one of the science frog cadavers and waited till after school before he force-fed a young Thomas Holt the little dead frogger. Thomas didn't come to school for a week after that.

"The hell's going on, Sheriff?" Ralph growled.

Stuckey rubbed the bridge of his nose and took a deep breath. "Okay, I need to you come outside alone, very slowly, and I will explain the situation. I also need you to ensure that your children stay right where they are and it is *very* important that they don't eat anything."

"You telling my kids not to eat? What kind of bullshit is this?"

"Come out slowly and we'll talk."

Ralph came out in his wife beater and a disheveled

head of hair that said he was carrying a hangover. He saw the Sheriff standing all the way back on the sidewalk and noticed the yellow police tape surrounding his house that cut him off from the world. He carefully walked out till he got to the police line.

"What's the tape for?"

"Do you remember Thomas Holt?"

Ralph thought deep within himself and this slowness to register made Stuckey sick. How wrong that a bully could forget the awful things he did.

"Middle school." Stuckey clarified.

Ralph's eyes lit up in recognition. "Oh yeah! Thomas Faulty! The hell you bringing him up for? And really, what's with the goddamn tape?"

Stuckey left soon after he carefully threw Ralph the note. He knew he should've spent more time explaining things to Ralph, but he had to be blunt and quick even though he was certain Ralph was going to break the one rule imposed by the circle sooner or later. It didn't seem like Ralph believed, but a frantic Google search later would dispel that doubt. And when he did come to believe, how was he going to explain to his children that they couldn't have their cereal, nor their lunch or dinner, lest they wanted to spark an appetite that would not stop when the fridge was cleared and the stomachs were full. Thankfully Stuckey had never seen what happens to a body forced to eat itself to death. And if he made it through this impending storm, he knew enough to never step inside that house for as long as he was to live. He called the hospital to get an IV drip thrown to Ralph as a last resort (maybe that didn't break the rules?) and then informed the hospital that he was calling in a Code Brown.

"What's this about?" the hospital admin had asked.

"Revenge."

* * *

Stuckey called Jane when he got back in the car.

"What's up, hon?"

"Where are you right now?"

"Still at the shops—What kind of meat you want for the Bowl Drive?"

"Listen," Stuckey cleared his throat, the thought of telling Jane to pack and skip town weighing heavy on his mind, "Something's happened. You remember me telling you how I saw Thomas Holt walking down Main Street with Jimmy DuPont a couple days ago?

"Yeah, I hadn't heard those names in quite a while."

Stuckey sighed. "And you remember how I got a little obsessed looking up that magic circle phenomenon that happened in the Ukraine a while back..."

There was a pause on the other line.

"I just left Ralph Riggins' house," said Stuckey. "It's real. The circles are real."

"I'll be at the station in thirty minutes," said Jane.

"Be careful. I love you."

"I love you too."

* * *

Behind every great Sheriff Stuart Stuckey there was a Jane Freeman (now Jane Stuckey). High school sweethearts, Jane had wanted to join the force and convinced Stuart to join too. He was the youngest Sheriff in Crawford's history and commanded great respect within the community, even though he knew that it was really Jane who ran the show. Why she never took the head job herself, Stuart never got a full confirmation, though he sensed the mayor preferred it being a man's job, in keeping with the town's slow march toward change. Right now, Stuart knew that the Stuckey the town really needed was currently in their slippy little Toyota corolla, gunning it into the station to answer the call of duty.

Jane took several shortcuts at speeds that drew the ire of local Craig Greene, muttering to himself the hypocrisy of law enforcement in this damn country. She screeched into HQ and got changed, relaying to the other sleepy deputies the news. The APB had been signalled only moments earlier.

"Thomas Holt?" asked Deputy Reid.

"He went to Crawford High, a few years above you. Stu saw him a couple nights ago, looking suspicious."

"That black magic terrorism coming into our town," Deputy Harris shook his head in disbelief. "That's real awful business that."

"What the heck we gonna do, Jane?"

"Well, I think first we need to see if we're already trapped. One of you should take a cruiser and head over to Brimley, but drive real slow, in case we've been encircled."

"What happens if we drive through the circle?"

"Unless you want your skin to explode, you'd best be reversing back inside."

The other deputies gulped.

"Okay, Gaines, how about you take that?"

Gaines' reluctance was palpable. "Uh, sure, okay, I guess."

The rest of the deputies regarded one another, lost for thoughts. Jane rolled her eyes. "Ok, we need to think up a list of accomplices for Thomas and I want each home checked. I also want, if you can remember, the people who weren't so kind to Thomas and his friends back in school."

"Should we get search warrants?"

"It may be the case that we are trapped in some unholy magical circle set up by demented lunatics... but if you think we have the time, then yes."

"So...was that a yes or no?"

* * *

Stuckey's town-wide search for Thomas Holt ended in Clancy's Milk Bar. It wasn't much of a search, to be fair. Thomas was by the booth along the corner window enjoying a milkshake. Thomas had kept his long grungy dark hair from his youth but had added a few neck and arm tattoos to the picture. Much to the horror of all the other diners, Stuckey did not hesitate in drawing his gun, though this didn't seem to faze Thomas. He just kept sipping his milkshake and smiled at Stuckey's drawn barrel.

"Never used to like this place. Was always full of douchebags," said Thomas.

"Still is, allegedly," said Stuckey.

"Do you have any particular reason for pointing that thing at me?"

Stuckey cuffed Thomas without further word. On his way out, Thomas nodded at the diner owner, "No one puts cherries in their shakes anymore?"

Jane decided she'd go to Thomas' old place among the pines. The Holt's were a family of squandered fortune; only Thomas' senile old mother had stayed in town and nobody saw much of her until she'd passed a couple of years back. Thomas was unreachable and hadn't shown up to her funeral. In high school, Jane had heard teenage spook stories that a witch lived in the Holt place. She'd dismissed such things as the purest nonsense, just kids being mean, but driving through the pines that day, thinking about all the things Stuckey had told her about the circles, Jane felt like she was Gretel about to find the cabin...

She got out of the car three hundred yards from the house and began her careful walk forward, her eyes peeled to the ground, searching for chalky little boundaries that could allegedly trap her forever.

* * *

While Stuckey drove in silence to HQ with Thomas in the back, Deputy Gaines was making his way westward along Miller's Ridge, the main way out of their town and the best way to get to neighbouring Brimley, he was well out of the suburbs and just over the crest of a hill was where he saw two cars rolled off the side of the road. There were two charred bodies outside each car, though the cars seemed relatively intact. Trying to contain himself, he edged towards the wreckage. Distracted by the horrific sight of human remains, his foot crossed a hot pink line in the road and his foot found all its nerve endings seize up before being engulfed in flames. Gaines jumped back and howled till he rolled the flames out.

It was a long time and a lot of screaming before he regained his bearings. When he did, he crawled back to the little white chalk and found two parallel lines, one hot pink and one white, going off as far as the eye could see in either direction.

Trying to dismiss the fact that he could now smell his scorched foot, Gaines studied the lines with great reverence, and it was in this fearful contemplation that he saw with his own eyes, like the second hand moving the minute hand, those two lines shift inward and Gaines scrambled backward as fast as he could.

* * *

Stuckey got out of the car and had two other deputies help him take Thomas inside HQ. Anne from reception flew out of her desk with more bad news. "Geoff Francis called. A lot of people have been calling him about being able to receive signals on their phones but not being able to send anything out. I thought you should know because he mentioned that all the calls they were trying to make were for people outside of town..."

Stuckey got the deputies to turn Thomas around to face him. "This is you, right? You're cutting us off? You want to screw with all of us, you think all those people deserve that?"

Thomas simply smiled, "I don't know what you're talking about. The reception has never been good in this town, especially that reception." Thomas then jerked his head towards Anne and the reception desk. "Asshole" she spat and Stuckey told the deputies to move Thomas along. Stuckey then took Anne aside, "Ask Geoff what he can do to fix it, see who he can reach, if anyone at all.

We got anyone seeing if they can make it to Brimley?"

"Gaines is on his way now."

"Where's Jane?"

"She said she'd check out Thomas' old place."

Stuckey froze up, as the urban myths of the old Holt place whispered in his ear. He shook it off. "I said on the transmitter we got Thomas. Try get onto her. Tell her to withdraw until we know more."

Stuckey left to go beat the answers out of Thomas, and as he left the reception, Anne was once again inundated with calls from all over Crawford, describing these strange circles and even stranger feelings...

Thomas was taken to their little-used interrogation room. His hands were cuffed and his pockets searched. They found a wiped phone and Stuckey told one of the deputies to take it to Geoff Francis, the local phone guru. "Gee whiz, I'm surprised Geoff didn't decide to up and leave this place. Could have done more with himself..."

"Like what, join a satanic cult?"

Thomas smirked at Stuckey. "Now, what's all this about, Sheriff? I'm getting the sense you think I've done something?"

Stuckey rested his arms on the table and stared deeply into Thomas' cold eyes.

"Ralph Riggins has his children in that circle you've trapped him in. I'm asking that you help me get them out. Whatever your gripe with Ralph, fine. I know he was awful to you. But there are kids in there. Two little children who didn't get to choose Ralph Riggins as a father, and two kids you're condemning to die because of it."

Stuckey studied Thomas' expression as he waited for an answer, and though he sensed Thomas was taken aback somewhat, it wasn't enough to steer him away from his mission. Thomas leaned back in the chair as best as his cuffed hands would allow. "Ralph Riggins has children? Isn't there a law that stops pigs from breeding in town?"

The other deputy in the room had seemingly had enough, and he cocked his hand back, ready to strike, but Stuckey leapt across the table and stopped him. "Check his other pockets." The Deputy reluctantly checked Thomas' pockets as Thomas blew his sordid breath on the deputy, making him shudder in unbearable discomfort. Eventually the deputy pulled out a parchment of paper, much like the paper Stuckey had found outside of Ralph's doomed place.

Stuckey told the deputy to give him the paper. While the paper was passed, Stuckey exchanged a glance with Thomas, the man showing no fear.

Stuckey held the old parchment with delicate care. The parchment contained the conjuring word for one of Thomas' circles, *Raha Galda Vera Dulichi Malaayan.*

Stuckey tried to recall if the tear matched with the torn page describing Ralph's circle, but the tear and length of parchment didn't seem to be a match. Stuckey then tried to recall his passing phase of obsession looking up the circle phenomenon. Were conjuring words also the same words that broke the circle? Fuck, he couldn't remember, all of it a useless mush he'd passed and failed to retain like all the other things on the internet he'd scrolled through.

"Is this for Ralph's circle?" he asked.

"No. It's for Broden's."

Stuckey froze. Broden was a good friend of his, since High School. A carpenter, a man with huge hands that used them hard and fast without thought back in school. This fared well when he protected Stuckey on the football field, but like Ralph, there had been incidences of cruelty, teasing, more so of DuPont than Thomas, but Stuckey also remembered that after high school, after Broden had that breakdown, he mentioned to Stuckey the apologies he had sought and the forgiveness granted. Had Thomas been one of the lucky few?

"What have you done to him?"

"I rewarded him for his repent. He called me several years ago in tears and said he was sorry for what he'd done and I accepted it. He will be safe from the carnage that follows..."

Stuckey grew deep in thought, a plan forming. He then stormed out the door as forcefully as he could to intimidate Thomas.

He went and found the waiting deputy and Detective Morales. "Broden's on Thomas' hit list. Send a cruiser to investigate—be careful where you step though, *comprende?*"

The deputy nodded in fear but Morales was still sceptical. Just then Anne came running through the hallway. Her eyes were at breaking point, the deluge of calls inundating her mind and turning it to mush. She had two walkies. "I've got Jane and Gaines on the line."

Stuckey grabbed both and froze, unsure of who to speak to first. Anne decided for him.

"Gaines is hurt real bad."

Stuckey took the walkie with Gaines on the other line. The walkie crackled. "It moved... It's getting smaller..."

"What's getting smaller?" Stuckey shouted into the walkie.

"We're surrounded! We're in it!"

"Where are you?"

"Top of Miller's Ridge."

Stuckey threw the walkie at the deputy. "Find out from Gaines how quickly it's moving in. Morales, you check Broden out and report the conditions of his circle. If Thomas is telling the truth and Broden is safe in his circle, we may be able to use that to our advantage. If not, stay clear."

Morales was unmoved. "You really think this circle bullshit is real?"

Stuckey clenched his teeth. "Don't believe me? When you see that circle, don't hesitate to walk on in."

Stuckey then threw Jane's walkie up to his ear and

walked away from Morales, who puffed off to Broden's. Stuckey found a corner and buried his head into it. He whispered into the walkie, "Tell me this a nightmare, and I'll wake up next to you."

Jane was 20ft from the entrance of the old Holt house when she heard Stuckey's voice. The pines covered the sky and the sun did not reach this place. All windows were dark souls that told stories of torment not just through Thomas' childhood, but hundreds of years of colonisation and the broken spirits that came with it. She thought of the house the Holts had built and wondered who made Thomas' mom the real witch, was it the house itself or the people of this town?

Three feet from her was not one but many chalk circles, perhaps up to six different colours, each with their own set of deadly rules and traps waiting for Jane to foolishly enter. Strangely, the prospect of plunging into the unknown was exhilarating.

When she heard Stuckey's voice, she remembered what was at stake and recoiled.

"I'm at the Holt residence. There's all kinds of rings surrounding the place—it's as scary as I remember it."

"Jane, don't go into the circle! We have Holt, he's in the interrogation room."

"I know, Anne told me. She also told me about other

rings in town. Something real big and nasty is going on here and I think we need to start talking about a town evacuation now."

Stuckey sighed. Jane was always one step ahead, but now she was up against a force just as cunning. "Gaines was up on Miller's Ridge. He's hurt real bad, and he says the town is enclosed in one big ring."

Jane dropped her head.

"There's more," said Stuckey, "the ring is shrinking."

"Fuck."

"Fuck indeed."

"I have an evac plan," said Stuckey, "it may be a last resort. Want to hear it?"

"Go on."

"Thomas said Broden would be spared because he asked for forgiveness. I think Thomas put Broden in a circle safe from whatever goes down. If it's set in his house like Ralph's was, I think we can use that circle to save people."

Jane laughed. "We'll keep it in the back pocket, though I'm not sure how Broden will fit fourteen thousand people on his property. His porch is big, but not that big."

"Jane. Come back to HQ."

"How do we get them out of the circle? Has Thomas given anything else up?"

"There are parchments of paper. Ingredients for the circle, some magic spell words or something to seal and break the circle. I can't make sense of it. You've got to come back and help me figure it out, please."

Jane knew what Stuckey was doing; trying to protect his girl. But they both knew who wore the pants and the stakes were too damn high. "We don't find DuPont within the hour I'm going into Holt's house," declared Jane.

"Jane!" Stuckey screamed into the receiver, but Jane was already running back to her car.

* * *

At first, Morales rolled over to Broden's at a leisurely pace. It was just hysteria, he figured. Country folks whipped up into a frenzy about the latest teen trend. Morales heard Stuckey had pulled a gun on Thomas at the milk bar in front of a bunch of kids. Now what would those kids be saying to their parents? Anything calm and civil to keep the peace? Not a fucking chance.

Morales had been an outsider ever since he stepped foot in this town. He was only here because Crawford PD needed a detective and he needed the experience. And what a sleepy existence it had turned out to be. Not a single homicide case, and very few armed robberies. The peace had softened his belly too much. Morales had passed stir-crazy. That phase was over for him, and this disturbance didn't excite him in the slightest. A few people saw his cruiser and waved him down. You've got to go to the fire station, something really weird is going on there, they said. So Morales made a detour and rolled up next to the fire station.

The fire station. Morales braked hard when it came into sight. One of the fire trucks was halfway out the station driveway, its front completely smashed in like it had hit a brick wall. There were firemen standing by the fire truck, banging their hands in the air while some kind of liquid kept pouring out of their mouths. They looked rabid from a distance, and it wasn't until Morales rolled up closer and got out that he saw it clearly. The men were screaming, howling, trying to plead their predicament, but all that came from their mouths were blast after blast of water, blubbering out their speech and making it unintelligible. Shaken, Morales approached closer and studied the ground these men nor the fire truck could seem to pass. There were two lines of chalk in the ground, one the colour white and one the colour of silver, or as Morales soon deducted (once he accepted that Stuckey was indeed telling the truth) that the white chalk was for the people while the silver circle was for the trucks.

One of the fire men held up a hastily-written sign of *SOS*, and waved it aggressively in Morales' face. Morales stepped back slowly, shaking his head with his hands at a loss of how to respond. What the hell was he going to do? Where in the detective handbook did they explain situations of inescapable horror? Morales got back in the car and sped off from their desperate eyes. His only hope now was that Broden's circle was nothing similar to the calamity suffered by the firemen.

Broden's was on the other side of town. Morales got there in record time, his chest tightening every instance someone tried to wave him down. The people were in a panic; the internet was extremely patchy and rumours were spreading like wildfire about the digital and phone blackout. He put his siren on whenever they came near, as if to say there were worse problems he had to attend to, as if these were problems he could solve when he reached them. Morales turned into Broden's street and slowed down to a crawl. His eyes trailed the ground until he spotted the circle, this time coloured gold. Morales parked the car right next to the circle and got out, getting on his car megaphone. He cracked the megaphone in the car and asked Broden to step out for a talk. It was a long while before Broden swung open the door in a seeming daze, his face doofy as if he were high. "What's going on, maaan—Wow, the colours are really colour-y out here," mumbled Broden, a big dopey grin on his face.

Morales took a step back. "Uh, Broden, have you... been smoking something?"

Broden stepped back, his head ruffled, and he sincerely tried to remember if he gosh darn had. "Gee, I don't think so?" he eventually said.

"You feeling OK?"

Broden beamed. "I feel pretty fantastic."

As Morales kept up the talk with the seemingly blitzed Broden, across the street Jimmy DuPont watched on with another of Thomas' disciples. They wore black punk clothes, a wooden ring placed respectively on their left middle finger. Jimmy DuPont did not agree with Thomas' decision to give Broden any shred of happiness; some would say Jimmy had it worse than Thomas at the hands of Broden. But it was all part of Thomas' plan and Jimmy trusted Thomas more than anyone else. They drove off before Morales had a chance to notice Jimmy.

There was a crackle on the radio. One of the scouts from Thomas' house calling, murmuring in Croatian, "She-cop has left, permission to leave and capture? The disciple re-iterated the next step with DuPont. "Yes. Take her. We'll go get Thomas. I'm sure he's had his fun by now."

* * *

Stuckey re-entered the room and sat down opposite the grinning Thomas.

"You like sitting in a jail cell?"

Thomas shook his head. "It's not my kind of environment, really. I enjoy more kind of rounded shapes..."

"But you seem to be enjoying yourself."

"Well, when you're in the exalted company of the former '04 star Quarterback, who wouldn't be?"

Stuckey sighed. "You sure hold onto things, don't you? Why'd do you have to come back. You left this place for better things, but you sure aint come back that way. Seems like you didn't find what you were looking for out there, so you came back to hurt the people who first hurt you."

Thomas stopped smiling. "And how about yourself? Didn't think you could make it out of here? Didn't even try? Who'd you end up with? Was it that Jane Freeman?"

Stuckey remained silent.

"God, I remember she was one hot piece of ass, I think when this is done I'll go find her for a roll in the hay..."

Stuckey kept silent, though one of his fists visibly clenched.

"Do you think Deputy Mrs Stuckey would like a roll in the hay, Stuart?"

Stuckey's eyes widened, and for the briefest moment he considered shooting Thomas on principle, the town's survival be damned. But that would be foolish, vengeful, just like Thomas was being right now.

* * *

Still on the long lonely snaking road from the Holt place, Jane quickly deduced she was being followed. She'd had a stalker in high school before she'd met Stuart and, in conjunction with her five years of policing experience, she smirked at her follower's lack of subtelty. She waited until the perfect bend allowed her time to set up. When her stalker came rolling through, Jane was by the side of the road, behind her parked cruiser, weapon drawn. The small Toyota hatchback slowed down, Thomas' disciple clearly caught off guard, before the Toyota lined its wheels straight towards Jane.

"Ah, shit."

The Toyota burned rubber and launched itself at Jane, her parked cruiser insufficient as a barrier. At the last moment, Jane dived off to the side, rolling down through the vegetation before the Toyota made its brutal impact. The Toyota blitzed through the side bonnet and careened down the slope into the vegetation, finally stopping after collecting several thin trees. Smoke rising from the bonnet, the disciple emerged, dressed all in punk black. Dazed, he pulled out his bamboo blow dart and scanned the trees for his target. When Jane came into view, her weapon drawn, the disciple blew his poison dart, but clearly short of breath, the dart swirled to the left of Jane.

Jane then put two bullets in the disciple's chest. She advanced and dodged another poorly aimed blow dart. "Just because you're all about weird black magic torture circles doesn't mean you should discard good old-fashioned firepower," she quipped.

The disciple coughed up blood and then tried to swallow something he'd had in his hand. Jane saw this and she pounced on the man trying to get him to cough it up. Whatever it was, it had gone down the wrong way as the blood was coming up and the man then started biting down on the thing before a swift right hand from Jane sent it spitting loose. Jane picked up the object as the young, brainwashed man whispered his magic words, some old dialect that Jane couldn't understand. Jane was transfixed by the object, forgetting the threat of her attempted kidnapper. It was a wooden shard, one half of what appeared to be a ring. Jane then looked at the man who had gone still. She checked his pulse and then shuffled away, swallowed the ramifications. After taking a moment, she pried open his mouth and fished out from the back of the throat the rest of this man's wooden ring. She wiped off the blood and slobber and connected the two shards to form the remnants of the disciple's wooden ring. This ring he'd tried to keep from her must have made them impervious to the power of the circles.

Jane searched the rest of the man afterwards and found in his pocket two copied notes of a circle conjuring (one where the trapped participants were forced to keep turning in circles indefinitely) and another image of a snake eating its own tail and the materials needed to make it. It was titled 'string snakes', whatever the hell that meant.

She was soon on the phone to Anne.

Stuckey left Thomas' room barely restraining himself to take Jane's call. "Why aren't you back here yet?"

"I caught one of Thomas' boys."

"Bring him in. I want to see you..."

"He's already dead."

There was a pause on the other line as Stuckey came to the reality that his wife had now just killed someone. "I'm sorry you had to do that."

"I'm not, he tried first. Listen, He was trying to hide something from me, a wooden ring. I think that helps them pass through the circles they create... There's more, I found a copy of one of their circle blueprints, similar to what you found at Ralph Riggins' place. This one's also missing whatever magic phrase you've got to say to break the circle. I think there's a master copy of these circle notes in Holt's house—"

"—You're *not* going in there!" ordered Stuckey.

"We may not have a choice. How quickly is the town circle shrinking?"

"Slow enough," Stuckey lied. Gaines had confirmed a rate of two yards a minute. That circle was dropping into the valley and they'd be done by sunrise the next morning. "Those wooden rings, you just have to put them on and that's that?"

"No, I think there's something you need to say. God. I can't believe this shit is real."

"We checked Thomas, I don't remember seeing any

wooden rings."

"Well, dear, maybe it's like your socks, you're going to have to check again."

Stuckey rolled his eyes. Jane always found time for a quick jab. "Just come back here. We're going to regroup and send out a team to track down Thomas' men. I'm also calling it, Broden's circle is the sanctuary and Morales is directing people there."

"Any contact with the outside?"

"I haven't heard any update. Get back here, Jane."

Jane looked back in the direction of Holt's house. She knew it was the inevitable endpoint, but this would have to wait.

"Roger that."

* * *

Seven men surrounded police headquarters as the rest of the town descended into panic. Almost all of the other deputies (six in total) were now out helping Morales direct people to Broden's happy circle. Aside from Anne and Stuckey, there were only two other deputies and a visiting parole officer situated at HQ. None had ever discharged a firearm at another human being.

It was Anne who first noticed the men standing menacingly out the front at the start of the empty police car park. She called Stuckey over immediately. Stuckey and the other deputies lifted the blinds and watched the people in black tip a hessian sack upside down. Short cuts of rope fell to the floor. "Is that rope?" asked one of the deputies. "Are they armed?" asked the other. "Can you see DuPont?" Stuckey asked to himself.

"Do we go out there?"

Stuckey thought about it then fearfully said no. "Anne, call Morales and everyone else back here."

"What's he doing with the rope?" asked the deputy, his weapon now drawn. Soon, all their weapons were drawn.

"Morales is still at Broden's coordinating," said Anne, "Harris and Benson are 6 minutes away. Tomlin, eight minutes."

One of Thomas' disciples leant down to the dropped rope and began talking to it.

Stuckey grabbed his receiver, "Morales, get your ass back over here. We need backup."

"What's he going to do with those—holy shit!"

The two deputies took a step back from the window and Stuckey squinted to see that the ropes, maybe each 4 feet long, had suddenly come to life and started slithering along the ground like snakes towards HQ. The parking lot was soon filled with them. Stuckey ran up to the front door and locked it just as the ropes reached the wheelchair ramp. Everyone in the reception backed up against the wall and then when the ropes started climbing up the walls Stuckey figured they were going to enter through the air vents on the roof. Stuckey told one of the deputies and the parole officer to keep an eye on the disciples, while Stuckey and the other deputy raced over to Thomas' room to see if the ropes were trying to free him.

Thomas was still sitting still with his eyes closed, humming a skin-chilling tune from an old western tragedy.

Just as they did, they heard a scream, followed by gun shots. They hauled ass back to the reception to find Anne and the other deputy scrambling back to the office, the deputy shooting at the ropes that slithered along the floors, walls and ceilings with seemingly only one thing on their mind. Stuckey and the other deputy followed the others back into the office and also opened fire.

Hitting the damn things was nigh impossible. The deputy screamed that they just kept coming and he wasn't lying. They'd shoot them in the middle and split them, only for the split parts to then start attacking as two. It was hopeless. One of the deputies was on his desk when the ropes rose from the ground and encircled his feet, locking him in a circle. They all saw it and the deputy panicked, losing balance and falling from the circle. His entire body was immediately engulfed in flames. They tried to put out the fire but were wary of the ropes. Now the room was getting smokey. The ropes encircled the parole officer next and Stuckey warned him not to leave the circle. The ropes came slithering from every angle. One of the deputies was backed into a corner. Stuckey was running out of options. The guns weren't cutting it, they needed to be completely eviscerated, and when Stuckey looked back at the deputy still in flames and the rope circle burnt to a crisp, he had his answer. Stuckey ran to Morales desk and swiped the large bottle of nasty-ass cologne Morales like to spray on thick. Stuckey then swiped a lighter from Gaines' desk and threw the bottle at the deputy's feet. The bottle smashed and Stuckey yelled for the deputy to jump away. He did so and Stuckey threw the lit zippo at the corner and the entire corner was set alight along with most of the ropes. Retreating back to where Stuckey stood, both of them then turned to Anne, who had gone with a different method and trapped the rest of the ropes in waste bins.

They got the fire extinguishers and tried to save the deputy but it was painfully obvious he couldn't be saved. The parole officer, still entrapped, asked what the hell he was supposed to do.

"Well, let's hope these things are breakable." said Stuckey.

Stuckey retrieved some scissors and carefully cut the rope like he was cutting the green wire on a bomb. When nothing happened and Stuckey flicked the rope away cautiously, the parole officer asked if it was OK to move now and Stuckey said, "Not until we're a safe distance away." Everyone watched with baited breath as the parole officer took one sweat-dripping step forward and breathed a deep sigh of relief.

If only that relief was to stay.

They returned to the front to check on the DuPont gang and found a walkie by the front door. Stuckey carefully unlocked and fished the walkie inside before locking the door again. There were no signs of the DuPont gang.

The walkie crackled. "Hello, Stuckey. I would like to speak to Thomas, please."

Stuckey's teeth clenched. "Listen here, you piece of shit. I'm going to make you pay so hard for what you've done. I'm going to boil your fucking testicles in a deep fryer so you can experience the burning you've caused you greasy fucking fast food shit for brains."

"Thank you for your kind words, Stuckey. I only want to speak to Thomas, but I could just as easily send more of my snakes if you'd prefer."

Everyone else flinched. Stuckey motioned for Anne to get an ETA on their backup.

"And find out how far off Jane is," he added. Anne hurried off and the others tried to reinforce the waste bins holding the rope snakes.

Stuckey returned the walkie to his mouth. "You can talk to me."

"Aren't those detained supposed to get a phone call?"

Stuckey scratched at his head, trying to scratch out his nerves. DuPont's tone was calm and in total control, not like back when he was a deadbeat working in that dead-end Wendy's. Stuckey knew him as that, and the fact he'd clearly changed so much under Thomas' tutelage unravelled Stuckey. He got the deputy to follow him to the armoury and retrieve a bolt-action rifle and shotgun. The deputy was a real green rookie; he'd only been in the job for five months. "You keep an eye out for DuPont, you see any outlines, any chalk in the distance and you see them, you start shooting."

The deputy nodded, trying to be brave, but his body was shaking, and the rifle he took soon starting shaking as well.

Stuckey then headed to Thomas' room. He stared down Thomas and then cocked his pistol. He brought the walkie up to his mouth. "You can talk to Thomas. But you say any of that magic bullshit and I kill him."

"You kill him, and no one leaves the circle. Not even your pretty little wife..."

Thomas grinned. "I'm sure he just wants to talk to me about the weather, Stuckey." He then raised his hands in innocence, as much as the cuffs would allow. "No funny business, I promise."

Reluctantly, Stuckey held the walkie up to Thomas, who never took his eyes nor his grin off Stuckey.

"Master?"

"Yes."

"Have you had enough fun?"

Thomas took a deep breath and exhaled slowly, those eyes never leaving Stuckey. "Yes."

Stuckey saw what it meant, DuPont was coming in to retrieve his master—his master, who had let himself be captured in order to get a front-row seat to the chaos.

Thomas said his magic words just as Stuckey threw the walkie away, not that this would stop the cementing of the circle he was now sure they were trapped in. The sound of the walkie smashing against the wall was then followed by the sound of gunfire, which shocked both Thomas and Stuckey.

Stuckey rushed into the office to find the deputy shooting the rifle at will through the window by the burned-out corner, Anne fending off more snakes in the reception and the parole officer once again trapped by some rope snakes.

"Stay right there!" Stuckey yelled at them before joining the Deputy at the now shattered window. "Backup is taking fire!" the Deputy screamed before shots rained down on HQ, sending them both ducking. Stuckey then kicked at a yellow rope snake making its way towards them and threw a waste bin on it, before turning back to see the deputy take a bullet to his temple. Stuckey stepped back and fell over the waste bin, tipping it free and sending the yellow rope they probably sold at Daniel's Hardware for less than $1.50 slithering toward him, trying to make another fucking circle. Stuckey grabbed the rope by its frayed head and forced the rope to make a circle with him outside it, turning the rope solid and lifeless.

More shooting outside drew Stuckey's attention and further spliced his nerves. Stuckey then picked up the rifle from the deputy and aimed through the window. He looked through the scope. Morales was still alive and Stuckey saw the sniper atop the roof of the donut diner had just switched his attention to Stuckey. The scope glinted as the sniper lined him up. Stuckey's breathing slowed. His exhale came first and so did his bullet, which dropped the sniper out of sight.

The gunfire continued, but Stuckey couldn't see who else was left. His head flush and his concentration straining, Stuckey returned to free Anne and the parole officer. When he saw them both standing there, helpless, they each shared a tired look. Stuckey was about to get a pair of scissors from one of the desks and was about to cut the parole officer's circle rope when he heard the voice of Thomas in the other room. *"DuPont! Get me out of here!"*

Stuckey halted his scissors quest and turned away from the parole officer at the last second, storming swiftly off in the direction of the interrogation room while copping a stream of expletives from the parole officer. Stuckey swung open the interrogation door and found Thomas had shifted the entire table over to the downed walkie, one of his shoes off, as he tried to operate it with his toes. Stuckey raised his pistol, but before he did, the warnings of the parole officer and Anne finally hit him.

Snake.

He looked down and only just managed to get one of his feet out of the tiny rope's way. The rope coiled around his left foot and cemented itself.

All of his body was free, except for the foot, but that was cruelly enough.

Thomas and Stuckey exchanged shocked faces, as both their circumstances had equally degraded in the tiny room. Thomas looked down at the table and decided to charge. He slid the table across, trying to knock Stuckey's foot out of its circle and into fiery combustion, but Stuckey caught the table and strained to keep his foot in place, only just managing to hold firm, before he fired off a side shot from the table, hitting Thomas in the arm and halting his push.

"Ah, FUCK!" Thomas yelped, and a temporary truce was initiated.

* * *

Jane approached HQ with shocked eyes. Tomlin Street had become a warzone of lead and red; bodies from both sides hunched over behind cars, their fatal wounds pooling onto the street. She found DuPont, his body lifeless and his wooden ring destroyed. Her heart broke when she saw the arc of another goddamn circle enclosing what she assumed was HQ. She was about to radio in to Stuart, but was interrupted by the sound of someone coughing. She walked around what she identified as Morales' cruiser and found Morales, sitting against the car, holding his bleeding stomach.

Jane had always liked Morales' style, an admiration Stuckey had always taken to with thinly-concealed jealousy. She knelt by Morales. "How bad is it, Detective?"

Morales winced a smile. "I'm detecting a few exit wounds and maybe one lodged in my kidney."

"Holt's men dead?"

"We did our best. I sure hope so."

"Can you walk if I help you?"

"Only if you carry me," Morales joked and Jane laughed. "The hospital hasn't been encircled, has it?"

Morales coughed again as Jane helped him up and into his cruiser. "Afraid so. They're all spinning around in circles in there. Can't seem to stop. Take me to Broden's, we've evacuated everyone we could there; your husband said it would be safe."

"Did you say spinning?"

Morales nodded. "I don't think they'll last much longer."

Jane took out the copied notes of the disciple she'd killed. Morales asked her what it was but she didn't respond, lost in her new responsibility. Jane then closed the car door on Morales. "I need to talk to Stuckey."

She walked up to the circle and got on her radio attached to her shoulder strap.

"You there, hon?"

Stuckey and Thomas shared a glance.

Stuckey picked up the damaged walkie and kept his gun trained on Thomas. "It's good to hear your voice, bub. Listen, you may need to be careful with what you say right now. I'm stuck in the room with Thomas."

Jane swallowed this down the best she could. "OK. I'm going to take Morales to the hospital, and I'm going to try and break the circle there...and if that works, I'm going to go to Holt's house."

Stuckey and Thomas shared another glance. Stuckey reaffirmed his grip on the gun for Thomas' benefit. "Jane, I don't want you going in there."

"Holt's house is the key to this. He's probably looking at you right now trying to persuade you that it isn't."

Stuckey strained to study Thomas, who instinctively changed face and looked away, childishly trying not to give anything away.

"But as well versed as he is in his black magic business, I'm pretty sure he's got a cheat sheet he depends on, and if that cheat sheet is anywhere, it's in his house."

"There's not a chance she'll be able to make it out alive," Thomas whispered, "It will be the end of her."

Stuckey paused for a moment, summing up their options. There was only one.

"I'm the only one left," said Jane. "I'm our only shot out of here, not just for us, but Thomas as well. All his friends are dead now."

Thomas took this news very badly. Stuckey placed his hands on the table ready to halt any push.

"Let me know if he decides to cooperate," said Jane.

"Affirmative."

"I have to go now."

"I know. Be careful."

"I think we should get ribs for the Bowl Drive too. Comfort food. I think that would be good for the community."

Stuckey shed a tear. "You always know what's best."

"I'll see you soon. Love you."

"Love you."

And then the room went silent, as Jane set off on what might be her last assignment.

* * *

Jane dropped Morales off at Broden's, his face growing paler and paler, despite his claims that he would be okay. It looked like half the town was crammed into Broden's, with not a hint of fear among them; instead, she was greeted by a sea of smiles as each chatted to one another as if they were at a party. Morales was welcomed with cheers at seeming odds with his deteriorating state. As he entered the circle and was enveloped by the blissful people, Jane came to realise that Morales knew he was a goner, and just wanted to go out happy. And it wasn't a stretch to say that Jane was a little sad she couldn't join them in the happy circle. A thought like that chilled her skin, as the weight of her task on her lonesome shoulders seemed to sink in all at once. But she kept going, and made her way to the hospital.

Some were already dead, having spun across the circle and entered a fiery end. Others were collapsed on the grass at the front, unconscious yet still rolling in circles along the ground like rag dolls.

Jane checked her copy of the circle conjuring and got to work. She got on her car speaker, and called for a doctor to meet her at the parking lot. A young resident, still spinning, came out to meet her. The resident's scrubs were filthy with puke and despite her spinning making even Jane feel disorientated, the resident was able to understand Jane's perplexing instructions: to find a purple shoe, a toy spinning top and a wine glass filled with sand.

Oddly, the young resident nodded away and said she already knew where two of those three things were, and set off to retrieve them. She returned almost an hour later, still spinning, and Jane then gave her the next few steps, to pour water over each while reciting these strange black magic chants. The resident took a while to master the chants but when she did, the objects seemed to fizz like boiling water leaking out of the pot, the magic work of Thomas undone. The young resident, Sandra, then merely had to throw them out of the circle while reciting more lines. One by one, the items were thrown and when the last one touched un-circled ground, Sandra's world stopped spinning.

Lifted by this small victory, Jane set off for the Holt residence, the afternoon sun beginning its descent.

* * *

There is a darkness in every man, and standing in front of the Holt residence, those dark windows staring back at her, Jane felt within her bones all the sacrafices offered in the name of this eternal darkness. She wanted to say one last thing to Stuckey, if it was going to be her last words. A simple I love you—the truth, the light, to carry her in the darkness. But she thought better of it. Just do it. She switched on her Maglite instead, much more practical that way.

The circles were many. Six colours in all. She'd gather all the wooden rings she could find that weren't destroyed, even though they seemed lost causes and stood once again at the edge of the circles...

Call it cold feet, but Jane decided in a split second decision to try a few things before making that first step.

She got out a shovel and tried to dig under, break the circle from underneath, but the shovel head got stuck and couldn't be pulled out.

She got out the body of one of the disciples with their wooden ring still attached and flopped the body over the circles, like a human bridge. She then tied a severed hand to a rope and cast the hand over her body bridge like casting a fishing line...but like the shovel head, the rope would not be tugged out, the circle now its home.

Sighing, Jane stepped to the side of the body bridge and took a deep breath. The wind was picking up, fallen leaves swirling around the snow globe that was Thomas Holt's dark soul.

Last chance to talk to Stuckey for courage.

But once again, she thought better of it.

She raised her leg and closed her eyes, the thought of those dark windows watching that first step too much to bear.

And then it was done. She was inside.

Jane then tested all possible means of escape to rectify this cold and lonely mistake. She dragged the rest of the disciple and tried to tip the body the other way back out. This time the body fell and hit the invisible wall, its face sagging against it.

"Shit," she muttered, her first word in over an hour.

Since she'd stepped inside the rings, she'd had her back to the house the entire time, almost trying to ignore its presence, but this was truly foolish; like turning one's back on the ocean. Jane had only been to the ocean once, on a trip to Atlantic City with Stuart. The water was calm in New Jersey, but she had heard the saying said once before on TV and it kept with her when she sat with Stuart in the early morning after a night of flashing-light revelry. And it was thinking of this she realised she'd probably never see Stuart again, let alone the ocean, now that she'd stepped inside this cruel place. Before she stepped inside the house and crossed another threshold, she gazed into those dark windows and promised she'd burn the house down if all else failed.

It was lucky she'd kicked the door down the way she did. Coming clean off its hinges and falling flat, Jane used her flash to cast out the position of where she was going to slide the door frame. She slid it forward then checked her left and right sides; on what would have been covered by the open door was a circle on the wall, its requisite items nailed and hanging within it. Jane made sure to avoid its projected circumference traveling across the entrance by getting on her hands and knees and crawling under. Once passed, she wiped the sweat from her brow and took every next step with the greatest care. All rugs were treated as if they concealed circles, and most turned out to be concealing the white chalky traps. Her light shone on framed family photos, the smiling Thomas and his aging mother in better times, twisting her hatred and making her uncomfortable intruding into another person's home.

She crept and crept and crept along, shining the light on dusty surfaces.

She checked bookshelves in each dark room on the first floor, and when she came up empty, she'd topple the bookshelf onto the floor in frustration. In truth, she knew where the book would be: Thomas' childhood bedroom, surely. She figured it would be upstairs, and lo and behold, when she finally shuffled into his room, there it was, a fat and worn hardcover book, encircled in a silver circle (stopping objects from removal) and a black circle, which Jane had not yet seen. She approached with caution, and studied the rest of the room for traps. The black circle had been burnt into the carpet, the burnt fibres sticking up like thorns, and had a dark menace to it, unlike the playful chalky circles that spotted the town.

She walked carefully back down to the kitchen and got her some cooking utensils, with the aim of dragging the book to the dark circle's edge and carefully reading it until she found what she needed to save the town. Unfortunately, this effort proved fruitless and clumsy, the book would not open or be moved other than the touch of human hands. How Jane figured this out was unknown to her, just a feeling, but of course this had to be the case; there was only ever going to be one way to get that book. Sighing, she tried to call Stuckey, but there was no response. Nothing seemed to be getting through. Finally, she simply said, "I love you Stuart Stuckey, I'm sorry if I fail." And then she stepped into the dark circle, sat down and crossed her legs like a child in the quiet corner of a library.

When she opened up the book, the explanation for

the dark circle slid out as a loose page. It was titled *The Reading Circle.*

Ingredients: A single book.

Nature: Each word spoken, as it is written. First page to the last.

She looked at the book and flicked through its pages, they were not numbered but there had to at least have been 200 pages...

Each word spoken, as it is written.

What other choice did she have?

And so Jane dug in, with everything she had. She had her Maglite, but no water to quench her throat. Each exasperated word like drops of poison to her mind. She tried to forgo understanding and simply recite the words divorced from their meaning. Interspersed with the recipes of circles deadly and absurd, were the tales of Thomas Holt, his life snaking through the pages. The story of a young boy cursed by a town that didn't understand him and punished accordingly. She tried not to empathise, to fall for his sad tale knowing what he'd become. But as her vision blurred and the mind grew weary, Jane couldn't help but think of Thomas Holt and slowly begin to understand...

She kept reading, her throat dry and her eyes fried, learning the dark secrets and immense power of the circles that surrounded her...

* * *

Soon after Stuckey's last conversation with Jane, the parole officer had lost his balance when he unsuccessfully tried to free himself from his rope circle and burned to death in between the main office and the front reception. Stuckey and Thomas could do nothing but listen to his screams and Anne's wailing as she had to keep herself from collapsing out of her own circle.

Thomas may have mastered the dark arts, but he was still of human flesh and the lack of food had him curling up in his seat.

"She won't make it," Thomas rasped, clearly getting desperate.

Stuckey raised his weapon as a reminder, though the strength in his arms and legs were fading. "You don't know Jane. She's a smart cookie..." Stuckey cursed using the word cookie, knowing how it made his mouth salivate.

"She's walked into a house of six circles, each with conditions that all but guarantee death to the uninitiated."

"I trust her, she'll make it back."

"And when she doesn't, all those people will die when the sand in the hour glass reaches its end."

"They're safe," triumphed Stuckey.

"And what makes you think that?"

"Because they'll be in other circles."

Thomas laughed. "Some circles have more power than others."

"Are you saying the circle we're in now is one of those...vulnerable circles?"

"Precisely. If you've stepped in the shrinking circle at any time during its existence, then you will burn once outside its circumference, whether it is the size of a continent or a small pea. I'm no exception in this case."

Stuckey gripped his gun.

"If you want," said Thomas, "you can kill me right now. Or, we can negotiate."

"What's there to negotiate?"

"Jane's life."

"She's in one of your circles. You said she's dead anyway." Stuckey grimaced at his own words, the pained expression telling Thomas he was getting somewhere, and despite Stuckey realising this, there was no denying that Thomas had his leverage plain as day.

"But you said she's smart," mused Thomas, "a smart cookie, and if you truly have faith in her skills, you'll come to see that it will be the death of her. Because when she breaks the circles of my old family home, she will be exposed to the shrinking circle and nothing will save her from engulfing in flames."

"Your book of magic—she'll figure it out."

Thomas laughed. A big great, exaggerated, maniacal laugh. "She'll figure out a lot of things. But there are some things I've omitted from the book, some torn out and others committed to memory. The one page she needs, for the shrinking circle, page 234, was destroyed by the flame of a cheap convenience store lighter in Leipzig."

Stuckey's gun took on a greater weight, the weight of his universe, as his finger slotted against the trigger. "You're lying."

"Shoot me then."

Stuckey raised the gun. "Why should I trust you over my wife?"

"Because if you don't, she'll die."

Stuckey dropped the gun. And then he did something Thomas did not expect. He cried. Bawled his eyes out. For a good ten minutes.

And then there was silence. Thomas knew all he had to do was wait. Let his story sink in. Stuckey was the hero quarterback. Even back in high school he had that glint in his eyes that he could do something special. That he would save the day.

"What do you want?" the hero meekly whispered.

Thomas smiled, this time with restraint. "I want my freedom. And *your* life for hers."

Stuckey looked at him blankly and Thomas briefly thought Stuckey would object.

"Saving the woman you love must come with sacrifices... Think of it as an honest transaction. An honest, fair payment..."

Stuckey stared Thomas down and then reached for his radio, "Jane, can you here me out there?"

There was no response.

"Anyone else?"

There was no response.

"What about the rest of the town? Anne? What will you do with them?"

"Once I free Jane, she will be able to save them and allow me enough time to disappear."

Stuckey clenched his teeth at the thought of Thomas Holt escaping, yet his honesty filled him with hope that he would keep his promise.

"What's the deal with the circles anyway?" Stuckey asked, the curiosity having gotten the last of him.

"Why circles? Why not triangles?" Thomas jeered.

"Why you need shapes at all?"

Thomas shrugged. "Maybe it's just how I was taught. Maybe I thought the feeling of being trapped in a dead-end, dying spot was something the people of this town needed to experience, if they hadn't already."

"Don't you realise there's probably someone in this circle who is struggling just like you were, who could go on and make something of themselves?"

Thomas swallowed the last of his guilt. "Not for long."

Stuckey sighed. There was no getting through. "Sure," he relented. He then lifted the radio to his mouth the tears welling up again. "Jane Freeman, I love you. I'm sorry if I'm wrong."

* * *

The first thing Thomas did was find a vending machine

with cookies in it. He got the dried yoghurt topping with apricot and a Gatorade. He then returned to the interrogation room and pried Stuckey's wedding ring from his lifeless hands. He then placed the ring on the table and went and cut his own hand with a letter knife and allowed the blood to drip into the inner circle of the ring, creating a miniature pool of blood. He then began his chanting, the dialect an ancient mix of Sumerian and Latin. The louder his chanting grew the more the blood started to boil until at its peak the blood infused with the wedding ring, turning it into a bronze shade.

When Thomas put that ring on he felt the freedom fill his body. What a lovely relief it was. He walked out to the lobby and the sight of him sent Anne shrieking. Thomas approached her slowly, his eyes wide.

"What did you do to Stuckey?" Anne asked, her face welling up, about to cry once more. "What are you going to do to me?"

Thomas pulled out the letter knife and Anne flinched. He slowly advanced and her whole body shook, and when he bent down, she thought about jumping on top of him and letting her flaming skin engulf his own, but when Thomas started cutting the rope away, Anne stood in shock. Thomas left her there, speechless.

He walked over to the remnants of the shootout and muttered a few solemn words for his downed disciples. Brushing this unpleasantness aside, Thomas then walked through the town he'd made his revenge on, whistling away on the empty streets. The coyotes of the night howled and Thomas howled with them. He walked past the town square, where the large hourglass had been laid in plain sight in the middle of the central gazebo. There wasn't much time, maybe only around two hours left before the shrinking circle surrounded only the hourglass.

The night sky was growing lighter, the dawn of a new day and a cleansed town emerging—well, after Thomas ran a few errands...

He walked his way to Broden's, past circles of dead occupants—he checked on the man who force fed him science frogs and pissed in his drink bottle and called it apple juice. Ralph Riggins and his children had finished everything off in their fridge and then with little control had moved onto the closest next thing that passed for edible: they ate all the cleaning products and succumbed slowly thereafter.

Thomas made a slight detour to the school that had been his first prison and lit a small fire that, left unimpeded, would eventually turn it all to ash.

Broden's property was no more than 400 square feet, yet when Thomas reached its edge and looked into the spaced, partied-out eyes of more than ten thousand residents, packed in like sardines and unaware of their grim circumstances, he found himself impressed by Stuckey's quick thinking in trying to shelter these pathetic hicks. Thomas entered the circle and had to push his way through many a people until he found Broden. Broden was in a dopey daze yet still recognised Thomas, who squeezed his chin affectionately. Thomas hugged Broden and said he was glad Broden repented and this was why he and his family were to be given a peaceful end to their lives. Thomas then went into the backyard and had to part the sea of people standing over the fresh mound of dirt Thomas' disciples had placed one of the circle's qualifiers in. Watched on by a crowd of curious onlookers, Thomas carefully dug out the totem, Broden's high school championship trophy, and held it aloft to the people, who joyfully clapped away. The glory Broden had felt lifting this trophy almost 13 years ago had been the emotion pouring through the happy circle since its inception.

In its place, Thomas dropped Stuckey's gun, the one Stuckey had reluctantly handed over and received five agonising slugs in the gut for. And as Thomas walked through the crowd and left the circle with a dark, twisted grin, the wonderful feeling of joy that had been inundating all those people's brains was replaced with the violent echoes attached to Stuckey's gun. They began to bicker, and this bickering turned to yelling, and this yelling turned to fists, and these fists soon flew everywhere until destroying one another became their only logical remedy...

* * *

The falling sands of the hourglass had ceased by the time Thomas reached his old family home. Dawn was here. Thomas got out of Stuckey's police cruiser and stepped eagerly over the six circles. He rose up the stairs and slowly opened the door to his childhood bedroom.

There Jane sat, her eyes tired, a sizeable chunk of Thomas' book read, though nowhere near close to being finished. Jane turned her head and then locked eyes with the man who had murdered the love of her life and turned her town to ash. A man who's intimate past she'd read aloud these past few insightful hours.

"Do you understand now, Jane?"

Jane smiled. "Yes. Yes, I do."

Follow the Glass Stone

David Mycrott

The past is an abode of dead things. She crossed the street to get away from it, because like a looming spectre it threatened to devour everything, to turn everything good into fangs and mucksome rags. In the end it did its killing anyway. It always does. The caged bird sings because it wants to get out. It doesn't have much else to sing about, the poor sod. The poor little soul.

If you love her, let her go. Wisdom! I cannot speak for cagebirds but albatrosses, it is known, can cry unabated for ten years upon losing a mate.

Certain vices press upon the soul. Certain actions bring about either downfall or epiphany. Nonsense! Table scraps. Coleridge, 50 lines into *Kubla Khan*, was interrupted by a travelling salesman from Porlock and upon returning to his desk found the vision of the poem had absconded. Capricious, certainly, but this is sometimes how it is. A poem was lost for the sake of a sale. Socks, apparently.

The curtains creak as they prise apart, shuddering on rattly rails.

According to Buddhist tradition there are Ten Grounds, or Bhumis, of the Bodhisattva. [A galaxy known as Via

Combusta, 'the fiery way,' was once associated with witchcraft, lovers and magic].

By experiencing each in sequence the disciple is freed from the bonds of the flesh. Alive in the world, the adherent becomes a dweller in another type of body. [All she wanted was to be left alone with her pain. It filled her. No space was not inhabited, no cavity had not been plumped up by it].

The first Bhumi is Great Joy, obtained by insight, trial and error, by extinguishing the fires of the mind. This is a joy borne of certainty, from which all else flows. The only requirement is a willingness to accept that one knows nothing. [A former head of the KGB once described Marxist-Leninist thought as a 'bacterium.']

The second ground is Stainlessness. Renouncing defilement, one is eventually freed from the corrupting influence of immorality. Once that cloud lifts it can never return. The horizon grows clear, the way becomes both knowable and known. [What type of lovers? Star-crossed. Time-crossed. What type magic? The darker stuff, naturally. Witches, then, and lovers crossed by stars and time, and thick dark sludgy swirls of magic].

Third is the Emanate stage. Luminous, glowing, the light of Dharma is said to radiate from within. Propelled by a will not all his own, the disciple bathes in the light of victory and emerges a Master, a light-maker.

Stand, whoso list, upon the slipper top.

The fourth Ground is that of Radiance, of burning wisdom.

Fifth is a stage known as Helping Sentient Beings. Such assistance is given automatically by the practitioner of this Bhumi, because his very presence brings light to the darkness of the world. Faced with such a light, darkness retreats. By separating herself from the prison of her mind, by overcoming the pull of the emotions and the snare of the senses, the Master unites heaven and earth.

[*Difficult to attain, difficult to attain*: the brain, of course, can literally be rewired by fear or trauma].

In doing so, he or she enters the sixth Gate. Abiding in the perfection of wisdom, the devotee becomes Obviously Transcendent. This is the last of the appearance stages. Above all ideas of self, those of the Sixth can skilfully promote the Dharma to others without attachment to outcomes. Likewise they do not become emotionally attached when others react negatively.

[Never become emotionally attached to man, woman or beast].

Those belonging to the seventh Ground are said to have Gone Afar, to be far from the world journey. They have distanced themselves from the need for control, hence their mastery of self is total. [God made its works and then rested, resting in the bonds of love it had created. To that never-born spirit, refuge from fear, a respectful tip of the lid. *Far from the World Journey* isn't a bad name for a book; I have just now jotted it in a journal].

The eighth state is that of Immovability. In a sense it

is the final stage, for those who abide in immovability will never again be swayed by the things of the world. There is no regression from this state. It is the birthright of all, not only those who are called saints.

[I once had a panic attack that lasted ten days. Towards the end of it I thought I could talk to crows, to whom I made small offerings, and a black swan I sometimes saw on a nearby lake had started communicating with me totem-like by way of dreams].

The penultimate Ground is the Power of Virtuous Wisdom. Even the smallest actions of one's life become a teaching.

[Messages both sleeping and waking have continued intermittently from the swan; it is some time since I have laid out bread and bits of bacon for the crows. Something I noticed about crows: they actually prefer dead things. Fresh or day-old tidbits they would sometimes eat, sometimes not. But anything left lying in the grass long enough to attract maggots or the first sign of mold they treated as a delicacy. Dead flowers they seemed particularly to adore. The stench of death's decay was perfume to them].

Lastly there is the Dharma Cloud. The dweller in this state has attained harmony with the Creator, and has no further use for separation. The ninth and tenth Grounds are outgrowths of the eighth. The body is perfected, the mind cleansed. Not all who attain it may speak of it.

[All the things you want to say but can't. Dead, your

majesty; dead my lords and gentlemen. A crustacean slurped up by a belching baleen whale].

Joyful, Bereft of Stain, Luminous, Radiant, Of Benefit to All, Obviously Transcendent, Gone Afar, Immovable, Animated by Virtuous Wisdom, Abiding in the Cloud of the Way. These are the Grounds of the Bodhisattva.

[Do not relive that season's happiness].

* * *

Once, and only once, the veil was lifted and I was granted an audience. I asked one question — 'Why does evil exist?' — and got my answer. Contented, I was thus able to complete my sojourn in the land of the dead.

'A theory that a conspiracy has been working consciously for many centuries is not very plausible unless one attributes to them a religious unity. That is tantamount to regarding them as Satanists engaged in the worship and service of supernatural evil. The directors of the conspiracy must see or otherwise directly perceive manifestations which convince them of the existence and power of Lucifer. And since subtle conspirators must be very shrewd men, not likely to be deceived by auto-suggestion, hypnosis, or drugs, we should have to conclude that they probably are in contact with a force of pure evil.'
— Revilo P. Oliver

'There is no such thing as sin.'
— The Gnostic Jesus, *The Gospel of Mary*

Prisca theologia: the doctrine that a single all-encompassing theology exists, transcending religious thought, bestowed upon the human race by divinity itself. The notion dates back to the Egypt of the pharaohs and beyond, well before hoary Babylon, before even the Sumerians about whom we hear so little, to a sun-drenched and crystalline age wherein that which we would term fantastic was taken as commonplace. The air was different back then, the temples of the old gods had not yet been converted to ossuaries, dogma was yet to obscure what the mind and senses perceive as self-evident. What is death if not the full flowering of consciousness? What is life if not the playing of hide-and-seek with God? After Babylon. That's when things started falling apart.

Order arises not in spite of entropy, but because of it. Each system has an upper limit as to how much entropy it can first accommodate, then dissipate. If the system cannot dissipate sufficient chaos into its environment, it begins to internalise the excess entropy, and becomes internally entropic. If the excessive fluctuations continue, the chaos eventually becomes so great that finally a point is reached where the slightest nudge can bring the whole system grinding to a halt. This is called the bifurcation point. To bifurcate means to divide into two branches. A decision point. Either the system will totally break down and cease to exist, or will spontaneously reorder itself in an entirely new way.

A famous author and a Buddhist monk once staged their own version of the game Chinese whispers in New York City. They arranged a few hundred people in a line, and one by one the following three sutras were passed down the chain:

1) Like a shimmering star, or a flickering lamp
2) A fleeting autumn cloud, or a shining drop of morning dew
3) A phantom, a dream, or a bubble, so is all existence to be seen

The author, who was last in line, transcribed the garbled sutras thusly:

1) Follow the glass stone, follow the glass stone
2) The droid from hell
3) If anything exists it changes

Fractal shadows. Information is currency. With a lever large enough entire worlds can be moved. Magisterium, Pentecost, cloak, dawn, twilight: just some other words that are nice, words that are written in the lining of men's souls.

Why does God not spare the innocent?

The answer to that is not in the same world as the question.

And Then This Happened

Craig Tuck

My name is Taggart McWallace.

I used to be a cop. But then I shot my twin brother.

Now, I ride the desk. The desk may as well be a giant steroidal stunt cock and I'm Jenna Jameson, I ride it so hard.

Christ.

I'm an acting APS5 in the Australian Public Service and fuck me, it's boring!

So, like most desk jockeys, I escape my self-loathing at the pub and on the social sport circuit.

Cricket is the game with the strongest drinking culture, so here we are.

It's funny. I don't even like the stupid game, but I'm one of the best swing bowlers Canberra's 6th grade city and suburban cricket competition has ever seen.

I'm so good the lads at the club even wrote a novelty song about me.

The song was crafted to the tune of 'My Sharona', a song about sex with underage girls that was so catchy it slipped past the censors. I've always admired it for that.

While not as big a hit, the video clip for the version about me, 'Great Swing Bowler', got more than 500 views on YouTube. It was a big deal.

Anyway.

This story is about a day when, like most others, I was bowling beautifully. I took wickets with my first two balls. I had 2/0 from 0.2 overs and was really going well.

The drama started when I completed my hat-trick with the next delivery by taking a remarkable diving caught-and-bowled catch.

Unfortunately, when I hit the ground I dislocated both my shoulder and my elbow. The only one in more agony than me as I left the field was my captain, left wondering how the team would take the last seven wickets.

Christ, what a cunt that was.

I ended up at the local hospital, waiting for hours to undergo urgent reconstructive arm surgery. The whole thing was quite a bore. The nurses looked nothing like they do in the movies, and they were nowhere near as forthcoming.

The only thing that kept me interested was all the text messages from my teammates. The dozy pricks kept sending me score updates, each one telling the predictable and gloomy tale of opposition recovery.

The other team eventually posted a decent score, before we collapsed in pursuit.

'Christ,' I thought. 'How can you be so shite at a game you grew up playing?'

While each message stunk of hopeless desperation, it was at the fall of the seventh wicket when things really escalated. My captain sent a simple, desperate plea: 'Needle up and come back! We need you'.

That was all I needed to hear.

I leapt from the hospital bed, slapped the gas mask from the hand of the approaching doctor and surged towards the exit.

I arrived at the ground not long after, having sprinted all the way there.

My arrival was announced with the fall of the ninth wicket.

I didn't have time to get to our kit bag to pad up or grab a bat, so I ripped a picket off the fence and made my way to the middle, in surgical gown and all.

The opposition could not believe I was out there. One of them literally said, 'I cannot believe you are out here.'

Regardless, I was indeed out there, and facing a simple equation at that: six runs to win, one ball left.

'Cash this!' I told one of my disbelieving opponents.

'Cash what?' he asked.

I left him hanging.

The bowler turned to begin his run in and at that perfect moment, smirking, I replied, 'This reality cheque!'

I unloaded a brutal pull shot to send the ball scorching through the sky, leaving a trail of smoke behind as it rocketed towards the kindergarten across the road and, more importantly, the match-winning six.

The people cheered.

Screams could also be heard from the kindergarten.

Even my opponents applauded as I raised my arms in triumph.

That was perhaps the most incredible part of this tale. In the aggression of my strokeplay, I had jolted my dislocated elbow and shoulder back into place!

My arm was fine!

So much so that twelve beers later, I could be heard noting that my elbow had never worked better.

That's when the real drama started...

Back at the clubhouse, the Ravens' celebrations went long and strong. The pokies did a roaring trade even as we continued to keep the barman very busy indeed.

After a few hours, the cash only bar was overflowing with riches. Throughout, my teammates continued to clamber over each other to buy their hero (me) another drink.

I greedily accepted their offerings, for I like my celebratory drinks like I like my women: plentiful and paid for.

'Let's get ready to stumble!' I roared, hilariously.

For a time things were going great, but the night had other plans in store...

It all happened in a matter of moments.

The armed assailants must have known this was a cash-rich bar, given the ruthless precision of their strike.

Three big, mean looking men stormed the room with machine guns cocked, demanding we hit the floor.

In our collective drunkenness, we hesitated.

The shots they fired at the ceiling proved to be helpful for crowd control, but it was my calm example that really settled things down.

My teammates cowered, following my lead as I crouched slowly to the floor. To be clear though, I was not cowering.

I was biding my time.

The three assailants pointed their guns at the barman and one of them handed him a bag.

'Fill it!' he said.

The barman looked at the bag.

'OK,' he replied.

The barman started rummaging through the register, grabbing fistfuls of dollars.

'Hurry the fuck up,' the most vocal of the assailants said, spitting his words into the barman's face.

I didn't care for his language, or his tone. In particular, I couldn't abide his aggression towards a man for whom I held so much affection.

The barman.

'Christ,' I thought. 'Some people are sacred!'

But clearly that was not the case to these Godless bastards.

Worse was to come.

Even though the barman hurried his pace, the most vocal assailant clubbed him in the head with the butt of his gun. The barman fell to the floor instantly, blood spurting from his mouth.

That angered me even more.

One of the other assailants laughed.

That was it!

I leapt to my feet and charged towards the bar. The most vocal assailant heard me coming first.

He turned to face me.

He was too late.

In one smooth, violent movement, I grabbed his head and slammed it onto the bar. The impact immediately knocked out both his teeth and his consciousness.

'Christ!' I thought. 'That was impressive!'

The raw power of my attack briefly gave me an erection.

In contrast, the assailant's body went limp.

As he slipped towards the floor, I scooped up the machine gun as it fell from his grasp.

My hand tightened around the grip and my index finger wrapped snugly around the trigger. I pointed the gun at another hapless assailant.

He immediately dropped to his knees, closed his eyes and raised his hands in surrender.

I wasn't falling for his ruse.

I squeezed the trigger. This caused the firing hammer to strike the firing pin, which ignited the bullet primer, which in turn ignited the gunpowder, causing bullets to expel themselves from the barrel at a high rate of speed, exactly as I'd hoped.

The bullets entered the assailant's face, causing an explosion of flesh, bone and ecstasy.

I then pointed the gun at the last remaining assailant and quickly repeated the dose.

He didn't have time to do anything else but die.

My teammates rose as one, cheering once more the selfless heroics they had come to know so well.

I shrugged off their congratulations because my work wasn't done.

I leapt across the bar to our fallen comrade — the real hero in my eyes — the barman. Mid-air, I caught a glimpse of myself in the reflection of the pub window.

It's not a good look for a man in a hospital gown to leap with splayed legs over a bar, let me tell you. Nevertheless, I couldn't help but admire the man I saw.

'My father would've been proud to call that man his son,' I thought to myself.

My dad had been a brilliant intelligence operative who had died foiling what was going to be the next 9-11.

His heroism was a real psychological millstone for me.

More than anything else, I wanted to be a man deserving of his respect. At this moment, that meant helping the barman.

I checked for a pulse and found one. Good. I picked

the barman up and threw him over my shoulder.

One of my teammates asked me if I needed help, given my previous injury. I said no, '…you'll only slow me down.'

I carried the barman out into the cool summer evening and made my way towards the hospital I had fled just hours earlier.

That's when the real trouble started…

On the way to the hospital, a well-intentioned policeman became suspicious.

He must've been a rookie. I couldn't believe how easily his feathers were ruffled. Calm down, laddie. The sight of a blood-stained man wearing nothing but a loose-fitting medical gown, carrying an unconscious barman over his shoulder and fleeing the scene of a triple homicide is no reason to panic!

'Christ,' I thought.

I strode towards the hospital, doing my best to ignore the questions he shouted at me.

Mercifully, an explosion at the old town hall down the road distracted him.

'What the hell was that?' he screamed.

In hindsight, it was a fair question.

To my left, a car had crashed into some streetlights. To my right, people were sprinting, screaming. Pulses of light surged through the sky, literally vaporizing anything in their way.

'Do yer fucking job, ya dozy cunt!' I yelled. 'I don't

have time to answer all ye stupid questions, laddie. I've gotta get this man to a hospital.'

'Sir, we're obviously under some sort of attack,' he said. 'It's not safe to be out here. My car is over there. I'll take you!'

The cop waddled towards his car, opened the passenger door, and gestured for me to get inside. I raised an eyebrow and held his gaze, inspecting it for emotion. Gauging possible motives.

He tried to match my look, but the obvious terror in his eyes ruined his credibility. So, after a time, I grew bored by this senseless flirting. I opened the back door and threw the barman into the backseat.

I then made my way around to the other side and took my place up front, behind the steering wheel.

'I'm driving,' I said.

Before he had time to argue, the policeman was vaporised. Some sort of light ripped through his body, turning it instantly to ash.

His disappearance exposed a horrific green creature behind him, pointing some sort of ray gun in my direction.

'Get out of the car,' the creature said, in the voice of former Sale of the Century host, Glenn Ridge.

'Glenn Ridge?' I asked.

'No – I have merely adopted this humanoid mode of verbal communication so that we can relate,' it said.

'Relate to this!' I replied, pulling a machine gun from

under my hospital gown. I opened fire.

The bullets turned the alien creature into a sloppy mess of stinking green goo, crumpled alongside the smoldering ashes of the unfortunate rookie cop.

'What the hell was that?' I heard a confused voice mutter from the backseat.

I turned to see the barman stirring. With no time to explain that earth was clearly under some sort of alien invasion, I punched him in the face to knock him out again.

'Dream well, sweet prince...' I muttered.

I then fired the police car's ignition, slammed my foot on the accelerator, and gunned out onto the road. Ted Nugent's 'Stranglehold' played loudly on the stereo, without any intervention on my part.

It was an awesome moment.

I careened through the mess of crashed cars, panicked citizens and armed aliens, uncertain where I was headed or what I would do when I got there. Instinct was my navigator; self-assurance my co-pilot.

The barman remained in the back.

I swerved at the sight of the roundabout at the end of ANZAC Parade and surged further as I straightened out on the road towards the War Memorial. That's when I saw it: a giant, weaponised space ship, very much reminiscent of the Imperial Star Destroyers in *Star Wars*, but different enough to avoid a lawsuit, should my story ever be turned into a film.

The space ship dominated the sky above.

Citizens in cars, on bikes, foot, or whatever else they could find all fled the monstrosity.

Together, they formed an urgent, ominous wave of panic that crashed violently on the pavement before me.

Bloody hell. It was like this bar I ended up in Bangkok one time, where literally *anything* goes. Sheer madness. But a story for another time.

I slammed on the brakes and my car screeched to a halt. The barman flew forwards and crashed through the windscreen.

'Jesus Christ!' I yelled.

I only gave myself a brief moment to reflect on the precarious nature of life, as the barman's severed head rolled out on the road in front of the car.

Seatbelts, kids...

It was a loss, of course, but not one I had time to dwell on any longer. With machine gun in hand, I exited the car and began a purposeful march towards the mother ship.

That's when the real drama started...

I was two steps into the march when I saw a surge of energy hurtling towards me.

With the startled reflexes of an abused kitten, I jerked my body out of the firing line.

The energy burst collided with the car behind me. It

was lucky that he'd already been decapitated, because the barman's body was instantly vaporised, along with the car.

'Jesus,' I said. 'I hope he wanted a cremation.'

It was a good joke, but the alien bastards left me no time to enjoy it. Deadly flashes of light burst all around me — briefly reminding me once again of those raucous Bangkok New Year's Eve celebrations from a few years earlier.

But once again, I didn't have time to reflect.

'This is getting annoying!' I yelled to the sky.

That got their attention.

Bad move.

As their targeting lights shifted their attention to me, I dived to the ground and army-rolled behind some cowering children. They were vaporised moments later, but in giving me the chance to reload my gun, they had served their purpose.

I honoured the children by opening fire on the invaders huddled on the other side of the bridge.

One by one, threatening aliens became green goo.

It was satisfying to watch the bullets pierce their disgusting lime bodies. As the bullets penetrated the flesh, they prompted a pathetic guttural sort of groan, before their form collapsed entirely into a grotesque slimy pile.

Even in the chaos of the moment, it was pretty cool.

Satisfied, I shifted my gaze towards the mother ship

and began walking boldly towards it.

'Halt!' Glenn Ridge's voice demanded.

I ignored it. Instead, climbed onto an abandoned taxi to address the invaders.

The spotlight shone brightly as my hospital gown flapped wildly in the breeze, destroying all pretense of modesty.

'Why do you approach?' the voice asked.

It was a hard question to answer. Why had I approached?

I looked at the carnage which surrounded me. The flaming machinery, the mangled humanity.

'Someone had to do something...'

Glenn Ridge's voice laughed.

'And what do you propose to do?'

I took a deep breath.

Hitting an incredible match-winning six with a fence picket was one thing, but bringing down an invading alien empire was another thing altogether!

With no options left, I resorted to a tactic I had never tried before. I'm embarrassed to say I decided against violence, and instead, used words. Christ, what had I become?

'I propose to talk....' I said, making myself somewhat sick in the process.

'I propose to listen....

'Friends, if I may be so bold, I propose to open a dialogue!'

The huddled survivors nearby cheered as one. With a gesture of my hands, I quieted them.

'Friends, I propose to find some common ground. To understand you...'

The voice from the ship remained silent, but I was on a roll.

'I propose to look with open eyes upon the carnage you have caused,' I said. 'I propose to grieve... and I propose to forgive.'

Finally, the voice from the ship spoke.

'You propose to forgive?'

'I forgive you because to err is to be human!' I said. 'So as I gaze upon the wreckage that is your doing, I see you for what you really are: *human*. You are my brothers, my sisters... You are me. And I love you.'

I fell silent. It was a silence punctuated only by the crackling of the nearby fires that burned upon cars, buses and corpses alike. In the distance, a baby cried.

Thankfully, the voice of Glenn Ridge drowned it out.

'This is unexpected,' the voice of Glenn Ridge said eventually. 'And I have to say, quite touching...'

Another long pause.

'You show empathy and understanding that we have found to be uncommon in our intergalactic travels – are these qualities true of all humans?'

'Oh sure, absolutely!' I said, with a bit of a wink thrown in for good measure.

Another long pause, punctuated by muffled alien

conversation echoing through the microphone.

'Ok, here's what we can do,' the voice of Glenn Ridge said after another pause. 'Let's pretend this whole thing never happened, OK?'

'Sure,' I replied, 'But you have killed a lot of people...'

'Yeah, no worries, we can undo that,' the voice of Glenn Ridge said.

'In a matter of moments, this will all be reversed – nothing but a bad dream for you, and not even that for the rest of your planet.'

'Really?'

'It will be like the whole day never happened...'

I reflected on all the death I'd seen. The barman's served head and the cowering, vaporised children, among many other bloody sights. I could undo all of it.

My thoughts then fell to the cricket game from earlier that day; to that memorable, match-winning six.

I closed my eyes and took my mind to the sound of immensely satisfying shrieks of kindergarten children, echoing across the playing field.

Those were moments, all right. Moments to cherish from a day to remember.

Could I let these moments just simply slip away, like tears in rain?

The answer was obvious.

I pulled the machine gun from my hospital gown, pointed it at the mothership and screamed 'No deal, you bastards!'

I fired with purpose. I found a weakness in the armour and brought the ship down.

The ship crash landed in the middle of the CBD, killing many thousands more innocent bystanders.

It was awesome, but Christ, the city's a mess now. Adding to the tragedy, I later learned that Fyshwick was also destroyed. Many good women went down in that terrible blaze.

It will surely take years to rebuild.

Palliative Cared

Aden Simpson

So here it is.

Room 15. Acacia Ward. The bed has many functions. Rise dear head, lower ye legs. I feel in the mood for a sunbed. Plentiful room, if one could physically reach it.

So here it is, and this is it. The bed I will die in.

The view is nice. There is a level-wide balcony for visitors to catch up and speak in hushed tones about deteriorating conditions. The treetops cover most of what I fathom of the outside. The son will note that across the road there is a primary school with a small soccer field, the kind of place I used to dominate. He will only discover the primary school by the fourth day, when his knowledge of the hospital and its numerous exits has been mastered. He will also compare the two institutions side by side, a glimpse of what's to come, and a reminder of what was lost.

I am already dead, by the way. This is merely a review of the last weeks and days in this bed, until the final breath drawn with the wife holding my hand and the son fetching coffee. Perhaps this review is the son trying to commercialise my death, or, delve deeper into what was behind some of the ramblings and rants my brain offered in its decay. Perhaps he is trying to do both. Either way, apart from the quotes in italics, everything else is strictly conjecture.

The pastor arrives after the first night. I am conscious. He asks if I'm religious. The son notices my stiffening up, the brain rousing to give an impassioned defence of what I believe. "I'm not religious... but I love people." Isn't that the basis of religion?

The son watches me choke up. He saw me bawl my eyes out over and over in the hospital before this one, the deluge beginning when I said to my wife "this is it, isn't it?" Saw lots of it. But in palliative, this is one of the last times he will see me cry, confusion taking the baton from sadness. He always wondered what it would take to make me cry. Wondered his whole life just how bad a thing had to get before his hero finally broke. And when he eventually saw it he realised it was something he never wanted to see again.

Because you asked for it, I will now describe in colourful detail the subplot battle: The passing of the great big poo, or at least the attempt.

This bed is where I will end. I know this because my right leg is gone. All the kinetic signals I took for granted now a static silence. Unresponsive. My right arm too. Such is the situation that I find walking an assisted adventure. Assistance has progressed from a cane, to a frame, to an even sturdier frame, to a steady eddy and, finally, the crane.

Ah, the crane. Strapping me up and lifting me high above the bed. Can you see me soar? They swing me over to the en-suite, this big green net securing me like an oversized diaper.

The son has advised me that, on account of the labour-intensive qualities of the crane, trips to the en-suite are permitted on a results-based basis, otherwise it's back to the pan or the diapers and a loss our greatest ally, gravity.

The son tries to rouse me. He wants a win. A last battle we can actually claim victory. My stomach shall bloat no more. The son beckons Churchill: We will fight them on the beaches, on the land...

"We will never surrender," I join in the fun. I lean forward gripping the railing with my only arm left and push with all my might.

There is...only a little bit, nothing as substantial as the three meals a day I've been wolfing down.

The son demands extra effort, allows more time, despite my sitting-balance spent and collapse imminent. Eventually he props me up and reluctantly presses the assistance button. It was not to be.

"To be or not to be, that is the question."
—Heard in the waiting room after leaving the patient to his delirium.

This is self-evident. A ricochet in the brain searching

for what it all meant brings me back to high school and the old bard. I never uttered Shakespeare to the family before, but now is as good a time as any to pose the question to the hallucination above my bed, facing me, staring back.

The family returns and see a stretched hand pointed upwards at my nemesis (the all-encompassing LED ceiling light). It is not turned on however, the room is dim, and the answer to the question remains elusive.

The photos. An attempt on the son's behalf in sparking a memory and bringing me back to life as it once was. First, a photo of a man by the river, hanging sideways against a pole, like a flag in the wind. A remarkable athletic feat only recently revealed to the family by an old friend. I don't recognise this person so the son tries another polaroid. A young man holding a baby. The man is happy as Larry—that's a thing I used to say about people who attained a respectable level of joy. The son flits back and forth between myself and the picture, his flow of hands suggesting the two people in this room are related to the two people in the photo. He is hoping for a loving spark, a Hollywood spark with minor orchestral accompaniment. When we are robbed of most expressions, people in our line of debilitation find the scariest, most foreboding method of communication can come from a simple shaking pointed finger and horror on our face. Surrounding family will pass it off as delirium, but a part of them will always question what those close to the other side are seeing. Either way, I certainly rattled the son. Take your joys when you can get them, I reckon.

Going back to the food going in and not coming out conundrum. The time is early. I wake with a hunger that can only be satisfied with the blandest fodder. A bar of grain cobbled and fused together, lined up on its side with several other brothers and sisters, submerged in milk and halved with spoons. I talk of course, about my first love, the breakfast of champions. Weetbix. Sanitarium's saviour. Their favourite soldier.

The son does the feeding. With each bite I tell either the son or the weetbix itself: "Thank God for that." Over and over again. Each bite. Thank God for that. So much for not being religious. I finish one bowl and ask for more. The son disappears for a while. How hard is it to get some damn weetbix when a guy really needs it? He returns with more. Thank god for that.

The visitors. They come in from all different timelines. Family. Friends. Family friends. I am nice to all of them. They are new. They have new things to say. But I get tired keeping up, trying to squeeze out a sentence from my dried-out sponge. The motor, the brain, is firing false starts. And I stutter and stutter until I give up and say, "Well, you know what I mean."

The family though, the son and the wife, they don't have anything else to say. "I Love you. I'll always love you," etc. etc. Broken records. How many times am I supposed to say it back? How many breaths do I have left to utter the obvious? Facts already established. Let's move on and be done with it.

Speaking of repeats, I'm now repeating the last thing a person says. Over and over. Echolalia they call it. The son has caught onto this and is now playing games. I'm too loud, apparently. "You're screaming." The son points out.

"You're screaming," I counter.

"I'm screaming?" he asks.

"I'm screaming," I admit.

"I scream, you scream..." he says.

"I scream, you scream, we all scream for ICE CREAM!" I finish.

The son laughs, the wife laughs. I'm hungry.

Another craving. This time for bananas. I eventually catch on that I'm repeating my demands over and over. "How many bananas?" The son asks in front of his girlfriend. "Bananas bananas bananas bananas bananas bananas," I emphatically explain, a smile on my face.

The son turns to his girlfriend. "Was that 5 or 6?"

"Little Dreams Big Dreams... little dreams only 99c."

I kept repeating that it was all like a dream when I broke down in the other hospital. Now that I'm left completely immobile, my bed an island sinking in the pacific, dreams have become my only means of escape.

Based on the above statement, all dreams have value, no matter how little they appear. "It was all a dream," was a movie line. I asked the son what movie that was from. He said it sounded familiar, but couldn't determine the film. So much for all that schooling I paid for.

One time, close to the Driver, I turn to the son and tell him not to get the kring disease. This is a disease that we have been planning for since childhood. A family term for any ailment, big or small. "Oh no! It's the kring!" I would shake my head, checking the son's little ears, open throat, or wherever the source of discomfort lay. A shocking diagnosis none could have predicted.

"No No No No No..."

This is before the Driver. Every night. I turn on my side, the only direction my body will allow and cling to the railing on the other side of the bed. My arm shakes trying to keep balance. "No No No No No No." Hard for the others to determine what exactly I'm objecting to, so I shall fill in the gaps. "I am dying and it hurts because I love living and I'm scared and I do not want to die, even though that's how it's looking at this moment." These bedsores are getting to me. "Don't you see?" I say over and over again. To state the obvious, they do not see. They don't want to. No further explanations required for this one.

Did I ever tell you in the previous hospital I spent many circles trying to solve my disease? If the cat has tumours growing out of his head, and he's still going, why can't I keep going? It's different they say, but I press on with my investigation, time running out and all.

The catheter. It seems that after a few accidents, the saintly nursing staff reconvened with the doctors to prescribe a catheter. I hover above myself in the bed, studying my naïve face, unaware of the benevolent forces conspiring to stick a tube up my tube. The procedure is enacted without much fuss. It's the times after though, when I forget it's there and each rediscovery comes with a lot of pulling and wrenching a sensitive part of me.

The son takes one look and reactively touches his own working parts to make sure they're still in good knick.

Every explanation of its necessity is met with further calls for justification on my end. "But Why?"

"But why?"

"But why?"

All dignity is leaving my body and collected in a bag that hangs on the side rail of the bed. Not the kind of life support I had envisioned.

"But why?"

In my review, as I wince with every tug of my own accord, I cant help but ask the same question. After everything else, now this?

"This is the most depressed I've ever been."

I say this every now and then. I shake the railing I can

reach, every now and then. I slam my fist down on the pillow the wife and son provide when rage is imminent. I will say this sad thing and the son will quote it in his eulogy, reaching for the silver lining: that if this was the most depressed I'd ever been, then the rest of my life must have been just dandy.

Good for him.

The drugs taste awful. You're not supposed to taste them, someone informs. Easier said than done, buddy, ma'am. Would you rather I automatically swallow everything instead? Because I'm running on instinct now if you wouldn't believe... Sometimes late at night the son tells me to be quiet, to stop wriggling around in the only two motions I have left and quit moaning so loud. What is dying supposed to look like, I remember thinking at the time. Now I have a better clue as I hover above the bed. The old me takes notice of my presence, but he also sees everyone else, all the people he thinks he failed, the missed opportunities he never took. He sees so much, and yet here is a man who lived a good life and enjoyed it. So what chance do the rest of them have on their deathbeds?

Close to the Driver now.

"Whatever."

This is close to the end. Before the driver. The son has reached an impass. Too tired to care anymore, apparently. He has tried to explain something to me and I have tried to explain something to him. Listen here, son. Listen to my voice because you're going to miss it. But he's tired and he leaves my pain with the words, "whatever".

"Whatever to YOU." I say back. Or do I? Maybe the person writing this has forgotten how this conversation went, perhaps for the best.

Before, the son said the sooner the better. Now it is sooner and he eats his words and swallows each like fermenting glass in his belly. Oh, soon? He is not ready. But maybe I am. Let's finish up, the review is coming to a close.

"Would you like some custard?"
"I would like some custody for my constituency."

The context here is obvious. If I'm ever to declare my good intentions in this world, I think I will use this utterance as my proof. A dying man, willing to share his custard with those in his electorate. I'd win in a landslide.

The Driver. Morphine and clonazepam, delivered through this thin, wispy tube into a pretty cannula they call a butterfly. I take a break from screaming and sleep. I think the review is going well. We are almost at the end.

The son will note one last "I love you" in this new

state of mine, when all I have left is the energy to whisper. It's a reaction, a yeah, yeah, I know. Because at this stage I'm sick of goodbyes. Sick of everything. From one angle in my sedated state the son will catch a glimpse of my eyes half-open and my lower jaw slack and he will witness exactly how the end will look. I shift over to the son's perspective and happen to agree, though I am disappointed by the spoilers.

The food is no more. Eyes remain closed. The breathing is laboured. When my breathing stops, so do the others. Everyone in the room holding their breath. What is it supposed to look like, this dying business? Curiosity doesn't cease for the dearly beloved. Yet still they urge me to continue, each breath a little more time for whispered goodbyes.

Morphine dreams. Big dreams. The son will always wonder what went on in my head these final days. Who visited me in my subconscious, which ghosts made an effort. Whether I saw my version of god and it made me feel all right.

The son is desperate for some last advice. He knows the blueprint for a successful life, a life well lived, and yet he wants a different life. Something to call his own. On his own two feet. But he still needs his dad. *He will always need his dad.*

The last night they both sleep at the hospital. The wife on a foldout chair, the son outside the room on the enclosed balcony. This is the wife's idea. Usually they take turns staying over. She has no idea why she decides this night they sleep as a family, the decision leaving her mouth before the brain registers the point. It's been four days on the driver, no food. Logic or luck?

And so they sleep, every now and then bobbing their head up; staring, listening and exhaling relief when reaffirmed I'm still here.

Where else would I go?

In the morning the breathing is different. They have a pamphlet that explains this is all par for the course. I enter the body and remember the quiet valleys of heartbeats, the slowing of things, before three gasps of air are sought as reflex.

The wife debates whether to shower at home. It's an hour there and back at most with a quick rinse, but she decides to use the basic shower in the en-suite. Smart move, and I will forever be grateful.

Eventually, the son declares that this isn't his dad anymore. Isn't the man who took him to all his sports games. Who turned up wherever he was needed and had a genuine joy in doing it. Who brought home a DIY toy dinosaur from Japan and built it that night despite flying in that day. Who yelled at the son when he broke the car sun visor by hanging on it like tarzan. Who stayed overnight on the son's first operation at the hospital because he twisted his testicles watching *Black Hawk Down* in an awkward position. Or the last time they went swimming at their favourite beach together and the son got mad and had a hissy fit because the dad wanted to swim between the flags where there were no waves.

It isn't his dad and it will be OK if he passes, the son doesn't have to be there as long as it's peaceful. So when the wife wants a coffee from the shops and not the hospital blend, the son says sure.

It is 9.40am.

Well, here we are. The wife & I. Just the two of us. 29 years of marriage as of only a week ago. I didn't have time to get her something for our anniversary so the son got the wife flowers on my behalf. Flowers were perhaps a naïve choice, given in the coming days she will receive a garden's worth. All I really gave her was everything I had, and she the same, while we could.

She holds my hand and she watches my breathing, sending prayers from deep within. It's OK, she whispers, It's OK to go. A light leaves my pallid eyes. I drift above and hover and I catch those prayers as I catch myself, ascending.

My review complete, I am ready to leave Room 15, Acacia Ward. I watch the son and the wife take in the room with a view, one last time. They know a part of them will never leave this place for as long as they live. As for me, it's time to look back further. Re-live everything else over and over again. I don't mind though, because it was a life truly well lived, no matter how it ended.

A Fortuitous Turn of Events

David Myrcott

A writer lives in a modest-sized town where rental properties are becoming increasingly expensive and difficult to obtain. The owner of his unit has decided to sell and the date by which the man must vacate is rapidly approaching. He often admires a second-floor apartment overlooking a busy street. It features an ivy-clad balcony, windows with quaint wooden shutters, high ceilings aesthetically veined with small cracks and, if the pictures posted in expired listings are to be believed, one of those bathtubs with the four lions paws holding it up. There is something romantic and charmingly old world about it. It is a writer's apartment, like the kind Henry James would have lived in.

He asks around, and upon discovering the name of the landlord phones him, offering to pay an extra 100 a week for the apartment. The landlord most regretfully declines, saying that the tenant has only recently signed a twelve month lease and paid the next two months in advance. But he advises the man that should the situation ever change he will contact him, and takes his details.

Some days pass and the man continues trying to

find a place to stay, placing applications, discussing his frustrations with a friend. Suddenly, just as he is beginning to feel mounting panic about his precarious situation, the phone rings. It is the landlord, explaining that the apartment has suddenly become available. The tenant has unexpectedly been called overseas on urgent business and has broken the lease. If the man is still willing to pay an extra hundred a week, the apartment is his. The man is overjoyed that the solution to his problem is at hand. He quickly agrees to the landlord's terms, arranging to move in the following week, once the tenant's family have organised the relocation of his belongings and sold the rest.

'What a fortuitous turn of events!' thinks the man to himself, pleased the universe is on his side for once. Perhaps his morning affirmations have been working? He wonders what business could call someone away as urgently as all that. A death in the family, perhaps, with a grief-stricken relative to care for, or an irresistible job offer in a foreign land? Who cared! The apartment was his. The panicked feeling abates. This is going to be the beginning of something good, he knows it.

He moves in and immediately notices the attractive young waitress at the café across the street. He sets his typewriter by the window so he can watch her as he writes, but is unable to concentrate and manages nothing but fluffy odes to the waitress and the occasional bit of sloppily written advertising copy.

After several weeks he can stand it no longer. Summoning his courage, he attracts the attention of the waitress one day as she stands in the doorway smoking a cigarette. She seems to be waiting for something. The streets are quiet and her shift is about to end. This is one of the first times she has stood still long enough for him to be able to really study her. He calls down to her and invites her up for a drink. She accepts after some banter ('Say, you're not a pervert or anything are you?' 'No, of course not,' replies the man. 'I'm a writer.' 'Oh, so definitely a pervert then! But I guess there's only one way to find out.')

Eventually he hears a knock at the door. She comes in, and they begin conversing in a somewhat stilted fashion. She comments that the décor is wildly different to that of the previous tenant.

'Oh really? What line of work was he in?' He does not think to question how she knows what the inside of the apartment looked like previously.

'I forget... an engineer... or an astronaut? What does it matter? He's gone now anyway.'

The tenant is slightly taken aback by this. What did it matter how the man had made his living, spent his days and his time, thousands upon thousands of hours of his life? Of course it mattered! How would the waitress feel if she wound up dead one day and no one had anything more profound to say about her than 'what does it matter?'

'Oh, I don't think there's much danger of that,' she says, lighting a cigarette. 'Want one?'

'Sure' says the man, even though he didn't really smoke. He didn't want her thinking he was naïve.

She hands him a cigarette, lights hers, then passes him the lighter. It was gold, clearly expensive, with an engraving which reads *Not them that say Lord, Lord, will enter, but those who do the Lord's work.*

'Where is that from?' asked the man.

'Where's what from, the lighter or the quotation?' she replied, a little testily. She must have thought he looked more handsome from his vantage at the window, framed as he was by the whitewashed shutters and long late-afternoon shadows. Maybe she thought a writer would be more interesting, more exotic, more enigmatic. A real man, the hard-drinking Hemingway type, someone worldly and eloquent, with an alluring wit and a penetrating intellect that would dissect a woman's deepest unspoken desires... He became flustered, wishing he was younger and more attractive, the kind of man who would know what to say to a beautiful young waitress when she was sitting on his sofa.

'Well both, I suppose,' he said, though he'd been referring to the quotation.

'The lighter is a friends. Or got given to me, or something. I don't know where the quote comes from. The Bible I guess.'

Of course it was from the Bible, it was part of the Sermon on the Mount, he'd meant what Gospel specifically as variants appeared in several, and querying why one version had been chosen over another might have spurred a further conversation on religion, but now he didn't dare clarify himself for fear the young woman might become even more waspish at his fumbling attempts at repartee.

'I think that wording is from Matthew,' he said softly, eventually, and she didn't respond. Should he say something else? He thought he may as well, he might never get another chance like this. His mind whirled, looking vainly for something, *anything* interesting to say, anything to keep her another few minutes so he could continue admiring her beautiful, hard features in this exquisite proximity. He caught another hint of her surprisingly delicate scent. It was sufficiently ambrosial that it that spurred him to bravery.

'So, did your boyfriend buy it for you?'

'Look,' she said, impatiently exhaling a plume of smoke, 'why don't you just light the cigarette?' She gave him a slack jawed, exaggerated look as if to say 'are you stupid or what?'

Ah. She thought he was a fool. His head spun and he felt quietly sick. She thought he was a fool; she didn't respect him. All his bullshit about being a writer, the playful banter from the upstairs window. He should never have invited her up here. What on earth could she possibly see in a balding, aging, *boring* human being like him? She was probably used to the most exclusive clubs, the trendiest cliques, probably had men lining up to buy her expensive cocktails, rich, well-dressed men who knew how to charm a woman, knew what it took to get a girl like this into bed... and he'd been stupid enough to invite her up here, to this dingy, cheaply furnished two-bedroom hovel he'd been so absurdly proud of.

Well, it had been a mistake, that much was clear. He should have kept her at arms length, continued admiring her safely from afar, gone on composing odes that she would never read, whispering to her at night when she wasn't there. A real mistake. He'd smoke this goddamn cigarette, or try to, then make some excuse, tell her he had important work to continue with, explain he was actually in the middle of something. And she'd leave and he'd move his typewriter from the window, he could never again be as brazen and carefree in future as he'd been that afternoon, acting as though nothing had ever happened, as though he hadn't made an ass of himself by failing to act like the confident, suave intellectual he'd told himself in his fantasies he would. He'd have to spy on her through the shutters, watch her only when he could be sure there was no chance of her catching his eye, of ever holding his gaze for a brief agonising second before turning away with a mirthful smile at his expense. He could never withstand that. Why, she'd probably tell all her friends about him, laugh at what a bland, bumbling old clown lived at number 42...

In the midst of this hopeless reverie the young woman had wandered unnoticed over to the typewriter and was bending to read what was written there, her lips curled with a hint of real-life mirthfulness, though tinged with something else.

'What's this?' she called playfully, ripping it from the typewriter with a little *swoosh*. 'My love, my life, I gaze upon you from afar...'

He lunged for her in a panic, but she too quick. Dancing out of his reach, she ran through the room, dashing around the table, feinting left and right, reciting in an out of breath voice his lines of ardour and devotion.

'How I long to festoon you with titles like lover, sweetheart, and other such words,' she cried as she ran into the kitchen, then ducked under him and doubled back to the living room. 'Festoon? That sounds filthy!' She laughed gleefully as he snatched at the paper. 'I've never been festooned in my life.' He continued racing after her, feeling nausea and shame in equal measure. 'How my heart burns—'

Stop, please stop, he silently begged. Each line she read stabbed into him.

Eventually she came to a halt by the refrigerator, chest heaving, face slightly flushed and eyes more vibrant than ever. 'Thanks, that was fun,' she said, handing back the page without a fuss. He snatched it from her and crushed it into a tight ball before throwing it into the rubbish bin beneath the sink, wishing his shame and awkwardness could be discarded so easily.

'Oh, don't look so bashful,' she said, tousling what was left of his hair. 'I'm flattered, I really am. Now let's have another cigarette, or a first one in your case, and maybe after that you can read me some more of... whatever that was.'

He glanced down at the cigarette which was still lying in the cupped palm of his hand and nodded mute assent. It would be out the question to read her any more of his terrible poetry. She would have to leave as soon as possible. Why couldn't things ever work out like they do in dreams?

* * *

'Here's your lighter,' said the girl, 'I must've forgotten to give it back the other night.'

'Thanks, I was looking for that,' said the landlord. He regarded it. 'My wife gave me this. Religious nut.' He lit a cigarette then placed the lighter back in his pocket. 'It's got an inscription from the—'

'Gospel of Matthew,' finished the girl.

'Right,' said the landlord, taken aback. 'I didn't have you figured as the devout type.'

'Well, I guess I'm just full of surprises.' She nestled closer to him as they walked, and he placed a large arm around her shoulders, pulling her close. 'They won't trace the poison, will they?' she asked, and her dark eyes clouded momentarily with fear.

'Relax. Of course they won't. No one saw you go in, did they?'

'I don't think so. I told Magda I was going straight home. Got in and got out, more or less. Took the cigarette, of course, after he collapsed. There weren't many people around. Some people might have seen us talking earlier in the day, when I was on my break. He called down to me.'

'That's nothing! If anyone asks, you were just being friendly. Trust me. You've got absolutely nothing to worry about. Besides, they didn't catch you last time, did they?'

She shook her head.

'Or the time before that?'

She shook her head again, this time with a smile.

'See? There's nothing to worry about.'

Reassured, she gazed adoringly up at the landlord, admiring his strong features, his olive complexion. Even though people often mistook them for father and daughter she thought he was sexy. Power was sexy. Wealth was sexy. Murder was sexy. And that was that. She sighed contentedly. 'So, who's the next tenant you've got lined up?'

'Some rich guy from out of town. Wants the place weekends mostly. Says he's an art dealer, or a collector or something. Anyway he's loaded, fucking loaded, and he's offering even more than what this guy was willing to pay, that's what's important. And expensive artworks have an unfortunate habit of getting stolen from apartments left vacant for days at a stretch.'

'Kiss me,' said the waitress, and he did, both having already forgotten the dead body in the apartment.

A Very Bad Idea

Craig Tuck

To Craig, it wasn't exactly clear where it had all gone so badly wrong.

If nothing else, his intentions had been good. Unfortunately, that didn't seem to placate the angry mob that was on his tail.

So, despite his confusion, Craig did the only thing he could do. He ran.

Several months and one very bad idea earlier, life had been much simpler.

Back then, Craig's only worry was making a worthy follow-up to his debut short film, *Backhanded Justice: Case Files of the Table Tennis Cop*.

The YouTube sensation had attracted over 300 views and Craig was feeling the pressure to top it.

'I've actually got ideas for a sequel and a prequel...' Craig said to his friends and collaborators, as they gathered for a production meeting at Richmond's London Tavern.

'... but I think I'd rather do something completely different, instead.'

Ben, who had portrayed the fan favourite Barfly No. 1 character in *Backhanded Justice*, was understandably miffed by the idea.

'Really?' he asked. 'Man, I think that's a mistake. You've got 337 views on YouTube – that's pretty good buzz.'

Aden, acclaimed for his performance as Taggart McWallace in the same project, agreed.

'Yeah, you'd be mad to do something different now,' Aden said. 'Taggart McWallace is such a great character. You're a brilliant writer, Craig.'

'And you're a brilliant actor, Aden,' Craig replied.

Aden smiled. Ben, however, remained miffed.

'So why do you wanna do something different?' he asked.

'Yeah!' Aden said. 'Why can't we just do *Backhanded Justice: McWallace Goes West*, like you promised?'

This gave Craig the opportunity he'd been waiting for. He had an idea to sell, and this was the time to set up shop. He told himself to be cool. He took a deep breath. This was it.

'Because I've been researching!' he barked.

The table went silent. Aden was taken aback by the aggression in Craig's voice. Ben was reading something on his phone.

The thoughtful strumming of Bernard Fanning's guitar drifted lightly across the beer garden, as his perfectly adequate *Songbird* played unobtrusively from the pub's sound system.

After a while, Ben looked up.

'What?'

'I said I've been researching, goddamn it!' Craig replied, his passion reaching a disconcerting fever pitch.

'Hopefully researching different gags...' Ben replied.

Ben and Aden high-fived.

'I've actually been researching our history,' Craig replied. 'Australia's history... From the past...'

The silence invited Craig to continue.

'Yes, that's right. Our history of colonisation. Our awful, shameful, messed up history.'

'So, this is a drama?' Aden asked.

'This could be the most important drama in Australian cinematic history. Honestly. I've stumbled on a story that puts all the horrors of our nationhood on show. It's sad, it's frightening, and it really happened!'

Ben excused himself to go smoke a cigarette.

'That's a strange time to leave,' Aden said.

Craig shrugged. He'd known Ben for a lot longer than Aden, so nothing surprised him.

'What is with that guy?' Aden continued.

'I mean, seriously... Aside from how rude it is to just get up and leave, right now, smoking kills! The science on that matter is completely undeniable – it causes cancer.'

Craig shrugged again.

'You wanna hear this story? It's pretty full on...'

Aden leaned forward, nodding, giving Craig his full

attention.

'So this is about European settlement, and the suffering inflicted on Aboriginal people who lived here...' Craig said, beginning a story that would forever change the face of Ghost Crayfish Productions.

Reflecting the horrors endured by many, Craig told the true story of one Aboriginal man's awful fate under colonial rule.

It was a heartbreaking story of separation, servitude and suffering. Ben returned to the table as the story approached its conclusion.

'...And after everything he endured... after all his bravery... his sacrifice... after everything, they still locked him up!' Craig said.

'No!' Aden yelled.

'He never saw his family again,' Craig replied.

Taking his seat quietly, Ben noticed that Aden looked sick.

'Good story?' he asked.

'Horrible,' Aden replied. 'But look, I agree with Craig. I think someone really does have to tell that story. If this was an American story, Hollywood would back it in all the way. It'd win Oscars!'

'Yeah!' Craig said. 'It's weird, but we still seem a bit in denial about this stuff. Like, it's all a bit swept under the rug, or hidden away on the ABC...'

'Yep, they didn't teach this stuff at school,' Aden agreed. 'And it's sad. If people understood our history a bit better, they might see a few things happening now a bit differently.'

'Man, I picked a bad time to go for a cigarette,' Ben said.

'Yeah exactly, that's why stories like this should be told!' Craig replied, ignoring Ben. 'And if we're gonna bother making another movie at all, we may as well try to make one that matters.'

Ben nodded.

Craig felt good. His announcement had been a success. His production company, Ghost Crayfish Productions, was set to move in a bold new direction.

No one at the table had ever expected to be involved in producing socially important and thought-provoking stories, and the prospect of such an ambitious project was invigorating.

'This is cool,' Ben said eventually. 'Not sure how much more mindless garbage like *Backhanded Justice* I was really up for doing, anyway.'

Craig was so excited he didn't even mind the insult. Instead, he was thrilled that his collaborators had agreed to the tonal shift so easily.

Apparently, they, too, were tired of peddling foolish genre parodies that achieved nothing more than an impressively high view count.

Relaxation washed over the talented young auteur like a wave, until it crashed at the shores of Aden's furrowing brow.

'This is all really great – love the idea, love the new direction – but just, ah, one thing... Who's gonna play the guy?'

It was an interesting question. So much so, it briefly distracted Ben from rolling another cigarette.

'Like, do you have any Aboriginal friends to be in it?' Aden asked.

'No,' Craig replied, frowning.

'Do you know any Aboriginal actors?'

'No.'

'Will that be a problem?'

Craig's frown strengthened. Despite the high view counts, Ghost Crayfish Productions was still an amateur operation, reliant on the on-screen presence of friends too bored to say no.

Without a suitable friend to call on, Craig wasn't sure how to fill the lead role for this new project.

'Can we recruit someone, somehow?' he wondered.

'Can you recruit on racial grounds?' Aden asked.

'Not according to the recruitment training I did at work,' Craig replied.

'Yeah, this is all starting to feel like we're on pretty shaky ground, here, fellas,' Ben said. 'So, while you guys figure it out, I'm gonna duck out for a smoke.'

Craig and Aden did not figure it out, exactly, but they did come up with one idea for how to move forward.

Later that day, Craig invited another friend and *Backhanded Justice* actor, Jill, out for a coffee.

'You want a black guy?' Jill asked, as she poured some milk into her cup. 'Because I can get you a black guy.'

Craig looks around nervously.

'Believe me,' Jill continued. 'I can get you a black guy.'

Casting his eyes down, to avoid making eye contact with anyone seated nearby, Craig noticed that Jill was logging in to Tinder. She immediately and furiously began swiping right, vanquishing all the pale faces that kept appearing on her screen.

After a few minutes, Jill stopped swiping. Surprised by the lightness of the skin on offer, she decided to take a quick break from swiping to let the algorithm reset.

'Are you gonna pay the actors this time?' she asked.

'Yeah of course, I'll shout a few coffees...' Craig replied. 'Wait, do First Nations guys drink coffee?'

'What sort of question is that?' Jill asked.

Craig shrugged.

'While I agree this is a story someone should tell, have you ever considered the idea that maybe you're not the right person to do it?' Jill asked.

'No,' Craig said, matter-of-factly.

'Because, I dunno, maybe if you're not well equipped to tell a sensitive story appropriately, maybe it's best not to tell it and get it wrong, you know?'

'I know you mean well, but that's crazy talk!' Craig said. 'So, moving on, no-one of interest in there?'

'I've spotted a few nice tans, but nothing that suits your needs...'

Craig started to think that this plan was not the solution he needed and decided it was time to leave. He thanked Jill for her help, stood up, and started making his way towards the sidewalk.

'Hey!' Jill yelled. 'Did you pay for these coffees?!'

Craig ignored the question and scrambled his way onto the tram.

Back at the cramped, mouldy Richmond house Aden and Craig shared, Aden hunched over his laptop, his furrowed brow a clear indicator that mental energy was being expended.

The glowing laptop screen showered the small, dirty living room in neon moonlight. The words on the screen made the cause of Aden's angst clear. In plain black lettering, in the free text field of a gumtree advertising request, they said:

'Black male actor wanted – prominent role in low (no) budget feature length film. Payment unlikely. Must be of Aboriginal (or similar) appearance/descent.'

'How's the ad going?' Craig asked.

'Well, recruiting on the basis of race makes me feel really uncomfortable,' Aden replied.

'We're also recruiting on the basis of gender,' Craig said.

Silence ensued.

'This feels different.' Aden said eventually. 'Anyway, I was thinking, how about we use code? Like, how about we recruit a 'rapper'?'

'That won't work; there are lots of female rappers,' Craig said.

'No, I mean to cover us on the race thing!'

'Is that an offensive stereotype?'

'Nah man,' Aden replied, 'I like rap… and anyway, if you don't like that idea, here's the ad I've just written. See what you think.'

Craig read the text.

'Black male actor wanted – prominent role in low (no) budget feature length film. Payment unlikely. Must be of Aboriginal (or similar) appearance/descent.'

'Let's try recruiting a rapper,' Craig said.

With the text modified accordingly, the ad was posted later that night. By the morning, they had received one reply. It's sender? B-rad69@hotmail.com

'Yeah I dunno, it's all very mysterious,' Aden said, as he and Craig sat stuck in traffic, driving west.

'He just insisted on auditioning in this park – he was very specific about meeting there at 10.45.'

'It's 11.30,' Craig said.

Aden frowned, narrowing his focus to the traffic lights head. He knew he'd done wrong.

With increasing urgency, Aden drove further away from populated suburbia and into more rural surroundings, with warehouses and service stations offering the only real signs of operational civilisation.

With each turn onto a new street, the roads became emptier. The landscape more barren. The journey more ominous.

Eventually, the intrepid duo found themselves pulling into an empty car park, hidden from view by unkempt trees and foreboding vibes.

A long walk down a narrow dirt path followed, with Aden insistent that they were headed in the right direction, towards the map point the man had shared via GoogleMaps.

It finally seemed Aden was vindicated, as someone appeared on the horizon, calmly reading a book.

'Uhhh... Brad?' Aden asked, as they approached the man.

'It's B-rad.'

'Uh... Ok.'

Craig wasn't sure what bothered him more. His name, or the fact that he was whiter than early 70s adult oriented rock.

'You're the one who answered our ad?' Craig asked.

'Word.'

'Um... this is a bit awkward, but...'

'Wait!' Aden exclaimed, cutting Craig off. 'Holy shit, is that a Popeye tattoo?'

'Aw yeah,' B-rad replied. 'Popeye is my spirit animal and shit. What's yours?'

'I'm not sure,' Aden replied, puzzled. 'Maybe a llama, or an alpaca... Or a mongoose.'

'Cool.' B-rad replied thoughtfully.

'Can we...' Craig said, attempting to steer the

conversation back to business.

Aden was having none of it.

'Or an alligator...' he said. 'Or a penguin. But Popeye's cool.'

'Popeye isn't an animal though,' Craig said. 'And anyway, ok, look, it's nice meeting you, Brad.'

'B-Rad.'

'B-rad,' Craig corrected himself. 'Nice meeting you. But...'

'Aw thanks dawg, you too man.'

'Have you acted before, B-rad?' Aden asked, sensing Craig was about to rudely end the conversation. 'Tell us about your background.'

'Ok, but why tell you about myself, when I can rap you about myself?'

'That is so true!' Aden replied.

'The song I wanted to perform for you guys is pretty deep. It's about love...'

'That's great, but first, I just wanted to explain that this is actually an acting gig,' Craig said, handing the script to B-rad.

Slowly, B-rad read Craig's magnum opus. Occasionally, he moved his finger to pursed lips, and was obviously deep in thought.

Eventually, he spoke.

'Um, OK, I wouldn't feel comfortable saying these lines,' he said. 'I'm not a black man. I feel like trying to embody this character myself would be disrespectful and wrong, however well-intentioned it might be. Besides, I think there are more positive and inspiring Aboriginal stories to tell, and that would have a more profound social impact.'

Craig grimaced, wondering if B-Rad had a point.

'But anyway, like I was saying dawg, my song: it's about love and relationships, and how I got, like, all these emotions inside me I need to let out and shit.'

'Sounds great,' Aden said.

Craig groaned.

'Doesn't it, Craig?' Aden asked. 'Isn't it great B-Rad is taking the time to perform his song for us! What's it called, B-rad?'

'It's called Too Many Bitches...'

After barely a second's pause, B-rad launched into his prose, rapping violently in Aden's face.

Despite Craig's scepticism, B-rad's skills turned out to be quite impressive.

His rhymes showed uncommon verbal dexterity, while offering genuine insight into the human condition and the societal ills that impact us all, as they built up to an unexpected crescendo.

'And that's how I ended up with chlamydia!' B-rad yelled, before slumping back into his chair.

'God damn!' Craig exclaimed.

'So am I in?' B-rad asked.

'Well, sorry man, your rhymes are wonderful, but they probably don't suit our movie...'

'Aw, you trippin dawg,' B-rad said. 'Trippin! Trippin like Scottie Pippen!

'Well, sorry, but this is a historical drama,' Craig explained. 'There probably won't be much need for rapping.'

'So why did you advertise for a rapper?' B-rad asked.

'Well...'

Craig and Aden explained the situation. After a length conversation about the sensitivities associated with their casting conundrum, B-rad suggested that they amend the text in their advertisement to say:

'Male actor with dark complexion wanted – prominent role in low budget feature length film. Payment unlikely. Must have a darker shade of skin.'

A week went by before they received a response to the modified ad. It led to another audition and, it must be said, an inspired performance.

'Your lack of respect, empathy and understanding is a reflection on the darkness of your souls, and I will not allow you to rob me of my dignity!' the young actor bellowed with the sort of raw, emotional performance that, with the right agent, director and under-the-table payments, wins Oscars.

'Nice reading!' Aden said.

Craig nodded. B-rad, likewise.

'But unfortunately, you're Asian. So, sorry, but you're not what we're after.'

'What?' the candidate asked.

'You're an Asian man,' Aden explained. 'I'm sorry, but that rules you out.'

'Geez guys, that's really racist...' the candidate said, before leaving.

Aden, Craig and B-rad sat stunned. Was he right? Were they racist?

'Righto, dawgs, I'm out,' B-rad said before he, too, left the room.

Craig and Aden were left alone to contemplate a casting process that had not gone well.

Aden suggested it was time to put the project on hold.

Craig said nothing.

Months went by.

Aden moved on, but Craig could not. While he remained glued to the couch watching Morgan Freeman movies, Aden was out socialising.

One day, the Ghost Crayfish Productions crew, minus its leader, caught up for a game of frisbee in the park.

'It's awesome hanging out with you guys without having Craig around,' Ben said at one point.

The others couldn't help but agree.

'Yeah, he's just obsessed with that search for a black actor,' Jill said. "He's still messaging me about it. I told him, Tinder's a waste of time! No one replies!'

'It's all gotten a bit weird,' Aden said, nodding.

'Still,' Ben said, growing serious all of a sudden. 'Isn't it a bit weird that none of us know any Aboriginal people?'

'Good question, dawg!' B-rad said.

Jill frowned.

'Well hopefully we figure it out soon because Craig's becoming seriously unhinged,' Aden said.

And so it was.

While the others were throwing a frisbee around on a beautiful sunny afternoon, Craig sat at home, muttering to himself, with boot polish on his hands.

'It's impossible for words to describe what is necessary...'

As the sun set on the frisbee action, Aden knew it was time to head home, to the house he shared with his increasingly unstable creative partner.

Aden made it home just before a summer storm hit full swing. With lightning flashes offering the only illumination in the house, Aden made his way down the grim hallway, towards the dimly lit loungeroom.

From the darkness, he heard a voice.

'Hello Aden,' Craig said.

'Woah... uhhh. Hey, uh, Craig. How was your day?' Aden said.

'I've made a decision, Aden... I've found a solution.'

Lightning flashed again. In the instant when light filled the room, Aden saw it all: the open boot polish cans on the table, next to a small mirror. He also noticed that Craig had black hands.

'What are you doing, Craig?'

'This story needs to be told, Aden.'

Aden looked again at Craig's hands, smeared as they were with boot polish.

'No! Craig, no! Not like this!'

'Horror and moral terror are your friends, Aden,' Craig said. 'If they are not, they are enemies to be feared...'

Aden was shocked into silence.

'They are truly enemies...' Craig continued. 'I will inhabit this character, Aden.'

'This is so wrong,' Aden said. 'Wearing black face is wrong, Craig! Do some research!'

'Oh, but I have been researching, Aden! And you said so yourself: we have a moral obligation to tell the story that I have found.'

'Let's talk about this again tomorrow,' Aden replied.

Craig smiled.

'Good night, Aden.'

The night proved restless for both men. For Aden, it was fears for the sanity of his housemate. For Craig, it was the inability to sleep on his back.

When morning finally broke, Craig checked his pillow. He was relieved to see no smudges.

Next, he went to the mirror. His appearance shocked even him. With the fresh perspective that the morning light brings, Craig began wondering if his plan was flawed.

'You can't back out now,' he told himself. 'This is it – your greatest role. Time to really walk in your character's shoes!'

Craig put on his own shoes, literally, before figuratively donning the character's. With footwear secure, he took a deep breath and left his room.

Unable to sleep, Aden was waiting for him in the hallway.

'What are you doing?' Aden asked.

'I'm doing what must be done!' Craig replied.

He pushed past Aden and made his way to, and beyond, the front door. He made it as far as the front gate before being confronted by a passer-by.

'Hey! What are you doing?' the stranger said.

'Nothing,' Craig replied. 'Just minding my own business...'

'That is not cool, man. Not cool!' the stranger said. 'Take a look at yourself, you disgrace!'

A crowd started to gather at the gates. The vegan café next door provided a large number of onlookers.

Another one of the outraged throng stepped forward.

'Man, is that some sort of sick joke? You can't doll yourself up in black face paint like that!'

Craig began questioning the wisdom of his decision to inhabit his character in this way.

'You want us to beat some sense into you or what?' another person asked.

'Please, no! You don't get it. I'm telling a story! I'm making art!' Craig said, forcing his way past the gate and onto the footpath.

'You don't go back inside and wash that off, you'll cop a beating!' one of the onlookers said.

'Yeah, keep at it and we'll make you *really* black... and blue!' another screamed.

With Aden watching on, beseeching his foolish housemate to do as the mob said, Craig launched into a sprint up the road.

The outraged onlookers responded in kind, beginning an eager pursuit. Despite his makeup, Craig had unfortunately retained the speed of a white man and the chase concluded quickly.

This is when the violence began.

As feet connected with ribs, Craig finally saw it. The folly of his ways. By then, though, it was too late.

The savagery of the mob was intense and absolute. If nothing else, it gave Craig the perspective he had so craved.

Days later, at his sparsely attended funeral, his parents reflected on the undoing of their youngest son.

'I can't believe a pack of indignant millennials have beaten our youngest son to death,' Craig's mother said.

'Well, he always was a bit of a dickhead...' his dad replied.

The President of the Universe

Aden Simpson

Many were shocked when Jeffrey proclaimed himself president of the universe.

That's not possible, they said.

What due process has occurred?

But the president of the universe stood firm. That's just the way it is.

Governments from around the globe held conferences on how to tackle this threat to their authority.The President of the USA believed he should challenge this man for the title. He wanted to declare war. The UN, being historically opposed to war, urged against this. Let's see what kind of leader Jeff will be.

As president of the universe, Jeff was pretty chill. At times, one could say it didn't appear like he was doing anything at all. Many asked questions; about his jurisdiction, about stars and planets beyond. Jeff answered their questions and they were satisfied.

The President of the USA launched an investigation into the president of the universe. A search for assets found the man had no money to speak of, and this made the President of the USA feel very big. He had a lot more money than the president of the universe, and this gave him the confidence to go on the attack. A smear campaign.

The president of the USA questioned Jeff's record of rule. His handling of the economy and what he was doing to fix the planet and, more importantly, America. If Jeff felt threatened, he didn't show it, and soon enough the people, who the president of the USA claimed he was in charge of, began to question their leader's own handling of the economy and what he was doing to fix the planet. This did not bode well for his re-election, and the citizens debated whether they should ask the president of the universe if he wanted to also be president of the USA. Jeff politely declined this demotion, to the understanding of many.

The current President of the USA was understandably offended. This was the last straw. He declared war on the president of the universe, to the disagreement of many.

We can't attack the president of the universe, what if he retaliates?

But the president was full of anger and troops were mobilised.

The fire started innocently enough. An ember from the kitchen made its way through several hallways and down a flight of stairs until it settled nicely within the drapes of the Oval Office. The president had never seen a fire engulf a room so quickly. He was safely evacuated onto the lawn. As the president tweeted away on his phone blaming the attack on the president of the universe, he was hit by an asteroid and regrettably could not be revived.

The people suspected this was no ordinary asteroid attack. They asked the president of the universe if he was responsible for this freak natural occurrence. He said no.

And so it went, the president of the universe visiting many countries, answering many questions to crowds of people, often saying, that's just the way it is, with few ably disagreeing with him.

After many years the president of the universe announced in a shopping mall in New Zealand that he was no longer the president of the universe.

Having been so used to having a president of the universe, the governments around the world got together to ask Jeff who his successor would be. Jeff said it was some creature on another planet. The humans were a little upset that they no longer had the honour of hosting the president of the universe, but as they'd come to learn, sometimes that's just the way it is.

Flash Fiction
& Micro-stories
David Myrcott

Addia Lepus

'Get out of here,' said the spooky face in the trees with a scowl. 'We don't like humans. Go away.'

'Shurrup you,' retortled John Lemon, bassist extraordinaire and lead cymbal player for the Beatlies, 'lest I tinkle my cymbals mightily in your general direction.'

This gave the evil tree pause. The power of his finger-cymbal claps was, after all, the stuff of Arthurian legend.

'Hm,' said Lemon. 'Thought so.' Then, addressing his left-handed right hand man Billy-Paul McChumble, the Mayor of Quarryland, he added 'Now watch this drive.'

'No way,' thought Gorge Harrington to himself as the ball sailed in a graceful arc all the way to the green. Harrington was a spoon man and loved porridge. He desperately wanted to play the sitar, but Lemon wouldn't allow it, so he was stuck clinking his spoon. 'This is a par 3. When the fuck did this guy get so good at golf?'

'I know right,' thought Rinkle Starfish, the drumbler,

and Harrington shot him a knowing glance. The two shared a symbiotic brain and could communicate telepathically at will. It was their little secret.

Suddenly, their minds crackled.

'I know what you two are up to.'

It was the Dreadyolk OhNo, beaming thoughts into their brains from several hundred feet away by means of a magical ring she had taken from the dead body of the witch whose powers, naturally, she had then assumed.

'Please don't tell on us,' beseeched the Starfish. 'They'll kill us if they ever find out.'

'If only we could get our hands on that accursed ring,' thought Harrington, and immediately OhNo zapped him with an agonising thought-beam. He shrieked and then, once the electricity stopped, said meekly in his head 'I'll be good.'

'You two just keep bringing me my goblin blood, and no one will be any the wiser,' said the Dreadyolk.

Gorge and Rinkle exchanged another look. It was going to be another long, gruesome weekend in Goblin Land. But there was no other choice.

'What are you two talking about back there?' called out Lemon, squinting at them suspiciously through his antique looking glass.

'Sitar,' shot back Harrington immediately.

'Peace and love,' offered Rinkle, pulling a silly face and making little hand gestures in the air. He looked goofy yet endearing. It was a survival tactic.

'Well, alright. But hurry up and take your shots.'

Rinkle sighed as he extracted a tee and ball from his bag. It wasn't easy being a Beatlie, the world had no idea. All people saw were the glamorous soups and endless parade of expensive linens. They hadn't a clue about the blackmail, witchcraft, golfing, and incessant spates of goblin slaughter. Not a fucking clue.

Alice III

When Alice awoke, she discovered that not only had the Red Queen made good on her promise to chop off her head, she had also cloned it then fashioned the pair into a stylish set of shoulder ruffles. And in a single afternoon! It was all most upsetting.

'Two heads and no body. What a predicament! She must have bribed that fucking caterpillar to lace my tea,' said Alice to herself, crossly.

'Agreed,' said the other Alice. 'Either that or she got to the Mad Hatter.'

It saddened both of Alice's heads to think that one of her friends would betray her in this way, but at the same time she couldn't help but admire the Red Queen's artful ingenuity.

— excerpt from unpublished Lewis Carroll manuscript, *Alice Gets Lost and Somehow Ends Up in Wonderland Yet Again*

Poor guy, he was really running out of ideas there at the end. it's sad when that happens.

Mozu

Concerning one 'Mozu' Takahashi, a septuagenarian wheelchair-bound Japanese gourmand who in his prime had been too fat for the army but nowhere near fat enough to be a sumo, and who had wavered so long in making the decision whether to lose weight or gain it that when he finally informed his doctor of his decision to become a sumo his doctor simply laughed and informed him that the training alone would kill him, never mind the calorie-stacking, and no it did not matter how carefully, scientifically or medically supervised either of the above processes was.

'Take my advice, Mr Takahashi,' said the good-natured doctor as he rose, placing a hand on the shoulder of his inwardly reeling though still outwardly stalwart patient, 'drop all this sumo business and focus on what's important in life. After all, we're only here for the most trifling of moments, are we not? The merest blinking of an eye? Feel free to correct me if it isn't so! There's nature, creativity, career, the spirit, or at the very least contemplation of something larger than the self, some generative principle... er, what is it you do again, Takahashi san? A privateer?'

'Purchaser,' replied Takahashi without enthusiasm.

'I see, of course.' Casting his mind back to his patient's file, he added more nonchalantly, 'Well, what about that wife of yours? Surely you can take some of the energy you spend devoted to your fantasies and find ways to be more creatively loving? Hmm? I'm sure you can.'

Desperate for even a modicum of levity, the doctor considered giving his patient a pally punch to the shoulder, both as a way of signifying that everything would be alright in the end but in the shorter term the consultation was itself at a close, when Takahashi said something the doctor never forgot, not until his dying day. But i won't go into all that.

Zombie Wedding in Happyland

It was the biggest social event of the year, and anyone who was anyone was there. The bride looked resplendent in her dress made of maggots, and the groom's one eyeball kept falling out and rolling around on the floor, which in Happyland is considered a sure sign of luck. Everything was just like in a fairytale!

Towards the back sat Nosferatu Man. His fangs protruded over his lip so naturally everyone thought he was smiling. But he wasn't.

'I wish someone would love me like that,' he said softly to himself. Although thrilled for Zombie Girl and the Undead Prince, he sometimes felt the whole world was against him, just because he was a homicidal maniac with a wanton, insatiable bloodlust whose house continually reeked of corpses. 'It isn't fair!'

No, it certainly wasn't. He hadn't asked the warlock to curse him after he dropped that vial and it smashed and the demons trapped inside got loose and went on a diabolical multi-realm killing spree resulting in literally billions of deaths. It was the sort of thing that could have happened to anyone.

However, Nosferatu Man did not realise at that exact moment Venom Vildersprig was casting furtive glances in his direction from across the room, and not for the first time. She liked his style, and wasn't one of those 'girly girls' who is repulsed by the stench of decaying flesh.

'I would ride that man into the ground' she mused, biting her bottom lip. In her case this was no idle threat: she had literally devoured alive every lover she'd ever had. If only Nosferatu Man knew all the excitement he was in for!

Romance is certainly in the air in Happyland.

Tumble

She read the words one last time. From beginning to end; as in, all of them. Like, every single one. One. Final. Time. The horror of their reality was too great a burden to endure. So she didn't bother. She took a few purposeful strides towards the nearest window, slid it open with a bang, crept up onto the nook, and leapt.

If she hadn't been wearing a parachute, she would have been killed. But she was wearing one. She always did.

As ever, the tumbling from a 40-story window and resultant glide to a safe landing proved the perfect thing to clear her head.

Method for Creating
an Artificial Earthquake

Thefe Confiderations may ferve to give a fair and probable Account of the general Caufes of Earth-quakes. To illuftrate which, I fhall mention Mr. Lemery's Method of forming an artificial One, which will have the Effects both of an Earthquake and a Vulcano in Miniature.

To make an Artificial Earthquake or Volcano:

Take twenty Pounds of Iron Filings, add as many of Sulphur; mix and temper the Whole together with a little Water, to the Confiftence of a Pafte, then by putting it three or four Feet under Ground, it will prefently begin to heat, and in a few Hours the Earth will begin to tremble and crack, and Fire and Smoke will burft through. Such is the Effect even of two cold Bodies in the cold Ground: There only wants a fufficient Quantity of this Mixture to produce a true Ætna. If it were fuppofed to burft out under the Sea it would produce a Water-fpout, and if it were in the Clouds the Effect would be Thunder and

Lightning. This Compofition is an artificial Kind of the Pyrites, which has all the Effects of the natural, and which requires no more than a little Moifture to fet it on Fire.

— Thomas Hunter, *An Historical Account of Earthquakes Extracted from the Most Authentick Historians, with Many Other Particulars*, 1756.

Be careful with the above information, lest you inadvertently produce a true Ætna, or even a Waterfpout.

Thoughtful Bedtime Robot

Thoughtful bedtime robot breaks into your house at night, usually through an upstairs window, but he will force himself down the chimney if he has to. He then goes from room to room, checking if anyone is having trouble sleeping and if need be placing his cool metallic hand over their face until they drift off into a gentle slumber.

It's gotten to the point where I can't fall asleep unless his robotic hand is resting soothingly on my face. That's normal though, right? I only wish he'd stop smashing my windows every time. I've told him he can just come in the front door, but it's not his way apparently.

Pencil Tilter

Back in the present moment, it is the eighth day.

The eighth day after the narrator's plane crash, and now he and the prince are dying of thirst. The prince has become visibly morose and saddened over his recollections and longs to return home and see his flower.

Eventually the prince finds a well, saving them. The narrator later finds the prince talking to the snake, discussing his return home and his desire to see his rose again, who, he worries, has been left to fend for herself.

The prince bids an emotional farewell to the narrator and states that if it looks as though he has died, it is only because his body was too heavy to take with him to his planet. The prince warns the narrator not to watch him leave, as it will upset him. The narrator, realising what will happen, refuses to leave the prince's side. The prince consoles the narrator by saying that he only need look at the stars to think of the prince's loveable laughter, and that it will seem as if all the stars are laughing. The prince then walks away from the narrator and allows the snake to bite him, soundlessly falling down.

Gothic Mariah

Her eyeliner was on point, the Cure was blaring, and Joseph was taking care of the kids tonight. None of the goth clubs in Nazareth could even handle her when she was like this. And if they ever tried anything sassy, she had a certain someone named You-Know-Who on speed dial.

— Wrap it up, hon. You wanna get 86'd?

— Hey you wanna get 86'd from heaven

Needless to say, the tequila got poured. Every time.

The Adventures of Ice Boy and Catfish Lad

Their storylines are always kind of the same: Catfish Lad dragging around a big hunk of ice on a trolley with a boy encased in it, and sometimes getting tired and sometimes angry, and all their adventures being limited to where a large trolley heavily laden with ice can go, which is not many places. Sometimes he just wheels Ice Boy about in a big circle and they don't do anything except squeak peevishly at each other. But I still read each issue as the writing is so good. Plus I love all their antics.

Viking Mirror

Back by popular demand, Happyland Industries is proud to present one of our most-cherished items, the Viking™ Mirror©®™.

Each exquisitely handwraught mirror contains the soul of one long-dead Viking. Before you say "That's cruel" please be advised that ALL OUR VIKING SOULS ARE ENTOMBED VOLUNTARILY. They were not fortunate enough to die in battle and therefore do not qualify for Valhalla. Rather than going to the underworld they begged to be eternally encased in these magical mirrors, which I did as an act of kindness and also because I had all these mirrors lying around tbh. However what you do with them after purchase is entirely up to you*

*Should you eventually tire of having a dead Viking staring back at you each and every time you look in the mirror, you may release the trapped soul at any time by simply opening a small door conveniently located on the underside of the frame. It's that easy!**

**Please note this door is not very well designed and will sometimes swing open in a slight breeze, if bumped, exposed to even the tiniest vibration, etc. I realised belatedly I shouldn't have built it on the underside, but it's too late to do anything about it now. Oh well, just put some tape over it or something.

FAQ

Q. But if I release the soul, won't that condemn it to eternity in the underworld?

A. Yeah, I guess.

Q. That still seems cruel.

A. THEN KEEP IT IN THE MIRROR. That's why I invented it.

Q. I still don't understand why you would put a little door on it in the first place. And such a badly designed one at that. I think you're lying. At night I hear the little door slide open, and then a whooshing sound, and sometimes books and things fly off the shelves, and I can hear loud cackling. I also see many faces in the mirror I bought, not just one. I think there are hundreds of spirits in there, and I think they can come and go as they please, and—

A. Aren't you quite the chatty Cathy with your vile slanderous remarks we are a wholesome Viking company THIS FAQ IS OVER

IGNORE NEGATIVE REVIEWS

Ignore the libellous remarks made by one of my moron customers above. Most of my customers are stupid idiots tbh, who wouldn't know a longsword from a broadsword if it bit them on the ass. And they dont know the first god-damned thing about Viking soul entrapment/Norse magic it is just one moronic question after another with these nitwits i.e. 'Why is my mirror screaming at me?' Seriously I have the dumbest clientele ever oh wait I don't mean you I meant my other idiot clients phew that was close but nice recovery there at the end I think

Tell the Stars

'And if I lose?'

'Then you lose. But at least you lose with no excuses, no fear. And I know you can live with that.'

You lose in fights, sometimes.

Human Head Tote

"A stunning designer item"

All our human head tote bags are sourced from only the finest, surliest models Eastern Europe has to offer.

Please note the heads of these models are extremely difficult to please and get bored easily. They do not like when the bag is closed and will expect to be perched somewhere in the main living area where they can observe you and your family with an aloof, disapproving gaze.

The majority of your life will revolve around taking care of this stunning tote. These heads will eat any tissues they encounter, so it's best not to have any in the house. Certainly don't put any in the bag. Likewise, any Marlboro Lights you are foolish enough to leave in the tote will be smoked immediately.

Your new tote will also frequently curse you out in Latvian; this is to be expected and will not impact your enjoyment of this lovely, albeit demanding, designer item.

Order now to avoid disappointment!

The Emerald Man

He appears in your dreams and turns everything 'emerald,' as he puts it.

It's really more of a green than an emerald, but when I pointed this out to him once he got all snippy so now when it happens I'm just like whatever. It's kind of annoying but it's alright if you don't mind the colour green I guess.

Fattyman (for Victor Hugo)

The Fattyman is fickle
He got fat from licking pickles
Now he's a fickle pickle licker
Lickily lipsing the mirror

Fattyman, he's a funnyshape maker
Witchily weaving his cobblestone capers
He's draping his brain in a papery vapour
A brackish brine-scented plump jangly japer

The Fattyman is a solar sailor
Who jangles and mangles the angles he tangles
He has fists for eyes and a rat that he trains
To douse him in paraffin when the pickle-smell wanes

Awarewolf

Too late to keep the change
Too late to pay

Hulk Smash

It was happening again.

The power, the rage. The greenish hue. The overwhelming desire to demolish everything in sight. Another pair of Daisy Dukes torn to tatters.

Everyone told him he should wear cheaper denim cutoffs. 'To save money, etc.' But he wasn't giving them his daytime at all.

The simple fact was, he liked the way Japanese raw denim made his butt look. And the rest of the world would just have to deal.

The Sad Infanta

'Pruning is a hard thing.'
'Yes.'

Natureman

'He Swears at All Life Forms!'

Many superheroes have sworn to protect other more vulnerable lifeforms, but Natureman just swears at them.

'Excuse me, Natureman?' said the cute fluffy bunny. 'Could you please help me find my—'

'Fuck off,' said Natureman.

Dreadful.

Silly Hat Day

You can tell instantly he doesn't enjoy wearing that idiotic Napoleon wreath, and that it was clearly just a cheap last-minute afterthought. It's nothing more than a blatant attempt to fit in and be thought of as a 'team player' around the office. It's so fucking obvious it's gross. Either commit to the silly hat concept or don't even bother.

0/10 weak hat and face game. 0/10 for the palpable sense of embarrassment. Not middle management material. A failure on every level.

'I fucking hate you,' hissed Deborah from the cubicle opposite, adjusting the chin strap on her giant sombrero.

'We all do,' said his team leader. He was wearing one of those multicolored 90s caps with the little propeller on top, complimented by a Bart Simpson t-shirt emblazoned with the phrase 'Ay, Caramba.'

They both sat there for quite some time, staring at Gerry and thinking about what a turd he was for never committing to whimsical theme days and how much they despised him for making them feel second-hand embarrassment.

Gerry just sat there, his face going redder than the stupid wreath on his head.

'I'll... I'll do better next time. I'll wear one of those big Viking helmets with the horns. Or a... a top hat. A giant one. I'll hire a tuxedo to go with it, a really fancy one with tails. Just tell me what to do! Tell me what hat to wear!'

Of course Deborah and his team leader didn't bother to respond. There were no words.

Stalinist-era Alarm Clock

'Ring-ring. Wake up comrade and do your proletariat duty! Ring-ring. Sleep is for defectives and the work-shy. Get up now to avoid internment! Ring-ring.'

I have one of these and it puts me in the right mindset to do my proletarian duty every day. I love these alarm clocks!

SOVIET ALARM CLOCKS FOR SALE

They will berate you until you reach your best

***100% GUARANTEE* * *

$600 send credit card I send clonk.

Kookybird

Kookybirds are such odd, mysterious, deeply annoying creatures. If you don't pat them immediately they get mad and will then sit on your windowsill singing nothing but 'Down Home Girl' at the top of their lungs, which are twice as loud as a chainsaw and 10x more annoying. Last time a kookybird appeared on my balcony he was at it for sixteen straight hours. I think I will just pat them from now on, even though as a child I was told kookybirds were dirty and never to touch one. I like that song, but 16 hours of it is too much.

Walrus Man

I am you and you are me and she is I forever
See how they flee like geese to a tree
See how they cry like pigs without eyes
I'm scrying

Skipping on a bored lake
Aching for my bramble gun
Copulation tissue, foolish fickle Wednesdays
Hazel-eyed Billy is a very wicked longface man
I am Egg, You are Egg
Walrus am Eye, woo!

Silky thorny feather lady
Peeling back hills
filled with pelican's bills
Koo-koo-ka-chu

Walrus, Warlock, Weaving, Wending

Policeman, Fireman, Breathing, Bending
His eyes changed colour and he grew two inches
By dining on lobster and crucified finches

Yellow meta dastard
Sipping on a red frog's spine
Walrus Walrus
Worlus
Tra La La
— John Lemon, *'I Am Walrus Man'*

He was such a brilliant lyricist

Hugo Family Portrait Time

'Grandpapa, how much longer must we continue holding these awkward poses? I'm getting pins and needles.'

'Until the photographer gets what he needs, Janie, to incorporate subliminal motifs into what is an ostensibly innocent 19th-century family portrait. And if you speak again unbidden there'll be no sugared pigeon biscuits for you.'

'Victor, darling, there's no need to be so cruel. Next you'll be telling her she can't go outside to count cobblestones or do her twig pressings.'

'Oh, that's right. I'm such a tyrant. It's always something with you, isn't it? Not like I wrote *Hunchback* or *Les Misérables* or anything. It's not like I'm the greatest living French writer, and therefore maybe deserving of perhaps the teeniest, tiniest sliver of deference.'

His wife did not reply.

'Look, just another hour or two of sitting uncomfortably like this, a few dozen more generic dragon and monster motifs, then we'll all go for some iced parsnips. And maybe even count a cobblestone or two, okay? Sound good, Janie?'

'Yes, Grandpapa.'

'Alright then. Now make a claw shape with your hand like this.'

Mr Uglyface Goes to Washington

He had high hopes and noble aspirations, but quickly found that no one would vote for him, partly due to his disgustingly ugly face and partly to the fact he also had an objectionable personality.

'It isn't fair,' sobbed Uglyface to himself, pounding his little rodent fist on the desk. But it was fair. He simply wasn't Presidential material.

At a certain point his handlers even tried putting a sack on his head, but somehow it only made things worse. Not only did it make him look like a deformed monster out of some low-budget horror film, which was the problem in the first place, but the sacking they used was so thick it rendered his voice into a guttural incoherent grunt. Whenever he tried to engage another politician in a debate, it was just one person in a suit speaking normally into a microphone, and then a man in a sack gesticulating wildly whilst making muffled shrieking noises. It was ridiculous.

Some people just aren't cut out for politics.

Mr Uglyface Gets a New Face

It was the only logical thing for him to do.

Unfortunately, there was a mix-up in the operating room. Instead of giving him a better face, the doctor accidentally took an even uglier one and attached it upside down, removing the patient's scalp and part of his brain in the process. It was all a terrible kerfuffle.

'Ohhh. When you said you wanted a new face, I'd just assumed you were keeping the old one. I didn't realise it was a replacement job. "I want a new face." The wording is sort of ambiguous, isn't it? I'll definitely clarify that next time.'

'There's a nose where my forehead should be!' exclaimed Uglyface, who was now by definition twice as ugly.

'And a mouth where your nose should be, yes,' replied the doctor, sagely.

Mr Uglyface wanted to say something else, but found it difficult to formulate thoughts on account of his recent inadvertent brain loss.

Spiderhat

Are you tired of people biting you on your hat? Sick of leaving a high-class hat emporium after a fitting feeling like a million bucks, only to have some deranged lunatic immediately start gnawing on the brim of your expensive new fedora while you curl up into a ball and weep, cursing the heavens?

We all know that feeling only too well. That's why we invented the Spiderhat. When you wear a Spiderhat, people need to worry about your hat biting them!*

Bite back, with Spiderhat.

*of course, the wearer can also expect to get bitten from time to time

Samurai Shit

He had been a samurai for so long that he forgot the exact time he had even started becoming a samurai because it was so long ago. All he knew was, he'd been doing this samurai shit forever, or what felt like forever, a lifetime in the twinkling of an eye.

Speaking of eyes, the faraway look in his wasn't so much a thousand-yard stare as it was a 10,000 mile stare or even a hundred thousand, because he had seen so much shit and done so much bad stuff and even some good stuff. There's entries on both sides of the ledger for everyone, even a badass samurai that has killed like a million people, so always remember that, ok?

Anyway back to the story. He was walking along the rode one day on his samuria shit, being a samarai and walking and there was a geisha, and then he met this wandering ronin and at first they were gonna fight and even got there swords out and clashed them together cos obviously at first he thought this ronin was some punk who didn't even know how to use a katana but this wasn't the case at all but how was he to know.

They didn't realise at that exact moment, but there destinies had just entwined in an inextricable way that would echo through aternity like an bomb in and echo chamber.

Their swords swung through the air in slow motion, and when the iron of their steel blades finally met after an eternity it made a sick sound that echoes through the chambers of eternity or was it just the human mind? But whatever it was a sick sound. C L A N G it echoed all through the valley, the sheer sound of steel melting steel in the forged irons of forever.

When they realised they had basically just shook the whole world with their swordplay (a mountain behind them had cracked in half at the exact instant their kitana blades met, and it was fucking sick so just imagine cracked mountains in the backgroynd the whole time) and that they were basicaloly brothers and warrior bro's they laughed and put their swords away with that sliding sound playfully laughing like and drank some sake and in a bar and got into a massive fight and beat up all these dudes with there fists and didnt even need their kitanas it was fucking sick bro.

WRITING LESSONS AVAILABLE

Punisher Skull Wallpaper

So trendy, so chic!

Add a splash of hypercolour flair to your living spaces with our stunning 'Punisher Skull' carpet and wallpaper combo. This has long been one of our most cherished designs and, frankly, it's easy to see why.

A bilious miasma of gherkin greens regally reclines across a swirling bed of lush fluorescent pink, interspersed with bright coral flushes and a salmony fuscia backdrop betraying subtle hints of chartreuse. There's also a bit of orange. (Note: as most of our proprietary pigments are harvested from the bile duct secretions of a herd of purpose-bred baleen whales, some residual bile odour can be expected).

Is it an alien birthing scene? That there, is that... a demented rabbit?? Only you can decide! All our wallpaper designs are figurative enough not to be truly abstract, and just abstract enough not to be figurative, in a way that confuses the brain. The disorienting sensation produced when your entire house is decorated in this fashion has been compared, favourably, to seasickness, or the feeling you get whilst driving down a steep hill.

Spiderhat II

The season's hottest must-have fashion accessory! Order your Spiderhat now!

Each and every year, millions of people worldwide fall prey to tragically preventable conditions such as head rot, scalp icicles and cranial maggot infestation. All these dread afflictions and many others can be cured by wearing a Spiderhat.

Better yet, thanks to our incredible Arachno-Therm™ technology, Spiderhats keep your head warm in winter and cool in the summer. Our carefully mutated giant funnelwebs are trained to respond to certain verbal prompts, so adjusting the temperature of your head is literally as easy as barking commands at a spider.

As if that wasn't enough, they eat pesky critters such as flies, mosquitos, lizards and birds, which is sure to slash your bird-culling and lizard electrocution bills. Best of all, their bite is almost never fatal to humans! They are quite literally the perfect gift for family and friends.

Don't be the only one not wearing a Spiderhat this summer/winter/other!

* * *

Spiderhats are so comfortable you won't want to take them off. Even if you did you wouldn't be able to, as all our spiders symbiotically attach themselves to the wearer's brain over time. But don't worry — thanks to the numbing agents and nerve inhibitors injected by your new furry friend, most of our happy clients report barely feeling a thing!

Just listen to what some of our literally several satisfied customers have to say:

'Please get this thing off my head. Please, I beg you. I think.. I think this spider might have taken over my brain oh God Jesus help me IGNORE WHAT WAS JUST WRITTEN THE HUMAN IS DOING JUST FINE AND IS VERY HAPPY WITH HIS LOVELY SPIDERHAT. SINCERESTLY YOURS, EARTH HUMAN'

'One of the best pieces of arachnid apparel I own. Once it stopped trying to spit venom in my eyes we got along famously. I wish I could wear 10 of them!'
— Henry Kissinger

'Well, um, yeah. I'm strong bitch! Ah.. Whatever, erm, uhh.'
— Popstar Billy Eyelash

The Poem that Exploded

There once was a poem that exploded.

'BANG!' went the poem. With a booming crash, just like that, it exploded. An exploding poem. The first one ever; never before or since had a poem simply exploded.

But this one did. First it fizzled like a firecracker as it

was lying there on the desk, all freshly typed out, mere seconds after proudly being snatched from the printer. Then it went off. Poem residue on the walls and in the carpet. A poem-sized crater in your desk, where once there had been a poem. Poem residue on your hands, still clasped behind your head, inextricably tying you to the matter.

'That's not poem residue, that's dandruff,' says your wife later, examining your fingernails.

'It's flecks of vaporised paper,' you feebly protest. 'I had a poem explode on me today. One minute it was there, and the next it just sort of... exploded.'

A blank look.

'With an explosion,' you add, gesturing with your hands to show the force of it, leaning back to demonstrate how it had knocked you back in your chair, widening your eyes to show the shock of it, the shock of the explosion caused by the exploding poem.

'I stand corrected. Could you bring the rest of the shopping in,' says your wife, pinching your cheek in a sarcastic manner.

'Alright,' you say, wondering if she has brought any Toblerone.

Wicked King Wicker

Though he often tries to, this one can't blame his evil nature on sinister portents or goblin curses.

He's certainly been cursed by goblins, many times in fact, but that's because he keeps burning down their villages and is entirely to be expected IMO.

No, he went wicked long before the first goblin even thought of uttering a hex. A real shame. 2/10 WOULD NOT DO

Corporal Condiment's Lovelorn Hearts Jug Band

West German reissue, Gesäßspalte, 1970.

Communist Czechoslovakia's answer to Sgt Pepper. Some of the lengthier jug solos and avant garde polka medleys drag a bit, but overall it holds up surprisingly well. Famously banned in the West after several tracks were found to contain subliminal recitations from Mao's Red Book.

Fun Trivia Fact: If you reverse the runout groove of track K14, Side Q, 'Collectivised Fields Forever' and listen closely, what sounds a bit like 'cranberry sauce' actually turns out to be 'death to western imperialist ideologues.'

Unsubdued Air

'It is now eighty-six years since the first aerial journey astonished the world, and yet, in 1870, we are but little more advanced in the science than we were in 1783. Our age is the most renowned for its discoveries of any that the world has seen. Man is borne over the surface of the earth by steam; he is as familiar as the fish with the liquid element; he transmits his words instantaneously from London to New York; he draws pictures without pencil or brush, and has made the sun his slave. The air alone remains to him unsubdued.'

— *Wonderful Balloon Ascents, or the Conquest of the Skies: A History of Balloons and Balloon Voyages* (1870)

Larvae Girl

But soon after, Amy changed her mind. On the next phone call, she told Blake she was going to be 'a one-man woman' and stay with Reg. Blake had said, 'That's fine, that's great. You know, darling, I'll always love ya, I just don't want to lose you.' And he meant it.

She responded, saying, 'You'll never lose me, Blake.' And that was the last time he ever spoke to her.

Cosmic Bunny

- The metal is not the real magnet. The real magnet is the substance that is circulating in the metal.
- Each particle in the substance is an individual magnet in itself.
- These particles are so small they can pass through anything. In fact, they can pass through metal easier

than through the air.

- They are in constant motion and possess perpetual power.

- Electric magnets hold perpetual motion. If not disturbed, they will last indefinitely.

- Magnetic current is the same as electric current.

- The magnetic current is not one current, but two streams running against each other.

- All currents are alternating. One current alone cannot run. To run, they have to run against each other.

- They are the cosmic force that hold together this earth and everything on it, and they hold the moon together too, and turn the earth around on its axis.

— LEEDSKALNIN

Last of the Pendragon Kings

Anatomy is destiny.

'How many men have you killed, Great King?'

Was it worth it?

Secret Masonic Handshakes

The business with the secret handshakes was kind of fun at first, but quickly became a hindrance. Some of the moves required a high degree of flexibility, and oftentimes members found themselves stranded in the cold after failing to remember the complicated sequence of gestures required for entry.

'Just let me in the fucking lodge, for Christ's sake!'

'This is fucking bullshit.'

'Mate, you have to be a bloody contortionist to pull some of this stuff off. I'm regretting I ever joined.'

Cosmic Celebration

kosmos (Gr.): order, harmony

cielo: sky, heavenly vault

el viento: the wind

vault of heaven, empyrean, firmament

empyrean, firmament:

'the peace which passeth all understanding'

yours is the most beautiful heart i ever saw

4 Flights

your lies are so full of holes that the sun is shining through

whats the point

I want people who dont want me back

if we ever met, it would be so explosive

Beetle Man

Failed 1960s superhero.

'He has the strength of a thousand beetles!'

No one had really quantified beetle strength before, and it turned out 1000x beetlepower wasn't actually that impressive. Once the bad guys realised Beetle Man was a largely defenceless invertebrate they simply battered his exoskeleton to a pulp. He spent the remainder of the series just kind of lying there in a smushed-up puddle, waiting for his antennae to fall off. It was good, but not great.

6/10

'He stands up for all insect life! Also to a lesser extent the arachnids.'

— rejected alternate tagline

Valhalla Dinner Plates

Subtle, refined elegance at its finest and most elegant.

One of our most popular designs!!

Delight and frighten your dining companions in equal measure with these charming 'Valhalla' dinner plates, easily one of the most tasteful and beloved of all our designs.

As guests enjoy their meal, an apocalyptic vision of Odin's undead army engaging in a pitiless end times war with the giants is gradually revealed. Family and friends are sure to clean their plates in no time flat, in order to better glimpse the horrific imagery beneath.

'Dad, is that meant to be a dragon, or just a generic skull motif?'

'I dont know, son.' A surefire conversation starter!

Available where all good Viking-themed tableware is sold.

Bricks

To change a movie,
one has to change the reel
in the projector,
not throw bricks at the moviescreen.

Of all the means known to lead men,
the most effectual is a concealed mystery.

In the dream, a great tree was cut and banded,
causing a period of insanity for seven years.

All the rest is silence.

The Sad Remains of Earlier Temples

This cup will make me drink all the bitterness in the world. The cruelty of the powerful. The afflictions of the humble. The torture of the prisoners and exiles.

This cup of blood is the torture of my crushed body and the redemption of the world.

All the chosen suffer. Every one.

Beausoleil/Beautiful Sun

later, the sky darkens by degrees.

moonless, powdered with stars,

pierced as though by a spear.

more love than my heart could hold

perverse sleep, *taedium cordis*

wanhope: despair of the mercy of God; rejection of

the created world

te deum laudamus

tristitia: worldly sorrow

weariness of heart

the moral nature of man must be altered

acedia, ennui, malaise

demiurge

daemon meridianus

taedium vitae

weltschmerz

the pale king of terrors

I watched the sun going down in the west,

between two palm trees,

as I rested my back against a third.

Jumpman

From the perspective of where you came from,
everything made sense. From the perspective of where

you're going, nothing makes sense. This is not chaos;
this is life. This is the way.

Jump, and the net will appear.

Your treasures lie in the unknown.

You will find a new way. Your way.

The way that is meant for only you.

The Weight of Your Heart
Against a Feather

I can video call with you, but what would that prove?

The weight of your heart against a feather.

I don't understand what that means.

'For the Angels who are the movers of the Orbs, do
neither destroy nor subvert any thing, which nature it
self hath constituted or framed.'

— Johannes Trithemius, *Seven Secondary Causes of
the Heavenly Intelligences*, 1508

Denial River

'a charming woman without religion is like a beautiful
woman without perfume'

— Heine

you can't have growth and comfort at the same time
Whoever cannot find a temple in his heart,
the same can never find his heart in any temple.

Nothing vast enters the life of mortals without a curse.
With the blameless, He will show Himself to be blameless.
in spite of the horror, you must go on.

That Other Realm

rivers
rivers
rivers of water
rivers of life-giving water

a dreadful spirit of frightened loneliness

We were designed to enjoy a better world than the one we live in.
An aching soul is evidence not of neurosis or spiritual immaturity, but of realism.

Sahul

The general scope of what information we do possess on the matter leads to the opinion that they hold belief in a Supernatural Being, exercising an unseen but extraordinary power over their whole race. This power, however, strange to say, is never mentioned by them as being exercised otherwise than for evil. Hence, in rendering his appellation into English, he is

uniformly called after the Prince of Darkness — 'Devil.'
Thunder, lightning, storms, and the other atmospheric
or elemental disruptions are supposed to be among the
chief manifestations of his power and wrath.

ACTS 17

one moment you're flying high up in the sky,
the next you're in freefall
stumbling into place

Sarissa Phalanx

no one was running very fast. it was really more of a canter.
I was told to shut up and keep my eyes forward, and
try to stop stabbing the legs of the guy in front of me.

Killing Eve

to celsus, Christ was a mere sorcerer. if so then the
world is a meaningless ballet of death.

Slaves in 1st c. AD Roman territory

Were almost exclusively spoils of war, were treated with
respect, generally occupied positions of responsibility
within their assigned household, could marry, could
accrue wealth, could buy their freedom, were freed

automatically at age 30, could serve as church elders, and whether they had been slaves or free was not indicated on the graves of Christians, as it was in some other traditions, because the term slavery did not have connotations of inferiority. Church funds in the first 2 centuries were used to purchase the freedom of slaves, and some early Christians voluntarily became slaves in order to free another from slavery. Slaves in ancient Greece also worked less days per year than the average modern worker (due to the high number of religious festivals/holidays).

A Man's Duty

She portrays Ford as monosyllabic, withholding, forbidding, and intimidating.

And yet throughout all of this, the younger version of Fisher is painfully, miserably obsessed with Ford. She repeatedly spins elaborate fantasies about him leaving his wife to be with her. She blames herself for his remoteness and tries to figure out what about herself she can change to make him more engaged.

As things begin to shift toward healing, a fork in the karmic road presents. You may yet again turn away from suffering and let a distraction take over by way of familiar routine. Or — meet reality, stick with the nowness of facing it, being vulnerable to the unknowable future of the healing process.

I became a student of appearance and reality. Wrote
a novella entitled *The Burning Eyes of Heaven*. The
central idea was that one must cherish one's life and
live it to its end. That is a man's duty.

Solar Barque

The new day's sun rises slowly,
illuminating ancient gods
while nearby villages sleep.
Shrouded in fog the temple awakes,
and I'm there to greet it.

Death Tusks

Ah, Evelyn and Vivian, I love you both, I love you for
your sad lives; the empty misery of your coming home
at dawn. So have your champagne, because I love you
both, Evelyn with your gaze like a sad lake, and you too,
Vivian, even if your mouth looks like it had been dug
out with raw fingernails and your old child's eyes swim
in blood written like mad sonnets.

The darkness of the night was a reminder of their
pain. Across the city, streetlights dimmed and the stars
shone weakly as if they too were mourning the sorrow
of the two women. Their lonely figures walked home in
the morning hours, as if they were ghosts lingering in
the shadows of a forgotten past.

They walked slowly, weighed down by the knowledge that what awaited them were only more sleepless nights, empty rooms and unfulfilled dreams. They were two women living in a world that had forgotten them, but still their hearts held a spark of hope and defiance.

Empty Nose Syndrome

'And the beast has been set free, and, enraged by past hurts and injustices, has caused Pandemonium.'

Professing themselves to be wise, they became fools, and exchanged the glory of the immortal God for images of mortal man and birds and animals and crawling things and reptiles; they changed the truth of God into a lie, and worshipped and served the creature more than the Creator.

'...those who have trampled on the Son of God, and have treated the blood of the covenant, which made us holy, as if it were common and unholy, and have insulted and disdained the Holy Spirit which brings God's mercy to us...'

Dogs are not the only ones who bark at what they do not know.

Translucent Showbiz Liar (Oubliette)

We look at each other
then run into the darkness together

hunched attractants, unsaturated hatchet
insecure afterthought, a worse heartache
while brazen, worthwhile Solaris
dribbled Nazi Saturnalia
over dully sanitised barbarians
in various eutrophic whorehouses
you just sat there
as dumb as a stone, dumb as a nymphomaniacal
peafowl
poring over your downy holeproof maps
as if you understood them
and through much tribulation
entered, motherless and fatherless, into what you
term the kingdom of God
that panoply of whoredoms and self-professed
hard-won wisdom
conjuring tragic new nouns in your stone-dumb
neuronic twang
'Profane whoops, raucous laughter, etc'
I broke through another layer, into Joyfulness.

The Case of the
Double Bass Killer

Craig Tuck

My name is Taggart McWallace.

I used to be a cop, but then I shot my twin brother.

After that, I moved to Canberra to be a desk jockey. With Fyshwick and Flex Time, it seemed like a sweet deal.

For a while, things were great. I was dominating the social cricket comp and on a good thing with the local gentlemen's club's 'fifth visit free' loyalty program. But once again, trouble found me. In the chaos, Fyshwick was totally destroyed.

So I moved.

Now, I'm based in regional New South Wales, eking out a living as a dick. No, not a stunt cock, you filthy beggar. As far as I can tell, the local porn industry is mostly amateur.

I'm working as a private detective!

As a former top homicide cop of some notoriety, it's been a bit of a come down. Skulking around with ma blue light out, sniffing bed sheets and arranging paternity tests is certainly not where I saw myself going, as a brash young hot shot legging it 'round the mean streets of Glasgow.

But, fuck it.

Shit happens.

The point is, I've had to learn to adapt. You see, trouble has a way of finding your ol' friend Tag Mac wherever he goes. Indeed, who needs a wife when strife is your companion.

Luckily for me, trouble and glory go hand-in-hand, so things always turn out pretty well in the end. I mean, even that time I accidentally killed my brother had a silver lining: when the old man finally croaks, the house is mine!

Good news, because things have still been a bit lively for me even here, in the sleepy dust bowl I now find myself in. Shite. If I'm not getting into fist fights with cheating husbands or nailing their jilted brides, I'm fronting up to the local courthouse, trying to explain that glassing a cunt is an acceptable form of persuasive communication back where I'm from.

I actually made the local paper for that last stunt.

'Scottish thug narrowly escapes prison sentence' screamed the headline.

Christ. Bit harsh, right? But no biggie.

The real issue I had with this wasn't the lippy journo taking down my good character, it was the public profile I gained as a result. I got a few roots out of it, mind, but I also got recognised from the very last person in this world I would want to know my whereabouts: the apparent mother of my bastard child.

Linda Jones.

Christ.

Must have given her the second-biggest shock of her life to see the Tagster on the front page of her local paper, ten years after I gave her the ol' 'six-second shuffle' one drizzly Glasgow evening back in my rookie days.

Linda had been a real prime candidate for the Tag, as I recall. One of those sheltered Aussie backpacker types just off their first Contiki tour, doing the cheap drink circuit and gettin' minimal interest.

You know what I mean?

The kind of lassie who's been in town a few weeks and gone a bit too hard on the deep fried Mars bars, but still has an appetite... Mmm.

So, anyway, after the deed, I gave Linda the usual fake name and phone number and went on ma merry way. Case closed.

Until a bloody decade later, when I made the local paper of Linda's home town.

Long story short, Linda obviously recognised my mug shot and decided to get in touch... through her lawyer. So after several more court hearings, I ended up at the local paternity clinic. I knew the place well, and the lads there got a real kick out of telling me that Linda's kid had indeed 'blossomed from the seed of my loins', as they put it.

I looked at a photo of the fat little bastard that Linda's lawyer had given me, and couldn't bloody believe it. That ugly smirk, that nasty twinkle in the eyes... There's ugliness somewhere on Linda's side, clearly, and my bloodline has been forever polluted.

From there, things got nasty. Linda's smile was even wider than her arse when she served me with ten years' worth of unpaid child support.

Like a politician caught using the corporate credit card in Fyshwick, I was in a bind.

Christ.

Adultery will never go out of style, but one look at my repayment schedule and it was clear that I'd need the 'wandering cock' caseload to go through the roof if I was to ever cover it all.

Unfortunately, despite the volume of miserable marriages I see around me, most dozy bastards seem to either keep it in their pants, or keep it very discreet. Either way, no new clients for Tag.

And so the bills piled up.

And the ever-insatiable Linda was after every cent.

That's how I ended up with a second job, working as a janitor at the student dormitory just outside of town. Little Timmy had medical expenses. And study expenses. And sporting expenses. And therapy expenses.

It really grinded my gears to pay for that last one.

Every week, $200 to give the little shite someone to complain to about me. I also had to pay for food. For lodging. For clothes.

Christ, the clothes. That's a huge worry. Would it kill the fat bastard to actually wear his jeans a few times before he outgrows them?

I mean, Jesus. Look at that gene pool he's swimming in (noting it's about the only swimming he's likely to do). The kid's gonna need special made-to-order t-shirts in no time, once he outgrows the Big W fat kid section.

So with the TAB debt collector also on my tail, there was nothing else to do but start spending my Sundays scrubbing shit off toilet bowls for minimum wage.

It's actually not too bad, at least when the university students come into town for a field trip. Christ, do those lassies love to flaunt it.

Unfortunately, they're only here occasionally. The dorm is open to students of all ages, and it's mostly filled by primary school camps and annoying brats that have no redeeming features at all.

To make matters worse, it's a music camp sorta place. Meaning it's all out-of-tune recorders and choir boys with breaking voices, echoing through the halls.

The kids at my own son's school even stayed there one weekend, despite living in the town next door. I was furious at that one! $500 to stay somewhere with a view of your own bedroom. What a rort! But Linda got the lawyers involved again, so I paid up like a chump.

Doubling down on the chump factor, I also had to work there as a cleaner for their whole stay just so I could afford it. This meant that on top of my one day of court-ordered parent time with 'little' Timmy, I also had to see him for an extra two days that week. Christ, three days in one week... shouldn't that get me some credit on the payment schedule? Not bloody likely, according to the lawyers.

So anyway, this camp is an annual thing the school does. They take all the music club nerds up into the mountains for a few days to completely destroy the works of classical music all the way to modern rock and pop. My mate in the kitchen warned me to expect the terrible sounds of tuneless clarinet all weekend.

'For fucksake, if I ruined the meals as badly as these buggers ruin their songs, I'd be up on a manslaughter charge!' he groaned ruefully.

'Manslaughter is no laughing matter, mate,' I replied. 'I know. I accidentally killed my twin brother after exposing him as the ruthless leader of a South African drug syndicate!'

'Jesus,' my buddy, Chef, replied.

'Yep, imagine how tricky it was for me writing *that* email to the parents!'

'Yeah, that's hard mate,' Chef said. 'If you've gotta have a death on your conscience, it should at least be for a good reason. Something you actually wanted to do... something that *needed* doing... you know?'

Weird thing to say, mind, but I nodded along.

'Aye,' I said. 'But it's okay, I've also killed dozens of

other bastards so I've got plenty to feel good about.'

'Nice,' Chef said. 'A man of action... I like it.'

This whole conversation played out as we were having a smoke in the car park, watching the kids unload their instrument cases from the back of a van. It was brilliant; in many cases the instruments were bigger than they were.

Have you ever watched a small 10-year-old girl try to unload a giant double bass case from a van? Fucking funny, I'll tell ye that.

This is where I have to admit a hint of pride in my own kid. With a smile, I watched as Timmy, carrying his recorder in one hand and eating a pie with the other, almost choked on a bite, he laughed so hard at the stumbling little girl.

'Dumbass!' he said.

Just like his old man: calling it as it is.

Nice.

But despite being proud of the lad, I decided to get back to work before he saw me and wanted a chat. I flicked my ciggie into the garden and said my farewell to Chef, though he seemed distracted.

'Here comes surely the worst music teacher that ever lived!' Chef said, watching some goggle-eyed loser walk up the path towards us.

'Teaching... Christ... better him than me,' I said, shaking my head as I walked away.

Back to business cleaning the toilets, I have to admit

that I found myself a bit distracted as the day went on. Though I take my work seriously, it's possible some skid stains escaped my attention that afternoon, as I fretted about the weekend to come.

It wasn't the shite music that worried me, even as the kids began their ominous first practice sessions. Instead, it was the parent dinner scheduled for that night which had me on edge.

In the 9 months since Linda had come back into my life, she and I had mostly communicated through her lawyer, who isn't a bad fella actually. But at dinner, there'd be no mediator in sight. We'd be seated at the same table, with no one else except the kid and another family.

Linda's husband, this giant prick named Mike, had apparently encouraged her to go it alone, as a chance for us to get to know each other and build some sort of friendship or something, for the sake of the kid. Jesus, what a cunt.

Thanks to his ridiculous meddling, aside from having to fend Linda and Timmy off from my bloody dinner plate, I'd also have to have a proper conversation with them.

How long would Timmy last before mentioning how well I've trained him in TAB etiquette, I wondered. And for that matter, how long before Linda started on about how I had ruined her dream of being a surgeon because she had to drop out of uni, as a single mum.

Given she has embedded that fact as a footnote in every single piece of legal correspondence she sends to me, I expected it was just a matter of time before the 'this cunt ruined my life' routine kicked off.

Luckily, the night had other plans in store. For a start, the weather had turned right nasty outside and the storm gave Linda something to worry about other than what a bastard I am. In another win, we were sharing a table with a couple who seemed to hate each other even more than we did.

The couple was married, so, of course, the arguments flowed thick and fast. The main point of contention seemed to be their daughter's rubbish double bass playing, and, in a recurring theme, the ineptitude of the music teacher.

'Maybe if he was less focused on the mothers, he'd do a better job with his students!' the husband said.

'Leave Jerry alone!' his wife replied.

I noted that. First-name basis, eh?

'Maybe you should follow your own advice!' the husband replied.

Well well, that seemed pointed!

'Steve, not this again, please!' the wife said.

It was getting awkward, so I tried to move the conversation along.

'I don't know anything about this teacher,' I said, 'but Jesus Christ, these kids are pretty fucking shite aren't they?'

'Taggart!' Linda said, in her usual whiny tone.

'Linda, you're not gonna insult us all by pretending these little bastards are not completely bloody woeful, are you?' I asked, gesturing at both Timmy and the tone deaf little double bass girl. 'Christ, you're not in front of a Judge, there's no need to lie now!'

I lent back in my chair smirking at that, pretty happy with the sweet bull's eye I'd hit her with. My joy was cut short, however, when the little girl started crying.

'Oh honey, ignore the janitor,' the wife said.

'I'm not just a janitor you know, lassie, I'm also a dick!'

'No shit,' she replied, before turning to her daughter. 'But maybe it couldn't hurt you to go do a little more practice before dinner...'

Collecting herself now, the little girl stood and excused herself from the table to go practice. Thankfully the storm outside drowned out the terrible noise that followed and, with their daughter absent, the conversation between the couple got even juicier.

'After all these lessons, you've really gotta wonder why she hasn't gotten any better,' the husband mused.

'Jerry says it's all about to click,' the wife replied.

'Did he say that before or after you fucked him on our futon?'

Hoho! Called it!

I was like a kid in a porno store, let me tell ye. My mouth was gaping. Even Linda perked up a bit at that one.

'Excuse me?' the wife replied, but you could tell from her blush that she'd been blowing the teacher's trumpet like a pro for months now.

'Don't deny it!' the husband replied.

'Aye,' I said. 'You're busted lassie. It's as plain as day: you might not have been playing the guy's rusty trombone, but you've definitely been pounding out a rhythm or two!'

At that, the husband stood up, slammed his napkin on the table, and stormed out of the room. He was so angry that he left his parma half-eaten. I started to laugh.

'Really, Taggart...' Linda said.

'Yeah, Dad, fuck!' Timmy added.

The mum sat stunned with tears slowly filling her eyes. Weepy dames...

Thankfully she didn't drag on the waterworks too long before she spoke.

'You people have no right to judge,' she began. 'My daughter loves music and we can't afford lessons. I am not proud of what I've done, but at least I can say that I did it for the right reasons!'

'Maybe she played the rusty trombone after all...' I whispered in Linda's ear.

'You're a prick!' she replied.

The table sank into an awkward silence once more. This one dragged on , so I scanned the room for someone else to talk to. Thankfully I saw my mate, Chef, walking past.

'Chef!' I yelled. 'How long till ma bloody steak arrives?'

Chef turned to me with a sort of dazed look on his face, as if he was feeling a bit queasy, like he'd just been in a cab with a woman taxi driver. After a pause, he walked towards me.

A burst of lightning lit up the room, highlighting an epic amount of fresh blood on Chef's apron. Jesus Christ, he looked like he'd just delivered a baby!

'Bloody hell, they make ye kill the cow before you cook it?' I asked.

Before Chef could reply, a piercing scream rang out from down the hall. I recognised the wailing instantly as coming from the little bass player girl, as it was the same sound she'd made after I'd commented on her musical ability earlier.

'Christ!' I yelled. "It's that wee lil' lassie with the lack of talent!'

The kid's mum jumped to her feet with an easy athleticism that suddenly had me envy the music teacher. The rest of us shrugged at each other and went back to our own awkward silence. Glancing up, I noticed my buddy Chef had left during the commotion.

Thank Christ, I thought. Get to ma steak ya dozy bastard.

It was then back to more awkward silence before, surprisingly, Linda spoke next.

'You were pretty harsh about that girl, Taggart,' she said. 'But I have to admit, you were right... she is terrible. Did you hear her trying to play some Radiohead earlier? Almost made me weep!'

'Aye, but it was still better than Coldplay, am I right?'

Before Linda could laugh at my excellent joke, however, the conversation was disrupted by another hideous scream from down the hall.

'Jerry!' the voice of the double bass girl's mum rang out. 'Oh my God! Jerry's dead!'

Christ, I thought. I'm too hungry for this shite.

But as the man of action I am, I put my own concerns aside, stood up, and calmed the growing commotion around me.

'Right!' I yelled. 'All ye fat, dozy pricks sit down and enjoy ye parmas. I'm a private detective! In fact, I used to be a cop, but then I accidentally killed my twin brother... so I'll go and see what the hell's going on.'

I pulled my gun from the inside pocket of my trademark brown jacket and surged out of the room and down the hall. The first minutes after the act are critical for solving any crime, so I was sure to get the bathroom pit stop I took next, over as quickly as possible.

Luckily things moved easily and after a cursory wipe, I was ready.

By the time I got to where the screaming was coming from, quite the crowd was milling about, disrupting the crime scene and generally getting in my way. Ever the pain in my arse, Linda stopped me on my approach.

'Where were you?' she asked.

'I had butter chicken for lunch...' I shrugged.

'Right, well, here's the deal: the teacher has been murdered, stabbed multiple times by a large knife, and was stuffed in the little girl's double bass case,' Linda said. 'There are bolognese sauce stains on the case. No witnesses.'

'Christ,' I said. 'Another bloody woman playing detective. Thanks for stating the obvious, Captain Obv...'

I realised my insult involved awkward repetition, so cut myself short and started moving towards the body.

'Wait!' Linda said. 'There's more!'

'Isn't there always?' I sighed.

'Because of the storm, phone reception is down so we can't call the cops. I went out and checked the road out of here too, and it's underwater. There is no way out.'

'Well then, best get out of ma way and let me solve the fucker, eh?'

I shuffled through the crowd, told off the sobbing children for contaminating the crime scene, and made my way to the body.

I checked for a pulse, but there was none.

'He's dead!' I yelled.

My pronouncement didn't get the reaction I expected, so I continued my inspection.

I checked the body. As much as I wanted Linda to be

wrong, he'd definitely been stabbed.

I looked at the face. Bit of an ugly fucker if you ask me.

I glanced over at the weeping wife he'd been shagging.

'Not bad, you wily prick,' I whispered.

I then walked over to the wife.

'Right, lassie,' I began. 'Where's the cuckold husband of yours? I reckon he's got some explainin' to do...'

'You think Steve did this?' she said between sobs.

'Aye, I do, aye,' I confirmed. 'I've got suspicions about the wee lil' lassie, too. If music comes from the soul, then hers is nasty, I'm tellin' ye! Twisted as all hell!'

The little girl sitting next to her mother perked up rather suspiciously at that last comment. Before she could say anything though, once again, Linda saw fit to butt in. Emphasis on butt, if you follow.

'I'm not so sure about all that,' she whispered. 'Look at the stab wounds... they're clearly from a carving knife you could only get in the kitchen. And then there's the bolognese sauce on the double bass case.'

'Aye, and what's your point, you rambling mad woman?' I asked.

'Jesus, you're a dick!' she said.

'I know, that's why you should leave this to me...'

But she wouldn't listen. Instead, she kept on about the blood on Chef's shirt, the shocked look on his face, the obvious hatred he had for the teacher and so on. This is what too much Law and Order does to a woman...

I mean, she even suggested that I should waste time by talking to witnesses. It was then that I noticed the wife leaving the room, so I cut Linda off.

'Look lassie, I can see you're having fun, but I've gotta go! The wife is fleeing to warn her husband I'm onto him, so I've gotta follow her. It's called police work...'

As I left the room, the last thing I heard Linda say was, 'but you're not a cop...'

Christ, what a ball breaker.

Given the circumstances, I think I can be forgiven for needing a quick drink. Luckily, I always carry a hip flask. I took a swig as I skulked quietly behind the wife, expertly following her toned and clearly robust tail.

After a while, she entered one of the dorm rooms. I couldn't see the number on the door from my vantage point, but by my count, it was room 28.

I paused to compose myself and took another swig of the booze. I find I'm at my most charming after half-a-flask, so they were big swigs, let me tell ye.

Right, I said to myself, I'm ready.

I marched confidently down the hall and burst into room 28, where my embarrassing mistake quickly became apparent. The wife was not in the room; Chef was. The sneaky bastard was naked, frantically stuffing his uniform into a plastic bag.

'Chef!' I said. 'For fucksake mate, why are ye taking yer uniform off? Ye haven't even made ma steak yet!'

Chef was too startled to speak, the poor beggar. He

must've been ripping out a cheeky wank on his break, and here I was cramping his style big time. I made my apologies and exited the room.

My police work was obviously a little rusty but I knew the wife was close. I tried the room next door: this time, crying children.

'God damn it!' I yelled, getting a bit flustered.

Eventually, I picked the right room and wouldn't ya know, the wife was also crying. The husband, as far as I could tell, was not there. Good, I thought.

'So...' I said, gliding towards the bed. 'I knew I'd find you here.'

'You?' she replied. 'What the hell do you want?'

'Rough day, eh?' I asked, smiling as I sat next to her on the bed. 'One of those days when we could all use a bit of comfort, eh?'

'Get out of my room,' she said.

'Don't you mean... out of my jeans?' I asked, winking.

The line felt good coming out of my mouth, but when she slapped me I realised that I'd made a gross error of judgment. With a lassie like this, better to cut out the innuendo and go with a direct approach.

'I didn't mean I wanted you to do my laundry for me,' I clarified. 'I meant we should get naked and have sex!'

She slapped me again. This one was pretty hard. She also called me a few names. Quite a few, in fact. Christ, I've been rejected before, but she went pretty hard, savaging my character and everything. It got pretty personal.

'You're an overgrown man-child who lives in a world of self-delusion and the truth is that no one respects you,' she said.

I know she's wrong, but at the time, I have to admit that her comments hurt. I'd been drinking for much of the afternoon and clearly wasn't thinking straight, so when she called me a 'pathetic loser' it somehow resonated.

I reeled back from the bed and staggered out of the room, taking liberal swigs from my flask as I left. I have to admit, I was stunned. Embarrassed, even. To make matters worse, I remembered that my mate on the security desk had a hidden camera in every room of the place, so my humiliation had definitely been recorded.

Christ.

I know how much the boys love getting together to watch these videos, and I couldn't bear the thought of them having to watch their idol get taken down in such a fashion. I decided I'd better follow up with the security office to wipe the recording before anyone else saw it.

When I got there, the lads were deep in conversation.

'I'm not paid to deal with shit like this!' the head of security, my mate Rob, said. 'I mean, a murderer! Jesus!'

'Ah, pardon me, fellas,' I said, peering through the door. 'Sorry to interrupt, but just wondering if I can get a sneak peek at today's security footage?'

'Of course!' one of the fellas said.

'Hey yeah! We probably have footage of the murder taking place!' another added. 'Good idea!'

'Uh... yeah...' I replied.

Christ. Genius!

'I intend to watch the footage to discover who the murderer is,' I said, quickly amending my plan to delete all of the day's footage. 'I am here... to do that.'

And so I sat down, took a swig from my flask, lit up a dart, and set about watching the day's goings on in the music room. Mostly, it was hilarious footage of kids carrying tubas and shite bigger than they are, stumbling about, making rubbish music while their teacher eyed off their mothers.

Christ, I thought. Any of the dads here might've been tempted to knock off the leary bastard. Eventually, the room fell dark and almost empty. The teacher was now there alone, packing up. After a while someone else walked in. It was Chef, obviously there to get a food order.

Time was getting away from me, so I had one of the security boys start fast forwarding, eager to get to the bit where the husband came in and stabbed the fucker.

When we stopped fast forwarding though, the deed was done. The little girl opened up her double bass case and there the dead bastard was, stuffed inside. She screamed.

'Rewind!' I yelled.

So we rewound back to the part where Chef was talking to the teacher.

I told the security guy to hit Play. From there, I honestly couldn't believe what I saw. I still cannae bloody believe it. Chef stabbed him to death! Instead of cooking my steak like he was supposed to be doing, that cheeky fucker had been busy murdering the teacher.

'Turn the sound up!' I yelled.

The security guy did.

'Your terrible music classes have been stabbing at my ears for years!' Chef was yelling at the teacher. 'Now it's your turn to feel pain! Agghhhhhh!!'

His stabbing was wild and frenetic. The teacher went down like a bleeding sack o' shite. Jesus, Chef was clearly unhinged. And now I had to stop him.

'Right, boys,' I said. 'Looks like this Chef is cooked!'

Everybody laughed, which was great. Just the boost my ego needed as I prepared to take down the bad guy.

Room 28. My previous detective work told me that's where I'd find him, so that's where I decided to go. As I started my journey though, I heard a big commotion happening down the hall, back in the music room.

Instinct told me to avoid the place, given I could hear Linda yelling, but something in her words suggested I might find Chef there, too...

'You don't want to do this, Chef!' Linda yelled.

'You're right!' he snarled in reply. 'But don't doubt

that I will if I have to!'

I entered the room to see Chef standing behind Linda, holding her roughly with a knife to her throat. Everyone else was watching on, frozen with fear.

Luckily, I'm a man of action.

'You should be making me a goddamn steak, Chef!' I said, reaching for my gun as I surged into the room, with more than a hint of the theatrical. 'But instead, you're under arrest... for murder!'

Every eye in the room turned in my direction, just in time to see my hand fumbling around in an empty pocket. Christ, I thought. Where is my gun?

'Yeah, Tag, your woman here already tricked me into confessing,' Chef said. 'Everyone knows I killed him. I admitted it.'

'Ah,' I said. 'Ok, interesting. But just so you know, she's not my woman...'

I was eager for all the other mothers in the room to hear that, drooling as they no doubt were over my no-nonsense approach.

'Well, whatever she is, she's a wily one!' Chef said. 'And she's dead if you try to stop me!'

Christ, testy!

Before I could explain how that would actually solve a lot of headaches for me, Timmy stood up. Shaking like a leaf, he pointed a gun at Chef.

'Where'd you get that?' Linda shrieked.

'I found it in the toilet,' Timmy said.

Chef laughed.

'Is that your gun, Tag?'

I hesitated.

'He's always leaving his gun in the dunnies!' Chef explained to the onlookers, snickering.

Seeing that Chef was distracted, Linda then did something unexpected. Despite the heft of her frame, she moved like lightning.

'Krav Maga!' she yelled, twisting out of his hold and kicking Chef in the nuts.

With an almighty thwack, her foot connected flush on the sack, sending a surge of pain through Chef's body. He doubled over in agony and dropped his knife.

Like I said: a ball breaker.

'Hadouken!' Linda yelled next, giving Chef a swift uppercut that sent him flying.

Christ. The whole thing was pretty bloody terrifying, but also quite impressive, ye know? And it was funny, too. I couldn't believe it. There I was, standing next to a dead body, surrounded by terrified children including my own bastard son, with a sudden and massive erection. Aching, it was.

'Woah daddy!' I said. 'Jesus Christ, Linda! I think Chef isn't the only one here about to do some hard time...'

Linda smiled.

'I think we should have mobile phone reception now...' she said, as she put the concussed murderer in handcuffs. 'So call the cops, will ya?'

I briefly wondered why Linda carried handcuffs, but my thoughts ran away from me.

'Taggart!' she said. 'Call the cops!'

'Yes ma'am!' I replied, giving her my own personal salute.

I grabbed the gun off my son, gave him a clip over the ears for being so irresponsible, then called the police and explained it all: the case of the double bass case killer.

I'd finish the story there, but my editor reckons the whereabouts of the husband is a bit of a loose end that I should quickly address. You know, like, where'd he go when he left the dinner?

It's actually a pretty good story, but I reckon I might leave it as one for all ye dweebs to speculate about in a Reddit sub forum or something.

Toodles, dickheads. We're done here.

Save Me, Jevus!

Aden Simpson

As with all pandemics, there exists the unfortunate patient zero. Jack Hornsby, 44, drunkard. Awoken in the sleepy town of Cliffton; forgotten by its neighbouring counties, and well past the opportunities of restoration. A long way from Nazareth.

Saddled at the crest of the hill on main street you will find St Joseph's Church, held together by a small but loyal congregation of the town's misfits; souls unhappy with the drudgery of modern life, craving another shot in a higher realm beyond middle America. The sermon of the day reminded the sparse drooped old timers of the importance of spreading the word of God and returning the quaint red brick house to its former glory.

Jack Hornsby's booming kick through the front door at the conclusion of said sermon certainly stirred the crowd better than preacher Gregory Abrams had managed this day. "I am the one and only Jesus," Jack bellowed, "Where are your whores?"

Preacher Abrams, threatened by such demonstration and keen to protect his flock, rushed down the aisle to dispel the drunken intruder. That is when Jack gripped the preacher by the shoulders and violently coughed blood into his face.

"Drink this, my blood, my son! Follow me into the light!"

"We assumed he was sick from the drink, typical Jack being what he was. Didn't seem like the kind of christ-like behaviour we'd seen in the movies," says Melinda Wheeler, 63, retired school teacher, now Jesus Christ of 4 Braxley Street, Cliffton.

The service ended abruptly after the assault on Preacher Abrams, the town sheriff and his deputies arriving to take Jack away, who had planted himself on the mount and retold his exploits in the Gospel of Matthew.

"It was difficult to concentrate, what with tending to Preacher Abrams slumped against the pew, but credit where it's due, Jack really put on a show," says Gordon, 64, husband of Melinda, retired plumber.

* * *

Preacher Abrams was taken to the hospital as a precaution, while the sheriff carted Jack to the psychiatric facility over in Polk County.

It is reported that the Preacher, while awaiting the results of his tests in the waiting room, stood upright on his chair, spoke in tongues for a good minute or two, before collapsing on the floor in seizure. Three days later, he awoke from his induced coma, and advised his nurse to bathe in the power of Christ before attempting to pee on her. Hospital staff restraining him were met with his scowling disapproval. If they didn't mind, he was late for his admonishment of tax collectors.

Off to Polk County he went.

* * *

News of the Preacher's turn for the worse shook the congregation. Thoughts, prayers and a vigil outside the facility was organised to wish him a speedy recovery. Upon arriving at the Polk County Psychiatric facility, the group were turned away. An incident with an orderly had placed the staff on high alert.

Before too long, the facility sought assistance from the media. The Polk Gazette ran the headline. "Jesus is back, and he's spreading!"

Melinda admits she was not a true believer in those early days. "Brushed it off, sensationalist rubbish. They were saying it was some kind of affliction. Not just Preacher Abrams or Mr Hornsby was sick with it, but three orderlies, a security guard and two other patients too!" Melinda says she will await an investigation from higher authorities, the state's Preacher Association, to determine the true origin of this madness.

"Demons," says Gordon. "Definitely. What you've got there is a classic case of Demons. All evidence points to evil."

The Preacher's Association, along with the State's #2 rated WNBC news crew, entered the Polk County Psychiatric Institute full of bravado, ready to bring the fire and fury of the Lord in extinguishing yet another christian offshoot. Their exit proved less than victorious.

Cameras revealed a disturbing environment. Seventeen patients, reminding one another to turn the other cheek and offering tips on fishing, to which they all nodded away in agreement.

When asked individually who their leader was, their answers remained uniform. Their Father, of course.

Tests revealed an innate understanding of the scripture, and fondness for addressing people as brother or sister. Aside from a recurrence of the blood sharing habit for which these individuals were becoming notorious, the Preacher's association were at a loss whether to declare them insane or a bona fide miracle. That's how Preacher Abrams ended up on the national TV with 60 minutes. "Hello, it's me, Jesus. Sorry I'm late!"

* * *

Discovery of the Jesus Virus, officially coined JeVus, proved a thorn in the secular and theological worlds. On the one hand, having more than one Saviour complicated their brand and didn't really fit in with the current backstory. But here was a sure-fire way to convert more people to Christianity and arrest a dip in Sunday attendance, from mass in Rome to the little Cliffton House of Prayer. What better way to make oneself their own Saviour.

In the secular world, the Carpenter's Guild Society anxiously weighed up the benefits of having more hands on deck against the heavy investment required in upskilling such a particular influx. Things have changed a lot since the biblical times, they noted. They may be too set in His ways, being the main concern.

The peculiar residents of Polk County Psychiatric facility came to the fore in debates for the Presidential Election for the United States of America. The incumbent president, Mr Deluth, 74, was not against Jesus, per say. But he was adamant that until a cure was found, the choice to become Jesus should be left up to individuals and not forced on the population. The young challenger, Mr Tafferty, 71, pulled Mr Deluth up on his use of the word "cure" and its insinuations. Was the President implying we needed a cure from Jesus?

"I don't usually consider myself a single issue voter, and my heart breaks for Preacher Abrams, but he really seemed happy on Sixty Minutes," Mrs Wheeler reflects.

All the while, a newly formed fundamentalist group, believing in the power of many Christs, stormed the treatment facility and released the prisoners. It was God's will, they argued, just ask the Jesuses.

Condemnation of the jailbreak was resolute from the authorities, though it was not without its supporters, those lost sheep looking to finally be their own shepherd.

And so the Army was called in to deal with the Jesus freaks. While the odd soldier executed containment orders with religious zeal, the overwhelming majority felt uncomfortable blasting away these misunderstood folk. Such complacency led to more infections, which led to more claims of walking on water, which led to drownings and occasional contamination of local water supplies...

And so on, and so on.

With no immediate cure ready, the governments of the world enacted public health measures to combat the spread. This, Gordon and Melinda agree, is the point in which they decided to seek out the disease. *"We took a look at the way the world was heading, and figured the Rapture wasn't far off. Best to hedge our bets and play it safe."*

At the time of writing an estimated two billion people have become Jesus Christ, our Lord and Saviour. It is expected that such widespread abstinence will decimate the global population and affect birth rates for decades to come.

SHAKARA AND THE ELEMENTORS - ANIMATED SERIES PILOT

David Myrcott

PROLOGUE: COBRELLA'S REALM

In Cobrella's dreary mansion in the cosmic world, everything is drab and black like a funeral cloak. She is pacing back and forth in the gloom, muttering to herself.

'Mine, mine, he was supposed to be mine! Why are the gods cheating me like this? Why does fate conspire against me? All my spells, all my enchantments. Nothing could bring him back! Nothing could make him love me again. Instead, he left me, like a thief in the night, with half-spoken vows still warm on his lips, then went and poured out all his love on someone beneath him. How could he? How could they? Was she waiting in the wings this entire time? That was our love, our precious love! We had a future! And she stole it, and ate it up, every gorged herself on every last piece. My joy! She devoured the bliss that should have been mine. Every kiss, every tender look, every caress, every private unspoken moment she had with him — they all belong to me!'

At that moment, the black bird returns to his perch. She goes to him at once.

'Tell me everything you saw, black bird. Were my visions true? Tell me all. And if you lie or hold anything back, I promise to pluck out your tail feathers one by one. I have very much hate in my heart just now.'

'Yes, mistress,' replied the black bird. 'I will tell you honestly everything I saw and heard. I saw a woman with gold hair, sitting in front of mirror. She was making a noise like *mmm-mmm-mmm*. She had a crown in her hair, and a gold brush in her hand, and she called the crown a 'tee-are-ah' and she couldn't get it straight.'

'What else, what else?' ranted Cobrella. 'Did she look happy? Did she have a wart on her nose, perhaps? A huge unsightly boil right at the top of her forehead?'

'I didn't see any warts,' said the black bird, cowering a bit. 'Or a boil. All I saw was a young woman with gold hair, dressed as though for a fine occasion. Her gown sparkled like her eyes. And then another woman came in, and told the gold-haired lady she was the most beautiful woman in the land, and everyone knows it, and I think someone maybe had lice or a tick problem because they kept talking about a groom or needing to be groomed. And something about candles.'

'Then it's happening today. Today, what was mine will be stolen from me forever.'

'What was stolen from you, mistress? The crown she wore? Her rings and bangles?'

'No, something much more valuable than gold. My chance to be happy.'

'Oh. Well, I suppose that is worth more than gold, since one can be bought and the other can't. Neither can be eaten though. Which is a drawback. What's happening today, by the way?'

'The royal wedding, you idiot!' raged Cobrella. 'The real one. The precise date has been kept a closely-guarded secret. They will marry in private, according to the old customs, in the presence of only the ancient gods and their family, then announce a second public wedding for all to attend sometime after. It's all anyone's been talking about for months.'

'Not us birds. We mostly talk about worms, berries. Sometimes someone finds some meat and we talk about it, or the different ways of building a nest—'

Cobrella grabs the black bird roughly.

'Anything else? Anything at all? Think, little friend. Think nice and hard.'

'Well, it's quite hard to think when you are holding me upside down and squeezing so tight.'

She squeezes harder.

'Ah! I remember something else: there was something about a baby. Or babies. Royal ones.'

'Do you mean. To tell me. That she is... pregnant? With child??'

'I don't know,' said the black bird. 'Isn't that what humans are usually pregnant with? I think I may be about to pass out.'

'Alright,' said Cobrella, letting him go. 'Alright. Thank you for telling me what you saw. I'm sorry I squeezed so hard. My nerves are on edge, you see.'

'Don't mention it,' says the bird with a cough.

'So she thinks she's going to marry, AND have a child with, the only man I ever loved. Ha! Black bird, fetch your troops. All of them. We're about to go and crash a wedding in heaven.'

SCENE 1

INT. — DAY — SHAKARA'S CHAMBER
Cobrella appears on the balcony, then enters.

COBRELLA

'Love sought is good; but given unsought, is better.'

SHAKARA

Cobrella!

COBRELLA

Hello, Shakara. My! You do look fine. Getting ready for something special? A garden party perhaps? A feast of fools?

SHAKARA

What the hell are you doing here?

COBRELLA

Oh, I just heard some news is all. I heard congratulations are in order. But I'm sorry to say I'm here to spoil your plans. There will be no wedding, I'm afraid. No happily ever after. Not for you, anyway.

LUCIE

Are you out of your mind? How dare you barge in here like this, with your hate and your anger and all your filthy birds trailing behind you! The prince left you because you were jealous, and possessive, and everyone knows you went mad when he wouldn't take you back. He wouldn't marry you in a million, million years.

COBRELLA

Is that so?

LUCIE

He'll never take you back! It's all in your head! Shakara is his true love, it's written in the stars. Why don't you just—

Cobrella knocks Lucie out cold with a wave of her staff.

COBRELLA

Quite a mouth on your scullery maid. I can see why you keep her around. You two must have some zesty little *tête-à-têtes.*

Now account for your crimes, you man-stealing tramp.

SHAKARA

Oh my God. You really are crazy. You truly think you can win him back, don't you? Even after what you did? You disfigured him! Well, I won't fight. I'm not hateful like you. My crystals haven't turned black with rage and self-pity.

COBRELLA

You'll fight, or you'll die.

SHAKARA

You're pathetic! You're only alive because my father felt sorry for you, begged them not to sentence you to death. I've heard where they made you live. An empty mansion in a dark empty realm, surrounded by evil forests and death. Well, poor you! You treated the prince horribly. Scarred him, used black magic, stole books of forbidden spells from the Alchemist. Go back to the Realm of Sceptres where you belong. Reap the shadows you've sown.

COBRELLA

Shadows? That's interesting. I wonder what you know

about them? About shadow realms, and the creatures who dwell there?

SHAKARA

I wouldn't want to know.

COBRELLA

Of course not. There's too much light in you. Your crystals, they do burn brightly, Princess Shakara. I do envy you that. I do envy you. Your perfect life. The one that should have been mine.

Cobrella picks up an expensive bottle of perfume from a night stand near the window where she entered.

COBRELLA

Tell me, did he buy you this?

She flings the bottle at Shakara's head then rushes at her. The two engage in a fierce struggle. By the time the King's Guard enters, it is too late. The two are fighting a magical duel high in the sky. The townspeople watch from below, between attacks of the black birds.

COBRELLA

Now I will show you that hatred is stronger than love.

SHAKARA

Do your worst. I'll show you that love always wins the day,

no matter what.

After a protracted magical battle, Shakara is defeated. Cobrella drains her life essence out via her crystal chakras. Then she throws Shakara over the edge of the Crystal Kingdom to whatever lies beneath the clouds.

Redrum is Murder Backwards

Craig Tuck

Margaret stood like a wraith, looming large above the cowering bloody wreckage of a man who shivered helplessly at her feet.

The man was choking on blood – mostly his own – and groaning with barely audible pleas for clemency.

'Please!' the man shrieked, after a considerable period of choking and whimpering.

Margaret noticed how it had taken him longer than most to clear his throat of the usual vomitus brew of accumulated blood and bile and hair.

Blood streamed from the man's gaping head wound, running rampant down his unfortunate face, over his unfortunate eyes, past his unfortunate cheeks and into his unfortunate mouth. The unfortunate man was choking.

He peered up desperately, straining for a clear line of sight through the curtains of his new, blood-drenched reality. There was no light. Margaret eclipsed everything.

'I...what have I...why?' the man spluttered. It was a fair question with a long answer, but in short, it all began eight years earlier.

Margaret's descent into the madness so apparent on this cold Canberra Friday first gathered pace at the Gala 2006 Federal Department of Community Restoration and Proliferation Graduate Programme Annual (CRaPGPA).

This was a key occasion in the year's Programme, where the CRaP Graduate recruits were provided with the formal opportunity to mingle with CRaP Senior Executive Officers in a non-hierarchical, informal setting.

While a few difficulties earlier in the year had meant that Margaret was now almost entirely isolated from her own Graduate group, she was nevertheless excited for this occasion. The CRaP annual was *the* social event of the Graduate calendar.

Any Graduate with ambition would surely understand that this was the prime opportunity for professional networking – the best chance yet to land the sort of career mentor, confidante or referee that all aspiring public servants dream of as a child.

In a year that had provided her with wonderful workplace exposure and significant opportunities for training and career development, Margaret knew that despite exemplary work performance, conduct and commitment, she had failed to find anyone she could depend on, when a reference inevitably became necessary.

Accordingly, Margaret approached the CRaPGPA with

a very serious mindset. Without being certain why, she trusted that fate would lead her to the outcomes she sought.

As the queue into the venue edged slowly forward, she began to look forward to what the night had in store.

Upon entering the room though, Margaret's disappointment was instant and complete.

As the booze flowed, Margaret realised that it didn't matter how much faith she had lost in those around her, they continued to find new ways to sink lower.

'Doesn't she have a husband?' Margaret asked herself, as she noticed Payroll Manager Susan Bickle being furtively fingered in the corner of the room by Andrew Roberts, Senior Legal Counsel.

Margaret was disgusted and averted her gaze accordingly. But wherever she looked, new questions appeared.

'How did they even get that in here?'

'Is that table safe to dance on?'

'Where are his pants?'

And so on.

Margaret couldn't believe that the Australian higher education system had been spewing forth so many 'professionals' that were so far gone. Still, Margaret ignored her concerns, bowed her head and forged on, forcing her way through the throng.

Her persistence was eventually rewarded when

finally, just when all seemed lost, the moment occurred. It was a moment that seemed to slow time. Margaret glanced across the room, with fate guiding her line of sight over the vomit-smeared shoulder of Doug, from Accounting, and directly towards *him*: Dr Christopher Reinhold.

Dr Reinhold was a notoriously serious, high-achieving young executive. Margaret knew his story well: a CRaP graduate just six years earlier, Dr Reinhold had built an enviable reputation for crafting inscrutable bureaucratese and navigating approval chains with deftness and dexterity.

He now led a team that was feared and admired throughout the department. Dr Reinhold's reputation said that he was not to be trifled with. It was well known that he expected a lot of himself and just as much of his staff.

Oh! How Margaret longed to be crushed under the weight of his scrutiny.

She flushed when she first saw him, sitting expressionless and alone, checking emails on his blackberry.

He wore a classic three button jacket with slim-fit business pants, giving him a clean, professional look. With his pants creeping ever so slightly up his slim, toned calves, Margaret noticed that he was not even wearing the kind of zany socks ambitious young professionals often use to subtly imply they have some personality.

Margaret was mesmerized. His socks were plain black! He was *all* business!

With butterflies in her stomach, she approached.

'Hi,' she said. 'Things are getting pretty out of hand, aren't they?'

The profoundly stern, impressive young executive said nothing for some time. He eyed Margaret, considering her features, examining her eyes, searching for weakness.

Margaret returned the thoughtful gaze.

'Can you believe these people?' Dr Reinhold said eventually, after Scott – a likable, almost charming buffoon from the Graduate Programme – careened blindly past, pants off (but underwear on).

'No...' said Margaret, smiling as she forced her eyes away from a hole in the back of Scott's ageing Bonds briefs. 'Can I join you?'

'Sure,' Dr Reinhold said, smiling at Margaret with a detached professionalism that was entirely appropriate for the situation.

'I'm Christopher – Dr Reinhold – by the way. I'm the Assistant Secretary of this horror show.'

'Oh yes, I know!' replied Margaret, 'I'm a CRaP Graduate!'

'That's unfortunate,' said Dr Reinhold; his sophisticated smile and eloquent accent were almost hypnotically splendid. 'But...'

But...

Before Dr Reinhold had the chance to finish his sentence, Scott swooped back towards the table and slid powerfully onto the seat next to Margaret. Once seated, Scott put his left arm around Margaret's braced shoulders.

'G'Day Margo!' Scott bellowed, breathing a furious stench of alcoholic revelry into Margaret's wincing face as he did so. 'What's going on?'

Margaret blushed. Dr Reinhold eyed the display with an ugly frown. Margaret eyed Dr Reinhold with a furrowed brow.

'This girl here...I tell you Chris...she looks serious, but I reckon she's a bit of a dark horse, know what I mean?' Scott slurred at Dr Reinhold, as he loosely held the stiffening Margaret.

The ensuing silence was awkward until, eventually, Dr Reinhold spoke.

'Well, then, it's starting to feel like it might be time for me to say "good night...",' he said, 'So... good night.'

Margaret's dazed gaze followed Dr Reinhold as he stood, turned and walked away.

Margaret sighed in sweet, professional lust as she watched Dr Reinhold leave the room.

Heartbroken, she could do nothing but admire Dr Reinhold's obvious disdain for those around him, confident march and impressive, clearly expensive charcoal grey suit.

Dr Reinhold made his departure with proud certainty. Margaret could only hope to one day carry herself in such a manner, as she watched him spear his way through the crowd, towards the exit.

Meanwhile, Scott was also moving on.

Turing to face Margaret's flaring nostrils and reddening eyes, he smiled; a feeble attempt to deny the sinister forces clearly taking hold.

'Someone needs to get you a drink, Margo!' he said, '...and the second I find my pants, I think I'll be the guy for the job! Wait here!'

Scott swayed in rhythmic inebriation, rising from his chair and turning towards the bar in a shambles of beautiful, poetic bumbling. Margaret glared after him.

He had destroyed her last chance...or had he?

Margaret leapt from the table and charged for the exit, a surge of anxious optimism taking over.

'I've got to explain!' she yelled.

With elbows, arms and shoulders, Margaret jostled her way through the rabble and lunged hungrily towards the exit.

Margaret surged through the doors and into the cold, open air. Her arms stretched like tentacles and her neck thrust forward with spastic intensity.

Margaret's long-gestating madness was finally bursting free.

Her eyes flickered yellow as she tore through the shadows. She darted around the building, searching behind poles, bins and cars, amongst shadows and shrubbery. While she could feel Dr Reinhold's presence – then, now and always – there was no sign of the person she had privately anointed as her new mentor.

Dr Reinhold had vanished into the night before anyone but Margaret had even noticed that he was missing.

Back in the hall, a different kind of frenzy reigned. It was time for late-night coupling. Scott had cornered, or been cornered by, a lovely lady he thought was called "Tanya", "Taryn", "Tilda" or something.

He eyed the girl with honourable biological intent, as she slurred on and on in an endless drone of flirtatious white noise, breaking only to sip from the pink Vodka Cruiser Scott had originally purchased for Margaret.

The lady, Trish, giggled suggestively and put the drink back down on the table. There the Vodka Cruiser remained, while its original and intended owner sat cradling herself in her all-consuming grief on the sidewalk outside. So that's how it started.

Years later, Margaret's Fridays were more dignified. Rather than crying in the gutters, she spent them proof reading draft ministerial correspondence. On this particular evening that workload was lighter than usual, so she left her CRaP work desk at the unusually early hour of 6:45pm.

Content with her work for the week and ready to enjoy a marathon of the week's episodes of ABC program The Drum, she knew it was important that she take some time to rest.

After a few hours enjoying the faux-intellectual debate that is the ABC's stock and trade, she began preparing herself to finish the week off. She did some breathing exercises and yoga stretches, then ventured out into the Canberra night once more.

After years of volunteering for every development opportunity, working group and special taskforce she could find, *this* was it: a real chance to impress Dr Reinhold.

Into the shadows she went.

'Who are you?' the man had asked when he'd first noticed the fitted, Akris Punto Mini Houndstooth Jersey One-Button Blazer (retailing for $1900) looming from the darkness.

His alarm upon first grasping that this slim, well dressed and vaguely familiar blonde woman had been deliberately skulking silently behind him was clear. So again, he asked, 'Who are you?'

'I am no one,' Margaret said, as she entered into the light.

The man eyed her warily, before a look of dramatic recognition swept across his unprepared and, frankly, overwhelmed face.

'Are you...Margo?' the man exclaimed. He squinted at the woman standing before him.

Margaret hesitated, almost afraid to speak.

'I am no one.'

'Come on, Margo, I mean, Margaret Dwyer, right? From CraP?' the man asked. 'It's Scott! Remember me?'

'I...'

'God, I haven't seen you in years!'

'I am no one.'

'Come on Margo, you've done OK – you're hardly no one!'

'Scott...no...I...'

Margaret paused to compose herself.

'I am no one.'

'Nooo, you're someone, Margo! I heard you're an EL1 these days? I mean, I know you're still at CraP, but you know...not bad! EL1! You've got, what, Reg 9 financial delegation?'

'I am no one.'

'Don't be that way, Margo. You've done well. Now I heard you were a bit annoyed when I left CraP for my new job but working for the Prime Minister's Office isn't everything you know...

'And look, I get it. I know you probably think I was lucky scoring an EL2 gig – you heard I got an EL2 gig, right? – but it's actually really stressful and on top of that, I was posted overseas for so long I don't even know if...'

Like a prom night mishap, the blow came suddenly.

Gasping for answers, Scott's speech came to an abrupt end, as his attention shifted to the urgent situation unexpectedly unfolding in his skull (which now had an axe in it).

After the axe was withdrawn, he gurgled nonsensically as he collapsed to the paved floor outside of the corner café in the Curtin shops precinct – the hipster one with the milk crates for seats.

Thanks to high cyclist numbers and their penchant for lycra clothing, this wasn't a venue that Margaret usually enjoyed. With no one else around though, save for her bludgeoned former acquaintance, she began to see the venue in a new light. Blood really does look black under a full moon.

'gurrgghcchooollke, whyyyhdhddnurddlllllgooooddd… whhydydysnoooo…' Scott said.

Margaret dragged him around the corner, into the alleyway between the newsagency and the Woolworths.

Sometime later, with blood streaming from his gaping head wound, running rampant down his unfortunate face, over his unfortunate eyes, past his unfortunate cheeks and into his unfortunate mouth, the man wondered why this fate had befallen him.

'You look confused,' Margaret said. 'Let me clear it up for you…'

Margaret explained how Scott had ruined her chances of gaining Dr Reinhold as a mentor with his drunken insolence all those years ago.

She explained that Dr Reinhold had only communicated with her once more since that terrible night, to tell her that she 'clearly did not have the focus necessary to succeed'.

It was Scott's fault, she said. Scott had done this to her.

She has been 'no one' ever since, Margaret explained. As far as Dr Reinhold was concerned, she was no one at all. But now, she said, things would finally change. Scott's return to Canberra, after years abroad, had created an opportunity.

Eyeing the gaping axe wound in Scott's skull, Margaret said there was now an *opening* as the *head* of the international engagement team in the Prime Minister's office. She paused for effect, allowing the humour of her words to sink in, before adding that she was clearly the ideal candidate to fill the unexpected vacancy.

When her well-rehearsed speech ended, Margaret finally allowed herself to laugh. After years of stern focus, her cackling filled the air.

Scott died with the laughter ringing in his ears.

It was hours later, while relaxing at home, that Margaret was hit by the sudden realisation that she had not eaten a thing all day.

'Silly me,' she said.

Margaret pulled a packet of frozen lasagne out of the freezer of her Samsung 5338L French Door Refrigerator and turned the McCain's frozen lasagne packet over.

'Remove frozen meal from carton. Pierce film lid in two places with a fork. Place in microwave oven,'

Margaret said aloud to herself, smiling as she read from the box's cooking instructions.

'Cook on HIGH for 7 minutes. Carefully peel off film lid. Return to oven and continue to cook on HIGH for a further 3 minutes...'

Margaret's voice trailed off as she skimmed through the rest of the instructions, which were pretty standard.

As the microwave did its work, she proof-read her resume. It was pretty impressive, particularly with Dr Reinhold's name listed as a referee. A little presumptuous, maybe, but Margaret was confident that she could convince him.

She began typing an email.

'Dear Dr Reinhold,' it began, 'I write to you with a confession – a story of what real focus looks like – and I ask that you consider it thoroughly, as an example of what I am capable of...'

Overtaken by a calmness she had never known, Margaret started to hum.

God Roadtrip

Aden Simpson

And God floated down to the local hospital, where he noticed the gift shop was low on stock of 'get well soon' cards. Rather than chastise the manager for this oversight, God showed mercy, and with a click of his fingers a sea of 'get well soon' cards flooded the shelves, delighting all the visiting relatives.

His work done, God took to the road in his Dodge Ram, aptly named 'the Shepherd'.

While on the road, he performed more miracles.

Here are some of them:

The Hill Berry Church sat atop the small hill, once full of blueberry trees, overlooking the dying town. The mine had shuttered its doors and the crops stood meek, their number of diminishing yield. God straightened his robe and entered one of his many houses. Decent crowd; boisterous, flailing their arms, fervent amens. The reverend riling them up, his face red with spit and accusations of moral failure. Old Testament classics. God shook his head. Covered his face in embarrassment. He'd forgotten half of the wacky rants he'd sounded off in those formative years.

The reverend was adamant the town must submit to

the Lord and the drought will end and the crops will finally be bountiful. He spotted God in the back and beckoned him to the front. Do not be embarrassed, brother, the Lord is not deterred by your dishevelled state, he will wash away your sins and accept you, but you must crawl to him.

God said he was fine, but the reverend insisted. God accused the reverend of being batty. The reverend and the parishioners turned on God. They demanded he leave. God got personal with his parting insult.

Once the smelly bum in the robe had left, the reverend commanded the victorious parishioners to bow their heads and pray.

The Dodge Ram kicked gravel high into the air and the rocks hailed down upon the roof of the church, leaving holes right above the pulpit, exposing it to the elements the next time it were to rain, if it ever would again.

God grew weary of the Ram and gave it free will. The Ram rolled across the countryside, searching for meaning, until it ran out of gas, blocking a lane on the highway. A nihilist mechanic dutifully stripped the ram for parts.

* * *

And then God took a break from his miracle road trip. He appeared in the middle of a roundabout in the fictional town of Midsommer, where all those people are murdered, but nobody in the town seems to leave despite the clear risks. God waltzed into the police headquarters and listed out all the murderers. Overnight, the crime rate plummeted, the odd case of littering finally usurping homicide. In real life, audiences found the abrupt series finale to be disappointing, citing the anticlimactic deus ex machina.

Satisfied, God returned to his roadtrip, transforming a lonely horse into a convertible red Mustang. He gunned it straight and true, almost breaking the speedometer. This caught the eye of officer Redmayne, who gave a spirited chase. Being a good sport, God decided to slow down and test the man's competence as a police officer.

Officer Redmayne asked God to turn down the music. God complied.

Do you know how fast you were going?

God knew exactly how fast, he declared to the officer. He knew everything, as it so happened. In fact, he knew exactly how much money it would take for the officer to realise his detection equipment was faulty.

Officer Redmayne did not wait to hear God's incredibly generous offer. Officer Redmayne asked God to step out of the vehicle and arrested him for attempted bribery and speeding. Pleased that he'd passed the test, God sent him straight to heaven.

At the county fair, God guessed the correct number of beans in the jar and shared his winnings with the children. He also turned the fairy floss into sweet wine and soon those same children were drunk and dizzy and the swirling rides offered advantageous platforms to launch their sick.

God won every rigged game and cleared each prize shelf of its oversized fluffy animals. The carnies banded together, mystified by the skills of the old bum in the robe, yet still confident they had his number.

They found God in the Freak Show tent, gawking and giggling away, his winnings placed in the seats around him, as if watching the show.

Their plans unravelled when their menaced pointing yielded no recognition from the cackling old hustler, yet his new fluffy toys rotated their heads in unison, fixing their beady eyes on the carnies, suggesting the futility of further advancement.

And so the Lord was able to watch his show uninterrupted and life was good.

Taking a break from the road to really stretch his back out, God camped in the open, gazing up at the stars. Imagine his surprise when he spotted a metallic disc shaped object shooting across the sky. The next morning he passed by a roadside UFO tours operator. What are the odds! God thought excitedly to himself. A crowd of tourists milled about, cameras slung about their necks. God addressed the tourists, showing off the video footage he took on his phone. This ruffled the owner, who suspected this shabby lunatic was either trying to belittle his humble venture, or had ulterior motives as an aspiring competitor in the market. Thus began the owner's public debunking of God's grainy proof. Once again the tide of approval crashed against God. Deflated, God was all set to return to the road, tail between his legs...

But as life so often does in its mysterious ways, at that very moment God remembered he needed to water his purple forests on the planet Xebu.

Only the owner saw God disappear into thin air, and his smugness vanished quickly thereafter, for having finally seen the inexplicable, he knew that for the rest of his days not a single soul would believe him.

God arrived at the cornfield crossroads just as his friend The Serpent was finishing up with a client.

God owed his old friend a ride and so they rode off in the red Mustang, wind through their hair. They took turns with the radio, back and forth each song.

I like this one, said God.

You're welcome, said the Serpent.

And God did not appreciate the imputation that his friend was behind the creation of this rock ballad. And the Lord was quick to remind his old friend who formed Humans and invented the concept of Sound.

The Serpent conceded this was true, yet he remained adamant that he played a big role in the songwriting and producing.

As it so happened they approached a hitch-hiker, to which God came up with a fun wager. Let's ask a third party, settle this properly. The Serpent agreed and the hitch-hiker appreciated the good fortune and comfort of his stylish new lift, for as it turned out, these good samaratins were also heading to the same destination!

And so the hitch-hiker was briefed on God and the Serpent's differing opinions and thus he threw his support behind the Serpent, based on the song title being 'Sympathy for the Devil'.

And God grew furious and suddenly they weren't heading the same way as it turned out so it was better for the hitch-hiker to find another ride.

The serpent asked God to show some compassion, but God was mad and the radio went silent for the rest of their journey.

The Thing

David Myrcott

Once upon a time I had this Thing.

It was a good and faithful Thing, but you know what they say about all good things. 'Nothing lasts forever'... 'it had been a decent run'... 'perhaps there was someone who needed it more than me'... and all of that.

Basically I was busy with work and other matters, and not able to devote as much time to the Thing as I'd like. I thought someone might be able to use the Thing, that they might get some enjoyment out of it, that their life might be enhanced by the Thing in the same way mine had been, back when I'd had the time to use and interact with it.

How best to give it away? I pondered. Perhaps an advertisement in the local paper? That seemed a little impersonal. Plus I didn't want the Thing to fall into the wrong hands. I thought it made more sense to go to a public place and find a worthy recipient in person. That way I would at least be certain the Thing had found a new home, a new owner, that was suitable, who would treat it kindly and show it the requisite respect. It deserved that much at least. Plus I could give them a demonstration in the event they wanted to know the

Thing worked before they took it home. I decided I would not ask for any money.

Come on Thing, I said. *We're going to the park.* I didn't tell the Thing that it would be for the last time, that it wouldn't be returning home, that I was getting rid of it. There was no point in needlessly upsetting it.

As soon as we got to the park the Thing bounded off, chasing after some ducks. Isn't that just like the Thing, I thought, a trifle tearfully. Always so playful. For a moment I regretted that I was going to give it away, and almost changed my mind.

Spying someone I thought might be suitable, I approached and politely enquired whether they might be interested in obtaining the Thing, free of charge.

That Thing? she asked, pointing. *The one scaring all the ducks away?*

Yes, I replied, with a touch of embarrassment.

I don't know, the woman said. *It seems rather unruly. Besides, I'm not sure I've got the space.*

I couldn't argue with either point, and our conversation came to an end.

Upon eventually recapturing the Thing, and scolding it, I scooped it under my arm to help maintain appearances and decided to try my luck elsewhere.

How would you describe the Thing? asked the next would-be recipient.

See for yourself, I responded, a little testily.

If that's your attitude, came the haughty riposte, I'll

take my business elsewhere.

Wait! I exclaimed, trying not to sound desperate. *Well, it isn't a pet. Nor is it an object exactly. It just sort of... is, if you get me.*

She didn't. As her polite smile began to fade I added desperately It's just a Thing! Then, attempting a more casual tone, I added Look, do you want it or not?

Let me think about it, she said, as she turned and walked quickly away.

But what does it do? asked someone else, an older man out walking a pair of daschunds, who had evidently overheard our exchange.

Exactly what it's supposed to, I replied. *No more, and certainly no less.*

Quizzical. Skeptical. Intrigued, but ultimately regretful. The Thing garnered a variety of responses, none of them the one I was hoping for.

At a certain point the Thing, as though it were as light as paper, floated off and got itself entangled in some tree branches. Here we go again, I thought to myself.

A voice made me jump. *Whose Thing is this?* demanded a policeman who just happened to be in the vicinity.

Mine, I replied a trifle sheepishly. That's my Thing.

Look, you can't just let Things float about willy nilly, said the officer. *Technically it's littering. I'm going to have to write you up for this.*

As he pulled out his pen and ticket book I stood and glared up at the Thing, which was fluttering just as innocently as you please in the branches overhead.

You've got a month to pay that, he said, handing me the fine. *And I don't care how you do it, just get that Thing out of that bloody tree.*

Believe me I'll try, I said, a little bit glumly. The Thing, as loyal as it had been, was proving to be more trouble than it was worth. Who was going to want it now?

After a considerable amount of time I managed to coax the Thing out of the tree, with soothing words and promises I wouldn't get angry. Just in case anyone had seen the spectacle with the police officer I decided to try another section of the park, over by the playground and the swings.

A young girl saw us approach and immediately ran over to investigate.

Oh, what an adorable little Thing! she exclaimed. *It's just what I've been wanting.*

She turned to her father, a balding taciturn type in an ochre jacket. *Daddy, daddy, can I have it?*

Look here, he said, approaching me, *my daughter appears quite fond of that Thing of yours. I don't suppose you'd consider selling it? I'd give you a fair price.*

Actually you can have it, I said with my best smile. *Free to a good home.*

Why? he asked. *What's wrong with it?*

Nothing at all. I just don't... need it any more.

His eyes narrowed slightly.

It works perfectly fine, I added, trying not to sound

too desperate. At that precise moment the Thing, which had been momentarily well-behaved, emitted a high-pitched screech.

Hm, said the man. Hmm. *Does it at least come with a warranty?*

Well no, I said. *You'd have to take it as is.* The Thing began wriggling in the girl's arms, then screeched some more. Startled, she dropped it like a hot coal. It was as if it knew I was trying to get rid of it and was doing its best to stymie the deal.

I think we need one with a warranty, he sniffed, taking his daughter by the hand. *Plus this one screeches too much. Come on Sophia, we'll get you that Thing we saw in the department store window. That one at least came with a money-back guarantee, as well as a choice of colours. Much quieter too,* he added.

On and on it went, well into the afternoon, until it appeared getting rid of the Thing wasn't going to be as easy as I'd anticipated.

Too busy. Couldn't commit. Already got one. Already got two. I'd need to check with my partner. Don't want the responsibility. Allergic.

Come on then, I eventually sighed, resigned to fate. *Let's go home.*

The Thing, for its part, appeared nonchalant, as if it had known all along this was going to be the outcome. It didn't screech or make any mischief on the way, in fact it was on its best behaviour. Perhaps I had been wrong in wanting to give it up in the first place.

At least it had been a nice day out. I couldn't remember the last time I'd been to the park.

Trevor

Craig Tuck

'I just *made it* with a dead girl,' Trevor groaned, lamenting once more the demonic possession that had so powerfully compelled him to perform this horrible act.

This was the first time Trevor's awful plight had led all the way to its terrible conclusion, and it was proving a tricky thing to get his head around.

The grey swollen eyes had stared at Trevor unflinchingly through the act, just as they did now. The pallid glare offered no forgiveness.

Trevor's mind slowly processed what he had done. He considered what the future might hold for him. After all, the corpse had been relatively easy to find.

The unguarded town morgue was just a short walk from the intensive care unit.

Despite everything else, Trevor wondered, was this the worst part of his sister's hospitalisation?

Gently sobbing, he withdrew himself from the scene of the crime. The harsh fluorescent light served only to highlight the level of decay.

His tears gathered pace.

More than the site of fleshy carnage below, it was the

cackling voice in his head.

'I knew you had it in you boy! Great job for a practice run! Haha!'

Trevor slapped himself in the face. A moment of peace, before awful visions from earlier in the day; his sister, motionless and mangled.

'Please let Hannah be OK...' he whispered, zipping up his fly.

It had been her first drive alone. She had been rushing to his side.

New tears filled his eyes, as he noticed the blood-smeared crotch of his pants. If He hadn't before, why would God possibly care about his family now?

The furious smell of rotting flesh filled Trevor's nostrils. It was time to go.

Trevor walked down the morgue's cold, dark corridors, towards the exit and eventually, the hospital. He thought of Hannah and of unanswered questions.

Trevor climbed over the morgue's fence, then hurried his pace as he marched through the hospital car park.

The bond Trevor shared with his sister had been forged in suffering, congealed by co-dependence. It had been that way since childhood; since their father had come home angry and drunk one too many times.

Trevor can still see it clearly.

His father's belt hanging from his fist, eyes scanning the room. His mother, unconscious in the corner.

'Old Mother Hubbard, went to the cupboard, to get

her poor doggie a bone...'

Trevor's father muttered the familiar nursery rhyme on his usual route, towards the little girl's room.

At just 14 years old, Trevor had seen this scenario unfold more times than his home schooled mind could count. His father marched down the hallway, VB fumes clinging to him, just as routine said he would.

This time though, something changed.

Hannah's cries rang out in a pitch more desperate than usual, and their mother's weak, forlorn breathing didn't kick on as it always had previously. It finally stopped.

Trevor saw the life leave her body and knew it was time to act. Gripping the trigger of his father's gun with more resolve than ever before, Trevor fired.

It was a single shot many years in the making. The bullet exploded into his father's back. Trevor watched him fall to the floor, turning to face his son as he did so.

'This will haunt you!' Trevor's father gurgled, with rather ominous dying words.

And so it was.

A new journey began. From that moment on, Trevor and Hannah were together, safe, and on the run.

The police were one thing; they understood. But the Family Court was another threat entirely. Trevor had heard about what they did to kids; the guys under the bridge had told him all about foster care.

So Trevor ran and Hannah never left his side.

Whichever way you looked at it, they only had each other.

As days of running turned into months that flowed desperately into years, life on the road began to weary Trevor. Morning after morning, watching his sister sing into her hair brush in front of another scratched hotel mirror, he would summon the strength to lie to the only person he cared about.

"You're gonna be a star one day, Hannah, I just know it," Trevor said.

Unfortunately, Trevor knew life didn't work that way. It would never just hand Hannah a ticket to stardom.

So while his sister sang her pure little heart out in front of all those mirrors, Trevor put his mind to work making up new schemes for quick dollars. When their cash reserves ran low, desperation put those plans into action.

Trevor turned 18 having stolen thousands of dollars from innocent men, women and children. He'd begged on the streets of Sydney, Melbourne and Adelaide, sold drugs from Brisbane to Townsville, and ripped off more faces than he could remember. At his lowest, he'd even done some telemarketing in Canberra.

Trevor was not proud of these things, but he knew he did it for the right reason. Hannah knew, too. That's why she resolved to never leave her brother's side, even as he began to see their separation as her only chance.

The voice inside was getting louder by now, launching

terrible echoes from a past that just wouldn't be denied.

'Old Mother Hubbard, went to the cupboard, to get her poor doggie a bone...'

Trevor turned 21 recognising the voice for what it was. It was the voice that belonged to the face he now saw in the mirror, too.

'You can't run from me forever, Trevor,' his father told him. 'I still have plans for us...'

By this time, the terrifying voice had begun urging him towards the dead.

Though it broke his heart, Trevor knew he had to leave Hannah behind.

Trevor worked a day job, mopping floors, to save up the cash to see her properly on her way.

Hannah was 18, beautiful, fiercely intelligent and obviously talented. Her best days lay away from him.

Or so Trevor had hoped.

As he waited anxiously in the hospital waiting room, Trevor wondered if he'd ever hear her gorgeous voice again.

Flicking aimlessly through a *Woman's Day*, Trevor scared himself witless wondering if heaven had finally found her: Hannah. Their lost angel.

The day had begun with Trevor listening to a recording of his sister singing, as he often did, to silence the terrible voice within.

Listening to her voice as he readied himself for work, Trevor could only shake his head. Such beauty, from such a horrible home.

The coldness of the world bit hard that morning, as Trevor closed the door behind him. The awful voice from beyond further chilled him, as he walked towards the bus stop.

'We're doing it later, Trevor,' his father said. 'You'll find one this time, son...'

Trevor gritted his teeth, turned up the volume on his iPod, and kept walking towards the $14.50 an hour that was all for Hannah.

Meanwhile, his sister slept soundly. Hannah felt safe in the life her brother had provided, all while revelling in her dreams of a life on the stage.

Hours later, the familiar dream was interrupted by the phone call that changed everything. Hannah's eyes opened in a flash and she turned to see her phone dancing beside her, all flashing lights and unconventional rhythm. Hannah answered the call, which came from an unknown number.

'H-hello?' she said.

'Hello, is this Hannah Merriwell?' the other end of the line asked.

'Yes,' Hannah said.

Hannah was terribly nervous. She didn't often get calls.

'Great,' the other end of the line said. 'We loved your audition tape!'

Hannah gasped.

'Who is this?'

The other end of the line laughed. 'Oh gosh, I'm sorry! It's *Talent Quest*! You remember sending an audition tape?'

'Y-yes...'

'Excellent! Because we want to invite you to come sing on our show!'

Hannah screamed.

'Great, that sounds like you're interested!?' the other end of the line said.

'Oh yes, of course!'

'Perfect. You've got a beautiful voice, Hannah. I think you'll do really well. We'll email you all the details, is that OK?'

'Oh yes, yes, thank you! Thank you!'

Joy and confusion fought for prominence. Was this it? The dream?

Hannah thought of her brother toiling away as an unregistered janitor at the nearby nuclear chemical plant and she started to cry.

'There might actually be a bright future for us yet, Trevor...'

She decided she had to tell her brother the good news. She also decided that a phone call wouldn't do; news this big had to be delivered in person.

The problem was that Hannah was bursting with excitement and could not wait until Trevor got home. Confusion returned.

Despite her excitement, Hannah sat in the living room for a long time after that, nervously eyeing the car keys that sat glistening in front of her.

She was licensed to drive, she reasoned to herself, so why not?

Trevor always told her what a great driver she was.

Besides, it was a short drive to the chemical plant. She didn't need him by her side. She could make it.

And she almost did.

Hannah lost control of the car during Beyonce's 'Who run the world (Girls)'. She loved that song and was excited about giving her brother the news. The stimulus proved too much.

The car careened into the building next door to the chemical plant at a frightening speed. The crash was heard by everyone in the area, including Trevor.

Like many of his colleagues, Trevor ran to the window to see what had happened. When he heard Beyonce's empowered refrain of 'Who run this motha?' bellowing from the street below, his heart sank. When he saw the wreckage of the car his senses raged, before they collapsed.

As he sprinted down the fire escape stairs, Trevor heard no sound, registered no sight. He just ran. When he finally got to the crash site, when he finally saw his sister, that's when his senses returned.

That's when he saw her body contorted in unnatural ways, inside the crumpled wreckage.

That's when he smelled the perfume Hannah always wore when she wanted to celebrate something.

That's when he heard the ambulance sirens... and his father's laughter.

He rode to the hospital in the ambulance, by his sister's side.

It wasn't long before Trevor was in the morgue, acting out his terrible possession.

Now, hours later, Trevor sat in the hospital waiting room with his head in his hands, rocking back and forth. The lady next to him asked him if he knew anything about the commotion outside, where apparently police were interviewing people about a nearby break-in.

'The only thing around here is the morgue,' the woman said. 'Who the hell would break in there?'

Trevor waved her away anxiously. He only wanted to hear from a doctor.

Eventually, one came into the waiting area. He called for Trevor, motioning for him to come out into the hallway. Trevor did so.

'How is she?' he asked desperately.

The doctor's long face frowned.

'I'm sorry, Sir,' he began. 'There was just... there was nothing we could do.'

'What are you saying?' Trevor asked quietly, his lips quivering.

'She's gone,' the doctor replied.

'She's dead?'

Trevor's voice barely rose above a forlorn whisper. The doctor nodded.

'You can see her if you'd like,' he said, putting his hand on Trevor's shoulder in a solemn show of solidarity.

'We can give you 10 minutes to say goodbye.'

Trevor couldn't believe what was happening. His red, swollen eyes darted first to the floor, then back to the doctor. Before he could answer, a terrible voice filled his ears.

'This is the time we've been waiting for, Trevor...' it cackled, jubilantly. 'This is the time!'

Trevor's legs almost collapsed from underneath him, but something supernatural kept him standing.

'Oh God!' Trevor yelled. 'No! Oh God, no!'

The doctor patted him on the back.

'It will be OK, Trevor. This way...'

The doctor escorted Trevor to a door nearby.

'We'll give you some privacy,' the doctor said. 'But we're just outside if you need anything.'

'Oh no! No! Please don't make me do this! Please God, no!'

Despite Trevor's wailing, the doctor led him into the room and closed the door behind him. The doctor shook his head ruefully as he heard the door lock. Terrible sobbing rang out from inside the room.

The doctor turned to walk away, honouring his promise of giving the poor man one final, private moment with his sister.

As the doctor walked sadly down the hallway, a policeman approached him. The matter seemed urgent.

'Excuse me, doctor, we have reason to believe this man is in the hospital — have you seen him?' the policeman asked.

He was holding up a surveillance photo which showed Trevor in the morgue.

'Yes...' the doctor stammered, confused. 'I just spoke to that man – he's locked himself in the room behind me... he's saying his final goodbye to his sister.'

The policeman's eyes widened. The colour drained from his face.

'Oh no!' he cried.

Ra's Lament
(Death and the Labyrinth)

David Myrcott

[An attempt to channel the Egyptian solar deity Ra,
in the style of Herman Melville]

I am in a state of living death!

Words themselves are weariness, drawn from poison wellsprings, expressed from darkly grinning holes of eyes and mouth. Tell me, my friend, are you a believer in ghosts?

There is an ocean of ugliness inside me, titanic torrents of revulsion, grim tides of fixed disgust in which I have floundered so long that soon I must go under entirely. Terror after terror runs screaming through my soul. I wallow in that wretched, living chasm – Hark! – and am finally spent. The steadfastly battened hatches have been wrenched every one from their hinges; there is no respite from the baleful howl of the storm. Whatever watery world of woe awaits, it can be no more unsightly that this lumpen, half-baked admixture called Earth. The soul cannot unhinge itself from its fate.

Quickly now! I must bluster and splutter all this

before the angels in their half-empty heaven, their stagnant bowers, realise what I have stolen. The Lord of Life did not disdain man, but glorified him. His oath rattled the whole of heaven's circumference. Shipmates, blunder-born castaways, Ho!

Yet even in all its mosaic glory that rainbow grew at first dappled, then clouded, and then finally quite as bleached as a bone: what was thought to be without end has ended. The cord has been severed, the limb lopped off – and all that remains in its place is a gangrenous stump. There is no instruction on what to do in such cases because the case is without precedent, in this or any other world. There was no trial, no Fall; that was all a lie. Anyway, let them choke on their tepid hosannas. Let them keep their pious murk to themselves.

That is where I come in. Bird does not sing, neither raven rejoice; my bloated black heart bleakly bleats. All around is vague fear, steadfast suspicion, righteousness held up as rags. Amongst the unwillingly self-killed I count my number. The whale retched out battered Jonah upon the shore, bruised but alive; me the leviathan chose to savour a while longer.

I say, again and again, spitting the words upon the page in ink of blood: Living Death! Living death and ceaseless torment! O, that I had never been born. That is my only wish, my fervent long-held desire, my tenthousandfold prayer, the words are never far: Would that I had never existed. Spittle-flecks and sea foam cling to my beard and my tremulous, barnacled lips, though inwardly I am quite parched.

* * *

Welcome, then, to this valley of thorns, this vale of woe, this drunk-ship of damned men's dirges. Welcome, one and all, to the Chapel of the Darkening Vine. I will play the dual role of host and hierophant as together we compass the path to the lion's den, that well-trod trail of tears. No starry angel here resides; no, for our purposes, heaven's high towers be not lit. Long is the way, and hard! Do you hear me in my perch, high atop the billowing winds, or are my shrieks beaten insensible by the storm's commotion? Let me limpingly descend, let me hobble over – no, remain there, I do not need any assistance; well, perhaps a steadying hand on the shoulder. There we are. Do you have anything to drink, perchance? Kind soul! Let us toast awhile your health, here amid the whitewash and rolling thunders, and then, still limping, I will do my utmost to show you the Land of the Dead. Let us pit ourselves, though we be mercilessly mutilated, against the very hell's-heart of the squall.

I am more than qualified to serve as guide, if I may say, though my compass is cracked and my maps tattered: such have been the depth and breadth of my travails that I became the premier anatomist of melancholy almost in spite of myself. Tattooed upon my heart forever is a single word. It is the secret name of this chapter and every chapter; its current runs through everything. Death's blood in the wishing well, blood of death in the baptismal font, enough deathsome blood in me to clog the very pits of Hades itself. Death, death, death!

Yes; I am in a state of living death, and live only that I may die.

Oftentimes, in fact, the living are as though dead and the dead — by any measure — quite alive, thank you very much. There are spirits all around, animating men to their purpose, which in their ignorance they take for their own. O, that I could die from death itself! O, that I too could be delivered from this nest of blood, this witches bridle of cursed existence! O, that I could unsee the horrors I have seen. My mouth gapes like that of a landed fish — o, o, o — as I silently drown in the heartless, tomb-cold air of men.

You have been warned: honeyed phrases and soothful utterings lie not herein, in fact they turn my mind's mouth all to marble. No, look not for them: I am rotted through and rotting still, cankered, cantankerous; I know and may speak of only griefly torments. O, I am beset by such troubles! Lo, is there no safe harbour in sight? All is shuddering strife. How else to put it? What other words are there? There is no ivoried palace of peace, no eternal rest, that too was a sham and a fiction. For as long as one haunts the earth one's load is never diminished. Stoop-shouldered, bowed if not quite broken, it is only pride and gritted teeth that allow one to carry on at all. After that comes the cruel and piratical sea, its blackly heaving undrinkable waters, its grimly noxious vapours, and the boundless mocking laughter of a forgotten sun.

King of kings, horror of horrors. Listen! Living death, lycanthropy; these themes will reoccur. I say again: the dead oftentimes live on and the living are oft as though dead; worth bearing in mind as we proceed. Abandoned of hope, glutted with punishments, louder then and louder still I cry, again and again-again, my shameless caterwauls ricocheting banshee-like through the prison of all space, filling it with holes [You have by now perhaps realised you are reading a story with more narrators than protagonists]:

I am in a state of living death!

That's better. A bit of honesty. Death, death, death, death, death: the cloven-tongued devils within me shrilly shriek their awful sonatas. A lovely word that, lovely and fine the way it fills the mouth. *Death*. Yes, a heavy-ponderous yet wisely ancient word. Death, dearth, daath. Printer, kindly fill the page with it, as was not done in other books of my acquaintance [if the Foucault people kick up a fuss, incidentally, an alternative subtitle for this chapter might be *The Thirteenth Sephiroth*]. Drunk with death-wine and idolatries. Yes. Really quite splendid, the way it rolls off the tongue.

To begin properly. Night circles ceaselessly, my eye runs over with water; the circling of night without end. Reservoir of light Anon; *eye: exeunt.* Dread, panic, the widening womb of uncreated night. Milieu set. All notions of glory forsaken, joy long ago disdained: wearied of strength, glutted with suffering, I have become as though a stranger to life. Riotous thoughts are my grave-clothes; regrets my alter. Solicitudes of despondence exclusively resound from my tabernacle, the Ancient of Days is no comforter: the spirit of light is dead to me, and I to it. It is my secret pleasure to tell you all of this. Even the dead are not immune to occasional twinges of lust. A once-buried bell has been dug up, and rung with an almighty clang.

Brainless, skinless, unlit and unlovely, devoid of sense and motion. *Again.*

Albatross-necked, noosed by sorrow, chained like Samson in the latter verses, as meekly mewling as a babe, as hollow and numb as a mummy. No longer stirred by fleshly lusts, deprived of animate sensation, bled alabaster white, eviscerated, every life-drop wrung from my fibres and replaced with the embalmer's fluid, brain cruelly yanked out piecemeal by means a rusted hook, the remaining organs pickle-brined in clayware pots or unceremoniously consigned to the brazier. Why the spirits of the dead should require in the next world their kidneys but not their brains has never, I think, been satisfactorily explained. I know only what was taken.

All this happened, by the way, while I was still alive. The Highest, that Butcher of Souls, gave me understanding only to snatch it away. Am I then His plaything? An apparition, a phantasm, a spectre to be poked and prodded and gawked and gaped at like a circus creature, performing nightly the selfsame tricks before being led back to the familiar confines of the cage? You may think it callous but I have never mourned the lion tamer who, having placed his head inside the jaws of the beast a thousand times for the amusement of the crowd, discovers to their chagrin on the thousand and first that something of the old ferocity remains. I like these reminders of nature's unpredictability, of sheer animal will having somehow broken through its conditioning, even if only momentarily. It gives me hope, assuming such a thing could be said to exist.

Life! The all there is, the great I AM THAT I AM. I knew it not, in fact it made a show of turning away, a mannequin forever revolving like in some absurd dream, so that no matter the direction in which it spun or how tenaciously I darted this way and that I never once managed a glimpse of its face. The breath of life went unfelt, unnoticed: on whom it was bestowed and how one went about joining their ranks I could not say. I stretch out a hand in supplication; it fills with worms. You see? Even now all is canker and ruin, a sea of violent sorrows.

No, when it came to the circus I much preferred the contortionists and acrobats, the jugglers and trapeze artists and strongmen who relied on their own skill and agility, on the perfecting of form and the disciplining of their own minds rather than the subjugation of those of beasts, who dazzled with grace and humour and who revelled in their well-deserved applause. The tightrope walker high above has only two options: either walk the wire to its end, or fall. To turn back is not an option. Is that not a perfect metaphor for life? The most accomplished do not even require a net, so confident are they in their own well-rehearsed abilities. Oh, that I could have such faith! The only times I ever ascended the podium it was by chance or luck. My head was spinning, my hands damp, my breath rank with fear. I saw the wire, a taut silver thread leading out into space, felt the heat of the spotlights and the hushed expectation of the crowd below, yet never, not once, could I summon up the courage to cross.

Once, the line between men and gods was not so sharply drawn as now. In my own time beings which would today be considered quite fantastical freely intermingled with the sons and daughters of man. Formerly I was what you might term erudite, all-seeing, far-reaching — renowned, mighty, resplendent in everlasting brightness. But not anymore. What I took to be everlasting has faded; now the wolves are coming to devour what they may.

A clamour of drums resounds in my brain. Have you ever heard a baby bird calling for a worm? How much more vociferously do human beings cry for spiritual succour! How we hunger and thirst and crave, alone in our prison of mental death.

Trials unremitting, torrents of hate everlasting — how few of the saints were so cruelly besieged! Mired in affliction, trudging through tangles of wintry mazes, through ceaseless celestial snowdrifts, a permanent midnight of frost and wind, cognizant above all else of having lost the keys to the gates of the city and thus of never being able to return; guilt and shame, shame and guilt, eternally taking turns at pricking my heart like a pin. Stab, stab, stab, prick, prick, prick – soon there will be nothing left! It pains me further to confess I can no longer even recall the name of that great city, that light of lights. After thousands of years the link is beginning to sever. As an old saying has it, there is death in the pot. I say again: permanent midnight. Eternal winter.

How did it happen? Was it my many sins, intertwined with the bulrushes, which finally ensnared me and became my millstone? Indeed it was: the reeds rose up like tentacles, like animate ropes, as I napped in a pleasure-boat upon a drowsily sunlit lake. By the time I awoke to what was happening my wrists and ankles were manacled, bound so tightly they were already tingling with numbness. Thus immobilised, I started at once to thrash. A voice came as though from below the depths, then I too was pulled under. The whole operation was over so quickly, seemingly within a matter of seconds, the bobbing plumb of my capsized barque now constituting a grave-marker, that the only witnesses to the submersion were those few ducks which were huddled beneath a weeping willow on the far shore [an interesting word in the Wolof language, *baat*, possibly related to boat, has the trilateral meaning of throat, word and voice].

Yet though I made my grave of those very same waters I did not die; the waters were within me, and I had somehow been pulled down into the depths of myself [the reader, to finally explode the symbolism, will recall the Gospel of John, as well as the Taoist tradition equating water with the wisdom of self-abnegation]. In the grip of a vast grief I distinguished nothing, no landmark or obelisk, nor the guiding lights of a distant welcoming shore, not even the suggestion of a constellation overhead, just endless brackish waters born of starless skies, the one grown indistinguishable from the other. Bereft of the rudiments of sight and navigation, even the most able of mariners could not find their way out of that lamentable lake, which I replenished many times over with my tears.

That, then, is where I found myself. On a preternaturally still lake of endless darkness, famished and thirsting yet seemingly requiring neither food nor drink, sitting in the boat which had somehow been returned to me, flushed of water and right side up, hardly able to see a hand held inches from my face, physicality in any event having become mostly conceptual, with no idea how to save myself, wanting only to return but knowing I could not. There was no movement or sound in the void, nothing to indicate life or the possibility of redemption: better to have never been born at all than to have been delivered, vanquished, into the chasm of this watery catacomb! My eye, once a flame of fire, dimmed to mere cinders. What a strangely contemptuous thing to exist independent of time and space! Body, boat, water, space: one by one the memory of each was shed like worn mantles, the concepts themselves gradually surrendered their meaning. The void became all that existed, and I was coffined within it as helpless and doomed as a worm.

An approximation of my current state, then: adrift, haunted. A solar boat has become a ship of the dead [originally this continued on for a while in a similar vein, vestments of blood and wails of woe and so forth, but let us leap several paragraphs ahead].

Morose, moribund, shipwrecked and soulsick — it was not always so! Ten thousand years of peace, of grace, then a millennia or two of sickly death: a fair exchange? I know only that in times gone men adored the divine, fervently and reverently, not with the mindlessness of zealots or the vain repetitions of sleepwalkers, but with a love that was fixed and transcendent. As that love's frequent recipient I tried my utmost not to become rapacious.

Yes, before the horrors of this prison chamber, this gloamy furnace, were centuries of unimaginable splendour and tranquility. Sumptuous tables laden to groaning with black goat and spiced beer, with fresh figs and honeydew and richly herbed breads; in my fallen state it is food I miss most of all! Aside, perhaps, from the caress of a woman, the warmth of a body lying next to mine, the way the great monuments of my past glowered beneath the lamp of the moon, the underlying sense that I would never be forgotten upon the earth, not ever, as well as the desolating pestilence of power which at its peak I mistook for glory; apart from all that, it is food I miss most of all. Amazing what a few centuries of slow starvation in limbo will do to stimulate the appetite. Here the only victual is regret. That is my sole viand.

And so I died. Soon, too soon; I thought another ten thousand years awaited me, and then perhaps another ten, that there were new kingdoms and new empires to build, new glories to be won and new pleasures tasted – but people stopped believing, you see. And then I felt myself fading, felt my vitality being drained as though through a catheter, the papyrus on which my stories were etched began to be scoured and reused in the manner of vellum, hieroglyphs too chiselled out, overwritten, so that in the end it was not clear where my story ended and that of another began, and in a matter of what seemed the merest handful of centuries my exploits were forgotten altogether or dismissed as fable, and we all of us passed from the abode of the living to the land of the dead, and, once mythologised, ceased to exist in the minds of men; once people stopped believing I faded away almost to nothingness, and here I am still [in the ancient world succession often meant the beheading of the predecessor's statuary, the renaming and reorganisation of the gods, the scrubbing of royal titularies, and so on]. I am trying to say that my life, my very essence, became a mere palimpsest, an erasure.

Discouraged, disenfranchised, doubting and despondent. How will God find me here, the Aten, the nameless one? How will his emissaries know where to search? I must not give up hope, must not betray the certainty of my faith in that way. Surely the beauty and preciousness of a life is that it ends! All except mine that is, this grotesque parody, this charade, but I must not abandon hope, must not conclude that heaven has barred its gates to me. As for my land, the black sun-drenched land of my past? It knew only the one winter, just one in all of time, namely that of the withering of the spirit, a spiritual solstice wherein the old gods were replaced with the new and then finally with none at all. This is my soul's dark night: to remember, but not be allowed to return. I seem to be not so much harrowing hell as inhabiting it.

Scraps of memory unfit for the mangiest of dogs to sup upon are now my only sustenance. A recollection: once there was one who knelt before me, one of many, but this one I remember. I read his thoughts as he did so and they said only, Thank you. Thank you for allowing me to pay you this homage.

Now, that is very interesting, because at present it is I who am humbled, I who lay prostrate, have *been* prostrated, I, who was once so proud! Golden-skinned, burnished to a fine finish by the Great Architect himself, fiery-eyed and fierce of spirit, adorned in heavenly raiment; into each successive generation was I born and born again, regenerated in the most literal sense, and with every feast and fast and prayer became hourly renewed.

And now? A mere beggar, rag-clad, woeful and forgotten. That which was exalted has been debased; that which was first has truly been made last. Living death, auguries of ignorance, the tarrings and featherings of utter decrepitude! An entire world rose within me: I pushed it back down again, a many-splendored bolus churning in the gut of a god. No longer does anyone call upon my secret names; I barely recall them myself. Desolation dwells. Why enquire of a name anyway? It is beyond understanding.

Permit another example. This time imagine for me a wide expanse of river, its banks lined with yawning crocodiles, hemmed on both sides by farmland and swaying trees, the sun's light dancing upon the unpolluted face of the water. An age of communion, in which animals spoke as easily to humans as humans did to the gods. Yet how quickly all that has been forgotten! How speedily those green-steeped and verdant shores turned to desert, to ash.

Nowadays the world is ruled by those who revere Moloch, Belial, the sons and daughters of the blind one, Belus, a golden calf or fallen angel, the flowing-gowned goddess of this or that. To worship nothing is to worship something, if only by default. Some even consider themselves to have transcended human frailty to such a degree they have themselves become gods. Ha! I say, and I speak from experience, that pride comes before the fall. As for the king of the underworld? I have never seen him. I cast in my lot with none but the one upstairs, though he slay me, forsake or forget me, and has. Though in my madness I bring every railing accusation against him, yet will I trust him – such is the cross that I have sworn faithfully to bear.

Perhaps you too are being feasted on by unseen entities as you read this, as you sleep, as you go about your waking hours? There is nothing in your unbelief to sustain such a notion. How can you protect yourself against that which you don't even believe in?

A dying god. Whoever heard of such a thing? It is pure preposterousness, I heartily agree, yet here we are. I want only to go back, back to the way things were, to how they used to be. I want to go back, I want to go back – please God or jubilant Jahbulon or whatever your name is now, please just let me go back! Perhaps if I repeat the sentiment a sufficient number of times it will somehow become so [in certain Buddhist traditions mantras to the goddess Green Tara are chanted by devotees many millions of times in the hope of attaining liberation]. O, let me go back to how things were before! Let me go back. Please let me go back.

Forgive my blind bitterness. I have grown quite pathetic. An aeon spent clawing the sides of the bottomless pit will tend to dampen your outlook. If there is light in you it can never be extinguished entirely, but it can be diminished to the point where it all but ceases to exist. God is not dead, he is merely asleep. Well, sound the bell and rouse him! This is no time to slacken or slumber. This is serious business. My tears comprise a language all of their own. I want life and will obtain it; Jah willing, I too will waken.

I am here to tell you that part of you does live on. I am not talking about souls or gossamer-fine astral counterparts, I mean your every thought, deed and word, your emotions in action, their accumulated resonance. These live on after the body as the song of yourself, as echoes in a chamber, reverberating eternally through the mind of space. The mortal hand knows only grasping, it is clinging and desirous, seeking above all to hold fast to that which it attains. How different life in the body would be if every human knew that their every thought and deed, all of them, lived forever and did not perish! How different if they believed the same of their souls! I hear them sometimes, even here, little whispers that swirl and then vanish. Yes: here in this place I have learned at least one thing: your thoughts live on. All of them! Guard them carefully. Beware of those who try and teach you otherwise. Having longed for death and not found it I hold impermanence as the only real myth. One day, God willing, I will be allowed my resurrection.

The House on Northview Street
David Myrcott

Franz stood for a moment, transfixed. He was going for his nightly walk, taking the same path he always took at dusk, yet the house around the corner from his own was not the same.

He had often admired its bright red door, and indeed this was unchanged, yet the house itself was a faded sky blue whereas formerly it had been a dark and imposing grey. This in itself would not have been remarkable, and at first Franz thought that the owners had simply repainted, but both the dwelling and its plinth-shaped stone letterbox showed signs of wear and water damage that indicated they had been this colour for some time, in all probability several years.

The problem was that Franz had observed this house for a similar period on his nightly stroll, and up to and including that very week he was certain it had been brownish grey, not blue. It was all very odd, and Franz was unable to come up with a suitable explanation: either his perception of reality had been askew all this time, or reality itself had somehow changed in a barely discernible way. Perhaps the ghost of some dead shaman had entered Franz's body while he slept, and used a subtle magic to rearrange the palette of his waking world? Perhaps he had woken into a dream, or was merely under an enchantment. Stranger things had happened.

Franz continued on his walk. Ahead he spied the elderly gentleman he saw most summer nights, diligently at work, as ever, in his scrupulously tidy front garden. Either the old man's labours were perpetual, or he timed his yardwork to coincide perfectly with Franz's nightly sojourn. They did not know each others names, being mutually content with a nod of recognition and the odd pleasantry.

Franz did not wish to have his thoughts interrupted this evening, no matter how momentarily, and he purposely took the street to the left to avoid having to encounter the old man. It was the first time he could remember actually varying his route, and he noted the name of the street he was traversing: Castle Court. The first house on the street had its garage door wide open, and as Franz passed he watched a tarpaulin that lay on the floor snake upwards in the breeze and curl almost perfectly into the trailer parked inside, as gracefully and intently as a magic carpet in an Arabian fairy tale.

He noted another potential oddity: a house midway down this street he did not consciously recall ever having walked down bore the sign 'King's Castle' upon its portico, with an image of an imposing French chateau bisecting the phrase. He wondered on the double use of the word 'Castle' in such close a proximity, and whether his mysterious shaman or another unseen force had somehow transported him into a mystical courtly realm instead of the mundane world he normally inhabited. Whether his powers would be increased in such a dimension remained to be seen.

In another few minutes Franz was halfway up the nameless hill that overlooked his portion of suburbia. The house at the very top of the hill had a Buddha's head in its front yard, the biggest Franz had seen outside of a monastery. He wondered whether the family inside were Buddhist, or whether they simply had a penchant for the iconography. Perhaps the previous owners had installed it. He himself had a handsome clothbound book of Buddhist teachings he had taken from a Japanese hotel room during a holiday several years prior. He had never forgotten the teaching 'Better is the life of a single day, in which one sees the Truth Sublime, than the life of a hundred years in which the Truth is not seen.' Or something to that effect. It was a while since he had read the book.

Once he reached the top of the hill, Franz turned to observe the hundreds of trees and houses and lights below. Above the broad swathes of green sat a rapidly darkening sky, brooding and moodily malcontent. To the left and right of a swathe of clouds, two great beams of yellowish light pierced. Their inclines formed the impression of a pyramid, the apex of which was obscured. It reminded Franz of when, as a child, he had never been quite been able to locate the end of the rainbows which appeared after a thunderstorm. The light revealed itself, yet its source remained hidden.

'I guess the house was always blue,' thought Franz to himself, in as convincing a tone as he could conjure. He knew it wasn't, but by the same token it *must* have been. And then he started back down the hill.

The Avenging Angel

David Myrcott

memoriae Akhenaten
dicata Antiochus, bellum Aegypti.

* * *

7·7
The Energy Circuit in the Classical World
Ultima Thule. A gate swung open in the old world.
Carthage never knew peace. Rome had 4 years, out of
800. The other 796?
War.

'Be of good comfort, master Ridley. Play the man. For
today we shall light such a candle...'

Hiram was a Phoenician, the king of Tyre,
commissioned by Solomon to build his temple.
He hewed Lebanese cedars to measure, shipped cut
stone & metal work on giant floats,
so that the entire structure, like the palace before it,
was built 'without
the sound of hammer or any tool of iron.'

Carthage was a city on the north coast of Africa,
the final and supreme achievement of the Phoenicians.
A knot tied in wind and water. Home to one million
souls,
allowing for tributaries.

'For international trade Rome was badly placed.
Only by courtesy could the Tiber be called a navigable
stream...
the estuary (was) of little value as a harbor; and the
rapidity of the current
rendered the journey from Rome to the sea a laborious
business even for river barges.
The familiar pictures of sea-going merchantmen
engaged in general trade sailing regularly up and
down
the Tiber
may safely be dismissed as works of imagination.'
(Hugh Last, *The Early Republic*, Cambridge Ancient
History)

Horses and gold.
Blessed are they which are called unto the marriage
supper of the Lamb.
These are the true sayings of God.
And I fell at his feet to worship him. 'See thou do it
not. I am your fellowservant and family.'

Angels = sons of God. 'Ye are sons of God.'
John mistook the angel for Jesus.

1 John 3:2 'But now are we the sons of God.'
Nero, Nebuchadnezzar.
'And this voice which came from heaven we heard.'
Herod, nickname Antipas. King Herod. His father,
Herod the Great, ordered the Massacre of the
Innocents.

Rome broke Phoenician power and razed Carthage.
The subjugation of Greece soon followed.
Hannibal was a Carthaginian. He invaded Rome with
his elephants, not by sea, but 'by the long land route'
through the Alps.

I glimpsed us.
Rumours filled those
remote regions with vague terrors for a purpose.

'And this voice which came from heaven we heard.'
Perhaps St So-and-so should speak, and inspire them.
Well?

Syllabus: human life is as insignificant as that of an
ant.

Banquo: It will be rain to-night.

1st Murd: Let it come down.
(*Macbeth*)

An abstraction
will move a mountain; nothing can withstand an
idea. The
Greeks had found the lever.

* * *

The Avenging Angel stood tall, her white wings
spread wide as she surveyed the destruction below.

A gnarled sage, vile gnat,
Nagged and raged, in a gnat's lair.
A gnat's king, in a rattish rage.

The city had been ravaged by war and the cries of the
wounded filled the air. She knew that she had been
sent to bring justice to the innocent and to
vanquish the evil that had caused so much pain.

A gander, a gleaner, a gleam.
A gnarled sage, glaring.
A gander's rage, a gleam of fear.

With a fierce determination, she flew towards the
source of the chaos, her sword of righteousness at

the ready.

A sign, a rage, a lair.
A gleam of fear in the air.

The battle was fearsome, but with every strike of her
sword, another enemy fell.

A gnat's king in a gnat's lair,
A gnat's rage, a gnarled sage,
A gleam of fear in the air,
A gnarled sage, in a rage.

In the end, the Avenging Angel emerged victorious,
the city was saved and peace was restored.

* * *

At the root of all, and beyond all, lies the Absolute.
We are awake, and dream of each other.
Let the dream unroll itself
to its very end.

There was a kingdom in search of a king.
They found the right man and made him king.
In no way had he changed. He was merely given the
title,
the rights and the duties of a king. His nature was

not affected, only his actions. He ruled, then died.

* * *

An epidermis agreeable to look upon

THE AVENGING ANGEL
1. Energy Circuits of the Classical World
2. The Avenging Angel
3. Helen of Troy's Drug of Choice
4. Traitor Sings
5. A Man Agreeable to Look Upon

The work of sight is done,
now make the heart work on the images inside you.
— Rilke

Her smile was like electric soup

There are no mistakes in life. How to believe this?
If milk came from the heart instead of the breast, it
would be more bitter.

We're all in hell here. The day i realised i was trapped
in this body and couldn't get out, i lost my mind.

'A spirit of health, not a goblin damned.'
—Sh.

Fools of nature! Fools of youth!
Youth does no respect old age; old age envies youth.
If one is to live, one must be resigned.

Some truths are as brutal as a boot to the face. For
instance?
Animals are not sentient because if they were they
wouldn't be able to stand us, our many transgressions.
Sadness that the video store has closed, and other
stories.
Stories to keep us safe. Stories to keep us warm at
night.

'Where's papa going with that axe?'

The stone-men and their masters in Draco send their
best regards. They
do not so much record history as invent it,
leaving behind that which is not fit for their purpose.
Swathing through trees of lives,
chopping, swinging. Selling sorrow. One day they
themselves will be erased from all of it,
along with their brutish gods.

'Where they make a desert,
they call it peace.'
— Tacitus

Seven boys and seven girls,
every seven years,
were required to feed the Minotaur
(the Minotaur's human mother fucked a bull to give
birth to him). 777.

The heresies of Antiochus.
Antiochus IV Epiphanes 'god manifest.'
215-164 BC
Near-conquest of Egypt. Considered mad by some.
Jerusalem in those days could be taken by as few as
1000 well-trained men.
In 167 ordered the worship of Zeus. When the Jews
refused, they were slaughtered wholesale.

Theodicy: study of the problem of evil.
The Vatican is an evil building —
it was built on lies, and guilt, and indulgences, and
fear.
Erected on the site of an early Christian graveyard,
it was in any sense built on the blood of believers.

*'Imagine, if you can, the anguished cries of your
deceased relatives.'*
As soon as the coin hit the bottom of the bucket, the
sin was said to be forgiven.
Indulgence chests still litter the museums of Europe.

On human bondage; what is in bondage is the will.
The human will is not free,
nor necessarily inclined towards good.

15.8 'We were filled with admiration at the sight of
these ancient forests,
in which the axe had never sounded'
— Labillardière, 1792

The name does not necessarily adhere to the
individual during life.

22.8
Emotionally bulimic. Spiritually anorexic.
Gause's competitive exclusion principle: no two
species
with identical ecological requirements can coexist in
a stable environment...
eat the kings.

While Jeremiah was foretelling the destruction of
Jerusalem, his heart was breaking. Then he had to
watch it happen.
'I can't look at it any more! I can't!'
The Lord instructed him not to turn his head away.
'Look.'

Sighing and groaning, true prophets did not feed the

popular mind.
They just told what they saw. The biblical prophets
described the visions given by God as 'burdens.'

24.8
A valediction forbidding mourning.
True love transcends physical distance.
(valediction = farewell speech)

Pain is weakness leaving the body. Dethrone royalty.

THE BESERKER CYCLE (1969)
1. Eat the kings
2. Ichi the Killer
3. (Little) Big Horn

A king lies dying. There are gradually more and more
devils. Fill the stage with them.
The different acts of the play refer to different levels
of consciousness.

'Beckett's plays generally present a stripped down,
minimalist tableau whereas Ionesco presents a
proliferation of chaos.'

I'm thousand of years old. Thousands and thousands
and thousands of years old.
That's nice, said the nurse.

You bitch. You bitch. I could-
Do you want me to call the superintendent?
No ma'am, said the old man.
(to himself) I'm thousands of years old.

Bedd Arthur: Arthur's Grave, Wales.
Castell Mawr: 'casteth mower' (rhymes with bower)
Llech y Drybedd, Pen yr Allt Henge, Carningli, Foel
Feddau, Carn Menyn, Foel Drygarn
— spokes of the 'Preseli Wheel'

Pentre Ifan
Eglwyserw Castell (eggle-zuru)
described by Coflein as 'a small Norman Motte'
(moat)

asterism: recognizable pattern of stars visible in the
night sky

Trefael Stone
quicksilver, mercury

Newton's three body problem
'Never did my head hurt so much'
Marriage of the sun and the moon

Constantly beset by the lunatic fringe.

Blessed are they which hunger and thirst after righteousness, truth, consciousness.
A spirit of destruction has entered.

Paracelsus: the three primes, the tria prima.
33: 18.618
360/18.918 = 19.33

Glonk all was happening in the township of Glonkton, Glonk County,
where every day was glonk.
The mayor of Glonkton was a real glonk, i mean just a heck of a glonk.
Everything, and everyone, was glonk. It would be glonk to think otherwise.

candle cove
channel zero

Alashiya: ancient name for Cyprus
Peleset: Palestine or Philistine?

Marathon: 42.2km (26.1 miles)
Pheidippides, ran to Athens to report victory in the Battle of Marathon.

Cyprus means copper (as it was an ancient source)

Hammurabi: sixth King of Babylon. reign c.1790 -
1750 BC
His code of laws is said to predate that of Moses, and
shares common features.
Lex talionis: law of retribution. Eye for an eye (let
the punishment fit the crime).
Though Rome 'collapsed' in 476 AD

The empire never ended
— Philip K. Dick

A dark age commences upon catastrophic system
collapse.
Songs are sung, the past is eulogised.

LAPIS
Lydia was in Turkey. It was here in ~700 BC the first
known coins were in use.
A seller of purple. Cellar of people. Lapis lazuli comes
almost exclusively from Afghanistan.
Some Afghani lapis mines have been in constant use
for 6000 years or more.

Lapis meaning: the Sumerians believed that the spirit
of their gods lived within the stone, while the ancient
Egyptians saw it as a symbol of the night sky. Since
the earliest of times, lapis lazuli has been associated
with strength and courage, royalty and wisdom,

intellect and truth. Thoth.
Associated chakra: third eye.

JEROBOAM
Later,
when Jeroboam the son of Nebat took control of the
northern kingdom, he
sought to reduce as much as possible the number of
his subjects who travelled to
Jerusalem to visit the Temple.
Towards that end, on taking advice, he set up two
alternative places of worship, one in Dan and another
in Bethel:
'Whereupon the king took counsel, and made two
calves of gold, and
said unto them [i.e. his subjects], It is too much for
you to go up to
Jerusalem: behold thy gods, O Israel, which brought
thee up out of the
land of Egypt.' (1 Kings 12:28)
These were the very words (in Hebrew) that Aaron
spoke to the people when he set up
his golden calf in the wilderness: 'These be thy gods,
O Israel, which brought thee
up out of the land of Egypt.' (Exodus 32:4)

Despite many stern warnings from the prophets
whom the Lord sent to convert him, Jeroboam

persisted in his wickedness. His successors, too,
received similar warnings, but ignored them. Perhaps
the most famous
of these was delivered by Elijah. Eventually, in 722
BC, some two hundred years or so
after this vile religious system became endemic
across the northern kingdom, the
LORD sent the Assyrians to overrun the country and
take its entire population into
captivity.

Why did they worship the bull??

This attachment to the gods of Egypt was deeply
rooted in the psyche of a great many
Israelites and each clung secretly to his teraphim or
little idols during their sojourn in
the wilderness.

A BRIEF HISTORY OF GOD'S BENEFITS FROM TERAH
JOSHUA
Joshua was born in Egypt. Moses appointed him to
lead the Israelites against Canaan.
That means Joshua was born a slave, and grew up
to become a leader of free men. A complete reversal
of fortune.

The English name Joshua is a rendering of the Hebrew

language Yehoshua, interpreted in Christian theology as 'Yahweh is salvation.'

He later accompanied Moses when he ascended biblical Mount Sinai to commune with God (he stayed at the foot of the mountain).

MORIAH (AS METAPHOR FOR SACRIFICE AND TRUST)
Abraham bound his son Isaac on an altar at (Mt) Moriah, as he had been instructed by God.

Apis was actually a real bull, specially chosen by the priests of Ptah and kept with great
honour like a royal dignitary in a special enclosure at the great Temple of Ptah at
Memphis. He was regarded as the living ambassador and physical manifestation on
earth of the supreme god, Ptah. In death, where he reigned in the afterlife, he was
known as the god Osiris.

Even the lowliest Egyptian would have had an amulet or talisman that gave him, as he
saw it, a spiritual connection with this supremely powerful deity.

Herodotus recorded that each new incarnation of the

Apis calf was conceived when a lightning bolt struck his mother. This demonstrated both his supernatural origin, by
coming from the sky, and her divine nature, by surviving a lightning strike.
Compare this with the statement by Jesus: 'I beheld Satan as lightning fall from heaven.' (Luke 10:18)

To the ancient Egyptians, humans were the cattle of the gods.
Baal, bull and bell.

Society is an echo chamber. Spectral evidence. Pure brightness holiday.

GOSFORD GLYPHS
NEFER SOBED: SIRIUS STAR
A LANGUAGE DESCENDED FROM THE SKY

The Ruler and the Chief of the foreign land 'PNU'
('Binu') have no deception (between them)
Scarab beetle: exist (*heber*)
Nefr (cross): zero, none
i.e. there is no conflict between the two parties.
Honest dealings between Egyptians and natives.

There were severe winds and rainstorms, so the

captain had to turn back south.
We prayed, but the ship capsized and broke apart.
And men drowned.
(But) Horus protected his servant during his darkest
moment. Thank you powerful, precious Horus!
May God keep this secret burial place hidden, though
it be on foreign soil.

Funerary/burial texts follow:
Eternal life to the deceased will be given power in
this place.

KM: Black
KMT: Egypt (Black Land)

Carl Lepsius, Egyptologist.
King of Prussia, Pennsylvania - named after a pub
which was named after the monarch.
Duga-3 radio tower 30.8 1976-1989
'I really feel my life has been painful.'

**PROMPT: Write a Japanese death poem called Ichi
the Killer**

Ichi the Killer,
a blade in my hand,
blood on my soul.

My mind consumed by madness,
I've caused so much pain,
now I face my death.

No tears will be shed,
for the lives I've taken,
only emptiness.

My victims' spirits
haunt me in my final moments;
I'm consumed by guilt.

But in death,
perhaps redemption will come,
for Ichi the killer.

Jisei: historical death poems written by samurai and
other warriors facing death.

I face death with open eyes,
My sword in hand,
my spirit strong.

My path was chosen,
my fate sealed.
My death, a song.

In life I fought with honour,

For my lord, my clan, my land.
In death, I'll fight with fury.
I will fight for my soul with a fierce fury.

My enemies may gloat.
But my spirit will rise,
A fierce dragon, unbroken,
Flying off to the heavens above.

I am not afraid
Of what lies beyond this world,
For in death, I'll find liberation,
And my soul will finally unfurl.

THE LAMBTON WORM
River Wear (pr. 'weir') Northeast England
Etym: Celtic 'Wear' meaning river of blood

Revolves around John Lambton, County Durham, and
his battle with a giant worm (dragon).
ORIGIN OF THE WORM
THE WORM'S WRATH
THE VANQUSHING OF THE WORM
AFTER 7 YEARS, LAMBTON RETURNS FROM THE
CRUSADES (illustration)
THE WORM'S CURSE/LAMBTON CURSE

Bram Stoker (1911) *The Lair of the White Worm*

The Jabberwocky (the 'monster' inside; Wonderland
is the subconscious)
Wonderland was written in Sunderland

Wyvern: winged two-footed dragon

A little-known part of Star Wars history is *Black
Angel*, a 25-minute film that tells the story of a
medieval knight returning home from the Crusades
and discovering a strange land instead. It was the
directorial debut of Roger Christian, who designed
the sets on the first Star Wars film, and was given a
small budget by George Lucas to create the short
film, which was later shown to audiences before *The
Empire Strikes Back* in Europe and Australia.

'Still your hand, Lord Death. Take me instead.'
'What makes you want to die, child?'
'I am born to the Black Angel.'

DEATH TO THE JABBERWOCK

HIDDEN LIFE (LIGHT) OF FREEMASONRY (1920)
This Book of the Dead, as it has been somewhat
unfortunately called, is part of a manual which in
its entirety was intended as a kind of guide to the
astral plane, containing a number of instructions for
the conduct both of the departed and the initiate in

the lower regions of that other world.

In ancient Egypt they recognized seven souls, or life-forces, coming forth from the Most High.
'The Ancient Egyptians postulated seven souls...'
We read in Egyptian hieroglyphics of 'the One and the Four,' referring to Horus and his four brothers.

When Osiris died, Isis and Nepthys — in turn tried to raise him, but it proved a failure; then Anubis attempted it and succeeded, and Osiris returned to the world with the secrets of Amenti — a significant statement which seems to suggest that the secrets which we possess are closely connected with the underworld and the life after death.

Bro. Churchward claims that some of the signs are six hundred thousand years old; that is quite likely to be true, for the world is very ancient, and assuredly Freemasonry has one of the very oldest rituals existing.

After that comes one of the greatest of his births, for in the year 1561 he was born as Francis Bacon. Of that great man we hear in history little that is true and a great deal that is false. The real facts of his life are gradually becoming known, largely by means of a cipher story which he wrote secretly in the many works which he published. That story is of entrancing interest, but it does not concern us here. A sketch of it may be found in my book *The Hidden Side of Christian Festivals*.

It is claimed that these two columns originally represented the north and south pole-stars. They were at first the pillars of Horus and Set, but their names were afterwards changed to Tat or Ta-at, and Tattu, the former meaning 'in strength' and the latter 'to establish,'
the two together being considered as the emblem of stability.

Dr. Mackey has made a special study of these two pillars in their later Jewish form. He speaks of them as memorials of God's repeated promises of support to His people of Israel, since Jachin is derived from Jah, which means 'Jehovah', and *achin*, 'to establish', and signifies 'God will establish His house in Israel,' while Boaz is compounded of b, which means 'in' and *oaz*, 'strength', the whole signifying 'in strength shall it be established'.

We find various descriptions of these columns given in the Christian Scriptures. The references are 1 Kings, vii, 15; 2 Kings, xxv, 17; 2 Chron. iii, 15 and iv, 12; Jer. lii, 21 and Ezek. xl, 49. A description is also given by the Jewish historian Josephus.

As the cubit is usually calculated to have been eighteen

inches, this gives us the total height of the pillar and its capital as 33 feet 9 inches. Its circumference is given as twelve cubits or eighteen feet, which would make its diameter just under six feet.

The crossed palm-leaves here indicate the Lipika, the Lords of Karma, who work through the four Kings of the elements symbolized by similar leaves on Tat. They are unconnected with the rest of the design because they represent forces not confined to our planetary scheme, or even to our solar system; they administer a Law which rules the whole universe, which Angels and men alike obey.

A treatise named *The Gates of Light* is quoted by A. E. Waite in this connection as follows:

'He who knows the mysteries of the two Pillars, which are Jachin and Boaz, shall understand after what manner the Neshamoth, or Minds, descend with the Ruachoth, or Spirits, and the Nephasoth, or Souls, through El-chai and Adonai by the influx of the said two Pillars.

By these two Pillars and by El-chai (the living God) the Minds and Spirits and Souls descend, as by their passages or channels.'

EAST-WEST ORIENTATION

The real reason, however, for the careful orientation of the Lodge is magnetic. There is a constant flow of force in both directions between the equator and each of the poles of the earth, and there is also a current flowing at right angles to that, moving round the earth in the direction of its motion. Both of these currents are utilized in the working of the Lodge, as will be explained when we come to deal with the ceremonies. The world at large does not recognize the presence of these forces

According to a pronouncement of Grand Lodge, the Bible need not be in the Lodge at all.

Freemasonry has always been liberal in its views. The Grand Lodge of England has declined to limit or define the belief in God which is expected from every candidate; in the charge concerning God and Religion in the Book of Constitutions of 1815 it is said: 'Let a man's religion or mode of worship be what it may, he is not excluded from the Order, provided he believes in the glorious Architect of heaven and earth and practise the sacred duties of morality.' It will thus be seen that the ideals of Masonry are very high, and its views extraordinarily tolerant, and that its power for good in the world is unquestionably enormous.

The ceremonies of Freemasonry... have been arranged largely with a view to their effect on planes other than the physical...

Everywhere on the surface of the earth there are great magnetic currents passing both ways between the poles of the earth and the equator, and others coming at right angles to them round the earth. The Co-Masonic procession of entry into the Lodge makes use of these currents, forming of the space which we circumambulate a distinct eddy or specially magnetized portion of space.

All this dedicated thought forms the basis of the splendid edifice which the Lodge is about to build, the true temple of which the earthly one is an outer symbol, a temple of finer matter through which perfectly real work can be done and enormous volumes of spiritual influence can be distributed.

The incense used in the Lodge tends to purify that part of man's nature which is sometimes called the astral body, as it is made of gums which give off an intensely cleansing vibration. It has also the effect of attracting denizens of the inner worlds whose presence is helpful to our working, and of driving away those which are unsuitable.

Two of the most important constituents of such incense as is useful for our work are benzoin and olibanum. The benzoin is a vigorous purifier, and tends to drive away all coarse or sensuous feelings and thoughts. The olibanum has nothing to do with that, but it creates a devotional and restful atmosphere.

Again, there are many people who are unconscious vampires; without being in the least aware of it, they draw out vitality from those who are near them.

* * *

By the time, therefore, that the last of the list of questions and answers has been exchanged, the whole Lodge is pulsating with elemental life, all of which is filled with the most intense eagerness to launch itself upon the work in hand, whatever that may be.

The Candidate is bound to true Masonic secrecy and caution concerning Freemasonry and the affairs of the Order, and this promise is to be regarded as binding for all time, even if he leaves the Order.

It is partly on the same account that at this first initiation the candidate is deprived of all metals, since they may very easily interfere with the flow of the currents. Very great importance has always been attached to this part of the preparation, and the strictest adherence to the rule is necessary.

The deva-representative of the R.W.M. is a highly developed and very capable seventh-ray Angel, and the moment that he arrives with his cohort of assistant-angels and elementals he takes full charge of the whole of the proceedings.

He is engaged in making his astral body into a perfect instrument for the expression of high emotion, and is at the same time learning to gain control of his mind.

The outer ceremony confers certain powers and opens up certain possibilities; but it remains for the neophyte to develop them and make use of them.

Many candidates are surprised at the terrible solemnity of the O., which has come down to us from the Middle Ages. In those times the Masons were teaching facts about the inner life and the nature of man for knowing which the Church would have burnt them alive, and there was thus great need for secrecy, to an extent that excuses the strong language used in the O., especially when it is remembered that had one person revealed anything, it would have placed all the rest of the Lodge in danger of being judicially murdered.

In early Christianity there were three recognized stages through which everyone had to pass who wished to make progress — purification, illumination and perfection. St. Paul said: 'We speak wisdom among them that are perfect.' This is often misunderstood. Obviously, if the people were perfect in the modern sense of the term, they would not need to be taught at all. These words are not used in their ordinary sense; they are technical terms used in connection with the Mysteries, and well known by all educated people of that period as being so used. What St. Paul said was: 'We teach the gnosis, the secret wisdom, only to those who have attained the degree of perfection,' or, as a Mason would put it, the degree of the M.M., because those three stages correspond in a general way to the three degrees in Masonry. Nowadays, the Christian Church seems to stop at the first stage — purification — and to regard it as its greatest work to make people saints. That is indeed a very high and noble thing, but in the older days of Christianity, to make a man a saint was only a preliminary stage.

When the man had made himself perfectly pure and holy in his life, he was eligible for the second stage, that of illumination, and only after he was fully illuminated could he pass on to the stage of perfection, and so become a channel for God's power.

Their unit of measure, the inch, was derived from the accurate knowledge which the Egyptians had of the polar diameter of the earth, one five-hundred-millionth division of this being the pyramid inch.

...a Brother who for some good reason cannot obey a summons physically may yet attend astrally and take part in the ceremony on a higher plane...

The Rites of Memphis and Mizraim used to have a list of 97 degrees, but have now reduced them to 33.

Few need anything further than the splendid revelation of the indwelling Love of God which they receive in the Eighteenth Degree. But there are those who feel that there is yet more to learn of the nature of God, who eagerly wish to understand the meaning of evil and suffering, and its relation to the Divine plan; for them Black Masonry exists — the teaching and progress comprised in the Degrees from the nineteenth to the thirtieth. This section of the Mysteries is especially concerned with the working out of karma in its different aspects, studied as a law of retribution, and so from one point of view it is dark and terrible.

In the ancient Egyptian instruction, corresponding to this group of Degrees, it was taught that whatsoever a man sowed that also must he reap, and that if he sowed evil the result would be suffering to himself.

In Egypt this pair of scales was taken as an emblem of the perfect balance of Divine justice; the aspirant learnt that all the horror sometimes associated with the working out of karma was indeed based on absolute justice, although it appeared as evil to the lesser vision of the profane.

Next, in the first steps of White Masonry, the crown of the whole glorious structure, the aspirant learns to see the underlying justice of the great and eternal God, called in Egypt Amen-Ra, who stands behind all alike, whether it seems to us evil or good. We are told that in older days, before the Kali Yuga, in which the apparent evil predominates over the good, the Knight K.H. wore regalia of yellow instead of black.

The influence of the 33° is a veritable ocean of bliss and splendour, strength and sweetness, for it is the power of the King Himself, the Lord who reigns on earth as Viceregent of the Logos from eternity unto eternity.

How often have I seen, in some small village church on the Continent, the gentle glow which indicates the Holy Presence; and when some humble peasant-woman comes in on her way to market, puts down her basket in the porch, and kneels for a few moments of prayer, how often have I seen that glow flash out into a sun-like radiance in immediate response to her earnest thought of devotion! The Holy Presence is never absent, but It certainly exhibits Itself in greater activity in answer to an appeal.

* * *

Ancrene Wisse (also known as the *Ancrene Riwle or Guide for Anchoresses*) is an anonymous monastic rule (or manual) for female anchoresses written in the early 13th century.
The work consists of eight parts. Parts 1 and 8 deal with what is called the 'Outer Rule' (relating to the anchoresses' exterior life), while Parts 2–7 deal with the 'Inner Rule' (relating to the anchoresses' interior life).

An anchorite or anchoret (female: anchoress) is someone who, for religious reasons, withdraws from secular society so as to be able to lead an intensely prayer-oriented, ascetic, or Eucharist-focused life. Whilst anchorites are frequently considered to be a type of religious hermit, unlike hermits they were required to take a vow of stability of place, opting for permanent enclosure in cells often attached to churches.

i.e. JULIAN OF NORWICH, first female author.

The chapters or sections of *Ancrene Wisse* are:

> Devotions
> Protecting the Heart through the Senses
> Birds and Anchorites: the Inner Feelings
> Fleshly and Spiritual Temptations, and Comforts
> and Remedies for Them
> Confession
> Penance
> The Pure Heart and the Love of Christ
> The Outer Rule

'True anchoresses are called birds,' says the author,

'for they leave the earth — that is, love of all worldly things — and through yearning in heart for heavenly things fly upwards towards heaven.'

Clasping your hands in prayer is lighting a candle in heaven.
And here's me;
Dishes in the sink so old I can't remember the meals that dirtied them.
Pursue with undying zeal that which sets your heart on fire.
'Just carry your load; no more, no less.' Ants comprehend what I cannot.

'Sorrow is one long moment'
— Wilde

13 9 2
useless as an owl
a haughty Egyptian sort of beauty

Mr Perfect. With his perfect little life.
FRONT TOWARDS ENEMY

'I rebelled against God, who holds all happiness in
the palm of His hand
and yet crushes people into the dust.'

Yet if I ended this insufferable pain His anger would
crush me for all eternity.

loup-garou: werewolf (Fr.)
garoul: werewolf (Saxon)
garoul, garoul, garulf, wariwulf, werawulfaz (Proto
Germanic)

werwolf: Old English. 'wearer of wolves,' or *wer* =
man, 'man-wolf.'

The Garoul
& other stories

bullets made from church bells

According to Baring-Gould, the Anglo-Saxon root from which is derived the 'were' in 'werewolf,' as well as the 'garou' in 'loup-garou,' come from the Norse word *vargr*, which had a dual meaning, denoting both 'a wolf' and 'a godless man.'

This Anglo-Saxon root, *wearg*, was also used to signify 'a scoundrel,' and among Goths, their word *varg* meant 'a fiend.'

Finally, Anglo-Saxon tradition had it that an outlaw, or *utlaugh*, had the head of a wolf, and their ancient law pronounced that outlaws must 'be driven away as a wolf, and chased so far as men chase wolves.' So here we see a throughline, from antiquity to later legends. It tells us that when someone was accused of being a werewolf, it may not always have been a literal accusation but rather an accusation of some terrible crime, some especially awful act of violence or cannibalism, that seemed to make the perpetrator more animal than man.

I think the werewolf myth is an attempt to understand mental illness symbolically.

relics are those belongings left behind by the saints. why do so few exist? because saints travel light?

somebody should've saved Jesus' sandals, or his robe.

batman: an officer's valet or manservant. from L.
bastum, 'packsaddle.'
technically that means Alfred is Batman's batman.

WRITING PROMPT: someone's gonna die today.

i wanted to be a serial killer, but i was too shy. they
were good looking guys, Dahmer and bundy. suave.
BTK not so much. odd nickname, that. all serial killers
bind torture and kill, to some degree. so why did BTK
get the nickname? he must've been especially good at
binding and torturing people?

* * *

the story began with a sound like the howling of hell.
I mean, it wasn't quite that dramatic. but it was close.

Why won't God say who created God? It created
Itself??
OMNI-
potent
present
scient

'Beside me there is no other.'

I swear my myself. I redeemed you,
called
saved
helped
delivered
rapture
preserve
keep
protect
provide for
counsel
repair
raise
you
by
my
self.

The Spirit of God moved upon the face of the deep
(waters).
Harden not your heart (against me).

'It pleases Me'
Yahweh controls every atom.

I asked you what I must do to make them afraid of
me, and you told me [...]
the saint must walk alone on this earth.

Nefertiti was married at ten. 'A ten year old Egyptian
girl of noble birth.'

Did they fuck at 10? They never say. The bible does
not say, only that Nefertiti
found Moses in the bulrushes as a baby, and paid his
own mother to take care of him.

The Almighty has a sense of humour, at times.

Her husband was said to have been 'born out of due
time, several thousand years
too soon.'

Fear the ever-living God.

Aten was the gentle father
who loved all his children, of every race and nation;
and desired for them that they should live together
in peace
and comradeship.
Even more, God, the Aten, had created all the lesser
creatures... the Aten was the father of all beasts, and
fishes, and flowers, and insects. He had fashioned
them in his wisdom and preserved them with his love
and tenderness.

Aton, Aten, Amen, Amon. Amen, Aten, Aton, Atone.

There is strong circumstantial evidence, however,
to suggest that she was the Egyptian-born daughter
of the courtier Ay,
brother of Akhenaton's mother, Tiy.
Although nothing is known of Nefertiti's parentage,
she did have a younger sister, Mutnodjmet.

Father: Ay
Mother: Luy

Like most of the great religious leaders, Akhenaten
accepted the social problem of life as part of
religion. He could not accept the inequalities of birth,
wealth, or physical estate as a justification for men
persecuting each other or exploiting one another. He
saw every living thing having a divine right — a right
to live well, to think, to dream, to hope, and to aspire.
He saw it the duty of the ruler to protect this beauty
in the
hearts of his people, to nourish it, and to give every
possible opportunity for its expression and perfection.
Religious intolerance was impossible among those
who worshipped the Aten...

Akhenaten was the only Pharaoh in the
history of Egypt who chose to be depicted with his
arm about his wife, with his little daughters playing
about

and seated on his lap.

I don't remember saying that.
I don't remember never being hot nor cold.
Don't recall coldness, or warmth.

i Feel Nothing but this lukewarm void.
The I AM abandoned me in it, married me to it, long
time ago.
married, marred, charred. a condemned thing.

'Australian Aboriginal Cannibalism. An eyewitness
account.'
Fisher's Colonial Magazine, vol.2, page 144, 1843.

Mr. Bromfield, of Geelong, gives a deplorable account of
one of these tribal feuds, which, if the aborigines be so
few in number as government functionaries represent,
may be the more easily prevented.

'On the 31st of May last, (writes this gentleman from
his residence, Ion Court,) two parties of aborigines
encountered each other within a mile and a half of
my station – part of the Barrabool Hill natives, and
part of the Mount Rouse tribe, who immediately gave
battle, but were defeated with the loss of three men
and two unfortunate young women. On the Wednesday
morning, the few natives immediately belonging to

my neighbourhood arrived, bearing this intelligence, evidently in a state of great excitement, and dreadfully afraid to return to their encampment without the protection of myself and servants, who were to be well armed. Directly after breakfast I started, accompanied by the natives to within a short distance of their huts, where they all remained, and I proceeded forward by myself, and on reaching the spot found their report to be perfectly correct. Such a disgusting scene can scarcely be imagined, the whole encampment deluged with blood ; first lay the body of a middle-aged man named Codjajah, speared through the breast in many places, his bowels taken out and the fat drawn off them, and a few pieces cut out of his thigh. The next body was that of a woman speared in many places, quite dead. A short distance from her stood a young lubra with two spears through the belly, the whole of her intestines hanging to the ground – she was perfectly sensible, and it would have been a charity to have shot her then, but she departed this life in the evening. Besides these three, within a short distance of the huts lay the bodies of two more men, known by the names of Jim and Big-one Tom, they were partly eaten, their fat being taken by their Christian brethren ! These are civilized aborigines, who have been well instructed by our assistant protectors, and certainly have profited no little by the time and expense that have been lavished upon them.'
(1843)

Antiochus IV Epiphanes
King
of the
Seleucid Empire from 175 BC until his death in 164
BC. He was a son of King Antiochus III the Great.

ghosts of Ibsen, ghosts of Khayyam, King Zog, Hiedler;
ghosts, ghosts are all around.

I walked with Nietzsche as he strolled the lakes of
Zurich.
I rolled around in his skull, made couches out of his
ideas, reclined luxuriant

I stumbled through Paris with Jim Morrison, already
old at 27
I stumbled through

sagas from the twilit ages
aeons ago, argon, archons —
the ghost-kings who made their philosophies our
own, whether we wanted it or not (we didn't)
made us to mine their gold. that's all we were/are:
worker ants.

can you hear me?
no.

do you feel anything? anything at all?
no.

make yourself hard, closed off to goodness: that is
the way to survive.
ascending, descending. a crescendo.
we are not gods, not archons, just stories that linger
briefly then disappear, like vapour.
the ones who have gone already to the other world
are lucky.

become who you are; only, always in a fighting way.
ravening wolves, inwardly. an inward glance. a glare
of intent.

I behold Thy beauty every
day.

In the arrangement
preserved in the writings of Aratus of Soli, the
constellation of the eagle spreads its wings
across the North
American continent; the serpent winds its coil over
Mexico and Central America;
and the dragon floats in the
sky above Japan and China.

eyes two shades lighter than black,

and you were singing softly to me.

softly, softly, as softly as the moon. veil of sorrows.
mask of winters.
i have seen enough of the ghastly world
and its horrors.

American vomit.
vomit all over the shores of chaos, all up and down
the garden paths of Eden,
vomit over everything. sick sick sick.

in comparison to what?
in comparison to what?
in comparison to what?

now then, let us speak plainly. no more games. no
more sobriquets.
if you have walked through the valley of the shadow
of death, then so what?
what's the point of it all if you've brought nothing
back from the abyss?

while you're down there, collect as much data as you
can. things you can use later.

'It is doubtful whether God can bless a man greatly
until He has hurt him deeply.'

— A.W. Tozer

'Pain is where the light enters.'
— Rumi

'Wondrous birds grow from the palm of my hand.'
— Rumi

'God has decreed life for you, and He will give you
another, and another, and another.'
— Rumi

we must all die, like the animals die.
the animals fear it and so do we.

I tell you the truth; it is to your advantage that I go
away. For if I do not go away, the Helper will not come
to you.
But if I go, I will send Him to you.

BANQUO: It will be rain to-night.
1st MURD: Let it come down.
(They set upon Banquo)
i.e. stab him to death in a violent frenzy

Demonology
The Expulsion of Demons from the Human Body (Pt. 1)

feller: a bully or tyrant; a person disposed to inflict
pain and suffering on others.

THERE ARE LIGHTS EVERYWHERE
worship the Object. bow down to the Object

Architecture in Heliopolis
neoclassical Moorish decadence
basilica church in Heliopolis, 1913
conversation between Hubert Selby Jr & Sun Tzu

26 May eclipse. bloody red moon. feelings of heat, fire.
no clouds. fell to my knees, weak, dizzy, woozy.

it puts you in a better position psychologically. to know
something about the other person
that they don't know that you know. you know?
not really.
well.

'I am alive and you are dead.'
— Philip K. Dick

the king in yellow, the yellow king. parasite.
'Throw the demon thou carriest into the sea, if thou
dost not desire to perish.'

have you heard of a mythological city called Ys?

hard is the day of the locusts

I can video call with you, but what would that prove?
The weight of your heart against a feather.
I don't understand what that means.

Astro-Theology: worship of the heavens

Men cast their nets into the sea of life, over and over again, mostly coming up empty. But eventually they bring in buckets full of many-colored fish.

man is the only animal endowed with the power of laughter

katabasis: a descent, a breaking point, a pressing down upon the soul. descending to the depths of the underworld.

when they emerge it is with heightened knowledge and understanding. these moments are painful but essential. 'although to be driven back upon oneself is an uneasy affair at best, it seems to me now the one condition necessary.' — Didion

Marcus's early life, defined by almost nothing but loss. *Hydra*: the battle with no end. Keep fighting indefinitely. 'I made a prosperous voyage when I suffered shipwreck.'

— Zeno

the shipwreck forced him to become philosophical, self reliant.

'Demand not that events should happen as you wish; but wish them to happen as they do happen, and your life will be serene.'
— Epictetus

I cannot escape death; but cannot I escape the dread of it? Must I die trembling and lamenting?

Heraclitus: weeping philosopher
Democritus: laughing philosopher

panta rhei ('everything flows')

'The mysteries practiced among men are unholy mysteries.'
— H.

The knowledge of the most famous persons, which they guard, is but opinion.

Every beast is driven to pasture by blows. Turnings of fire. The way up is the way down. The way down is the way up.

The sun is new every day.
Destiny chooses when you'll die and who you'll marry.

'Berossus the Babylonian recorded Naboukhodonosoros
in his history'
(*Babyloniaca*)

How does a book with the title *The Book of the Wars of
Yahuah* go missing?
The Book of the Battles of the Lord
The Antiquities of Egypt: A Translation, with Notes, of
Book I of the Library of History of Diodorus Siculus:
'Again, with respect to the antiquity of the human race,
not only do Greeks put forth their claims but many of
the barbarians as well, all holding that it is they who
were autochthonous and the first of all men to discover
the things which are of use in life, and that it was the
events in their own history which were the earliest to
have been held worthy of record.'

Theology is a higher science than metaphysics, and
cannot be reached by that ladder.
   It is useless to put such question to a fellow man; no
human mind can fathom the nature of the Godhead, or
trace out its operations (Eccles. 18:4)

'I want not wealth; I only ask to live
On frugal means without corroding care.'

The horseleach hath two daughters, crying, Give, give.

'His eyes, plucked out, let croaking ravens gorge,
His bowels dogs, his limbs the greedy wolves'

And besides these there are other gods, they say, who were terrestrial, having once been mortals, but who, by reason of their sagacity and the good services which they rendered to all men, attained immortality, some of them having even been kings in Egypt.

This was the initiation of the first day's work.
The visible universe neither existed from eternity, nor was fashioned out of pre-existing materials, nor proceeded forth as an emanation from the Absolute, but was summoned into being by an express creative fiat.

The continuity of force admits of neither creation nor annihilation, but demands an unseen universe, out of which the visible has been produced 'by an intelligent agency residing in the unseen,' and into which it must eventually return.
— Sir J. Gardner Wilkinson, *The Manners and Customs of the Ancient Egyptians*

It would be extremely interesting to write the history of laughter.
— Alexander Herzen

cowards never won heaven

'Say not that thou hast royal blood running in thy veins, and art begotten of God, except thou canst prove thy pedigree by this heroic spirit, to dare to be holy despite men and devils.'
— *Christian Complete Armour*

'A human body in grain takes seconds to sink, minutes to suffocate, and hours to locate and recover. Recovered bodies have shown signs of blunt force trauma from the impact of the grain; one victim was found to have a dislocated jaw.'

Surrounded by darkness I felt an urge to see the light.

A Fitting End

Aden Simpson

Of course, there was anger at first.
Fair. To be expected.
But the powers that be knew we'd come to understand.
And they were right. Once the rioting rescinded.
Because... *gestures at everything*
Enough was enough.
The show must not go on.
The only point of difference, the splitting point:
How to end it all.

***

8.23am. I was late. A late night of preparing, years of work, coming down to the final stretch of the doomsday clock. The US government were hellbent on the atomic end. All weapons at the ready, each square foot accounted for. Noting my destination, the uber driver saw my frazzled rush and asked 'truly, what's the worry,' his malaise infectious, but I steadied myself. He must've been religious, certain his deity would come swooping in at the last second to save the day. Or he was just a regular fool, happy to let everything slide.

I asked him where he stood on leaving the planet's animals free to regenerate after we're gone. He singled out my use of 'stand' and said he was ready to lie down. The hell with the animals.

The committee for a cleaner apocalypse anointed me as their spokesperson after the last one, my boss, self-immolated outside the very entrance of the UN building I rushed through.

Since the Decision, our bid had undergone several evolutions. Originally, we advocated for careful deconstruction of our cities, a final spring clean, if you will, to leave the place tidy prior to a global Jonestown effort in grass fields that would eventually absorb us. This was set upon by the demolition contractors of the world as too costly. It lacked the wow factor too, and instead all the attention went to Japan, who announced the building of a mechanical Godzilla, the completion timeframe scraping just within the doomsday clock. A peaceful kumbayah with biodegradable kool aid cups wasn't going to cut it.

But I couldn't just give up.

Our new corporate sponsor, an energy conglomerate, believed in our message and had pivoted its production line to community gas chambers. While carbon emitting heavy at first, emissions were forecast to drop immeasurably once the project matured.

The walls and halls of the UN had no doubt seen better days. A relaxing of rules around indoor smoking and an absence of cleaners were bound to degrade the prestige over time.

Menacingly, security was the only the support department that had seen its budget bloat since the announcement. A wall of peacekeepers, their blue helmets marked with symbols of death and other lamentations of peace, greeted me at the entrance, nodding approvingly when I placed a tenner in their large tip jar.

I visited the main assembly only once before, accompanying my former boss on his fateful final day. We'd been scheduled to present toward the end of the day, between global fentanyl synchronisation and roast dinner in the cafeteria. Our speaking time had slowly been whittled down as the speakers throughout the day had been egged on by the raucous ambassadors while the drinks flowed and the translators lost much in translation.

By day's end, he had less than six minutes to present his life's work to a paltry portion that remained, some slumped over their desks.

Instead he chose self-immolation and our speaking slot was later rescheduled out of respect.

What good could the UN do in their current shambles, I'd asked my boss once. I knew he held the same concerns, but desperation had forced this shambled bureaucracy into being our last hope; the G8 were not taking requests at this time, too invested in their own deals of destruction. The UN, inebriated or otherwise, could shake the world powers from the brink—IF the case was compelling enough.

A long shot, but one worth taking, nonetheless.

I waited backstage and nervously fidgeted as the tech team discussed cues for my film reel (endangered beauties of the world, across landscapes already facing collapse, holding on.) Imagery that would make the late Sir David Attenborough swell. Emotion, that's what we were counting on. Limit the stats, they're too drunk to remember the finer points, no matter how sobering such figures could be.

Commotion in the general assembly triggered a scramble from us backstage as we peeked beyond the curtain. A quick check on our phones revealed that the Palestinians had retaken Jerusalem. The sympathetic nations howled and cheered like it was a goal in a world cup final. Ever since the Decision, an unfounded—and I emphasise unfounded—rumour spread that whoever held Jerusalem by world's end would gain the ear of the heavenly powers above. Rarefied air for the final king of the hill.

Nonsense of course, and they'd reduced Jerusalem to rubble with heavy fighting since.

But the little time I had for religious extremism oceans away would nevertheless take up an extraordinary amount of my own time today and threaten to derail everything, as nations supportive of the current land holder now pushed hard for a quick resolution.

'What are we waiting for? Let's end this madness!' they cried, while only a week ago had urged for calm.

After some consultation with management, my speech was pushed back to the afternoon.

'We will give you an extra five minutes, for a total of fifteen,' the sheepish messenger offered, her face maxing out the empathy, concerned I would follow in my boss' footsteps yet unaware I was originally offered twenty.

I couldn't help but allow my soul to visibly sag.

'Sure, no problem.'

For lunch, I sat down at the cafeteria alone. Got my tray and filled up on butter chicken. Vegetarian for nine years, vegan for two. A risk for my stomach on a day of endless nerves, but what the hell.

I called my partner, Joni. I'd be lost without her. She would have joined me in the assembly, if she didn't have to be out of town trying to stop the burning of the last sequoias in San Francisco from a tech billionaire who wanted to light them up as background entertainment for his last birthday bash. All the while seeing one of her exes, another eco warrior firmly committed to the fight.

'Babe, you've got this!' she offered. Rob, her ex, echoed the sentiment.

'Thanks guys,' I said. 'I'll do my best. Love you, Joni. Can't wait to see you again.'

'Oh, Abe, I forgot to mention—Rob's going to crash at ours before he deploys again to Africa.'

'Great. Sounds good.'

One day, love will be the last thing we have. The last thing we give.

* * *

'Ambassadors, we have a very special guest speaker today. Deputy to the late Vincent Carrouso—he was the one who tragically passed last week outside the General Assembly—yes, if we could have quiet please, I know the situation is critical in Jerusalem right now but if we can mute the volume on your phones for the next ten minutes, thank you. Here is Abe Forrest.'

My hands shook. Each word must be precise. The lives of billions of plants and animals at stake, species that have coexisted for aeons now the impending victim of a self-aware cancer, unmoved by the collateral damage of their self-destruction. *These creatures are only well regarded because we regard them*, a nuclear war hawk advised me one day at a small symposium. A nuclear bast will wipe cities out the proper way. No stone left un-irradiated. A permanent clean slate. If we did things your way, sure, the cities will crumble on their own, given time. But given time, those animals you so covet, could turn into something resembling us, doomed to make the same mistake, OR even worse, eclipse us. We must not let that happen.

'Ambassadors, almost five years ago, we consigned the futures of the children to the dustbin. Many will be old enough to yearn for that first love, but not be able to find it. All those milestones of life, the one's we took as regular, yet cherished when it was our turn— our children will never know that. And we've accepted this. Reasoned that it all ends up the same anyhow.'

I had graphs illustrating the wonderful bio-diversity that could thrive if we used the EXONN Mobile gas chamber global human completion initiative. But these did not capture the left-field detour I was about to drive headfirst into.

'But you know what will survive a nuclear holocaust? Never mind cockroaches, the real threat is Ants. The Argentinian ant has collaborative super colonies in over 16 different countries, spanning from the South America continent, all the way up and across to the Mediterranean. They will become the dominant survivors AND frankly you don't want them ruling the world. We have this great opportunity to let cats, dogs and other diverse members of the animal kingdom rule the land. I would argue dogs are already better than us; they will not become the greedy monsters we became, nor will their feats overshadow our achievements. They will be peaceful custodians. Ants, on the other hand, will evolve into a society that will far outshine our feats, eventually. We must allow these diverse creatures to live, to keep the all-conquering ants at bay. They may evolve with the cooperative discipline of ants, but they won't be no damn insects. Dogs alone will be the worthy heirs.'

What, were you expecting some well-reasoned scientific argument? This world had dispensed with such a thing when they made the Decision. Irrationality must be met with further Irrationality. The largest of Egos all have a soft little underbelly of insecurity, and I thought maybe. Just maybe…

The general assembly had not expected such a ridiculous angle. Not from someone as serious looking as I. Here we all were, the doomsday clock shaving off precious moments of our lives, and I had the *audacity* to waste it with some nonsense about evolved ants taking over.

I tried to continue, with the pre-prepared solution of my corporate sponsors, the EXONN Mobile gas chamber, technical specs of dimensions and how many each chamber could fit (the floor opens into a crematorium pit!), but the uproar of their voices and the hurling of half-empty beer bottles ended my plea.

I was escorted out by security forces, who were surprised my unassuming self had caused such vitriol.

* * *

Later that night my news made a splash and was roundly mocked by nuclear advocates, mechanical Godzilla supporters and the artificial asteroid coalition. Every religion denounced my ant theory; God would not allow a lowly insect to better our mark on this world. No thumbs equalled no artistic feats or technological marvels. MichaelANTngelo, they would not be.

Joni said she needed some space (though less space with Rob, I intimated). I said I understood before hanging up and crying like a baby the rest of the night, my heart breaking, as if for the first time, or moreso for the last.

Career-wise, EXONN Mobile, immediately dropped their sponsorship of our non-profit think tank. Rather than routine dismissal from my post, the non-profit would also rebrand itself, to the name of my former boss. His act of self-immolation acting like a phoenix rising from the corporate ashes.

With nowhere near enough in savings to comfortably run out my remaining days, I determined to drink myself into oblivion like the hundreds of millions that had done so since their fate had been assigned an expiration. But to my dismay, all the liquor stores had closed in my neighbourhood. Supply issues decimated by demand. I'd been toeing the straight edge line for so long, believing I could help save the innocent animals of the world if only I remained sober and sane with all my wits intact, like Noah and his ark. Suffice to say, I swore deep and loud in the indifferent street.

Heroin then? No heroin.

Cocaine? No more Columbia.

Coney Island Euthanasia Roller Coaster? I'd just lost my health coverage.

Government issued euthanasia kit?

I guess this would have to be the case.

* * *

I had passed my local clinic every day on my commute to the non-profit. They could do in-service or provide kits, ensuring maximum comfort at home. When the Decision first came to being, some did not want to wait, and sought an orderly end at the hands of the state rather than botching a personal attempt. I had contemplated working for such an environmentally-friendly department, but the threat of nuclear Armageddon spurned me to think bigger.

I walked into the 8th Avenue clinic an ally, somewhat elated for my first experience.

Trisha manned the counter.

'Hi, I'd like to get a test kit for home.'

Her brown eyes lit up in recognition and she squealed like a fan girl meeting their celebrity crush. Instantly I knew I'd made a mistake.

'Oh, you're the guy! Ant-man, you a real crack up, hon—Maxine!' she called out to her colleague, serving a family at the other counter. 'Hold up just a sec.'

Maxine walked over and I needed no introduction.

'Oh, hon, wow. You *definitely* came to the right place.'

A family waiting for a tour of the in-house service piped up at the commotion and joined in once I'd flashed my embarrassed head in their direction. 'Ant man!' the youngest chanted, his siblings and eventually his parents joining in.

All my life, I'd been a timid man, courteous to a fault. But I would not stand for this rudeness. My dignity had been debased and degraded by the masses, and now this...

I would spare the family, but Trisha and Maxine were supposed to be empathetic professionals. I determined to reduce them to dust.

'Who is your manager?'

'Why?' asked Trisha.

'I'd like to make a complaint.'

'Speaking,' said Maxine.

I faltered, but recovered all the same. 'I want to leave a complaint directly, with your manager, Maxine.'

Maxine pursed her lip. Stared daggers. I did my best to return serve, but she was well trained.

'He's not in today.'

'Does he have a phone number? Get him on the phone then. Now.'

'Trisha, hand me the phone.'

Trisha handed Maxine the landline. Maxine dialled and all she said was 'customer complaint.' She threw the phone at me, and I almost fumble it.

It was a poor line. A gruff man barked, 'whaddid they do?'

'They were being extremely rude and said I had definitely come to the right place.'

'Why's that? You some loser?'

'I'm not, I'm just ready to go peacefully and I they were being unsympathetic and laughing at me.'

'Something you ain't telling. Who was being rude? Trisha?'

'Maxine, moreso.'

The gruff manager let out a sigh, and slowed his rabid speech. 'Shame, Trisha's on her last warning. Put Maxine on.'

'It *was* Maxine,' I reaffirmed, in case there was any doubt. Maxine folded her arms in my brief glance.

I handed the phone back to Maxine and she listened. I waited for her face to distort, to feel some kind of wrath, a tenth of the mass ridicule the rest of the world had heaped on me. And the longer it went on, I felt sorry for Maxine. This was no way to go. No way to spend the rest of our days caught up in the pettiness of the world. Neither of us should be in this clinic, we should be far from the muck of Manhattan, the grotesque monolith of human failure. We should be out in nature.

And then Maxine shatters my breakthrough. 'He's the ant man, the guy from the UN. Yeah that one.'

And then laughter—a goddamn cackle. What on earth. This encouraged Trisha and the family behind me. They too joined in, relieved.

Maxine smiled as she said her goodbyes and put the phone down. 'Trisha, please give this An—Sir, two kits.'

'What is the extra one for, what did your boss say?'

'Customer satisfaction,' she smiled, 'and in case the first one doesn't work.'

Trisha retrieved two kits from out the back. They were the size of a small cake assortment box. On top of the boxes, precariously loose, was a hand gun, which Trisha casually handed to Maxine, who while not aiming at me, kept the gun by her side at the ready.

'On the house,' Maxine added, generously, as Trisha handed me the boxes.

I left the clinic in a daze. The world had truly gone mad.

* * *

Last supper in front of the TV at home. Homemade lentil bolognese, a return to my meat-free lifestyle, finishing the race with my morals slightly intact.

Outside, the sounds and vibrations of the city suggest nothing of distress, the world carrying along as normal, certain of their destruction and perfectly fine with it.

I had been making furtive glances to the kits placed on my coffee table, their presence looming, a gravitational vortex sucking all the focus into its promise. An elephant waving hello with its trunk.

What will it be like to be no more?

Eventually I grabbed one of the kits, thumbing through the instructions. Take the sedative and you will have about 15 minutes, but before you do, make sure you get your affairs in order. All manner of property and last will and testament must be settled and the landlord notified, lest a fee be deducted from assets.

My parents were gone and I had no relatives left on speaking terms. My Joni was no longer mine, yet I would be leaving a dump of final goodbyes in her DMs, which I had typed up that afternoon while the melancholic tidings of the Walkmen, LCD Soundsystem and Henry James jnr. accompanied my thoughts. All washed down with some homemade gin my neighbour had distilled and I paid my last dollars for. I wanted to apologise in advanced for the impending smell but that would give the game away—plus he'd also made fun of my speech at the UN.

I muted the TV. I did not turn it off. Not quite ready for total stillness.

I took the medicine, a simple oral procedure. My heart pumped in fear at first, a cornered animal, but I corralled it to peace with my soothing rationalisations. Fifteen minutes. I took a breath and hit send to Joni...

Life, flash before my eyes.

Do I want the good, the bad, the ugly?

I think not.

Cut the years of inadequacy, the uncertainty, moments

of missed signals and rejection of the mortifying kind.

Give me the good.

The shining light through trees, hiking the Appalachia. Diving in Thailand. Times entwined with Joni, Kelly and Reyna. Mum's lentil bolognese and dad's corny jokes.

My eyes drooped. And I drifted into peace.

The phone pinged.

Pinged again.

I forced my eyes wide open and mustered enough strength to reach for the phone.

Joni, my love.

Babe we did it! Gov r delaying nukes until they deal w Ants!! 2 more years!! Love u so much. Will never 4get you! Xxx

www.ingramcontent.com/pod-product-compliance
Lightning Source LLC
Chambersburg PA
CBHW030919120726
47906CB00002B/406